W9-BUD-642
RECEIVED
AUG 31 2018
By

Peculiar Savage Beauty

A NOVEL

Jessica McCann

Perspective Books

ISBN 978-0-9994602-0-7

Phoenix, Arizona

www.JessicaMcCann.com

Cover image by George Peters
Book Layout © 2017 BookDesignTemplates.com

Because of Mike.

For Mike.

Always.

“...the land wanted to be let alone,
to preserve its own fierce strength,
its peculiar, savage kind of beauty...”

– Willa Cather, 1913, *O Pioneers!*

June 1920

Rosa Jean knew it was foolish to believe her parents had been buried alive. But she couldn't get the idea out of her head. When she closed her eyes, she could see them sleeping in their wooden boxes. She could hear the rain of dirt pelting the casket lids. She would dwell on their terror – awakening in the darkness, lungs burning from the rank, oxygen-depleted air, and realizing their fate.

How must it feel to be buried alive? To be swallowed up by the earth?

She stretched out in the oblong hole she had dug behind her uncle's barn. The moist earth chilled her bare legs. She briefly peered at the black mud packed around her chewed fingernails and jagged cuticles. Then, she crossed her tiny hands over her chest and closed her eyes. When Uncle Lou came upon the girl lying there, he howled, grabbed her up by the arms and dragged her like a ragdoll to the house.

"There's something dreadful wrong with this child."

May 1934

The walkway and lawn below Rosa Jean's second-floor dormitory window was teeming with graduates, proudly sporting their ebony gowns and golden tassels, embracing family and friends. Her own graduation gown was already neatly folded and packed away in her trunk along with most of her other clothes.

A breeze wafted in through the open window, bringing the sweetness of Wisconsin spring grass and adolescent glee with it. College commencement provided them all with a chance at real freedom. It was the perfect excuse to shed old baggage and start life anew. Maybe her plan was backward then, packing up all her belongings and heading back to where her life began.

"I have to be going soon, Rosa Jean." Aunt May shattered the silence inside the small room. "Lou wants to get an early supper at a restaurant before we head on back to the farm."

RJ, as she had come to be known at school, nodded and folded one more blouse.

Aunt May ran her calloused fingertips over her niece's college diploma, somewhat disbelieving the words. How often does a young woman get a master's degree, in geology of all things? The dean at the ceremony that morning had said RJ was this university's first.

"Oh, I do wish you'd come to supper with us," Aunt May said. "This rift between you two has gone on far too long."

"And why am I always the one who has to take the first step, always the one to mend the rift?"

"Because that's what *women do*, Rosa Jean." Aunt May set the diploma aside and stood up, smoothed down the front of her faded cotton polka-dot dress and sighed. "Fine lot of good that college diploma does you if you haven't even learned that much in life."

RJ groaned. She had learned that, and a whole lot more, during her six years at college. That didn't mean she liked it, or planned to abide by it.

"It would just be nice if he made an effort for once," RJ said.

Aunt May's posture stiffened. "Giving you a bed to sleep in and food to put in your belly all those years wasn't effort enough for you?"

RJ's shoulders dropped. It was the same old debate they'd had a thousand times. She turned to face her aunt.

"I'm sorry, Aunt May. I'm so grateful for all you and Uncle Lou have done for me. I know I don't show it the way I should. But I truly am."

The air between them took on its familiar fog of silence. Once RJ accepted there was nothing more that could be said, she stepped forward and embraced her aunt for what she expected would be the final time. "Thank you for coming today."

Aunt May indulged her niece for a moment, then tapped her back and pulled away awkwardly. "You have a safe trip, now. And be sure to send a telegram the moment you arrive in Vanham, so I won't have to worry too terribly long."

"Yes, ma'am."

"And you put that diploma away somewhere where it won't get ruined."

RJ smiled at that, her aunt's roundabout way of saying she was proud.

"Yes, ma'am, I will."

With one last nod, Aunt May turned and left. RJ stood for a moment, staring at the empty doorway, fighting the urge to fly down the hall after the woman. She ran her fingers through her hair to tamp down her nerves, then turned back to finish her packing.

~~~

"Hey, you can't park there! Hey!" The residence hall dean stood at the top of the expansive stone steps of Barnard Hall, waving her arms, as RJ backed the Ford flatbed truck across the emerald campus lawn and up to the women's dormitory entrance.

RJ turned off the engine and jumped out of the truck. She bounded up the steps two at a time and into the building, the dean hot on her heels.

"Did you hear me, young lady? I said, you cannot park there."

"Yes. Yes, I heard you," RJ said, scrunching up her shoulders, smiling. "I'm so sorry, Miss Tubbs."

But RJ did not turn around, nor did she slow her pace.

The dean stopped chasing, her plump face flushed from the high neckline of her dress all the way to the tops of her fleshy ears. She stood a moment, wringing her hands. Then, she spun around, shouting back over her shoulder, "I'm getting campus police. Don't you think for a moment that I won't." The woman hurried down the stairs muttering to herself – of all the unladylike behavior, the impertinence, the gall. Good riddance, I say.

RJ pushed her trunk along the floor and through the hallway. She bit her tongue. *Go right ahead and get the police, you old goat.* She knew Miss Tubbs wouldn't actually make the effort.

The trunk bumped down the stairwell. RJ struggled to maintain control over its weight and bulk. When she reached the bottom, she dragged the trunk across the carpeted vestibule, down the stone steps outside and up beside the truck. She stood up straight, rubbed at her lower back, and took a long look around campus.

Coming down the women's dormitory steps was a classmate, flanked by her parents. The young woman carried her purse and a small suitcase, and chattered excitedly, though RJ couldn't make
~~~

out what she was saying. Her father nodded and smiled, while he fumbled along with a bulky box. Her mother laughed and looped an arm around the young woman's waist.

RJ watched the cheerful family move down the walkway until they disappeared around the corner of the building. She blew the hair out of her eyes with an exaggerated breath, then turned to plod back up the dormitory steps alone.

After she'd hauled all her belongings out to the lawn, RJ carefully loaded them onto the flatbed, arranging them like pieces of a puzzle and tying them down. She climbed into the cab and started the engine. Then, she leaned out the window and waved good-bye to Miss Tubbs, who stood at the top of the steps in the entryway, flabby arms folded across an abundant chest.

The woman shook her head slowly from side to side, then turned and disappeared into the building.

RJ wrinkled her nose, and drove off across the lawn.

"Good-bye, Wisconsin. Good-bye, UW," she said, pulling out onto the main road. "Good-bye, you old goat."

~~~

RJ scanned the landscape for a good place to pull off and set up camp for the night. After nearly a week on the road, she was no longer enjoying the adventure. The last forty miles had been nothing but the same monotonous montage – flat, brown, barren as far as the eye could see. For the first time, she began to question the wisdom of her decision to drive the nine-hundred-fifty miles from Wisconsin to Kansas, alone. Why hadn't she taken the train, as so many well-meaning people had suggested? Maybe she had wanted the trip to take longer than was necessary. Maybe she wasn't so sure, anymore, if going back to Kansas was, in fact, a very smart move.

Aunt May's voice bounced around inside her head now. "Cheese and crackers, Rosa Jean. What in God's name are you thinking you're going to do down there in Kansas anyhow, with
~~~

your test tubes and fancy college degrees? Mix a magic potion and make it rain?"

RJ took a quick look in the rearview mirror at her crates and trunks in the back. She had taken days before graduation to carefully wrap and pack her equipment, her beakers and test tubes, her droppers and "magic potions."

Inside the truck cab she had packed her Corona typewriter, in its spruce green case, her one luxury in college and the envy of all her classmates. Beneath it, her satchel held important papers – her birth certificate, her college diplomas and the letter from Washington, D.C. that said her application to the Soil Erosion Service had been accepted. Upon receiving her diploma, RJ was to "dispatch immediately for Vanham, Kansas to establish and manage a Department of the Interior soil erosion experiment station." It would be a dream come true, if she ever made it there.

A gray-brown haze hovered across the horizon. The hardscrabble road became less and less distinct, blending with the landscape. Dirt road. Dirt fields. Dirt as far as the eye could see. The sky began to darken. RJ's grip tightened on the steering wheel as the wind kicked up.

She slowed and pulled off to the side, letting the truck idle. RJ extracted a silver pocket watch from her satchel. It had been delivered by the postman to her aunt and uncle's farm when RJ was just eight years old, along with a letter from the Clark County, Kansas doctor saying her parents had finally succumbed to the flu that had claimed so many lives that year. RJ ran her thumb slowly across her daddy's initials before snapping open the lid.

The watch ticked half past three. The horizon had nearly disappeared now, sky blending with land as the sun faded away in a blaze of scarlet through the dusty haze. RJ turned off the engine and stepped out.

"A storm rolling in?" she asked out loud, though there wasn't a soul within a hundred miles who could answer. Drought and hard times had driven so many farmers and homesteaders off their land. RJ knew that. It's why she was there. Then it dawned on her.

"It's a duster!"

She felt a rush of jitters tumble through her gut, something between thrill and panic, as she began to assess her situation. RJ ran to the back of the truck and pried open a crate containing a bag she had packed for just such an emergency. Inside were a canteen of water, a bandanna, a wide-brimmed cotton hat, goggles, canned sardines and a small box of saltine crackers. Next to the bag was a wool blanket neatly rolled and tied with twine.

A steady, deafening rumble in the distance put to shame the worst thunder RJ had ever heard. She squinted at the horizon, at the approaching mountain of dust. Millions of fine dirt particles hurtled across the landscape in a frenetic rush, picking up still more granules that bounced off one other in a chaotic whirl. This created an electrical charge in the air that made RJ's scalp tingle and the fine hairs on her arms stand at attention.

It was coming. Her first duster. She had no time to lose.

She surveyed the land. There was nowhere to take shelter. Not a building, not a tree, not even a big rock lay in sight. Just rolling sand dunes across miles and miles of abandoned farmland.

RJ slung the bag over her shoulder and leaned back into the crate to retrieve the blanket roll. She worked her way to the front of the Model AA, walking straight into the wind and biting dust. She grabbed hold of the door handle and felt a jolt of static electricity shoot through her arm and into her body. She dropped to her knees, momentarily paralyzed by the heat vibrating through her insides.

"Brilliant, RJ. Just brilliant."

She knew all about the dusters, about the danger of electrical charges they could generate. She'd read news articles about unwitting folks seeking shelter in their automobiles who'd been burned alive by the powerful currents. She felt glued to the ground now, her limbs paralyzed by fear – not fear of the storm, but of her own stupidity, her carelessness.

The wind and earth continued its onslaught across the landscape, pulling a burial shroud over the sun itself.

The unnatural darkness jolted RJ back into action. She yanked the bandanna from the bag, soaked it with water from the canteen. She wiped the dirt from her eyes, secured her goggles in place, then tied the bandanna over her nose and mouth. The risk of electrocution made taking shelter inside the truck impossible. She'd have to seek refuge beneath it.

RJ crawled to the back of the flatbed and struggled to her feet. She retrieved an Army surplus spade, careful not to bump the metal frame of the truck. Then, she grabbed the crate lid and used it as a shield, pushing and fighting against the dust and wind like some ancient warrior headed into battle. She worked her way back toward the front of the Ford and braced the wood-planked lid on the ground, leaning it against the front bumper and grill.

The grit hurling through the air nipped at her exposed arms, causing tiny pinpricks of blood to emerge from her soft skin. She rubbed the sting from her arms, then dropped to her belly on the ground and shimmied beneath the low truck, pulling her emergency supplies in beside her.

She had shelter. Abysmal as it was, it would protect her from the storm. But how long would the duster last? How long would she last?

The truck above her rattled and quaked. Darkness descended.

It could have been four o'clock in the afternoon or midnight. RJ had no way of knowing. Fear crept through her every muscle, every stiff joint, every prickling square inch of skin as she lay wedged beneath the truck.

The wind and dust raged onward. RJ couldn't see, but she could sense the earth rising around her, inching higher up the wheel-wells, up the doors of the truck, cutting her off from the world, stealing her oxygen.

RJ gulped for air through the moist, muddy bandanna covering her face and fought to relax the muscles contracting in her neck. The mature educated scientist was at war with the small girl still within her, in an epic battle to wrestle control of her thoughts. She couldn't allow herself to crumble in a heap of girlish emotion at the first sign of adversity, as so many of her male classmates had predicted she would.

Of course, the massive dusters were dangerous, terrifying. She'd discussed the storms, and their causes, with her professors for hours on end. She'd known what to expect.

A shifting gust of wind threw stinging grit into her exposed cheeks. She turned her head and buried her face in the bend of her elbow. She thought of the many late-night conversations with her mentor, sipping stale coffee in a pristine lab, jotting new insights and ideas and plans into her notebook. In all of their discussions and predictions, never did they foresee her current plight – cowering beneath her truck in a howling storm in the middle of nowhere. In the dark. Alone.

Being alone wasn't the scary part. RJ was a solitary person, even as a child. While her cousins and their friends ran around playing hide-and-seek or Simon Says, RJ preferred to keep to herself. She walked the pastures and backwoods, stuffing her pockets with geometric leaves and vibrant petals and dead insects for her collections. It was yet another reason Uncle Lou thought she was peculiar. But Aunt May told him, "Rosa Jean's just grieving, Lou. She'll come around."

No, being alone wasn't the scary part. Getting swallowed up by the earth. Disappearing without a trace. That was the scary part.

Her pulse thumped in her eardrums, as the panic sank deeper into her psyche. *Get hold of yourself, RJ. Think about your plan.* She would find a nice piece of land in Vanham and set up the soil experiment station. She would rise before the sun, like a farmer, like her parents had, to connect with the land and feel the earth between her fingers. She would put her Corona on a little table by the window, and at night she would type her observations and ideas in neat reports for her superiors in Washington. She would meet with the Farmers Union and explain new ways of working the land – of working *with* the land – to fend off soil erosion. Terracing and strip cropping and contour plowing...

Lulled by her thoughts and the steady drone of the wind, RJ drifted off into a fitful sleep. She'd awaken from time to time, disoriented, lost. Then, reality would return to her. The ground, the truck, the wind, the dust. And she'd soothe herself again with thoughts of science and research and logic until she nodded off once more.

RJ was jarred awake by the sense of something moving beside the truck. It was more than the wind. She listened intently for a moment or two.

"Who's there?"

Only the wind announced itself. The dust continued its assault. The truck rattled and shook.

Then, she felt it again, a presence, now with her beneath the truck. Her skin prickled as she felt a body press up against hers. Warm, soft, not a person, some sort of animal. RJ fought the urge to push the creature away, or to bolt from beneath her only shelter. Carefully, slowly, she slid her body away a few inches. Then, just as slowly, the animal crept back toward her, pressing its body to hers.

RJ had no idea what sort of wildlife roamed this country. But she realized this animal was not intent on eating her, at least not for the moment. It was, like her, seeking shelter. And it was warm.

For the first time since the duster had rolled in, RJ became aware of the cold that had edged in with it. She began to shiver. She remembered the blanket from her emergency crate. She carefully unrolled it, spreading it over herself and the animal beside her. Within a few minutes, their collective body heat radiated beneath the prickly wool. The critter snuggled in closer still.

"Ain't that just the way of things," she said, marveling at the complete absurdity of her situation. All of that planning and preparation. And yet there's always something unpredictable that creeps in on you, something unexpected, unavoidable, untamed.

~~~

A bright ray of light glinted through RJ's safety goggles, and her lids fluttered open.

The sun.

It took a moment to wrap her mind around the idea. The sun was shining again. The darkness had passed. The air was still. The dust had settled.

RJ jabbed at the sliver of sunlight with the spade, pushing outward at the dirt drift that had formed alongside the truck. When she had cleared enough space, she shimmied out from beneath the
~~~

vehicle and slowly got to her feet. She stretched and massaged a kink in her neck. She removed the bandanna, dry and stiff and caked with dirt. Off came the hat and safety goggles. She shook the dust like dandruff from her hair and took a look around.

"Holy Moses."

The road RJ had followed had nearly vanished, covered over by the same pale dirt that blanketed the landscape as far as the eye could see. A three-foot drift had collected at the front of the truck, piled against the crate lid. The vehicle itself was transformed from shiny black metal over whitewall tires to a soft brown, top to bottom. RJ ran her finger along the fender, leaving a black line in its wake, cutting through the powdery dust. She rubbed her thumb and fingertips together, examining the sample.

"Silt loam. Soft as flour."

RJ inhaled deeply and tried to exhale. The dust caught in her throat and sent her into a fitful cough, dry and painful. Thirst gripped her. She opened the canteen still slung across her chest and took long, satisfying gulps, letting the water dribble out the corners of her mouth and run down her filthy neck.

When she was finished drinking, she heard a wheezing sound from beneath the truck and remembered her visitor. RJ squatted down and took a tentative peek to see what sort of creature she had on her hands. A dog. The animal lay there, ears flat, mouth open, panting roughly. Its eyes and nose were caked shut with dirt.

"Oh, you poor thing."

RJ scooted in a little closer to the truck, reaching out her hand.

"Come here. Come here, little one. There you go. Come on out, now."

The dog's floppy triangular ears perked up a bit. With each plea from RJ, the animal cocked its head to one side and then the other. After a bit more coaxing, it finally wriggled out from beneath the truck toward the sound of RJ's voice.

"Oh," RJ recoiled at the animal's suffering. "Let's see what we can do to get you cleaned up."

She retreated to the back of the truck and rummaged through another of her crates, returning with a tin cup and dusty dish towel. She filled the cup with water from the canteen and sat herself down in the dirt beside the dog. She soaked a corner of the towel and, taking the animal's chin gently in her hand, RJ squeezed water droplets over its sand-packed eye sockets.

The animal winced and jerked its head.

"Shhhh, I know. I know."

RJ kept a firm, gentle grip on the animal. Gradually, methodically, with a scientist's patient resolve, RJ dabbed its eyes clean and then worked her way down to its flat snout. At a loss for comforting words, RJ began to sing.

"Don't know why, there's no sun up in the sky," she crooned softly. "Stormy weather. Since my man and I ain't together, keeps raining all the time."

As the dirt washed away, it revealed a smooth brown face with a patch of white running between the brows and down around the nose and jowls.

"Why, aren't you a pretty little thing?" RJ asked. The dog stepped in closer, then laid down and rested its chin on her knee.

Now that its nostrils were clear of dirt, the dog caught scent of the water and leaned toward the cup. RJ held the cup steady as the animal lapped up the lifesaving elixir. Then, it sat up on its haunches and patted at RJ's knee with its front paw.

RJ laughed. "Feeling all better, are you?"

She patted the dog's head and stood up. "Wish I could say the same."

RJ looked around again, taking in the flat, barren, roadless land that stretched out for miles and miles in all directions. *You better figure some way out of this pickle, RJ.* She nodded with approval as her mind began to click again. She was getting back to talking to herself, getting back to thinking like a scientist.

Who needed roads, anyway? RJ had spent countless hours camping out and traipsing through the backwoods of Madison during her six years at the University of Wisconsin. It was actually a requirement of one of her favorite professors, who challenged his students with the idea that nature was the best teacher. Aldo Leopold had warned RJ and her classmates not to waste their leisure time doing what everyone else was doing.

"It is because the vast majority of people do not have the courage to venture off the beaten path that they fail to find adventure and live lopsided lives," he had said during one of their many class outings through the university's research fields, standing knee-deep in snow. "A good, healthy curiosity is better equipment to venture forth than any amount of learning or education. The beaten paths of conformity are literally a prison."

Now, Professor Leopold's unconventional teaching methods were paying off. RJ had prepared well for her cross-country adventure. She drank a bit more water, then broke out the crackers and sardines from her duffle bag. After eating, she retrieved and opened a second can of the small, salty fish and set it on the ground for the dog.

While the animal slurped down its oily meal, RJ used the crate lid to clear away the sand dunes around the truck. She unstrapped a broom from the sideboard and set about brushing off the truck windows, hood and grill. Among the many supplies in her flatbed were a five-gallon milk can filled with water and another filled with gasoline, which she tapped to refill both her canteen and the truck engine.

RJ carefully repacked her emergency supplies and pulled out a map and compass from her glove compartment inside the cab. After careful study and thought, she determined where the road *should* be and in what direction she should drive to make her way toward Vanham.

As she folded up the map, RJ felt a nudge at her knee. The dog was standing beside her, looking up with dewy eyes, its stubby tail buzzing happily back and forth.

"Sorry, pup. I don't make a habit of picking up hitchhikers."

Just the sound of RJ's voice sent the dog into a whirlwind of joy, hopping and spinning around in a circle, once, twice, three times. Then, it looked up at her again, wagging its stub of a tail, and barked.

"You must have a home around here somewhere," RJ said to the animal. She looked around again at the vast expanse of nothing that surrounded them. But where?

"Go on home, now. Go on."

RJ opened the truck door to climb in. The dog bounded past her, leaping up and settling on the seat behind the steering wheel. It panted happily, its tongue lolling out the side of its mouth.

"Lordy," RJ said, shaking her head in defeat. "Well, if you think I'm letting you drive, you've got another thing coming."

RJ gave the dog a nudge and it moved to the passenger's seat. She climbed in, popped the truck into neutral and closed the choke. There was no telling how all that dust might have clogged up the engine, even though she had brushed it out with the broom. She pumped the gas pedal to prime the carburetor, put the key in the ignition and said a silent prayer. Then, she pushed the start button. The truck coughed and sputtered and died.

"Aw, damn."

The dog cocked its head, eyes trained on RJ.

Beakers and specimen jars and Bunsen burners, those were RJ's world. Not combustion engines. She pumped the gas again. *Please start, please start, please start.* She held her breath and pressed the button. The engine sputtered again. Then, it coughed and chugged and rumbled to life.

"Woohoo!" RJ cheered and reached across to tousle the dog's ears. "Can't believe you ever doubted me, pup."

~~~

According to RJ's calculations, Dodge City was about an hour's drive from where she had pulled off the road the day before. Right on schedule, the outline of the town came into view. It was a damned blessed sight after the night she'd had.

Dodge City. The cowboy capital. One-time home to the infamous Doc Holliday and the Earp brothers, to drinking and gambling, to shoot-outs in the street. RJ's stomach fluttered at the idea of setting foot in a town with such a rough-and-tumble reputation. As the truck made its way closer, disappointment began to set in. She saw nothing of the folklore she had read about in her school days. Dodge was a proper city, with paved roads and electric street lights, barber shops and ice cream parlors. Spiffy new Ford sedans and sporty Packard convertibles lined the streets.

The truck rumbled down the main road. RJ spotted a gas station on the corner. She pulled in to refill her water and gas, get directions and ask around about the dog's owner.

"Stay put, pup," she said, climbing out of the cab and shutting the dog inside with the windows half down.

"Good morning," she said to an elderly man sitting behind the cash register inside the shop, thumbing through the latest *Saturday Evening Post*. "May I buy ten gallons of gasoline and refill my water can at your spigot?"

"You surely may... ma'am," he said, pausing just a bit, as he sized up his customer. She must have been quite a sight – five foot
~~~

nothing, short hair tucked back under her hat, her men's overalls coated in dust. If not for her reasonable curves, the attendant could easily have mistaken her for a boy.

He called over his shoulder to a fellow outside. "George! Give the lady ten gallons and fill up her water can, too."

George waved his acknowledgment and lumbered over to the Model AA.

"That sure was some duster last night, wasn't it?" RJ said, digging through her purse for money.

The man wobbled his head side to side. "We seen worse."

RJ looked up from her purse. She studied the man, contemplated his daily existence a moment. "Suppose you have."

George clomped into the store and crossed his arms over his barrel chest. "That your dog out there? That boxer?"

RJ craned her neck to look past him and out to the truck. The pup was right where she had left it, all perky-earred, looking out the front window.

"I rescued it in the storm last night, about 25 miles north of here," she said. "I was hoping someone in town might know who it belongs to."

"That's a Kraut dog. No one 'round here would be caught dead with that dog," George said. He and the old man exchanged looks.

"Oh," RJ said. "Well, I..."

"Are you a Kraut, lady? Don't know who else would be driving around with a dog like that, unless they was a Kraut."

"No. I'm not German. I only found the dog. Out in the storm."

George scoffed and stomped outside again.

"He don't mean no harm," the old man said. "Lost his daddy in the war, over there, you know. Got run through by a German somewhere in the Somme."

"I understand," RJ said. "Lost two uncles in the war myself, on my father's side. I had no idea that was a German dog."

They looked back toward the truck.

"So you don't think it belongs to anyone around here?" she asked. The old man just stared at her, wrinkling up his nose, and handed her some change.

"No, I wouldn't suppose," she said and turned to leave. "Oh. Can you tell me how far it is to Vanham? Would I be able to reach it by nightfall?"

"About eighty miles, straight south. Depends on the weather."

"Thank you, kindly."

RJ climbed back in the truck and fired up the engine, while George watched her from the gas pumps. She forged a smile as she pulled out onto the main road, heading south. The dog stuck its head out the window and growled a short, low rumble. Then, it sneezed at the fresh dust stirring in the air and settled back down on the seat.

"Lucky you found me out there, pup. Looks like you'll be hitching a ride with me all the way to Vanham," RJ said, glancing in her rearview mirror at the shrinking buildings of Dodge City. Maybe they're not having shoot-outs in the street any more, RJ thought, but Dodge still had a crackle of tension in the air. "I sure can't leave you to fend for yourself in that town."

The dog walked around the seat in a tight circle, once, twice. Finally, it plopped down in a little ball, tucking its nose under its paws.

The road lay long and open before them. The cloudless sky stretched overhead in an endless blanket of white light. Heat radiated from the ground ahead, creating the illusion of water on the horizon. Eighty more miles to go, and RJ would finally be home. Barring any unforeseen obstacles, they'd roll into Vanham before sundown.

RJ hummed softly, "Stormy Weather" again, singing the words inside her head this time. She glanced sideways at the dog snoring noisily beside her.

"Seems we might be in for some stormy weather, you and I, rain or no rain," she said, reflecting on their brief stop in Dodge

City and wondering what sort of welcome awaited them in Vanham. "Stooormy wea-ther."

This would be the first time RJ returned to her hometown since she'd been sent away in 1918, forced to leave her ailing parents behind, to escape the Great Influenza.

RJ could remember only bits and pieces from that morning, sharp-edged fragments from a shattered childhood: She hangs bed sheets on the line. The doctor carries her trunk to the back of his wagon. "Come along with me, Rosa Jean." *Where?* Inside, her dad sits hunched over at the kitchen table, a blanket over his shoulders, cheeks ablaze. "You be a good girl, now." He wheezes. The air reeks of fresh vomit and old sweat. Time to go. *Where's mom?* RJ bolts toward the bedroom door. The doctor seizes her arms. Time to go. *No!* "Your mother and I will always love you." *I don't want to leave.* RJ howls at the doctor in the wagon. She thrashes the attendants on the train. She locks herself away at Aunt May's. She closes herself off from the world.

All these years later, she still contemplated the fate of those she left behind in the small town. She still had nightmares that her parents hadn't succumbed to the flu after all, that they'd been buried alive. Perhaps it was why RJ had requested Vanham as the spot to set up the soil erosion lab when the State Department asked if she had a preferred location. Certainly, the irony that people across the Great Plains were actually now being buried alive in the monstrous dust storms was not lost on her. On a subconscious level, it was as though RJ believed if she could repair the environmental damage to the land and stop the dusters, perhaps her nightmares would finally stop, too.

~~~

After a few hours, RJ pulled off onto the side of the road to stretch her legs and allow the dog to run around a bit. Part of her hoped the animal would catch a familiar scent on the wind and happily run off, perhaps returning home to an unseen, loving
~~~

family. A bigger part of her was grateful that the dog stayed close. The five days RJ had spent on the road since graduation had been lonelier than she'd expected. Having a companion on the final leg was a pleasant relief.

"Stormy!" RJ called out. "Come on girl. Time to go."

The dog had been rooting around the base of a dead tree about twenty yards off, pressing her flat nose into the dirt, sniffing, snuffling, sneezing. Her head shot up immediately at the sound of RJ's voice.

"Come on!" RJ patted her thigh.

Stormy came running full speed toward RJ, stopping just short, dropping her front elbows to the ground, head low, hind end sticking up, tail waggling fast. Then she zipped around and around RJ, yapping with enthusiasm. RJ laughed out loud.

"Yes, yes, I understand. We're best friends now, Stormy. Isn't that right?"

The dog stopped beside RJ, standing still now, but for her perpetually wagging stub of a tail. She perked her ears and cocked her head to one side as RJ spoke.

RJ opened the truck door and Stormy hopped up to the assigned spot. When RJ climbed in, the dog leaned across the seat and planted a wet kiss on her ear.

"Uck!" RJ lifted her shoulder up to wipe away the slobber, smiling.

They continued their way south, past acres and acres of empty fields. Every once in a while, RJ spotted a weather-worn barn half buried in sand dunes or a lone tractor plowing dust in the distance.

She remembered the landscape from her childhood, watercolor works of art preserved by her eight-year-old mind. The land had been lush with wheat. Green and hopeful in the spring, golden and bountiful in the summer.

The first two decades of the century had been plentiful years for farming towns in Kansas and throughout the Great Plains. Plenty of rain. The whole world clamoring for their wheat.

Hundreds of thousands of acres of open grasslands still there for the taking – to be plowed under, tamed, sown with yet more golden wheat to feed the soldiers fighting overseas.

Everything had changed in 1929, RJ's second year in college. The stock market crashed. Wheat prices plunged. The rain all but stopped. RJ had studied it all in school, read the news in the papers, and heard her professors' conjecture as the world seemed to be crumbling around them.

Most fields failed to produce. Those that might have shown promise after a few precious inches of rainfall were eventually burned up by the sun, devoured by grasshoppers, or harvested and sold for mere pennies a bushel. One by one, two by two, homesteaders began to lose hope. Some packed up and abandoned the land. Others were forced off by foreclosure.

RJ scanned the barren landscape, shook her head and sighed. Reading about it was one thing. Seeing it with her own two eyes, that was something else altogether. So much of that land lay bare now, exposed, waiting for the next wind to lift and carry it far away.

Drought had always been part of the Great Plains. RJ remembered lying awake in bed at night, listening to her parents' anxious whispers at the kitchen table. They worried over the weather every day, prayed for rain that didn't always come, consoled one another when the crops failed to produce. "Next year," Dad would say. "We'll do better next year."

It wasn't until college that RJ realized drought wasn't the true problem facing farmers in the Great Plains. The problem, she came to believe, was that man had tried to control the land, rather than work in harmony with it. It was that failure to cooperate with the land that put man's very existence upon it in jeopardy. But convincing people that the land should be protected rather than conquered would be a tougher task than convincing the skies to open up and grant the rain.

"To change ideas about what land is for is to change ideas about what anything is for," Professor Leopold had said to her. Yet, with the right information and the right line of reasoning, he believed it could be done, and it must be done.

The worst of it, RJ came to understand, was that the soil was drifting away on the wind, and there was no way to bring it back.

"Soil is a basic natural resource," Leopold had said during a lecture RJ's senior year. "Destruction of soil is the most fundamental kind of economic loss which the human race can suffer. With enough time and money, a neglected farm can be put back on its feet -- *if the soil is there*. By expensive replanting and with a generation or two of waiting, a ruined forest can again be made productive -- *if the soil is there*. But if the soil is gone, the loss is absolute and irrevocable."

His words had become a rallying cry for RJ, to help stop the destruction, to save the soil, to heal the land and, in turn, to alleviate the human suffering in the Great Plains. Now, as RJ traversed the final miles of highway leading to Vanham, she worried that it might already be too late.

Much like the wheat fields, the small town of Vanham in 1934 looked vastly different than the town in RJ's pastel memories. There were more houses on the outskirts of town than before. Sturdy-looking brick buildings lined the roads of downtown – the post office and a barber shop, the feed store and a Catholic church. Where folks had once parked horse-drawn wagons beside the occasional motor car, there were now mostly cars and trucks – late-model Ford roadsters and Chevrolet sedans alongside older-model pickups with hard tires and crank handles.

Yet, despite its contemporary cars, roads and buildings, Vanham looked old and beaten down. A boomtown already past its prime. Gone were the green lawns and colorful flowerbeds, replaced by barren yards and twiggy trees. Once-brightly-painted houses and redbrick buildings were now sand-blasted, monotone structures. Brown. Everything in this part of the country seemed to be defined by shades of brown, as far as the eye could see.

RJ spotted the Motel Royal near the edge of town. The long, squat building of numbered doors was punctuated at one end by the registration office. Empty clay planters sat on either side of the double doors leading inside. On a flag pole atop the building, a faded, dingy Old Glory fluttered in the perpetual, dusty breeze. RJ felt a rush of excitement now, having reached her destination, knowing her work would soon begin.

"We're going to bring some color back to this town," RJ said above the rumble of the engine as she eased into the parking lot. Stormy shifted excitedly in the seat, stirred by the passion in RJ's voice.

She left Stormy in the truck and went inside. The sign touted rooms with indoor plumbing and electricity for two dollars a night. These were luxuries to which she had grown accustomed while at the university, and RJ knew this might be her last opportunity to enjoy them for a long while. Only a select few homesteads on the plains had such conveniences yet. She paid the clerk for three nights in advance and bought a newspaper to check the upcoming auction listings.

The clerk gave RJ her choice of rooms, and she picked the one furthest from the office. She didn't ask if she could bring Stormy inside the room. Better to apologize later, if necessary, than to be turned away now.

RJ moved the Ford to the parking space in front of room number eight. *What a handy invention*, she thought to herself, about the new "motor hotels" like this one springing up in towns across the country. She liked the convenience of parking right outside her door, of hauling her suitcase in without help from a bellboy.

The room was cozy, if not clean. A layer of dust coated the dresser, lampshades, even the bed quilt.

"You'd think they could have given me a clean room," RJ muttered, hoisting her suitcase to the top of the dresser. She popped open the lid and gasped when she saw her belongings inside were also covered in dirt.

~~~

RJ awoke the next morning feeling revived and eager to get to work. A real bath in a ceramic tub and a good night's sleep on a real bed were just what she'd needed after a week of camping out on the roadside. She slipped on a crisp white work shirt and fresh
~~~

pair of denim overalls. She ran a brush through her tangled hair and clipped it back on one side with a small mother-of-pearl barrette that had belonged to her own mother. Cutting off her long hair into a stylish bob was one of the first things RJ had done when she left her aunt and uncle's farm for college. She still loved the freedom and convenience of the flapper cut, even though it was no longer in style.

"Let's go for a walk, Stormy," RJ said, tucking her purse and newspaper under her arm and opening the door. Stormy bolted outside and stopped to wait. "Dang if you aren't the best behaved little dog. Somebody's got to be heartbroken over losing you."

The two strolled across the motel parking lot and down the road into town. When they reached the post office, RJ told Stormy to stay put outside while she went in to conduct her first official business.

"Good morning," she said to the clerk. "I'd like to inquire about a package and to send a couple of telegrams, please."

"Yes, ma'am," the clerk said. "The name?"

"RJ Evans."

"Golly, we sure do have a package for Mr. Evans. Three big old crates, too."

The clerk ducked below the counter for a moment and popped back up holding a thick, oversized envelope. RJ smiled as she reached for the parcel.

"You Mrs. Evans?" the clerk asked.

"No," she replied evenly. "I'm *Miss* RJ Evans."

She tugged the envelope gently from the clerk's hand, his fingers suddenly unable to let go. He sized her up from top to bottom and back again.

"You're RJ Evans?"

"I am."

"And all these shipments from the Department of the Interior in Washington, D.C., they're for you?"

"They are."

RJ smiled mildly at the clerk. He ran his fingers through his hair, then tugged at his ear. She'd grown accustomed to this reaction. It was nearly the same every time she had walked into a science class or laboratory at the university for the first time, and the professor had to come to terms with the notion that his new student was a young woman.

When she felt she had granted the clerk sufficient time to contemplate her gender, she spoke again.

"Would you be so kind as to have the crates carried over to the Royal for me, room eight?"

The sound of her voice seemed to snap the fellow out of his daze.

"Oh. Yes, ma'am. Motel Royal, room eight," he said, fumbling for a pencil and paper to take down the information. "And, um, you said you wanted to send a telegram? Is that right?"

"Yes, thank you. To the Department of the Interior."

He looked up at her, blinking and quiet again. Then, he bobbed his head.

"Sure thing," he said. "What's the message?"

RJ recited a brief message to her superiors to let them know she had arrived in Vanham and would be attending the land auction the following day to secure a site for the soil station.

The clerk's pencil stopped for a moment, stalled on the paper, before he finally jotted the word "auction." His eyebrows raised a bit. Then, he finished taking down the message and assured RJ he'd send if off to Washington straight away.

"That it?" the young man asked.

RJ asked for a second telegram to be sent to Aunt May.

"Arrived in Vanham safe and sound. Stop. Long drive. Stop. Will write soon. Stop. Love RJ. Stop."

RJ expressed her thanks and inquired about the charges. She paid the clerk, retrieved her package from the counter, and stepped outside. Stormy's nonjudgmental tongue-lolling smile was a welcome sight after the awkward exchange.

RJ crouched down to tussle the dog's ears. Then, she stood and shook the agitation from her shoulders. "I'm half-starved, Stormy. Let's go find some breakfast."

~~~

They walked along the wooden sidewalks, and RJ took in the sights of town. It all seemed vaguely familiar to her, though not familiar enough to give her the feeling of being home again. She remembered the saccharine fragrance of baby wheat and the tang of manure that had drifted into town from the outlying fields when she was young. Now, her nostrils prickled from the parched air scented with dust and a hint of gasoline. She remembered Main Street full of life on a Saturday afternoon – families bustling in and out of storefronts, arms loaded with parcels, shouting greetings to their neighbors, "Hiya" and "See you at church tomorrow." Now, the street was vacant, soundless, surreal.

The town from RJ's youth had been like a sweet slumber. Then her parents had taken ill, and she'd been jarred awake to the painful realities of life. She could still remember flashes of that lovely dream, fragments of her past. Yet, the more years that passed, she could never get her mind at rest enough to return to it.

RJ and Stormy turned the corner and came upon Ethel's Restaurant. It was bright and tidy, empty and welcoming. RJ slipped in and sat at a table by the front window so she could keep an eye on Stormy outside. The blue gingham tablecloth had a few toast crumbs from the previous patron, but that was it. As RJ looked around the establishment, it occurred to her that it was the first place she had been in Vanham that didn't have a layer of dust covering every surface. When Ethel came to the table, RJ told her as much.

"Thank you, dearie. The work's never done, that's for sure. I do appreciate it when someone cares to notice."

The woman looked to be about Aunt May's age, her salt-and-pepper hair pulled back in a neat knot at the base of her neck. She
~~~

set a white ceramic mug on the table and filled it with steaming coffee from a metal pot.

"Cream or sugar?"

"Both please."

"You eatin'?"

"Yes. I'd love some toast and eggs, scrambled, and a few sausage links for my dog."

Ethel followed RJ's gaze out the window to where Stormy sat looking in.

"Dog eats better'n I do," Ethel said and shuffled off to the kitchen.

RJ took a sip of her coffee, then spread out the newspaper to peruse the auction listings, circling the properties that met her criteria. From time to time, she'd glance up and notice a passerby looking at her through the window. She'd smile, and the man or woman would scurry off.

Ethel brought RJ's breakfast and asked if the dog would bite if she took the sausages out herself.

"No," RJ said. "She's sweet as pie."

Ethel delivered Stormy the plate of links and gave her a little pat on the head, then came back inside and disappeared into the kitchen. The bell above the door jingled again, and RJ looked up to see the postal clerk walk in.

"Oh, hi there," he said with a stiff wave.

"Hello again." RJ smiled and returned to reading her paper.

Ethel emerged from the kitchen carrying a plate covered with a blue gingham napkin. The clerk thanked her and the two had a hushed conversation. RJ could make out only snippets of what they said – telegram, government, auction. She resisted the urge to look up again.

Instead, she took a bite of the thick toast, sliced from fresh-baked bread, spread with just the right amount of salted butter. She was momentarily lost in the delight of it. For the past six years in college, RJ had survived on mostly canned beans and day-old bread from the campus market.

She heard the jingle of the door, and the cafe was quiet again. After some time had passed, Ethel refilled RJ's coffee mug and picked up her empty plate.

"So, you work for the government?"

RJ laughed. "News sure travels fast."

"It's a small town, honey," Ethel said warmly. "I think it's jim-dandy, a young woman working for the government. From what Bud told me, it don't sound like you're a secretary."

"No," RJ said. "I'm a geologist. I'll be setting up a soil erosion experiment station outside of town."

"A geologist. Ain't that something," Ethel pulled up a chair and settled in next to RJ. "Bud said your name is RJ. What's that stand for?"

"My given name is Rosa Jean, but my friends took to calling me RJ in school."

Ethel slapped her knee and hooted. "I knew it! You're Rosa Jean Evans, as I live and breathe."

RJ could only manage to nod and smile, taken aback by the idea that someone in town actually knew her from so long ago. The thought of that happening had never crossed her mind, though now she felt silly for not anticipating it.

"Oh, honey, I knew your folks," Ethel said. Her expression grew more somber, and she took hold of RJ's hand. "Do you remember eating here at old Ethel's restaurant? Oh, what am I saying? You were just a little thing."

RJ smiled and shook her head, unsure of what to say or how to respond to this friendly stranger holding onto her hand. They sat quietly for a moment. Then, Ethel stood up abruptly and picked up the coffee pot and empty plate again.

"Well I think it's just dandy that you've come back home," she said, her eyes glistening.

They took each other in for another moment. Then, RJ hopped to her feet, too.

"It was lovely meeting you, Ethel," she said. "I better get going though. I have so many things to get done today. How much do I owe you for breakfast?"

"It's on the house."

"Oh, I couldn't possibly." RJ tried to protest, but Ethel wouldn't allow it.

"It's on the house, honey. On the house."

"That's very kind of you," RJ said as she gathered up her belongings from the table. "If there's anything I can do for you, please let me know."

"Actually... I'd be pleased if you'd take a bit of advice," Ethel said.

"Advice?"

"Bud said you were planning to buy a property at the auction tomorrow. "

RJ glanced back toward the post office, then looked at Ethel again.

"Just be careful what you bid on, honey, that's my only advice. It's gonna be a penny auction, you know."

"I don't understand," RJ said.

The bell above the door jingled and a handful of men in dusty overalls lumbered into the restaurant yammering. A hush fell over them when they noticed RJ. She felt each and every pair of eyes inspecting her, and wondered just how many people that big-mouthed postal clerk had talked to that morning and what exactly he had been saying.

"Mornin', fellas," Ethel hollered with a smile. "Sit wherever you like. Be with you in just a minute."

The men mumbled their thanks. They moved en masse to a far table in the corner and plopped down into their chairs. Ethel winked at RJ and flicked her head in the direction of the door. "Thanks for stopping in, hon."

RJ did her best to push the cafe encounter out of her mind as she finished her errands. Ethel's so-called advice seemed more like a warning, and RJ didn't like the feeling that had crept into her gut when the farmers sized her up. As she scanned the shelves for canned horsemeat and a collar for Stormy at the general merchandise store, she could feel the stares from the other patrons and the clerk, could hear more whispers behind her back.

On the walkway outside the store, as RJ crouched to give Stormy the collar, a shadow came over her and the hairs on the back of her neck prickled. RJ spun around to see a man in faded denim looking down at her. His broad-brimmed hat shadowed his lean face.

"That a Kraut dog?" he said.

"Oh, for heaven's sake!" RJ stood up and slapped her forehead. "Yes, she's a German dog. Sweet as pie, by the way. "

Stormy slinked between RJ and the farmer. The hairs on the dog's neck and back began to bristle. She growled deep and low. The man took a step back.

"Oh," RJ blurted, immediately contrite. "Stormy, no. I'm so sorry. She really is so friendly. I, I don't know what's gotten into her."

The man took another step back and harrumphed. He pushed his hat forward, turned on his heels and hustled down the walkway. When he rounded the corner out of sight, Stormy bounded in a circle, tail waggling, and looked up at RJ with a sort of pride.

"Being sweet now won't get you anywhere with me, young lady. You've got to mind your manners," RJ scolded, then sunk down beside the dog, stroking her head, and whispered, "Sure is nice to know you're looking out for me, though. Nobody's ever done that before."

The noonday light shifted from bright white to pink. The easy breeze that had been constant all morning graduated to a mild bluster. RJ looked down the main road. A dried-up Russian thistle bush tumbled by and got caught beneath the fender of a dented sedan. Dust slithered along the pavement, rising up in occasional wisps, like a rattler rearing its head to strike.

RJ's jaw tightened. She stood and began to make her way back toward the motel at a brisk pace. Stormy kept at her side. As they approached the parking lot, RJ noticed a man examining her truck. *What now?* she thought, slowing down.

"You have an interest in my truck?"

"1931 Ford Model AA," he said, without looking up. "One and a half tons, four speed, four cylinders, one-hundred-thirty-one-inch wheelbase, updraft carburetor, six-volt generator, two-blade fan, mechanical water pump, electric starter, four-row radiator. Just like the Model A, except for the radiator."

RJ didn't respond. Nothing the man said had been in the form of a question, after all, and there wasn't anything she could think of to add. She watched him walk the perimeter of the vehicle.

"It's a real beaut," he said.

"Thank you."

"Just look at that paint. I ain't seen a '31 with paint in that good a shape in three years."

RJ chuckled, but the young man was deadpan.

"Was that funny?"

"Well, yes," RJ said. "A little. Three years ago it would have been new."

"Yep," he said. "Wasn't tryin' to be funny though."

The man angled his head and looked off in the distance. RJ looked in the same direction and saw nothing in particular. They stood quiet for a moment. RJ knew the polite thing to do would be to introduce herself, but she was rather enjoying being anonymous for the moment. So she simply observed him – his tall thin build, his curly mop of charcoal hair. She guessed he was about her age, mid-twenties.

Stormy whimpered and put her paw on his shoe.

"You have a boxer," he said, crouching down and putting his face level with the dog.

"Oh, please be careful. She can be a little..." Stormy shoved her nose right into the man's face and gave him a sloppy kiss. "...unpredictable." RJ laughed.

The man stood and wiped the kiss from his face with the back of his hand. "That's a German dog, you know."

"So I've been told."

"It's a favorite breed over there, except it was originally bred from the English Bulldog more than a century ago. Got some terrier blood in its line, too. Registered by the AKC in 1904. That's the American Kennel Club. The first champion was finished in 1915. But people around here don't like 'em much, on account of them being German, which I already said. That's a German dog."

RJ's eyes danced, and she did her best to hold back another laugh.

"Was I funny again?" he asked.

"No, not funny," RJ said. "Amazing is more like it. You sure know a lot of things about a lot of different things."

He looked off to the side again and shrugged his narrow shoulders. "I read a lot."

Stormy lay down between them and rested her chin on his shoe. The wind nudged another serpent of dust across the parking lot. The sky overhead was crystalline blue, but the horizon grew darker pink with each passing minute.

"That a duster rolling in?" RJ asked, when she noticed him looking down the road, too.

"Nah," he said. "Dusters come in tall and black. This here's gonna be a sandstorm. They come in low. Should only last a couple hours. But they got a bite to 'em, so you'll want to be inside when it hits."

RJ took mental note of his description of the different types of storms. It would make an excellent anecdote in her first report to Washington, D.C.

"Thank you for the advice," she said, extending her hand. "My name's RJ, by the way."

"I know," he said, still looking away, not noticing her invitation for a handshake. "You're RJ Evans, the government man, who ain't actually a man after all. You're a scientist. Here to buy a place at the auction and set up a soil experiment station for the Department of the Interior."

RJ couldn't contain her laughter after that. And it felt good to laugh, a nice release of the tension she'd been carrying in her muscles for days. The young man looked at her then, right in the eye for the first time, and smiled broadly. "You sure like to laugh."

"I'm enjoying our conversation very much," RJ said. She also enjoyed the fact that he knew exactly who she was, and he apparently didn't have the same problem with her the other locals seemed to have.

"Woody!" An older man jogged to the parking lot from the gas station across the street. "Woody, I've been hunting all over for you, son."

"Look, Pa, a '31 Ford Model AA. Ain't she a beaut?"

The older man rolled his eyes. "Sure, son, sure. A real beaut. I hope my Woody weren't botherin' you, Miss. He ain't so bright, but he's a real good boy."

"Oh no. On the contrary, I enjoyed his company," RJ assured the man, smiling. "It was my pleasure."

The man shuffled his son away down the street by his elbow. Woody turned back to wave and shouted, "Good-bye! It was a pleasure meeting you, RJ Evans. You're nice."

RJ laughed again and waved good-bye back.

~~~

The sandstorm struck just as Woody had said it would. The late afternoon sky turned deep scarlet and a brown haze of gritty, biting sand swept through the town with a vengeance. Tumbleweeds flew down the streets, crashing into cars and storefronts, getting tangled up in wire fences. The sand pelted and swirled and formed small dunes along buildings and doorsteps. RJ watched from the window of her motel room, until the glass began to rattle so violently she feared it might give way.

She pulled the curtains closed and tried to occupy her thoughts with the auction listings, jotting notes and organizing her preferences.

For three hours, the wind howled and the walls shook.

And then silence.

Stormy poked her head out from beneath the bed.

"Hello there, little girl. You don't like the storms, do you? Can't say I blame you."

RJ opened the curtains to survey the damage. The dust lay so thick upon the glass, she could no longer see out. She opened the door and the sand that had piled up at her stoop flowed in around her feet.

"Lordy, what a mess."

She stepped outside, traversing the remaining dune in the doorway, and ventured toward the street. Up and down the main
~~~

road, merchants were already outside, fighting back against the onslaught of earth, shoveling heaps of sand from their doorways, sweeping the dust off the windows. It was business as usual; just another day beating back the dust. RJ retrieved the broom from her truck and joined the fight.

The bell over the door of Ethel's place jingled and Earnest Tugwell came shuffling in. He took a seat at the empty lunch counter.

"Hiya, Ernie," Ethel said, emerging from the kitchen, wiping her hands on her apron. "Cuppa joe?"

Ernie set a tarnished nickel on the counter. "I'd be much obliged."

"Anything to eat?"

"No thanks, Ethel. Just the coffee. Black."

Ethel retrieved a mug from below the counter, carefully wiped it clean of dust and filled it to the rim with steaming black coffee. Ernie took a sip and smiled his approval.

"You headin' over to the auction today?" she asked him.

Ernie crinkled up his face. "No, ma'am. I ain't gonna be no part of that business. Don't care to witness it, neither."

Ethel sighed. Couldn't have said it better herself. She picked up Ernie's nickel, placed it in her cash drawer beneath the counter and began wiping down the counter. The restaurant had been quiet. More and more folks were eating at home these days. Or not eating.

"So I was at the filling station the other day," Ernie said. "And I asked the feller that works there, have you got any of that gas that stops knocking?"

Ethel stopped wiping a moment and looked over at him.

"And he tells me, yes, we sure have," Ernie continued. "So I says, then give some to my wife in the back seat."

Ethel raised her eyebrows, snickered. "That's a good one, Ernie. Just don't you let Minnie hear you telling that joke, or you'll be sleeping outside with the hogs."

He hooted. "Yap, that's the truth. I read that joke in the *Farmer's Almanac* the other day over at Meginnis'. All the fellers got a kick out of that one. Been waiting for the chance to tell it to somebody new."

"We can all use a good chuckle, that's for sure," Ethel said.

Ernie rubbed the back of his neck. The frayed fold of his shirt collar tickled his hand. "Yap. And it don't cost you one cent to tell a good joke, or enjoy a good laugh."

Ethel agreed. "How's that old poem go? Laugh, and the world laughs with you."

"That's right," he said. "But snore and you sleep alone."

Ethel snorted and gave his arm a tap. Ernie shot her a gap-toothed grin and then drank down the last of his coffee. Ethel took her cue to make a discreet exit.

"Well, those dirty dishes in my sink ain't gonna wash themselves," she said. "Can I get you anything else, hon? More coffee? Maybe a cup of hot water?"

He looked down into his empty mug. "Some hot water would be swell."

"Sure thing."

She filled his mug with hot water and placed a saucer with a few saltines on the counter.

"You'd be doing me a favor if you helped yourself to them crackers, Ernie. They'll go stale if someone don't eat 'em soon," she said and then disappeared into the back through the curtained doorway.

Ernie reached for the catsup bottle. He stirred a couple teaspoons of the red sauce into his cup, added a dash of salt and pepper from the shakers. Then, he crumpled the saltines into what now passed as tomato soup and would be his only meal for the day.

"Be a good girl," RJ said, stroking Stormy's head. "I'll be back in a little while."

After the dog's bristly behavior with the farmer the day before, RJ decided it would be wise to leave her in the motel during the auction.

The air was crisp and cool and as clear of dust as RJ had seen it in days. The fresh morning and the excitement of the auction put a skip in her step as she strode down the sidewalk in her Sunday best – a cornflower-blue linen jacket and skirt, black kid-leather pumps and jaunty beret angled to one side. In a few hours, she'd have a new home, a homestead on which to set up her soil experiment laboratory.

A crowd of perhaps a hundred men had already gathered behind the feed store where the auction would be held. RJ could hear the low murmur of their chatter as she approached the building. She stopped to adjust the angle of her beret – to buy a little time and help settle her jitters before she came around the corner of the store to the back lot.

A hush fell over the group as she drew near. Their faces were obscured by the shade of dusty felt fedoras and herringbone newsboy caps. The crowd seemed to part for her entry, and then it closed back in around and behind her.

Hanging in the wide open entrance to the grain shed in front of the group were two rope nooses, swaying in the breeze. RJ froze when she saw them. She couldn't fathom any purpose for them other than hangings. But did such barbaric acts still take place in this day and age? It was hard to imagine. She speculated the nooses were meant as some sort of warning. But of what?

"Nothing much worth bidding on today," said a man behind her. RJ looked back over her shoulder to see who had spoken, but all the men stared straight ahead.

"Nope," said another from RJ's other side. "Be surprised if anybody bid more 'n a penny or two."

RJ started to turn her head in his direction, but stopped herself, a crease deepening between her eyebrows. She looked down at the rolled up newspaper gripped in her fist.

She had never worried much about her petite size, or even given it much of a second thought, until now. As she stood in her proper dress and high-heeled shoes amidst a sea of beefy farmers in grubby overalls and work boots, she felt particularly tiny. She silently chided herself for not wearing denims and boots instead.

The crowd smelled of dirt and hard work. RJ could feel the heat radiating from their too-close bodies. Her chest began to tighten. She saw a gap in the crowd and decided to step outside the group and observe from the back.

"Excuse me," she said, moving toward the gap. The men continued their steely gaze over her head while stepping in to close the space.

"Oh, I'm sorry," she said, stepping back and moving to the other side. "Excuse me, please."

The men on the other side closed in. One man cleared his throat, and another behind her snickered. The auctioneer pounded his hammer at the podium and announced the bidding would soon begin. RJ turned herself back toward the front, and a gust of wind blew through, kicking up a cloud of dust and setting the nooses swinging back and forth. She found herself wishing she had brought Stormy along after all.

RJ sniffed and threw back her shoulders, steadied her focus straight ahead. She shifted her weight to one side, tapped her foot a couple of times and pushed her beret a little farther forward on her head. She put her hands on her hips and casually looked around at the men to see if any had noticed her bravado or given one damn about it. From what she could see, they hadn't.

The first property was a forty-acre lot about twenty miles outside of town with two outbuildings. RJ had no interest in the property, but she was curious to see how the bidding would play out. It would give her a good idea of the going price for the lot she wanted. According to the paper's listings, land value had dropped as low as two dollars an acre. Surely foreclosures would go for even less. RJ expected this lot to sell for around thirty-five or forty dollars.

"Do I have an opening bid?" the auctioneer shouted into the crowd.

"Five cents!" barked someone near the back.

RJ was aghast. She'd expected the auctioneer to have opened the bidding for at least five dollars.

"I have five cents," he hollered. "Do I hear any other bids?"

"I'll go ten cents," another bidder chimed in.

"We got ten cents now. Do I hear more? We got ten cents. Going once. Going twice. Sold!"

The hammer came down and the crowd came alive as the bidder made his way through the group. RJ heard several atta boys. The men shook his hand or slapped him on the back. She just couldn't figure it. The property was worth far more. Didn't anyone else have an interest in the land?

The next several properties went much the same way, selling for less than a dollar, even though they had houses and wells. One even had electricity. Is this what Ethel had meant when she said it would be a penny auction?

RJ felt like a fool. She couldn't seem to make sense of anything. When the property came up that she had been eyeing, her stomach turned to stone.

"A'right folks, we got the Clay property now. Forty acres, barn, well, two-room house with plumbing, two outbuildings. Who wants to start the bidding?"

The instructions she had received from the Interior Department told her she should open with a bid of five dollars and could go as high as one hundred. It had said nothing about nickel and dime sales, or about nooses swinging in the breeze.

"Ten cents," came a bid from the back.

The auctioneer smiled. "We've got ten cents from Mr. Harvey Clay. Do I hear any other bids?"

He quickly raised his hammer, but RJ found the courage to speak up.

"Five," she croaked at first. Then louder, "Five dollars."

A rumble spread through the crowd, like an electric current working its way in RJ's direction. Then, the auctioneer raised his hand, and a hush fell on the gathering.

"I heard ten cents. Going once..."

"I said five dollars," RJ shouted, louder this time, solid and strong, even though her insides were soup. She sensed all faces turned on her now. She kept hers trained on the auctioneer. A bead of sweat trickled down her rib cage beneath her blouse.

The space around her began to evaporate. The men shifted in closer.

"I heard ten cents. From Harvey Clay," said the auctioneer again, with slow fuming deliberation.

Someone took a firm hold of RJ's elbow.

"Maybe you never been to a penny auction, little lady," he grumbled in her ear.

"Oh, I... um, I...," RJ stuttered, trying to pull free from the man's grip.

He took hold of her other arm and spun her around. "Why don't you come with me," he said. "And I'll explain to ya how this here works."

RJ's heart flapped wildly in her chest, a caged bird in a panic to smash free. She struggled to break loose from the tight hold of his rough hands. She jerked back and thumped into the chest of another farmer close behind her.

"I'm not going anywhere with you," she said. "You get your meat hooks off of me."

RJ kicked the man's shin with all her might.

"Ow!" He tightened his grip even more and gave her a good hard shake.

RJ's beret was jarred from her head and fell to the ground, where it was stomped into the dirt by a dozen giant boots in the scuffle.

"Let her go, Milt," came a command from behind, and the crowd parted for a man in suspenders and a crisp white shirt rolled up to his elbows.

The farmer protested. "But we was just..."

"Godammit, I said let her go," Harvey Clay, the original bidder, repeated. "She can have the house. It don't matter no more. It's over."

"But, Harv."

"I said it's over!"

Harvey Clay was standing beside RJ then, eye to eye with the brute, who finally conceded and let go. RJ gasped in relief. The farmer's fingers left behind bright red marks on her pale arms.

"The lady bid five dollars," Harvey shouted to the auctioneer and then shoved his way back out through the hushed crowd.

The auctioneer brought down his hammer. "Five dollars for the Clay property to the government broad. See the cashier on your way out."

As if by magic, the crowd parted behind her, and RJ wasted no time in bolting through. Her knees were shaky. Her head spun.

Hold yourself together, RJ. She approached the cashier's stand in a daze. Somehow, she managed to produce the letter from her purse that guaranteed the Interior Department would wire the money. The cashier wrote out a voucher and gave RJ a set of keys. She fumbled the paper and keys, stuffing them into her purse, and croaked what was meant to be a thank you.

She walked around to the front of the feed store, then took off her high-heeled shoes and ran full out back to the motel. Outside the door, she struggled to find her room key, winded and wheezing. After what seemed like a lifetime, she burst through the door, locking it behind her, and flung herself onto the bed sobbing.

~~~

RJ stood before the bathroom mirror, barefoot in her torn stockings, taking in her reflection. Dark streaks and smudges of mud covered her nose, cheeks and neck, from where her tear-soaked face had been buried in the pillow – a pillow that had already been settled by a fresh layer of dust since she had shaken out the linens earlier in the morning. She pressed her fingers to her cheeks and smoothed the smudges into a velvety brown mask.

"Dust."

After another moment of staring down her reflection, RJ rested her dirty hands on the edge of the sink basin and dropped her head.

"What am I doing here?"

RJ twisted the faucet and let its cool energy run over her hands. She bent to the sink and splashed her face clean, watched the brown torrent swirl down the drain. Pulling the towel from the rack and shaking out the dust, she then blotted her face slowly, deliberately. She let out another gush of air from deep in her lungs and stared at her pink face and puffy eyes in the mirror.

"You knew this wasn't going to be easy," she said to her reflection. "You knew that."

RJ turned to leave the bathroom and nearly tripped over Stormy, who was sitting in the doorway, ears perked, head tilted in
~~~

that singular canine way that could melt any heart. She crouched down and gave the dog a tight hug. Stormy squirmed free, bounded in a circle and then ran to the motel room door. RJ laughed.

"You're absolutely right, Stormy. It's time for us to get out of here." RJ took off her jacket and unzipped her skirt. She rolled down her stockings and examined the gaping holes torn in the heels and toes. "Aw, hell."

She threw the bundle into the trash can under the nightstand. "I won't be needing those again anyway. We're moving on, Stormy."

RJ picked up her pace, suddenly energized. *Those thick-necked farmers think they can intimidate me?* She clucked through her teeth, as she slipped on her overalls and boots. *Those self-righteous mama's boys at the university thought the same thing, didn't they?* She buzzed around the room, organizing her belongings and packing them neatly into her suitcase. *Telling me I didn't belong there, that I was stealing a seat from a man who could do more with an education than a woman ever could.* She slammed the suitcase shut and buckled the straps.

"I showed them, Stormy," RJ said. "Graduated top of my class and got myself a government job they could only dream of getting. And I'll do a damned better job of it than any man would have, too. They'll all be thanking me someday for the work I've done. They'll be eating crow."

RJ scanned the room. She peeked inside each dresser drawer, even though she hadn't put anything in them, and knelt down to spy underneath the bed. She stood and brushed the dust from her knees.

"You'll be happier out at the homestead, Stormy. It's not like being in town. There won't be a thing out there to hold you back."

Stormy barked once, as if to say quit talking about it and let's get going. RJ clapped her hands, picked up her suitcase and the two set out for the homestead.

~~~

The crisp, clean air of the early morning had given way to a wispy veil of brown, stirred by the breeze and drawn up from the parched earth into the empty white sky. RJ considered turning on her headlights to help make her way down the desolate farm roads, but the idea felt absurd. *It's eleven in the morning, for heaven's sake.*

She slowed down and checked the map again. The auction clerk had included directions to the property, but RJ had begun to wonder if they were accurate. It wouldn't shock her if the men had sent her on a wild goose chase with spurious directions.

To RJ's relief, the outline of several small buildings became visible through the dry fog of dust. She continued down the road until she spotted the designated mile marker. At the turnoff sat a row of mailboxes, on a fence buried so deep within a dune that the boxes looked as though someone had lined them up along the ground.

The truck rumbled down the drive toward a one-story brick cottage with a gabled roof and a small front porch. RJ shut off the engine and checked her paperwork again. She let out a short whistle and shook her head in disbelief as she stepped out of the truck.

"Welcome to the Sahara Desert," she said, sliding a foot from side to side in front of her, through small drifts of soft dirt.

Stormy leapt out of the truck and began exploring the terrain.

A skeletal tree loomed at the side of the house, its trunk and craggy branches sandblasted smooth of any bark. The porch was level to the ground, its steps completely buried. The front door was ajar.

RJ walked up to the house and stepped in through the open door. She gasped. Earth covered the entire floor, at least a foot deep based on its proximity to the door handles. She eased further in, letting her sight adjust to the dark, taking in the devastation.
~~~

Dirt blanketed every surface. It coated the windows. It lay thick on the sills. It filled the kitchen sink. RJ peeked her head inside what appeared to be a closet without any shelves. An angled handrail jutted from the inside wall and disappeared down into the dirt floor.

"Oh," RJ let go of a gush of air she'd been holding in her lungs. "The basement."

She blinked and gave her head a little shake. RJ eased her foot through the doorway and pressed her toe into the soft earth.

RJ wandered through the rest of the house, making mental notes of the damage and the work to be done. She began to berate herself for rushing into a purchase. She should have checked out the properties before the auction. She should have found one in better shape. And she hadn't even seen the condition of the barn and outbuildings yet.

Stormy barking outside broke RJ from her negative thoughts. She stepped outside, blinking against the pink sunlight, to see what had the dog riled up. A truck eased toward them up the drive, creating a brown cloud that swelled and stirred around it.

RJ put a hand up to shade her view. She placed her other hand firmly on her hip and leaned forward on her toes, trying to make herself feel taller. She recognized the man's silhouette as soon as he stepped out of the truck. Harvey Clay.

She gave a short whistle to Stormy. The dog bolted over and stood beside her.

"Good girl," RJ whispered.

The man approached slowly, looking from RJ to the dog and back again. "That dog gonna bite me?"

RJ waited a bit before she answered. "Are you going to give her reason to?"

"No, ma'am," he said and flashed a dimpled smile.

RJ stood stone-faced

The wind drove through the crevices of the house like melancholy voices of owners past. The dust whispered its way along the ground between them. The man took a tentative step closer.

"I, uh," he faltered. "I'm sorry, you know, if the boys scared you this morning."

RJ held her gaze steady, remained silent.

"It's tough times," he continued. He looked down at his feet, dug the toe of his boot into the soft earth. "They was just trying to do right by me. They wouldn't of hurt you."

"They did hurt me," RJ said, finally, shifting her weight, but holding her ground. She resisted the urge to touch the red marks that still prickled on her arms.

"Well, like I said, I am sorry about all that." He looked up at her. His eyes were soft.

RJ looked away. She scanned the barren property for a moment. "What is it you're doing here, Mr. Clay? Is there something you want from me?"

He took another step toward her. "Naw, I don't want nothin' from you. Just wanted to apologize for the boys, and to return this." He held out her battered, dusty beret. "It'll need a scrubbing, but you might be able to save it."

RJ took the hat and sat down in the dirt on the porch. She turned the beret over in her hands, shaking her head. Stormy sat down beside her.

"You okay, Miss Evans?"

"Pfft, oh sure, I'm fine and dandy. Thanks for asking."

He walked past her and onto the porch. He looked up and around at the house. "It ain't exactly what you were expecting, huh?"

"No. It sure isn't."

Mr. Clay walked to the end of the porch. He peeked around the side of the house and then walked slowly back. His relaxed manner began to put RJ at ease.

"I'm starting to think you had the right idea," she said, "only bidding ten cents."

He shook his head, looking the house over again. "Oh, no ma'am. This place is worth every dollar you paid and then some. It'll clean up." He paused. "You really gonna build some sort a science laboratory out here?"

RJ stood and brushed the dirt from her behind. "Yes. A soil conservation lab."

"Is that right. All by yourself?"

RJ shrugged her shoulders and rolled her eyes. That had been the plan. But in this moment, in the face of all the dirt, it seemed ridiculous. She stepped beside him on the porch, keen to change the subject.

"What was all the fuss about this morning, Mr. Clay, at the auction? Ethel at the restaurant warned me to be careful. But I still haven't the slightest notion of what on earth happened or what I did wrong."

He turned to face her and, for a second, looked as though he was going to answer her. Then, he straightened his back and stuffed his hands in his pockets. He shook his head.

"That this morning was nothing. It's just tough times, like I said before." Mr. Clay walked back to his truck and tipped his hat as he climbed in behind the wheel. "Good luck with your science station and whatnot, Miss Evans."

RJ watched him turn the truck around and drive back down the road until he vanished into the dust like an apparition.

In the days that followed the auction, RJ had fallen into a comfortable rhythm of hard labor. She'd made a list of the many items that required attention, arranged them by priority and confronted them one by one.

RJ enjoyed quiet hours of study and reflection in a tidy lab. Yet, there was also something to be said for the gratification that comes with physical exertion. It gave her a narrowness of purpose and clarity of mind. The burn of her muscles reduced to ashes the anxiety of earlier days. The sweat of her skin washed away the dread of obstacles yet to come.

She took apart, cleaned and reassembled the well pump. She cleaned out the woodburning stove and chimney. Then, she began the chore of shoveling out the house. This task tested RJ's patience and perseverance as much as it tested her muscle and might. With each jab of the shovel, the earth took to the air in a lingering cloud that refused to be evicted from the building. Every few minutes, RJ staggered from the house, wheezing and choking for fresh air.

Figuring out where to heap all the dirt she shoveled from the house added to the challenge. RJ had noticed the wind blowing mostly from the west during her first few days at the property, so she decided to dump the dirt behind the barn. If another duster rolled through – *when* another duster rolled through – the barn would block all that dirt from blowing right back up into the house. By the fourth day, the winds had shifted, coming up from the south. And by the time she began dumping the first few mountainous wheelbarrows, it shifted again, blowing steady from the north.

On this day, she'd already made a half-dozen trips across the yard by mid-morning. She stopped with her latest load out behind the barn and squatted down to grip the wheelbarrow handles. She pushed up, her thighs and arms trembling, to dump the load. Then, she flipped the wheelbarrow upside down and sat down upon it to rest.

She removed her hat and wiped the sweat from her forehead with the back of her gritty arm. The wind lifted and rustled her matted hair, cooling her scalp and neck. It seemed to blow constantly. Yet, at the same time, there was a stillness to this land that RJ found unsettling.

Being alone in the fields and forests back in Wisconsin, you were surrounded by the click and buzz of crickets and cicadas, the chirp and twitter of a dozen different types of birds. Even the Kansas landscape from her youngest memories had had that hum of life to it. Not anymore.

It was all so clear, in hindsight, the damage man had done by plowing under mile after mile of grasslands. The destruction hadn't been intentional. RJ understood that. The world was clamoring for wheat, and there seemed to be no end to the plains' capacity to provide it. The land was there for the taking, and man took. Then, Mother Nature seemed to say enough. The rain stopped, and the plains no longer provided.

Now the land was desolate, depleted, silent.

The only thing that seemed to vibrate with life was the dirt itself. As it pulled itself up and crept along the earth's surface. As it ground beneath your feet when you walked across the floor. Even the dunes RJ created with her wheelbarrow loads seemed to be in a constant state of movement, as the millions of particles that formed them shifted and rippled and morphed beneath the wind.

RJ sat watching the earth stir, mesmerized, until another small gust of hot wind made her shudder. She stood up to stretch her sore muscles.

"One more load," she said, out loud, just to hear a voice, to shatter the stillness.

~~~

RJ had set up camp outside next to the porch. That way she could take advantage of the agreeable weather until the house was habitable. Yet, she was close enough to the house that she could duck for cover there if and when another duster rolled through. She slept in the Army surplus tent she'd used during her road trip, cooked her meals in cans over a makeshift fire pit.

The sun broke on the horizon every morning around five. It pushed through the dusty haze that covered the landscape, turning the rutted earth scarlet and white, and the sky a rich indigo, as if someone had unfurled a massive American flag from the heavens. RJ greeted the patriotic scene each new day, with a tin cup of steaming coffee and a renewed sense of purpose. She dreamed of the day when the barren land would once again ripple with native grasses, with wheat and essential crops, with life.

In the early evenings, RJ walked with Stormy to the different edges of the property. She surveyed every nook and cranny of the landscape. Later, she'd sit by the firelight and jot notes in her journal and draft topological maps until the day's fatigue overtook her. Finally, she'd crawl into the tent and cascade into a deep slumber with Stormy snoring beside her.

More than a week had passed and supplies were running low. RJ opened the last can of horsemeat for Stormy. The pungent gobs of meat slid into the dog bowl. RJ wrinkled her nose and sighed as she carefully scraped the can clean.

"I can't put it off any longer."
~~~

In the morning, she would return to town to retrieve her mail, stock up on supplies and try to mend the rift with the locals, just as her Aunt May would have advised.

"No can do, Miss Evans," said Bud, the postal office clerk, to RJ's request that her future mail be delivered to her new address. "Can't make deliveries out to the homesteads no more, not with half 'em being empty now anyhow, and not with all the dust always blowin'."

RJ eyed the young man behind the counter. The thought of coming to town every week simply to retrieve her mail gnawed at her. "So the postman doesn't make *any* deliveries outside of town?"

Bud busied his hands straightening stacks of letters. "Nope."

"Very well," she said. "Then, I suppose you and I will be seeing a lot more of each other."

Bud looked up to see her tight-lipped smile and head cocked to one side. His freckled cheeks flushed pink. "Suppose so," he mumbled.

RJ's obligatory smile faded quickly. She scooped up her parcels and hustled out the door.

Down the sidewalk a ways, she ducked into the A&P grocery store. The woman behind the long counter looked up briefly when the bell above the door jingled. "Mornin'."

"Good morning," RJ said, forcing friendliness into her voice. She picked up a basket near the door and began working her way up and down the aisles. The store was empty and quiet, which was a relief. RJ didn't feel ready to fend off a bunch of curious or menacing stares. From the shelves she grabbed a box of wood matches, a can of Maxwell House coffee, a loaf of bread and a few jars of fruit preserves.

A boy of about twelve years, wearing a canvas apron, shadowed RJ, a broom in hand. Whenever she cast a glance in his direction, the boy would swish clumsily at the dirty floor. RJ continued her shopping, adding several dusty cans of Libby's vegetables, Van Camp's pork and beans, and Campbell's tomato soup to her purchases.

The basket began to weigh on RJ's overworked muscles, so she walked back to the front of the store and placed it on the front counter. The woman there began taking the items out one by one, entering the prices on the cash register, and then loading the purchases into a wooden crate. The woman seemed to be taking her time, so RJ stepped away to grab a few more items – a box of raisins, some canned ham, a pack of Chesterfield cigarettes.

"Bring the crate back with you next time and you get a two cent credit," the woman said without looking up.

"Oh, that's good to know, thank you," said RJ placing her remaining items on the counter. "I'd also like to buy a case of canned horsemeat."

The woman placed the cigarettes in the crate, shaking her head and clicking her tongue. "That it?"

"I didn't notice any sweetened condensed milk," RJ said. "Do you stock it?"

"It's five cents a can," the woman said. "I'd have to order it special."

"I'd sure appreciate it if you would," RJ said, and the woman balked.

"Most folks can't afford that kind of luxury," she said.

RJ clenched her teeth against the sharp retort that swirled in her mouth, words stabbing at her tongue to escape.

The woman finished ringing the prices into the register. "That it?" she asked again.

"Yes, thank you."

"With the dog food, that comes to two dollars and sixty-five cents."

RJ opened her wallet and paid in exact change. "My truck is parked by the feed store," she said. "Would you be so kind as to have your boy carry the crates over there?"

The woman took RJ's money and shook her head impatiently. "We're too busy to run deliveries today."

The steady tick-tick-tick of the wall clock echoed through the empty store. RJ scrutinized the woman.

"I understand." RJ's words were measured. "I'll come back around with the truck when I've finished my business at the feed store."

"We close shop from eleven to noon for dinner. I'll have him set the crates outside the door for ya," the woman said, then turned and disappeared behind a curtain into a back room.

RJ sneered at the curtain and muttered a few unintelligible insults. It was childish, she knew, and she immediately chided herself for letting the woman best her. *Take the high road, Rosa Jean,* she could hear Aunt May's advice in her head.

She took her time walking to the feed store. The men there were going to be even more ornery, she knew, and she needed to regain her composure before taking a stick to that particular hornet's nest. Eventually, to do her job, RJ would need to convince the locals to adopt new farming techniques, to change the way they worked their land. And to do that, she'd have to somehow earn their respect and their trust. It would be a tall order. That much was clear to her now.

Seeing the feed store and the men hanging around outside gave RJ a more violent jolt than she had expected. The auction flashed in her mind. Her chest constricted. Maybe she ought to wait a bit. Think on it a little longer. Come back another time.

Just then, she noticed Harvey Clay leaning against the feed store wall. Their eyes connected for a second. He gave the brim of his hat a quick flick in acknowledgment before turning his attention back to the other men.

Well, he'd seen her. It was too late to turn tail and run now. RJ strode toward the wide-open double doors.

"Good morning," she said, sizing up the group as she walked past them, making eye contact with as many men as she could. "I'm looking for the proprietor, if you'd be so kind as to point him out."

A few of the men shuffled their feet or jammed their hands in their pockets. Several smirked and folded their arms across their chests. None spoke. RJ glanced in Harvey's direction. She could see he was stifling a grin beneath his thin mustache, but he raised his eyebrows and bobbed his head in the direction of the feed shed door. She looked and saw a rotund man teetering on a tall stool. A makeshift desktop jutted from the shed wall on rickety supports, a wooden crate lid topped with a stack of tattered catalogs and a rusty can full of chewed-up pencils. The man seemed to be riveted by the condition of his cuticles. RJ sauntered over to him.

"Good morning," she said again.

"Is it?" The man looked up at RJ and shifted his weight. The overworked stool wobbled and half the man's behind slipped precariously over the edge, causing him to jolt and shift again.

"Might be a better morning for you if you had a bigger stool to set on," RJ said, smiling sweetly and leaning to the side a bit to get a better look at the man's backside. The man sucked at his teeth, and a handful of the gang behind her snickered. Still, no one else spoke.

RJ continued to stand in front of the man, smiling. She let the silence linger.

Her years dealing with fat-headed professors and classmates had taught her that silence bothered a man much more than it did her. Most men were composed when their intentions were to charm a lady. But when a woman stepped foot on their territory as a peer, well, that was another matter. That's when they usually got all sweaty and tense and defensive.

She tilted her head to the other side and whistled softly to gain his attention. She heard a few whispers behind her back.

"You wantin' something from me, little lady?" The man finally caved.

"Yes, thank you," RJ said, extending her hand. "I'm RJ Evans and I'll be working outside of town on a soil conservation project for the Interior Department. So I'll be buying lots of seed and just might come by to see you for a bit of advice from time to time."

RJ's hand hovered in the air between them as she spoke, but the man made no move to reciprocate. "And you are?" she added.

"Mr. Meginnis."

"It's a pleasure to meet you, Mr. Meginnis," RJ said, giving up on the handshake and wrapping her fingers around the strap of the purse slung over her shoulder.

"Yeah, well, the pleasure's all yours," the man muttered, which tickled the men gathered around.

RJ smiled at him again, mostly with her eyes. Then, she leaned in and whispered, "I suppose I had that coming after my wisecrack about your big old butt."

Mr. Meginnis recoiled and nearly fell off the stool. He jumped to his feet and coughed. The fellow standing next to him was the only other person close enough to hear what RJ had said. He erupted in a rasping laugh, then suppressed his outburst, folded his hands beneath his belt and looked down at his feet.

"What?" The other farmers chimed in. "What'd she say to him?" But the fellow just kept looking at his feet and shook his head. He didn't dare open his mouth.

"If you're here to buy something, you better get on with it," Mr. Meginnis snapped.

"Yes, of course," RJ responded evenly. "I'd like to purchase a fall seed catalog and a *Farmer's Almanac*. I'll also be needing a bag of broom corn seed."

Meginnis shuffled over to a trunk just inside the door and pulled out copies of the catalog and almanac. He returned his large behind to its stool, and flapped the publications in his hands.

"These is fifteen cents apiece," he said. "Seed's a dollar for a hundred-pound bag."

"Here you are." RJ handed over the money. Mr. Meginnis took it and tucked it away in a small metal box on his desk. He jerked his head toward the warehouse. "Seed's over there. Help yourself, little lady."

RJ stiffened for a second before she smiled coolly. "Thank you, Mr. Meginnis. I'll just go put these things in my truck and come right back for that seed."

She turned and walked casually to her truck. Her mind raced. *How in the hell am I going to load a hundred-pound bag of seed?* RJ climbed in the cab and set her mail, publications and purse in the seat beside her. She started up the truck and backed it as close to the seed shed as she could manage.

The seed bags were stacked about four feet high on pallets just inside the wide double doors. RJ strolled inside the shed, scanning the tags to find the broom corn between the barley and buckwheat. She grabbed hold of two corners on the top bag and pulled with all her might. It slid about an inch, and the men snickered.

RJ rolled up her shirt sleeves to give herself a minute more to think. She barely weighed more than a hundred pounds herself. She grabbed hold of the bag again. Then, she hoisted one foot up onto the stack in front of her, and pushed and pulled at the same time.

The bag budged a little, then a lot, and then it came sliding off the pile in a quick rush. RJ stumbled back to get out of the way as the sack crashed to the ground. The men whooped and hollered and clapped.

RJ's heart was pounding in her ears. She stretched her elbows to her back and then to the front, rolled her head to the right and then to the left. She squatted down beside the bag and tried to roll it toward the truck. With her shoulder, and all her weight, she leaned in. The seeds within shifted, but the bag itself didn't budge.

She walked around to the other side of the bag and tried pulling it by the corners again. Her feet lost traction in the loose dirt and slid out from under her. RJ fell on her behind with a hard thud, still gripping tight to the sack. This time the men roared.

The hard landing sent a shock of pain from her tailbone all the way up her back. RJ winced. She rolled over to her hands and knees to collect herself. From out of nowhere, firm but gentle hands took hold of RJ's arms and lifted her to her feet. She looked up to see Woody towering over her.

He held tight to her, steadied her on her feet. When he was certain RJ wouldn't tip over, Woody gently released his grip. He turned and glared at the men.

"Shame on y'all."

The farmers quieted their laughter to a murmur. They watched as Woody knelt down and heaved the seed bag up over his shoulder like it was filled with air. RJ grinned and shook her head in disbelief. She got a sudden vision in her mind of him flinging her up over his other shoulder with the same ease, and it made her laugh out loud. Woody beamed.

"Aw shoot, Woody," one farmer muttered. The others guffawed and spit and kicked at the pebbles on the ground.

Woody dispatched the seed bag to RJ's flatbed, and she followed close behind him.

"Thank you so much," she whispered. "Good-bye now."

"I'll go on back with ya."

"Oh, you don't have to do that, Woody."

"How you fixin' to unload them seeds when you get there?"

RJ opened her mouth, but no words came, so she snapped it back shut. She blew a puff of air out of the corner of her mouth to drive her bangs out of her eyes. “Well, I... I’ll just... I’ll manage.”

“I’ll go on back with ya,” Woody repeated.

RJ smiled. “I’d appreciate that. I just need to stop back at the A&P first.”

She cast a glance back at the farmers, but none of the men looked her way. She waited a moment more, daring them to look at her. Only Harvey had the nerve. He flashed her a dimpled grin and tipped his hat. RJ shook her head at him. She turned her attention back to Woody and smiled again.

“Come on, Woody,” she said. “Let’s go.”

RJ peeked sideways at Woody while she navigated the lopsided road out of town. The small truck cab wasn't very forgiving to his lanky frame, but he didn't seem to mind. His hands were resting on his knees, which were bent up close to his body. He looked out the side window, watching the landscape roll by as they bumped along.

"Do you know why them fellers at the feed lot was so mean to you?" Woody's gaze remained fixed on some point in the distance, out the side window.

"I suspect it was because they're still mad at me for bidding at the auction," RJ said. "But for the life of me, I don't understand why they got so angry about *that*."

"Do you want me to tell you why they're mad?"

"That would be a big help, Woody. I wish you would."

Woody launched into a lengthy narrative, reciting the facts in chronological order, starting fifty years in the past. His voice was even, almost methodical, and he hardly paused to breathe. Lots of families began moving to Vanham before the turn of the century, he said, for a chance to own themselves a piece of land, something they could turn into something better than it was before and pass on to their children one day. There were the Wallaces and the Sharps, and the Rothsteins and the Tugwells, and the Cobbs and the Clines. The land was harsh, and the weather was worse, but there was rain and there was crops and there was hope.

"What does any of that have to do with the auction?" RJ interrupted.

"I'm getting to that," Woody said.

"Lots of families began moving to Vanham before the turn of the century," he began again, at the beginning, and RJ smiled. *Best not interrupt him again*, she told herself.

"The Clays were one of those young new families," Woody said. Harvey Clay grew up on a plot of land his grandpa had owned. Lived with his ma and pa and brothers and sisters. He went to school when he was little, and worked the land with his pa and brothers when he got big. The years went by and the flu came and lots of folks went to heaven. Harv lost his ma and his baby sister and one older brother. Then his pa died a short while later, but not from the flu, from a broken heart.

RJ's jaw tightened. She wondered which of her own parents had been the first to succumb to the flu. Which one had been left brokenhearted?

"When the Clay boys were grown," Woody kept talking, Harv's brother Ben married his sweetheart Nettie and moved in with her and her folks. That's the property you're at now. Nettie was the baby of her family, so all her sisters and brothers had already moved on by then. When Nettie's parents passed, she and Ben worked that land and started a family of their own. Meanwhile, Harv stayed on at his folks' place by himself, and worked that land. Ain't got married or started a family, but Harvey was doing good.

Then things got bad for everybody. The rain stopped falling. The crops stopped sprouting. For one year, and then for another, and another. The wind kept blowing. The wind never stops blowing here.

RJ was absorbed in Woody's story. Her eyes were on the road, but her mind and heart were in another place and time. As they approached a fork in the road, she slowed the truck, hesitated. Woody continued talking and looking out of his window, but he lifted his hand from his knee and pointed to the left. She turned left. Woody placed his hand back on his knee.

"Folks that did manage to bring in some little bit of a crop had to sell it for next to nothing," Woody said. For less than it cost them to raise up and harvest it. Things got tight. And times got worse. Then them sons-a-bitches at the banks started foreclosin' people. And then them sons-a-bitches at the big farming corporations bought up the farms and offered to let the families live there and work the land, just like before, only for even less money than they could manage before.

"Sons-a-bitches," Woody said again. That's when folks started losing hope, started packing up and moving away. And there was auctions every month. Men in shiny shoes and stiff collars would come into town on auction days and buy up our land, our parents' land, our grandparents' land. It wasn't fair. It wasn't right. That's when someone come up with the idea of the penny auctions. When someone's farm is going up for auction, you see, everyone goes to support the farmer. That's called solidarity. When the businessman tries to bid, the folks close in and explain why there ain't no reason for him to bid. If he protests, they escort him off and continue explaining it to him somewheres else. One time, I seen a group of farmers, Mr. Meginnis and Mr. Clay and a bunch of others, pick up a feller over their heads and carry him away while he was kicking and cussing and hollering.

Woody paused to chortle.

RJ's stomach grew hard. Her knuckles turned white as she gripped the steering wheel. *So he's telling me I got off easy?*

"Meanwhile," Woody said, "the farmer could bid a nickel or two and buy back his own farm from the sons-a-bitches who foreclosed on him. And that's where you come in.

"You ain't a banker or a farming corporation sons-a-bitch, but you're with the government, and that's near as bad. Folks around here don't trust government fellers. Of course, you ain't a feller neither, so that kind of thrown everybody off, too. But when they heard you wanted to buy a farm at auction, that's all they needed to know. Harv's brother had moved Nettie and their little ones up to Wichita and got a job working at the Stearman Aircraft factory. That near broke Harv's heart, being the only family he had left. He was hoping if he could buy back their farm, he could convince Ben and Nettie to move back, give it another go 'round."

RJ tried to swallow the lump forming in her throat.

"But you didn't really do no harm in buying the farm, RJ," Woody said, turning to look at her. "At least that's what Harv told me the other day. He said he didn't really think Ben woulda come back anyhow. So there was no real harm in you buying it, other than giving them sons-a-bitches bankers more money than they deserved for it."

And that was the end of Woody's story. He turned his face back to the window. They drove in silence a few minutes more. RJ turned onto the slender road of her property.

"Thank you, Woody, for explaining all of that to me," RJ said as they pulled up to the house. She stopped the engine and turned to look at him. "That's helpful information for me to have, and I appreciate your giving it to me straight."

"You're welcome," Woody said. "Most people don't like to hear it straight."

He opened the door and unfolded his limbs from the cab. RJ stepped out, too, and they slammed their doors shut in unison.

"You can always be straight with me, Woody. I just can't abide folks beating around the bush."

"Guess you moved to the right place then," Woody said, looking around. "There ain't a bush in sight 'round here."

RJ laughed.

Woody shrugged, stone-faced. He looked around again, as if to prove his point. Not a bush in sight. That's when Woody noticed

RJ's tent and fire pit beside the porch. He drew up his mouth tight and scrunched his eyebrows. "You ain't living in the house?"

"Oh, I mean to, Woody. It just needs so much work. It's been neglected for a long time."

Woody shook his head. "That's a shame. It sure is a nice house. All them big windows."

RJ smiled, looking up at the house. Woody was right. She hadn't fully appreciated what a lovely house it must have once been, before the dust gnawed away its paint and assaulted its insides like a cancer. She looked back at Woody. He beamed as he surveyed the house.

"When Ben and Nettie lived here, they used to let me come over after the dusters and paint all their windows," he said, a dash of whimsy in his voice.

"You mean *wash* the windows," RJ gently corrected.

Woody shrugged again. "I call it painting."

He stuffed his hands in his pockets and began to walk the perimeter of the house, examining every pane of glass.

RJ let him be and began unloading her packages from the truck. She put her mail and publications in her tent. She carried the food crates into the house, setting them just inside the door. She didn't want to attract animals to her tent by leaving food out in the open. Though, when she thought about it, she had yet to see any animals running wild or to hear a coyote cry in the night. Even the crickets were silent at night, as though they too had packed up and moved on, unable to make a go of it in this parched barren land.

"Where you want your seed?" Woody had suddenly reappeared, the colossal seed sack slung over his shoulder.

RJ put her hands on her hips and looked around. "In the house for now, I suppose."

Woody deposited the sack inside. When he came back out, he said good-bye, waved and turned to head off across the field.

"Wait," RJ shouted to him. "Don't you want a ride?"

"Nah. My house is only two miles and eight-hundred-eighty-five feet due west of here. I can walk that in no time."

Two miles and eight-hundred-eighty-five feet, RJ muttered to herself. "As long as you're sure," she said. "Good-bye, Woody, and thank you again for all your help."

Woody waved again and began walking. Then he stopped and turned back around.

"Say," he said, looking at the ground. "I don't suppose you'd mind if, well, if I come by again sometime and paint your windows."

RJ liked the idea of his company, but didn't think she could hire him. "That's a fine idea, Woody. But it wouldn't be fair of me. I wouldn't be able to pay you for your work."

"Why in blazes would you *pay* me to paint your windows?" Woody laughed. "Ben never did. That's the silliest thing I ever heard. I'll have to tell Pa that one when I get home. He'll get a good laugh at that."

Woody turned a final time and trekked across the yard and into the field. RJ just shook her head and watched his tall silhouette shrink in the distance.

After a month of hauling dirt, RJ decided the house was ready for an occupant. She was thrilled to pack away her tent and sleep indoors once again, on a real bed. That first morning, she awoke to bright sunshine glowing through her dirt-caked bedroom window. She had slept in until nearly eight o'clock!

A few more weeks passed as RJ continued to sweep and scour every surface in the house. She hung curtains she'd ordered from the Woolworth's catalog. She stocked the kitchen cupboards with the supplies she'd purchased. She placed a small desk by the front window and a worktable, cabinet of file drawers and bookshelves in the living room.

On the two-month anniversary of her arrival in Vanham, RJ awoke and dressed quickly. Today was the day she could finally begin unpacking her equipment and commence setting up the lab. *Her* lab.

With Christmas-morning giddiness, she pried open the lid on the first crate. A neatly-typed, though dusty, inventory list lay atop the packing straw. This box contained gadgets to track wind speed, monitor barometric pressure and, God willing, measure rainfall. RJ removed the top layer of straw, coughing on the dust being stirred up, and lifted out the first instrument. She gingerly unwound the cheesecloth wrapping. Her fingers left prints in the grit that coated the carved oak base of the barometer. She blew on the glass face of the dial, and the grit took to the air in a billowy cloud of brown.

"Dust."

Was there no end to its craftiness? The dust had worked its way through the tight seams of the well-built crate, through the layers of packing material, beneath the tightly wrapped cloth. It coated all of her expensive lab instruments with a layer of grime so thick it looked as though they had been carelessly left out in a storm. They would all need to be thoroughly cleaned.

"Shoot," RJ said, setting down the barometer and slumping into her desk chair.

She stared at the remaining crates for another minute or so, running calculations in her mind, estimating how long it would take her to properly clean each instrument, wash every beaker, dust every chemical bottle.

Her thoughts tumbled around and around in her head – in frustration, in disbelief over the endless onslaught of dust. And she'd only been at it a couple months. How on earth did other people manage it, month upon month, year upon year? It was maddening.

After a moment, RJ swung her feet around beneath the desk and removed the cover from her typewriter. She took a piece of stationary from its stack, shook off the dust and rolled the paper into the Corona with three quick twists. At the staccato sound of the roller, Stormy trotted over and curled up on the floor at RJ's feet. The steady clickity-clack of the keys soon lulled the dog to sleep.

... pleased to report the station is piecing together well, though unrelenting dust remains a challenge.

Even the simplest of tasks requires twice the time and effort...

At this pace, working alone, it is unlikely the station will be operational in time to monitor the fall harvest and winter wheat seeding.

... respectfully request additional funds to hire a hand or two to assist with daily labors.

When her report to D.C. was complete, RJ folded it neatly and tucked it into an envelope.

"I'll go into town tomorrow and post this, Stormy. You come along for company, and I'll get you a sausage or two at Ethel's."

The dog peered up at RJ, groggy, roused from sleep by the word sausage.

~~~

Stormy lay in the shade outside Ethel's, eating the sausages RJ had ordered. Inside, RJ sat alone at a table by the window, savoring her Blue Plate Special of meatloaf and mashed potatoes with gravy. Despite having a full kitchen now, RJ still hadn't gotten the hang of cooking and was mostly eating out of cans and boxes just like she had at college. A home-cooked meal, even if it was prepared at a restaurant, had become such a treat.

Ethel walked over to RJ's table and peered out the window. She clucked her tongue and drew her eyebrows together. RJ looked out and saw the blood-red haze on the horizon.

"Another duster?" RJ asked.

Ethel seemed to shrink a bit.

A sandstorm had just rolled through a few days before. The frequency of the storms seemed to be increasing, even in the short time RJ had been in Vanham.

"It's August," Ethel said, as if she'd read RJ's mind. "Should be getting good ole summer downpours a couple times a week. Not this. Not this constant dust."

The woman shook her head in defeat. "Well, we best start battening down the hatches."

She turned to the other customers in the cafe. "Bud, Margie, we got a duster rolling in."

The couple sprang to their feet. The man dropped a few coins on the table, and the woman started talking at her husband. "You
~~~

fetch the children from school. I'll head home, to round up the chickens and pump some water. Who knows how long this one'll last?"

RJ jumped up, too.

"Thanks for the supper, Ethel."

"Where on earth do you think you're going?" Ethel didn't even give RJ a chance to respond. "You're not going anywhere. You can't drive back to your place in this storm. You'll never make it in time. Go bring that dog of yours inside and help me get some things together."

"Oh, I couldn't possibly stay here. What if the storm lasts all night?"

"What if?" Ethel said, throwing her hands up in surrender, and hustled into the back room. RJ stood motionless in the middle of the restaurant, running her options through her mind. She loathed the idea of relying on Ethel's hospitality for the evening, or longer. Yet, she also couldn't shake the image of cowering beneath the Ford with Stormy again, while the wind howled and the earth piled up around them.

Ethel called from the back room, "Wind's picking up. Go get that dog of yours and bring in anything from your truck that you don't want eaten alive by the dust."

RJ snapped out of her haze. She hustled outside to roll up the windows on the Ford and bring in the crates of food she'd purchased earlier in the day. Then, she called Stormy into the cafe.

Ethel was outside, bringing down the awnings to cover the windows and locking them into place. RJ called to her above the din of the wind, "What can I do to help?"

"Clear the plates and gather up the tablecloths, take 'em into the kitchen. Then you can help me flip over the tables."

"The tables?"

"Makes cleanup easier," Ethel explained, as she moved from the windows to help RJ clear the plates.

"I've wondered how you manage to keep the restaurant so clean. I can't seem to keep up with it at my place."

"You learn new tricks with every storm," Ethel said. "I'll share a few more with ya in a bit. But we've got to move right now, honey."

The women flipped the tables and stowed away the plates, utensils and linens, then they dropped canvas covers down over the cupboard doors. It was time to head to the basement to ride out the storm.

"Storm'll knock out the electricity," Ethel said, as she lit an oil lamp. "Might as well get this lit now, so we won't be stumbling in the dark later."

The basement was tidy and cheerful, just like the restaurant. It had a small bed with a sunny quilt and a brightly painted rocking chair in the corner. A single shelf on the wall held a handful of books and a porcelain figurine of the Virgin Mary with the Baby Jesus.

Stormy worked her way carefully down the stairs, then scampered under the bed.

"Poor thing," Ethel said.

"She doesn't like the dusters," RJ said, frowning.

"Who the hell does?"

RJ laughed out loud. "You have a point," she said, relaxing a bit. "So, this is your storm shelter? It's cozy."

"This is my home," Ethel said.

"Oh," RJ said, stiffening. She hadn't given it much thought before, but had assumed Ethel lived in one of the tiny homes at the edge of town.

"I sold the house after Ed died," Ethel said. The woman seemed to have an uncanny ability to read RJ's thoughts before she spoke them. "Didn't make sense for me to try and keep up the house and the restaurant on my own. Living here suits me just fine."

RJ smiled meekly. For the first time, she realized that Ethel was alone. And RJ understood all too well how awful it felt to be alone when it wasn't by choice. The room became painfully quiet, despite the wind howling upstairs and outside.

"So what now?" RJ asked, looking around the small room, uneasy at the idea of being cooped up for who-knows-how-long, even in such a cozy place.

Ethel grinned and wiggled her eyebrows up and down. "I'm so glad you asked."

The hostess opened the top drawer of her small bureau and pulled out a bottle of Four Roses Kentucky bourbon and two empty canning jars. RJ stifled a gasp. "Oh, I couldn't possibly."

"That so?" Ethel said, thumping the bottle down on the small table in the center of the room and plunking the jars down beside it. "And why's that?"

RJ struggled to respond, but words escaped her.

Ethel added a tin of cookies to the table and sat down in one of the two straight-backed chairs. "Roosevelt put an end to prohibition last year, honey. Or haven't you heard? I read in the paper them Anheuser-Busch folks sent a team of Clydesdales over to the White House the very next day to deliver a case of Budweiser." Ethel snickered and poured two fingers of bourbon into each jar.

"But doesn't Kansas still ban alcohol?"

"The law only says you can't sell it by the glass. Doesn't say you can't drink it by the glass." Ethel raised her drink to RJ and then took a sip.

RJ smiled stiffly and lowered herself into the empty chair. She opened the cookie tin and removed a snickerdoodle, took a bite. "Oh," she said, savoring the pillowy texture in her mouth, the spicy sweetness of the cinnamon. "This is a little piece of heaven. Truly."

Ethel smiled, nodding immodestly. "They're one of my specialties. Try dunkin' it." Ethel demonstrated.

"It's just," RJ started, then paused a moment. She watched Ethel take a bite of the snickerdoodle, dunk it in the bourbon a second time and then devour it. "You see, my aunt and uncle are Methodist, so we never had such things in the house. Ever."

"Teetotalers," Ethel smiled.

"Even at college, some of the girls would sneak out after curfew to a speakeasy on the outskirts of Madison. But I never went. Who had time to drink and be silly, what with working and studying? I sure didn't."

Ethel reached for a second cookie. "Makes no never mind to me one way or the other, honey. I can put up a pot of joe, if you'd rather."

RJ felt her face warm. *Where are your manners, RJ?* Liquor or not, her Aunt May would be mortified with RJ's behavior toward this gracious hostess who offered her shelter from the storm.

"I don't want to put you out any more than I already have, Ethel. I so appreciate your looking out for Stormy and me. What you've got here is just fine."

To prove her sincerity, RJ took a cautious sip of the bourbon. She delicately cleared her throat as the liquid burned its way down her gullet. Ethel laughed and dunked her cookie. RJ followed suit.

Ethel pulled a pack of Chesterfields from her apron pocket. She angled the pack toward RJ. "Smoke? Or is that also against the rules?"

A twinkle of mischief lit up RJ's face. "Not my rules."

The women lit their cigarettes and blew their smoke into the dusty air.

"All the girls smoked at school," RJ said. "But when I bought a pack at the general store the other day, I sure got a nasty look from the woman there."

"Not many women smoke around here. Most folks think it isn't ladylike, I suppose," Ethel said. She made a goofy face to show she didn't really give a darn what most folks thought. "My husband picked up the habit fighting the war overseas. They gave packs to the soldiers as part of their rations. He got me started smoking after he came home."

RJ had been told that's how her Uncle Lou got started smoking, too, in the war. But she'd sure never seen him offer up a smoke to her aunt. Guess he was in the not-ladylike camp. RJ looked down at the cigarette perched between her fingers and wondered if Aunt May had ever snuck one when Uncle Lou wasn't around.

Ethel retrieved a deck of playing cards and began to shuffle, her cigarette dangling from her lips. She suggested gin rummy or maybe canasta. RJ was as familiar with card games as she was with drinking. The women finally settled on playing Fish. They played a few hands, and RJ ate a few more bourbon-soaked cookies. Ethel refilled their jam jars, and RJ dealt another round of cards.

A halo of orange light glowed around the oil lamp, the air getting thick with dust and cigarette smoke. Ethel took the two joker cards from the deck and placed one on each of their drinks to keep their bourbon from turning to mud. She studied her hand and asked, "Do you have a three?"

"Go fish." A soothing warmth filled RJ's body and her mind felt light, free of worry for the first time in years. She stared at her cards for a moment. "Do you... have... a three?"

"Honey, I just asked you for a three," Ethel shook her head. "Do you have a three or don't you?"

RJ studied her hand again and shook her head. "No. No threes."

The women looked up at each other and broke out in giggles. Ethel coughed a bit from the dust and took another sip of her bourbon. RJ set her cards down, propped her elbows on the table and leaned her cheeks into her fists.

"Ethel, tell me something. How do you put up with all of this dust and not lose your blessed mind?"

"Who says I *haven't* lost my blessed mind," the woman shot back without missing a beat, and the two exploded into another fit of giggles. After they settled down, Ethel got serious.

"Now you tell me something, RJ. How *does* a young woman become a geologist at a fancy college in the middle of the Depression? Did your folks have some sort of buried treasure that none of the rest of us knew about?"

RJ sat up straight and sighed. "No, no buried treasure. My granddad was my treasure." She took a sip of bourbon and let the heat travel down her insides.

"He passed in the spring of my senior year of high school. His will left half of his money to my Aunt May with the other half divided four ways between my cousins and me. My uncle was the executor for my aunt, of course, and for us kids because we were all minors. He put every last penny in the stock market like he was some big shot."

RJ gathered up the cards from the table as she spoke and stacked them in a neat pile, turning them from one side to the next, tapping them into a tight, even stack. Ethel leaned back in her chair and balanced her canning jar of bourbon on her stomach, the joker topping it off.

"Soon as I turned eighteen, I took the train into town to the broker's office, closed out my account and walked straight to the University of Wisconsin. Oh Ethel, you should have seen my Uncle Lou's face when he found out. Holy Moses. He was spitting nails."

RJ shook her head, her focus fixed on the deck of cards as she clumsily shuffled them again and again.

"But he didn't go on down there to get the money back?" Ethel asked.

"Oh, he wanted to straight away, but my aunt talked him out of it. She said the money was her daddy's, and that he gave it to me and he would have had no problem with me spending it on a college education. And she was right. Granddad was always tickled pink listening to me jabber on about going to college someday. I'm sure he was smiling down on me from above when I plunked down that money at the school."

Ethel smiled, pantomimed a cross over her breast and then took a long, slow draw from her bourbon.

"Then, the next fall, the stock market crashed and Uncle Lou and my cousins lost everything. But my money was safe, you see, because it was in a student account at the university."

"Cheese and crackers," Ethel said, sitting up and reaching for another cookie.

RJ set the deck of cards back on the table, crossed her arms and leaned back in her chair.

"You can bet my uncle charged on down to the school then and demanded the registrar empty my account, send my money back home, and me along with it. I was devastated. I couldn't imagine going back to the farm, putting up preserves all day long, milking cows before dawn, marrying a farmer.

"But the registrar refused to give my uncle the money. UW needed my money as much as anybody else, and they had it and weren't about to return it."

"So you got to stay at school," Ethel said, shaking her head, grinning. "That's some fairy-tale ending, honey."

"And she lived happily ever after," RJ said, a tinge of bitterness on her tongue. "Except that my uncle hasn't spoken to me since. And even with my inheritance covering tuition and board, I still had to work nights in the lab all through school, washing beakers and test tubes, to make a few dollars for food and other necessities."

"At least you had work," Ethel chided.

"That's true. A lot of other girls had to drop out, and the kids who stayed had to get creative at making money. My roommate went prowling at night to trap stray cats. Sold them to the animal lab for a nickel apiece."

Ethel wrinkled her nose. RJ sighed, shook her head to force the memory of mewling kittens from her mind.

"You worked hard. And now you're a bona fide scientist, working for the United States government, for Pete's sake," Ethel broke the silence. "That's a helluva thing."

A smile spread across RJ's face. "It *is* a helluva thing, isn't it?"

RJ awoke in Ethel's small bed, beneath the sunflower quilt. Her head pulsed sharply. She eased herself upright and winced. Stormy paced the floor, barked twice, and RJ's hands flew to either side of her head in an attempt to keep it from splitting in two.

"Shhhhh, Stormy," RJ mumbled, wondering who had stuffed her mouth with cotton. Then she made a silent vow that she would never touch alcohol again. Ever.

She pressed her temples with the heels of her hands, swallowed hard, tested her knees as she rose from the bed. Stormy bounded up the stairs, and RJ slowly followed. A joyful hymn in Ethel's husky voice drifted softly down the stairwell.

"Good morning, hon," Ethel sang out when she saw RJ emerge.

The young woman moaned, one hand bracing the wall for balance, the other pressing against her forehead. "Is it?"

Ethel chortled. "Help yourself to some joe and sit a while. You'll get your sea legs in a few minutes. There's a bottle of aspirin under the cash register. Meanwhile, I've got to get this place in shape so I can open for the lunch crowd."

RJ poured a cup of steaming coffee and drank it black. She helped herself to two aspirins and a seat at the counter. The clock above the kitchen door read five minutes past ten. *How long had the storm lasted?*

"It was clear skies when I came up at eight," Ethel said. "Don't know when it stopped blowing."

"How do you do that, Ethel? How do you always seem to know what I'm thinking?"

"You're an open book, honey." Ethel smiled while she wiped the chairs clean with a wet rag.

RJ bristled. The last thing she wanted was for people to be able to read her so easily. When you're a woman living and working on your own, RJ had learned, it's best not to let your guard down or let people get too close to your thoughts. She decided to tell herself Ethel must have a touch of clairvoyance. Aunt May always insisted there was such a thing and, maybe just for today, RJ would choose to believe it.

The coffee and aspirin began to work their magic after a bit. The pounding in RJ's head eased and the fog slowly evaporated from her mind. "What can I do to help you clean up, Ethel?"

"Oh, don't you worry about me, hon. I have a system. You should get on back to your place and see what needs doing there. You're sure to have quite a mess on your hands."

RJ finished her coffee, walked over to Ethel and threw her arms around the woman. It had been so long since RJ had felt taken care of by anyone, and she was suddenly overcome with gratitude for all Ethel had done.

"Ain't you sweet," Ethel said, patting RJ's back. Then, she gently pushed the young woman toward the door. "Get along now. We've both got work to do."

~~~

Back at her place, RJ took off across her experimental fields. Every fifty yards or so she stopped, crouched in the dust and opened her field bag. She scooped teaspoons of soil into small manila envelopes, carefully sealed and labeled the envelopes before tucking them into her bag. She jotted notes in her journal
~~~

about what she saw, what she smelled, what she heard and felt and thought. They would all go in her weekly report to Washington.

Nothing beat the time she spent alone with the land. It was when she came up with her best ideas. It was as though the earth whispered its secrets to her, and her alone.

During RJ's daily explorations as a child in the meadows surrounding her uncle's farm, she had listened to the hum of the bumble bee and the rustle of meadow bromegrass, the chirp of the goldfinch and the gurgle of the creek. They spoke to her about the beauty and mystery of the natural world.

During her weekly explorations as a student in the wooded areas surrounding the university, RJ had listened to the call of the red-shouldered hawk and the mortal shriek of the deer mouse, the crackle of lightening and the moan of the fallen elm. They preached to her about the brutality and balance of the natural world.

What, now, was the Great Plains trying to tell her? RJ longed to know.

She stopped and stood still, eyes closed. She listened. Only the wind spoke to her. It never stopped speaking here. It blew day and night on the plains. Just as it had for centuries. It missed the conversations it once had, the wind said to her, with its friends the bellowing bison and howling coyotes, the rippling grass and the chirping crickets. It had only the dust for company now. And the dust was no one's friend.

"You've got me," RJ whispered into the wind.

You're not enough, the wind snarled back.

RJ shuddered. She opened her eyes and turned toward the rumble growing in the distance. The winds always shifted in the late morning, the dust churned on the horizon by noon. She flipped open the case of her pocket watch to check the time. Her stomach panged with disappointment. It was time to turn back to the lab.

~~~
~~~

Down the road, at the Clay farm, Harvey tied his bandanna over his nose and mouth and picked up the shovel he kept just inside the door. The duster left behind a good enough mess, and he wanted to tackle the dunes around the chicken coop and work shed before the next one hit.

He surveyed the nearby fields as he headed across the yard. A moderate wind blew across the land, ushering along an orange haze of fine dust. A scattering of dark objects littered the north field. They fluttered with each gust of the breeze. Harvey's heart sank.

Meadowlarks.

Dusters served up a unique form of terror for each animal in its path. For the birds it took the form of frantic flight to somehow outrun the storm. They flew and flew, until they were overcome by exhaustion or dust or wind. They flew and flew, stressing their tiny hearts until the muscles exploded in their rib cages. Then, they plummeted from the sky by the dozens, spiraling down, down on the wind until their fragile bodies collided with the shifting earth below. Long after the storm had passed, their lifeless wings quivered and flapped gracefully on the breeze.

After a detour to the work shed to get his wheelbarrow and gloves, Harvey set off across the field to collect the tiny carcasses. One by one, he picked up the almost weightless bodies and dropped them into the wheelbarrow.

What am I still doing in this godforsaken place?

Harvey bent down to pick up another bird. The creature shuttered ever so slightly, its golden chest pulsed up and down, once, twice. Its eyes and beak were caked with dirt. Its brown-speckled wings were mangled, twisted in unnatural angles. A melancholy groan bubbled up from deep inside Harvey's gut. He drew in a deep breath, then lifted his mammoth boot and stomped down quickly, firmly, to end the suffering.

"I'm sorry, little fella," he said. "Jesus, I'm sorry."

He closed his eyes and let his head fall back. After a moment, Harvey squared himself and finished collecting the tiny carcasses.

Behind the barn, he dug a fire pit and dumped the contents of the wheelbarrow. They lit quickly, the feathers shriveled and melted in the orange flames. The hollow bones snapped and popped like kindling twigs. Black smoke spiraled up into the hazy brown sky. Harvey adjusted the bandanna on his face to block the acrid smell.

He shook his head slowly and watched the flames dance.

Y*ou can catch more flies with honey than vinegar.* That's what Aunt May always said. Until recently, RJ hadn't understood the desire or need to attract flies.

"Good morning, Mr. Meginnis." RJ smiled brightly as she sidled up to the large man perched on his stool at the Seed & Feed. Mr. Meginnis grunted hello.

"I'm just stopping in to see if the seeds I ordered have arrived."

Meginnis grunted again. "Yep, they come in yesterday." Then, he added, mumbling, "Still can't figure why somebody'd pay good money to buy grass seed. Who ever heard of sowing grass, for cryin' out loud."

RJ continued to smile. She glanced around the lot, as Mr. Meginnis went inside the massive shed to retrieve her order. A handful of men were crouched together in the shade of a late-model Hawkeye truck, discussing the weather. Woody paced near the shed entrance, talking to no one in particular about the history of the truck and the company that had manufactured it.

"The Hawkeye Truck Company of Sioux City, Iowa, started making trucks in 1916," Woody said. "Models ranged from one ton to three and a half tons. Early models were made of wood, except for the hood. The company closed last year, on account of the Great Depression. Of course, if you ask me, it ought to be called the Terrible Depression. Nothing great about it."

RJ laughed to herself. She had to agree with Woody's down-to-earth logic.

"Here you go," Mr. Meginnis said, plopping two bags onto the ground next to RJ's feet. "Twenty pounds each of African buffel and pangola seed. That's seven cents for ten pounds, so the total comes to twenty-eight cents."

RJ reached into her pocketbook for the payment. Woody approached the pair, muttering something to himself, wringing his hands. Mr. Meginnis gave him the stink eye.

"Um," Woody said, pacing between Mr. Meginnis and RJ. "You sure that's twenty pounds, Mr. Meginnis?"

"Course I'm sure," Meginnis barked. "Now you git, Woody. I've told you before, I won't have you hanging around here irritating my customers."

Woody shook his head, continued pacing back and forth. RJ watched him for a moment, then turned to Mr. Meginnis. The massive man had fat beads of sweat collecting on his forehead. The tips of his ears were Christmas red.

"You sure that's twenty pounds, Mr. Meginnis? You sure?" Woody muttered again, backing away out of arm's reach.

RJ tilted her head to the side and peered at the merchant.

"Maybe it would help put Woody's mind at ease if you went ahead and just weighed the seeds again," she said.

Mr. Meginnis fumed. His entire face had turned so red that RJ thought steam might soon shoot out of his ears. He picked up the bags in a huff and stomped over to the scale. RJ sauntered over and stood behind him, looking over his shoulder at the big white dial. The black arrow-hand bounced back and forth over the numbers a few times and then settled at thirty-three pounds.

"Three and a half pounds short on each," Woody said from his safe distance, though he didn't have a clear view of the scale.

RJ looked Mr. Meginnis square in the eyes, her eyebrows raised.

"Well, I'll be darned," he muttered. "Can't figure out how that coulda happened. Better get my scale in the back checked out. Something must be out of whack."

RJ didn't respond. She simply stared the man down, waited for him to make the next move.

Mr. Meginnis recalculated her bill. RJ paid the man and carried the bags to her truck. She looked around for Woody, but he had set off down the street.

She called out to him and jogged to catch up. He stopped walking and waited for her.

"I sure appreciated your help back there, Woody."

He rearranged the dirt on the sidewalk with the toe of his boot.

"Can I buy you a pop, as a proper thank you?"

Woody's face lit up. "That'd be swell. I ain't had a bottle of Coca-Cola in three months, two weeks and four days."

"What?" RJ laughed, then shook her head. "Never mind, Woody. Come on."

They walked side by side to the Nickel & Dime store, then Woody sprinted in and went straight to the icebox by the cash register. He took out two bottles and opened them on the bottle opener affixed to the counter. RJ placed two nickels on the counter beside the register.

"Let's sit over there," RJ pointed to a shady spot on the sidewalk in front of the shoe store. They sat down beside each other on the curb, and Woody handed her a bottle.

He took a couple of big slow swallows, head leaned way back. "Ahhh."

RJ took a small sip, let the bubbles play on her tongue for a moment, and then let the cold fizzy liquid dance down her throat. "Gee whiz, that hits the spot, doesn't it?"

Woody bobbed his head enthusiastically. He gulped down the rest of his bottle and let out a long, loud belch.

"You're funny, Woody." RJ laughed and took another dainty sip.

"Am I?" Woody blew into his empty bottle, making it hum.

They sat quietly for another minute or so, then RJ turned to him.

"How did you know Mr. Meginnis had shorted me on the seeds?"

"I could see it plain as day."

RJ scrunched her eyebrows, shook her head a little. Woody just sat beside her.

"But *how*, Woody? *How* could you see it?"

"Oh," Woody said, grinning wide, finally realizing the point of RJ's question. "That's easy. You see, there's about twelve-thousand red winter wheat seeds in a pound. I'm not too familiar with buffel grass seed and whatnot, but they looked to be about the same size as winter wheat, so I figured they'd probably weigh about the same, too. Judging from the size of the bags, I could see there were only about two-hundred-thousand seeds in each one, at the most. So that would only be sixteen and a half pounds, not twenty."

RJ leaned her head back and examined Woody for a moment. "You could tell just by *looking* at the bag that there were two-hundred-thousand seeds in it?"

"Yep."

"How?"

"I dunno. I've always had a knack for seeing how things add up just by looking at them," Woody said. When I was a kid, he explained, and we'd go to the spring picnics and fall carnivals and whatnot, I could always guess how many beans was in the jar to win a pie or something. After a while, folks wouldn't let me play no more, because they said it weren't fair how I always guessed right and nobody else ever got the chance to win.

And I used to hang out at Mr. Meginnis' all the time, 'cause I liked to count things and he always has lots of stuff to count, Woody continued. But whenever I told him he had it wrong, he'd get terrible mad at me, and try to smack me upside my head and run me off. So after a while, I just stopped telling him when he was wrong, and he let me stay around. When I got older, I realized he was cheating people on purpose, not just making mistakes. He cheats a lot of folks 'round here. But most of them folks are mean to me, calling me dim-witted and such, so I don't really care if they get cheated.

RJ couldn't argue with his reasoning for keeping quiet. She watched him closely as he shared his story, though he was looking off into the distance as he spoke.

"But you're always real nice to me," Woody said. "I didn't want you to get cheated. So I said, 'Are you sure Mr. Meginnis?' And I made sure to stand way back when I said it, so he couldn't smack me upside the head."

RJ laughed out loud. And Woody turned to smile at her, his cheeks crimson.

"Well, I sure do appreciate you looking out for me, Woody. How 'bout I buy you another pop?"

"Holy smokes!"

Woody had saved her about five cents, but the look on Mr. Meginnis' face was worth a hundred times that amount. She handed him a nickel, and Woody sprung to his feet.

"I'm gonna take this one home for Alice," he said, and bolted toward the store. He shouted back over his shoulder as he ran, "Alice is my sister!"

~~~

RJ parked the truck in its usual spot beside the storage shed and began unloading her purchases from town. She eyed the bags of grass seed. She carried one into the house and set it on her work table, the heart of her soil conservation lab.

Stormy ran circles around her feet. RJ pulled out the scale, wiped it clean of dust, and poured a handful of seeds into the small pan until the weights balanced at one ounce.
~~~

She scribbled some numbers on a piece of paper. Twelve-thousand seeds per pound would be equal to seven-hundred-fifty seeds per ounce. RJ poured the seeds from the pan onto the worktable and began counting, using a sorting spatula to separate them into manageable piles.

Five, ten, fifteen... one hundred. Thirty, thirty-five, forty... two hundred. Seven piles of one-hundred seeds each gathered across the table, and RJ worked on the last tiny pile. Ten, fifteen, twenty...

RJ blinked at the seeds.

"Ain't that something?" She smiled and looked down at Stormy, who had been watching her with rapt attention. "Seven-hundred and forty-six seeds."

August 1934

Clothes were strewn around RJ's bedroom – dresses and denim overalls, blouses and work shirts. She stood in her camisole and panties, barefoot on the dusty floor, shaking her head in disgust.

"Never in all my life," she muttered. "Just pick something, RJ. For Pete's sake."

The monthly Farm Labor Union meeting was to convene in town in less than three hours, and RJ wanted – needed – to make the right impression when she addressed the group. If she wore farming clothes, she wouldn't fool anyone. She'd never plowed a field or worked eighteen-hour days to bring in the wheat. If she dressed too fancy, she'd be viewed as an uppity government bureaucrat.

"What do *you* think, Stormy?"

The dog raised her head from where she lay curled up on the rug. Her ears were drooped, eyes half-closed. Stormy yawned wide, then tucked her head beneath her paws and grumbled in discontent for being disturbed.

"Can't blame you, pup," RJ said, looking back to the spread of outfits. "Nothing more irritating and humdrum than a woman in a quandary over what to wear."

RJ glanced at the alarm clock on the nightstand and scolded herself for dithering. With a determined huff, she pulled on a pair of denim pants and cotton shirt with a lace collar. She slipped on her brown leather oxfords, ran a brush through her hair and clipped back her bangs with her mother's barrette.

"Come on, Stormy," she said, grabbing her journal, keys and satchel. "You're riding shotgun."

~~~

Mr. Cline banged the gavel on the table, calling the meeting to order for the Farm Labor Union, Vanham Unit No. 37. About forty folks sat in folding chairs in the Town Hall meeting room. About a half-dozen women sat in the back row, fanning themselves with flimsy copies of the *Farmer's Almanac*, while men filled the rest of the chairs and stood leaning along the back wall. RJ, too, stood near the back wall. She nearly choked on the stale, fetid air and tried to ignore the prickle of perspiration at the back of her neck.

After taking attendance and summarizing old business, Mr. Cline announced new business. "We have a request from Miss RJ Evans from the Soil Conservation Service to address the assembly. Any objections?"

A murmur of discontent rumbled through the group, though no one voiced a formal objection.

"All right then," Mr. Cline said. "Miss Evans, you may step up and address the quorum."

RJ walked to the front of the room, her knees wobbling beneath her. She turned to face the crowd and reminded herself to breathe and smile. This was no different than the oral presentations she had made to her classmates at college, she told herself.
~~~

"Thank you, Mr. Cline. And thank you all for allowing me to speak this evening. It's an honor to be here." Looking out into the room she could already see the crowd shutting down. Legs crossing, arms folding, heads tilting with disdain. There was nothing she could do but press ahead and hope for the best.

"As you are no doubt aware, the United States government, under the direction of President Roosevelt, has developed numerous new programs to aid and assist farmers of the Great Plains who are feeling the burden of drought and unsustainable farming practices."

"Oh, no doubt," someone mumbled from the crowd mockingly and a wave of sniggers and chortles passed through the room.

RJ's mouth went dry. Yet, she pressed on.

"Well, yes, as I was saying, uh, the government wishes to assist you during this challenging time through funding and education in farming practices that will help fight soil erosion. There are several techniques I'd like to share with you."

"Idn't that sweet? She wants to *share*," a voice rose from the back of the room, followed by more chortles.

"All due respect, sweetheart," another chimed in, "but I don't need some pen pusher from the United States government telling me how to work the land my granddaddy broke and I've been farming my whole life."

RJ raised her palms to the group, hoping to quiet the heckling. "Please, please, if you'll only listen for a moment, I believe you'll be interested in what I have to offer you in the way of federal allotments and support."

"Handouts," said a woman from the back, shaking her head.

"No, no, don't think of it as a handout," RJ pleaded. "It's financial support. For your efforts in experimenting with new farming techniques."

"Why don't you support us by making it rain, little lady? Now *that* would be something helpful, wouldn't it fellas?" The group erupted with laughter and lively banter. Mr. Cline tapped the gavel half-heartedly, and RJ knew she had lost any small bit of respect she might have had from the group.

"All right," Mr. Cline piped up after letting the chatter go on just a bit longer. "Let's settle down now. It's getting late. I move we carry this discussion over until our next meeting."

Someone seconded the motion, and Mr. Cline banged his gavel to punctuate the end of RJ's opportunity to speak. She willed her legs to hold out, feeling the heat rising in her cheeks, as she edged her way toward the exit.

~~~

RJ walked to her truck, where she had left Stormy sleeping on the flatbed. She unhitched the leash from the sideboard and the dog hopped down onto the street beside her.

"Come on, girl." RJ gave a gentle tug of the leash and the two began a slow amble down the sidewalk away from the Farmers Union crowd that spilled out into the street with gay chatter.

The sun was a whisper away from setting, bathing the town in crimson light through the dusty haze. Stormy pranced close to RJ's side, working hard to match her slow pace, glancing up from time to time for an encouraging word or look. The dog wasn't accustomed to walking slowly, but RJ was in no hurry to go anywhere in particular, her mind tumbling over the chain of events from the union meeting, contemplating what went wrong and why.

Habit brought them to Ethel's door, just as the sun dropped below the horizon and the street lights buzzed to life.

"Cuppa joe?" Ethel stood in the doorway, propping the door open with her hip while drying her hands on a gingham towel. RJ smiled and nodded. Ethel nodded back.

The women went inside, RJ taking a seat at the counter, Ethel fetching the coffee pot and two ceramic mugs.

"Gonna be a quiet night," Ethel broke the silence. "Never much of a supper crowd on meeting nights. The union wives always put on a nice potluck."
~~~

After a moment's pause, she added, "Your invitation musta got lost in the mail."

RJ looked up, startled, then confused. She saw Ethel's devilish grin, and the two women laughed. "Yes, it must have," RJ said.

The bell above the door jingled.

"Well, look who's here," Ethel said.

Harvey Clay walked into the cafe.

"Not going to the potluck tonight?" Ethel asked.

"No, ma'am. Had a hankering for your meatloaf and rhubarb pie."

"Well, ain't you a charmer. You set on down wherever you'd like and I'll bring you a plate."

Harvey removed his fedora and said hello to RJ. His dark hair was combed neatly back with a generous dose of Brilliantine, his shirt surprisingly crisp and clean despite the heat and dust. RJ said hello, and then turned back toward the counter and stared into her coffee cup. From the corner of her eye, she spied him taking a seat at a table in the back.

Ethel emerged from the kitchen a few minutes later with a plate of meatloaf swimming in gravy beside a mound of creamed spinach and a thick slice of buttered bread. She paused, almost imperceptibly, taking in the distance between her patrons, then strode toward Harvey's table.

"You want some milk with that?" she asked, setting the plate down in front of him. "All I got is canned right now. Sandstorm held up the train shipment this week, and there ain't a drop to be had from any of the cows 'round here."

Harvey nodded soberly. "Canned suits me just fine, Ethel. Thank you. Boy, this sure smells good." He closed his eyes and inhaled deeply over his plate, tucking his napkin into his open collar.

Ethel laughed. "What a charmer."

After bringing out Harvey's milk, Ethel sat down on her stool behind the counter across from RJ and topped off their coffees. RJ added a bit more cream to her cup and spooned in a little sugar. She could hear the clink of Harvey's fork and knife on his plate in the hush of the empty cafe.

Ethel leaned in.

"So, are you gonna fill me in on what happened at the meeting or not?" she whispered.

RJ sighed. "I don't know what to tell you, Ethel. It did not go well."

"Why not?"

"I have no idea," RJ shook her head. After a moment, she added, "Actually, no, I do know why. I barely even got a chance to speak. They all kept interrupting me and mocking me. It wasn't fair."

"Fair?" Ethel scoffed. "Honey, a fair's where you get a blue ribbon for your hog. It's got nothing to do with life."

RJ rolled her eyes. "That sounds like something my Uncle Lou would say."

"Well, then your Uncle Lou sounds like a pretty smart feller after all," Ethel said, raising her coffee cup in a mock toast before taking a sip.

"They never gave me a chance to make my point. They wouldn't even hear me out."

"I'm sorry about that, honey. I truly am. Everyone deserves a chance to be heard."

Ethel reached below the counter and pulled a cookie tin from the cupboard. She set it down in front of RJ and popped off the lid. RJ gave her a sheepish smile and reached for a piece of spicy-sweet comfort.

"Let me ask you something, RJ. Now don't take this the wrong way, honey, but I'm just wondering if you gave them farmers a chance to be heard either. They might be smarting right now, too, for not getting a say."

RJ stopped mid-chew. "Oh, I sincerely doubt that. They're all at their jolly potluck right now, having a grand ole time and a nice laugh at my expense."

"Not *all* of 'em," Ethel said, raising her eyebrows in Harvey's direction.

"What?" RJ blurted. "You think he's got something to say to me?"

Ethel removed the glass cover from the pie plate and served up two thick slices of flakey sugared crust oozing with plump rhubarb. She pushed the plates toward RJ.

"Well, I sure don't think he's here for my meatloaf and creamed spinach. And if you would put your pride in your pocket for five minutes, and go hear him out, you just might learn a thing or two that those college professors didn't teach you." She nodded to punctuate her point, then turned and disappeared into the kitchen.

RJ put her elbow on the counter and leaned her forehead into her palm. She stared at the pie for a moment, silently cursing Ethel, wishing the woman was wrong. Then, she sat up straight, swiveled around on her stool and rose to deliver Harvey's pie.

"Hi," she said, standing across the table from where he sat, holding a pie plate in each hand.

"Hi," Harvey replied. He removed the napkin from his shirt, wiped his mouth and set it down beside his plate. The electric light bulb flickered and buzzed above them. He drummed his fingers on the table, once, twice. Then he pointed. "That my pie?"

"Oh, yes. Sorry." RJ felt her cheeks warm. She set his plate down. "I... I was wondering, may I join you?"

Harvey flashed his dimpled grin and used his foot to slide out the chair across from him. RJ couldn't help but chuckle and slid down into the chair.

"So, Miss Rosa Jean Evans is ready to be schooled by Professor Clay." Harvey wiggled his eyebrows up and down at RJ, while shoveling a fork full of pie into his mouth.

"Oh, good heavens," RJ said, her eyes narrowing. "Didn't anyone ever tell you it's impolite to eavesdrop?"

Harvey laughed and wiped the corners of his mouth with his napkin. "It ain't eavesdropping if the other party is yammering so loud you can't help but hear 'em."

RJ's mouth dropped open. Her back stiffened. She moved to get up.

"Oh, come on now," Harvey said. "Don't go running off. I'm just playin'."

She felt an all-too-familiar warmth return to her cheeks. *Why did men always have to be so difficult?* They're either bossing you, or teasing you, or trying to get you to do something you don't want to do.

"You don't remember me, do you, Rosa Jean?"

"Remember you?"

"From when we were kids," Harvey said. His face softened. "Our daddies were friends. We had Sunday supper out at your place a bunch of times, before everyone took sick with the flu and everything went to hell. You used to play with my little sis."

RJ took in a quick gulp of air. Memories flooded her mind like a creek breaking its banks, sweeping her away. Running barefoot, hand in hand with her friend out to the barn to check on a new litter of kittens. Digging in the moist dirt for pill bugs. Kneeling in the fragrant garden rows, picking string beans and tomatoes off the vines.

She looked down at her hands. "Anna."

"You two were peas in a pod," Harvey said. "The cutest little girls. I recognized you the minute I saw you walk into that auction. You ain't changed a bit."

RJ tried to picture a young Harvey Clay, but his face was elusive. At five or six years old, RJ's whole world had revolved around her best friend. She had known Anna had siblings, but the two played only with each other. Anna and RJ's parents were the only faces she could remember from that time, and even those seemed to be fading. RJ blinked several times to battle the stinging in her eyes.

"Oh, shoot, I'm sorry," Harvey said. "I wasn't meaning to make you cry."

RJ looked out the window, considered a quick exit.

"I'm not crying," she said. "I just, I feel like a fool. I was so young when I left. It never even occurred to me that anyone here would know or remember me. But Ethel did. And you. Who else?"

She looked back at him. He was studying her, his hazel eyes glistening. After a moment, he said, "A handful, I reckon."

He helped himself to another bite of pie, and RJ followed his lead. They sat quietly for several minutes, savoring the flaky crust and sweet-tart fruit. Harvey drank the last of his milk. RJ took a sip of her coffee. It had gone cold.

"Is that why everyone's been keeping me at arm's length? They're hurt I don't remember them?"

"Oh, I don't know about that." Harvey paused. "Maybe not so much that you don't remember *who* they are, but more that you don't remember *what* they are. You left here as one of us, Rosa

Jean, an regular little farm girl. And you came back RJ Evans, a book-smart government bureaucrat."

"So people are upset that I grew up?"she blurted. "Because I made something of myself?"

"That ain't what I meant." Harvey shook his head. He scraped his fork through the crumbs on his plate. "It's the way you talk to 'em, as though they're all bumbling country folk."

RJ's chest began to constrict.

"You assume we haven't tried to change and don't know what we're doing," Harvey continued. "But we have tried, again and again, and we're willing to try something else, anything else, if it means we can hold on to our land another year, until things get better. We just don't want to be talked down to, especially by someone who ought to know better."

The bell above the door jingled. RJ and Harvey turned, and the boy from the general store bounded into the cafe. He removed his cap. Ethel emerged from the kitchen.

"Evening, Mr. Clay, Mrs. Ethel, ma'am," he said. "Ma sent me around to let folks know we got a sandstorm coming up from the south. Probably an hour or two away, from what we can tell."

They all thanked him and the boy spun around and bounded back out the door and down the walk. Harvey stood up and put on his hat, dropped a few coins on the table. "Thanks for the meal, Ethel. You need any help battin' down?"

"No, no," she said. "You two best get on your way. Get yourselves home before the worst of it hits."

Harvey tipped his hat to RJ and left. She stood for a moment, in the middle of the cafe, watching Ethel buzz about, feeling suddenly exhausted from the evening's events and Harvey's blunt words.

"RJ," Ethel said abruptly. "Snap to it, hon."

RJ gathered her wits and rushed out the door. Stormy whimpered, pacing back and forth on her leash. She jumped up onto RJ with her front paws, panting.

"It's all right, girl," RJ said, unlatching the leash and heading toward the truck. Stormy bounded into the cab as soon as RJ opened the door. She fired up the engine and pulled onto the road, the wind at their backs.

The dog circled around in the passenger seat a couple of times before hopping down on the floor and lying there. She kept her head up, panting, her attention fixed on RJ.

"Don't worry, Stormy," RJ said, looking down at the dog and then glancing up in the rearview mirror. "We'll stay ahead of it."

Scratching sounds pulled RJ from her light slumber.

"Stormy," she croaked. "What are you getting into?"

She rolled over beneath her covers, silently wishing for just a little more sleep after another fitful night. The raucous wind had finally stopped sometime in the early morning hours and now the air was still and quiet, but for this incessant scratch, scratch, scratching.

Stormy lay quietly at the foot of RJ's bed, her head cocked in the direction of the window and the scratching sound. RJ sat up and pulled back the drapes. The dust-covered window let only the tiniest rays of light into the room, through fine lines in the dust. The soft, rhythmic scratching continued. More lines appeared – some long and thin, some swirling and fat.

RJ could make out a few objects as they circled and angled and swept across the glass outside – a thin paintbrush, a fingertip, a clothespin, the heel of a hand. She watched in breathless wonder as a scene was slowly unearthed on the window. A slender windmill was erected in one corner, its broad blades seeming to spin in the breeze. Beside it, a barn took shape, with wide open doors and a weather vane atop its slanted roof. In another pane, an orchard of trees slowly sprouted, one by one, their textured trunks reaching up into a cloudless sky, their branches dipping with geometric leaves and plump fruit. It was like watching a story unfold.

"Woody's *painting* the windows."

The more the picture was revealed on the glass, the more sunlight seeped into the room, setting alight the dust particles floating upon the air. Before too long, the whole room sparkled in golden morning light.

Then the scratching stopped. The story was complete. RJ sat for a moment or two, taking in the detail of the window painting, amazed by the depth and layers of the image. Stormy's head cocked toward the bedroom door, and she hopped down off the bed. RJ followed, filled with anticipation as she shook the dust from her housecoat and slipped it on over her nightgown.

They padded into the kitchen, leaving footprints and paw prints on the dusty floor behind them, following the sound of the scratch, scratch, scratching now coming from the window above the kitchen sink.

There, a herd of wild horses galloped across the panes and splashed through a glistening creek. Their nostrils flared. Their tails and manes were windswept behind them. The water spray sparkled around their hooves as the sunlight shone through the kitchen glass.

RJ made her way around the front room, throwing back the drapes one by one, letting in the sunlight, marveling at the artwork that had emerged from the dust while she slept. A field of wheat. Cows at pasture. A vase of flowers.

She picked up her boots, turning them over to tap out any critters that may have made a home in them overnight. Then, she slipped her bare feet into the boots and stepped out onto the front porch, where Woody was etching another masterpiece.

"I'm painting the windows."

"Yes," RJ said. She hugged her shoulders and watched him work. "They're amazing."

Woody gave one of his trademark shrugs. He gripped a handful of utensils in one hand. With the other hand, he feathered away some dust with his thumb to create smooth river rocks in the horse creek. Woody paused to scan his tools. Selecting a thinly whittled stick from options, he worked over the same section of his picture, skillfully adding detail and dimension.

"Come on in when you're through. Okay?" RJ said. "I'll make coffee."

"Okay."

She watched him work for a moment more before going back into the house. In the kitchen, RJ rinsed the dust from the coffee pot, filled it with water and lit the stove. She glanced back toward the front window, marveled at the detail of Woody's dust painting. How had he learned to create so much beauty from such a dismal medium? She took a wet towel to the table and chairs, to wash away the thick layer of dust that had settled there in the night. She paused a moment, then ran her finger along the dusty surface, drew a stick figure girl with a frowning face. Woody knocked at the kitchen door, and RJ jumped.

"Come on in," she said, quickly dragging the towel across the table to erase her juvenile art. "Coffee's almost ready."

"I don't like coffee," Woody said, making a face like she'd just offered him a spoonful of castor oil.

"Have you ever had it with sweetened condensed milk?"

"Nope. Ma says that's only for rich folks or for Christmas."

"Well then," RJ said, studying him for a moment before setting a can down on the table. "Merry Christmas, Woody."

Woody picked up the small Eagle Brand can and turned it over in his hands.

RJ finished setting the table with a can opener, spoon and tin of molasses cookies. She turned over the mugs and poured the coffee while Woody carefully opened the condensed milk.

"How much?" he asked.

"I like a couple of spoonfuls," she said, demonstrating as she spoke. The thick milk drizzled from the can onto her spoon and then disappeared into the black liquid when she dunked it into the mug. After her second spoonful, she stirred her coffee and handed the can to Woody.

He added two spoons of milk and stirred, exactly as she had, sizing up the inky coffee as it turned creamy brown. He set down the spoon and picked up the mug with both hands. He took a tentative sip.

RJ watched with curiosity and anticipation. She was surprised by how much she hoped he would like it. He smacked his lips a little and looked to the side the way he often did.

RJ smiled. "You like it?"

"Yes," he said vacantly. He added two more spoonfuls of milk and stirred the concoction again. Then, he quickly gulped down his drink and abruptly stood up. "I'm done. Thank you for the Christmas coffee, even thought it ain't Christmas. Good-bye."

He bounded out the door before RJ had a chance to respond.

"You're welcome, Woody," she finally said and admired the horses galloping across her kitchen window while she sipped her cup of holiday cheer.

Outside the Nickel & Dime, a group of farmers stood around jabbering. Some leaned against the wall, some stood with their hands in their pockets, one or two meandered restlessly around the group, listening in. The old-timers sat along the baseboards of one fellow's truck, their elbows resting on their knees.

RJ observed the group as she emerged from the post office. Woody spotted her and shouted out.

"RJ! Over here!" He grinned wide, motioning for her to join him and his pa. She smiled and waved, hesitated for just a moment before stepping off the curb and heading toward them.

She was grateful to be invited over. Engaging in farmer small talk might help her fit in, might help them see her as part of the group, as one of them. *This'll be good,* she told herself, even though her boots felt like they were made of lead as she crossed the street.

"Hiya, Woody, Mr. Parker," she said, then smiled at others in the group, "Hiya."

She received a few obligatory nods and hiyas in return.

"Them Hoover hogs are eating everything." The conversation continued, as one farmer lamented, "Shoot, they're even digging down and getting at the roots."

"Hoover hogs?" RJ interrupted.

The farmers shook their heads. The fellow who'd been talking rolled his eyes. "Armchair farmer," he mumbled and then continued his diatribe to the group.

"They's talking about jackrabbits," Woody explained to her. "We call 'em Hoover hogs because they're ruining everything around here, just like President Hoover done. And they eat everything, just like hogs do."

"The county's having another rabbit drive in a couple of weeks," Mr. Parker said. "I saw a leaflet at the post office."

"That right?" one of the farmers asked him. "They paying a penny a piece, like they did last year?"

"Naw, ain't payin' nothin' this time. It'd probably bankrupt 'em, with as many as we got," he said. "But they're bringing the fencing and whatnot for the pens, and they'll haul off the carcasses."

The men discussed the logistics. We'll need everyone to turn out, they said, the women and children, too. We'll get an early start, before it gets too hot, and the women can fix up a picnic dinner for after.

"What exactly is a rabbit drive?" RJ worked up the nerve to ask.

After more eye-rolling and muttering, Mr. Cobb explained how the drives worked. The entire town would gather in a designated field where a large pen would be set up, one side of the fencing left open. Spaced in a long line, shoulder to shoulder, the crowd would move toward the pen, banging pots and pans, clanging cow bells, herding the rabbits toward the pen. When the pen was full, they'd close it off, trapping the rabbits inside. Then they'd take up pipes and bits of lumber and whatever else they had on hand, step inside the pen and club the rabbits to death.

RJ gasped.

"We're fighting for our livelihood, Miss Evans," Mr. Parker said. "We're getting overrun by the critters. We'll kill probably eight- or nine-hundred in one drive like that. And there'll still be thousands more."

RJ had read government reports about the pests. The reports explained how one rabbit could cause ten dollars' worth of damage to a farm in the course of a year. Nearly two million rabbits had been exterminated in Kansas alone in the past couple of years during so-called "extermination drives." The reports also explained that hundreds of the rabbits were used in the soup lines to feed hungry families, and thousands more were converted to chicken and cattle feed.

The reports failed to explain precisely how the rabbits were "exterminated."

"But why force the children to participate?" she asked.

"Everybody needs to do their share," Mr. Cobb said. He turned and looked at Woody. "Everybody."

Woody pressed his hands over his ears, squeezed his eyes shut tight, shook his head violently. "No, no, no, no. I won't do it again. No, no, no, no."

"Oh, for Pete's sake." Cobb crossed his arms and shook his head in disgust.

Mr. Parker's face turned crimson. "It's all right, son. Settle down. You don't have to do it. We'll have plenty of other folks to help."

He placed his hand on Woody's shoulder, and the young man winced as though he'd been burned. "I won't do it. I can't stand to hear all them tiny screams. I won't do it. I won't! I won't!"

The men in the group shifted, creating space between themselves and Woody. They muttered and made faces, coughed and repressed laughs. RJ took it all in. She stayed close to Woody, but she also stayed quiet.

"You don't have to. You hear me, son?" Pa's voice was louder now, a bit higher pitched. Woody continued to shake his head violently. "I said you don't have to help with the drive. You don't have to, Woody. Now, just settle yourself down."

Woody retreated to the outer edge of the gathering, hands still pressed over his ears. He paced, head cocked sideways toward the sky, whispering to himself.

"Just as well," one fellow piped up. "Don't want that retard running around me swinging a club anyhow."

A few others in the group grumbled, agreed, shook their heads. Mr. Parker kept his eyes down. His whole body seemed to buckle under the weight of their words.

"Well, who can blame him for not wanting to participate," RJ said. She shot a quick glance in Woody's direction. "The whole thing sounds barbaric. Can't you shoot the rabbits, instead of bludgeoning them to death?"

"What difference does it make how we kill 'em?" one farmer debated. "They're pests."

"Besides," another said, "nobody 'round here can afford the ammunition to shoot that many rabbits." He paused a moment to spit in the dirt. "None of us here is getting rich collecting government paychecks like you, Miss Evans."

The jab knocked the air right out of her. *I'm far from rich,* she thought. *I've worked damn hard to get this job. I've earned it, and every cent of my salary.* RJ opened her mouth to speak. But the comebacks, the excuses, all of the words in her defense caught in her throat.

Woody paced behind her, talking to himself.

"Well, we best get going," Mr. Parker spoke up. "Almost supper time."

He turned and walked past Woody, and the young man turned and followed lockstep behind him. "I won't do it, Pa. I won't."

"I know, son. I know. I said you don't have to."

"I won't," Woody said again.

"I know."

RJ's mind flashed to the many times Woody had stood up for her in the short time she'd known him. Shame for not returning the gesture burned in her chest. *I should say something*, she thought and swallowed hard. *Anything.*

One by one, two by two, the group thinned. One fellow wondered aloud what the missus might have made for supper, then he shuffled off. The men tipped their hats to one another, ambled in different directions. RJ was left alone in the street. She suddenly felt feeble, shaky.

"Come on, honey." The mere sound of Ethel's voice revived her, made her strong again. "I just pulled a raisin pie from the oven."

RJ turned and saw the woman leaning in the open doorway of the restaurant. Ethel scrunched up her nose in a sad smile, then spun around and stepped inside. RJ shot a fiery look down the street at the retreating farmers, then she marched into the restaurant.

Ethel scanned the playing cards fanned out in her hand. She eased one from the group and set it face up on the stack. "Gin."

"Oh, for heaven's sake!" RJ playfully tossed her cards onto the lunch counter. "You're cheating."

Ethel chuckled and told her young friend to shuffle. RJ scooped up the cards, shuffled and dealt a new hand while Ethel topped off their mugs with fresh coffee.

It had become a routine for the women, one that RJ liked more than she would admit to herself. Once a week or so they'd sit across from each other at Ethel's lunch counter, play cards, and exchange chitchat about goings-on around town. Afternoons were quiet, and they usually had the place to themselves.

RJ studied the hand she'd just dealt, placed a three of hearts on the discard pile. Ethel picked it up and set down a jack of spades. RJ selected a new card from the deck. She narrowed her eyes and rearranged her hand.

"Your mom and I used to play rummy from time to time," Ethel said, waiting for RJ to make her move. RJ finally discarded an ace of hearts. Ethel plucked it up and snickered. "Guess you didn't inherit her skill."

The young woman snorted and rolled her eyes. They continued playing the hand quietly. RJ wished Ethel would tell her more about her mother, but she couldn't bring herself to ask.

"Your mom was a force to be reckoned with at cards," Ethel continued. Her eyes danced. "A group of us would get together every couple of months to play. Just the girls. The other gals and I practically wrestled to see who would get her for their bridge partner."

Growing up, RJ had listened from afar to her Uncle Lou and his friends playing cards around the kitchen table. They'd yammer and yowl half the night. Aunt May would pop in from time to time to freshen their lemonade and restock the snacks. Then, she'd scuttle back into the other room and leave the men to their game. RJ'd never heard of women gathering for anything other than quilting or making preserves or other work.

Ethel rearranged her hand a bit, discarded a five of clubs. "It was always a hoot. Your mom got goofy after a bourbon or two, just like you did that night you stayed over."

RJ's eyes grew wide, and she laughed. "No."

"Oh, yes," Ethel grinned.

They paused their game without even realizing it, each lost in her own thoughts, her own memories. RJ tried to picture her mom and the others sitting around a table, playing cards, sipping bourbon, being silly. She saw them, for the first time, as more than wives and mothers. And it made her chest ache.

"I miss those days," Ethel said, and drew a card.

RJ nodded and gave her friend a tender smile. She could sense Ethel didn't need any other response; the lump in her throat prevented her from speaking anyway. The sudden realization that other people missed her mother, too, churned up emotions RJ had never expected.

"Gin," Ethel said.

"Son of a biscuit! I give up."

Ethel laughed and pushed the pile of cards toward RJ. "Be quiet and deal."

~~~

The bell above the diner door jingled about half-past three. A boy of about ten slipped inside and walked toward the counter.

"Hiya, Donnie," Ethel greeted him.

"Hiya, Mrs. Ethel," he responded, then turned to RJ with a nod. "Ma'am."

Ethel asked what brought him in today.

Donnie quickly took off his newsboy cap, rolled it up and shoved it in the back pocket of his shorts. He asked if Ethel had any work needing to be done. She told him it was a good thing he stopped in, because she could sure use his help. She directed him to get a bucket of sudsy water and a clean towel and start wiping down all the tables for dinner. When he'd finished with that, she said, he could shake out the tablecloths and get them laid out.

"Thank you, Mrs. Ethel," the boy said with a wide grin, and he shot off into the kitchen.

"He seems to know his way around," RJ said.

"Oh, yes," said Ethel. "He drops by here at least once a week looking for work. He's a good boy."

The women continued to play cards, while Donnie buzzed around the empty diner. RJ watched him work from the corner of her eyes, his knobby knees bowing as he hauled the bucket across the room, his sharp elbows zigzagging across the tables as he cleaned. She also couldn't help but notice that the tables were already nearly dust-free, since Ethel had previously completed her usual scouring after the lunch crowd cleared.

When it was nearly four o'clock, Donnie had finished his work and it was time for RJ to get back to hers. He came to report to Ethel, as RJ stood to gather her personal affects and say good-bye.

Ethel pulled a penny from her apron pocket and placed it in the boy's eager palm. "You go get yourself a candy at the drug store."
~~~

"Thank you, Mrs. Ethel!" he beamed.

"And you take this meatloaf and fried potatoes home to your ma," she said, handing the boy a pan neatly wrapped in wax paper and tied with a string. "Tell her you worked good and hard for old Ethel, and you earned it."

"Yes, ma'am. Thank you, ma'am."

RJ walked ahead and held open the door for Donnie as they exited together. The weight of the pan made his tiny biceps bulge from his spindly arms and his pointy shoulder blades protrude from his narrow back. She heard his stomach grumble as he passed her, presumably in anticipation of supper, possibly the first decent meal he and his family would eat since the last time he worked for Ethel.

Word finally arrived from D.C. authorizing RJ to hire one full-time hand to assist her at the soil conservation station. She considered placing a help-wanted advertisement in the Vanham weekly newspaper. But, honestly, there was only one person she wanted to hire.

"Come on, Stormy. Let's go for a drive to Woody's house."

Outside the air was thick and still. A slow duster had rolled through overnight, and the usual morning breeze was absent. The fine dust lingered in the air, enveloping the landscape and its inhabitants in a rose-tinted fog.

RJ swept off the truck and climbed in, Stormy taking up shotgun. She closed the choke, pumped the gas pedal, turned the ignition key. The engine clicked, sputtered and died. RJ tried again, but the truck wouldn't come to life. She blew her bangs out of her eyes and tried one more time. No luck.

"Damned dust," RJ said, looking out across the dry empty field and rosy-brown air. "Guess I'm hoofing it."

Back in the house, she soaked a bandanna at the spigot and retrieved her goggles from the hook beside the door. "You better stay home, girl. I don't want you out in that foul air any more than you have to be."

With her goggles and bandanna securely in place, RJ set off across the field in the direction Woody always had. *Just two miles and some hundred-odd feet.*

~~~

RJ trudged across the barren field and pastures. Her mind became fixated on the heartbreaking crunch, crunch, crunch of dry earth beneath her boots. It was the only sound in an environment devoid of life. No rustling of leaves. No twittering of birds. Not even the occasional scamper of padded paws since the jackrabbit drive.

The sun rose higher in the colorless sky, its heat intensified by the lingering dust in the air.

She pressed on, one foot after the other, under the pitiless sun. *Just two miles and some hundred-odd feet, huh Woody?* It felt further. Much further. Had she veered off course? In such a massive expanse of nothingness, it was absurdly easy to lose one's way in even the shortest hike. She chided herself for leaving her compass behind.

By the time RJ spotted what she hoped was Woody's place, her shirt was soaked through with sweat, her arms and face coated in a thin layer of mud. The bandanna helped keep the dust from her lungs, but breathing in hot air through the moist cloth was stifling.

The Parker home was a ramshackle structure that obviously began its life as a one-room farmhouse. As the family had grown, Woody's parents had tacked on a room here and there with whatever building supplies they could muster – bricks made of mud and grass, and salvaged wood, perhaps from a collapsed barn. The odd-shaped additions sprouted from the sides of the house like wild mushrooms on a tree.

RJ paused to take in the sight. She wondered if her childhood home looked the same, but she had no desire to seek out the old homestead and know for sure. Part of her hoped the house had been torn down after her parents died. That part couldn't bear the
~~~

thought of some other family having lived there and stolen what should have been her happy memories.

Her head began to pound, and she resumed her walk toward the Parker house. The structure seemed to shift in the white-hot sunlight as she approached. Geometric flashes of light glinted in her peripherals. When she finally reached the house, RJ steadied herself at the porch railing, working up the energy to knock on the door.

"Heavens!" Woody's mother opened the door, assessed RJ in an instant and ushered her inside to the kitchen table. The woman retrieved a pitcher and poured water from it through a cheesecloth into a canning jar to strain out as much dust as she could. She eyed the light brown water in the jar, shook her head and handed it to RJ. "Drink this. It ain't pretty, but it'll do you good."

"Thank you." RJ's voice came out dry, nearly inaudible. She removed her bandanna and goggles, then drank the water down in greedy gulps until it was gone. Woody's mother stood by waiting, then whisked away the jar for a refill.

"Don't you know better than to be out on a day like this without a canteen?"

"I do. I just didn't realize how hot it'd be."

Woody's mother placed the drink on the table and sat down across from RJ. "Yep. Been getting hotter 'n hotter these past few summers. Ain't never seen nothin' like it."

RJ thanked the woman again, and took another long drink before she realized she hadn't properly introduced herself.

"I'm so sorry to put you out like this. I'm RJ Evans. I own the property next door."

"Don't you apologize for calling. I've been a poorly neighbor. Should have brought you a pie when you first moved in." She paused, drawing up her mouth tight. "Been so busy around here, well, never mind my excuses. It's a pleasure to finally make your acquaintance. I'm Olive Parker."

She gave RJ's hand a light tap. Then, she picked up the bandanna from the table and took it to the wash basin. She rinsed out the dirt as best as she could, rung out the cloth and draped it beside her dish towel.

RJ could feel her wits returning. Water was an amazing elixir, despite the dust infusion.

"I must admit, the reason for my visit isn't terribly neighborly either," she said. "I've actually come to speak to Woody about employment. Is he home?"

Olive pressed her hands to her heart. "Employment?"

RJ smiled.

"Go get your brother in from the barn," Olive called out, and a small figure shifted from the shadow in the living room doorway, bolted through the kitchen and sprang out the back door like a gazelle. RJ laughed.

"She seems eager to please. How many children do you have, Mrs. Parker?"

"Call me Olive. I was blessed with five. She's my youngest. My two oldest girls are both married and moved on, one in Topeka and one in Dodge. Got a baby girl up in heaven. And then there's Woody. He's our only boy."

Olive looked out the small kitchen window toward the barn. Yet, it was as though she was seeing far past anything truly visible. She smoothed her coarse gray hair back over the top and sides of her head, tucking a loose strand into the thick braid at the base of her neck.

The kitchen door flew open and Woody lumbered in, his father right behind him. Both men wore black leather aprons soaked with blood. Olive threw up her hands.

"Stop right there! Not one more step into this house."

"Sorry, Ma," Mr. Parker said, "but you're the one what called us in. You know we was butcherin' the cow."

Olive cringed, then turned to RJ. "Lost our last milk cow in the storm over night. Poor thing fell to her knees in the pasture, and we couldn't get her back on her feet and into the barn. By morning, she was gone."

"Her insides is filled with mud," Woody said looking down at his feet.

RJ's hand flew over her mouth. She shook her head. "Oh. That's awful."

She reflected a moment on the cow's fate. Her eyes dropped to the canning jar of brown water, and her hand fell to her stomach.

"Well, all that aside," Olive said. "The reason I brung you in was because Miss Evans called to speak to Woody about some employment."

"Employment?" Woody and Pa said in unison.

RJ explained that she was in need of full-time help at the soil station, for a wide variety of tasks, and that she could offer a salary of forty dollars a month. Woody whistled through his teeth and then opened his mouth to grin so wide she could see his tonsils. Olive told him to close up his mouth before he started catching flies. Mr. Parker took a step back as though he might fall right over.

"But why do you want to hire *Woody*?" Olive's youngest peeked her head in through the kitchen doorway. Mr. Parker turned and yelled at her to git, but when he looked back at RJ, the same question was etched on his face.

"Woody has already helped me in so many ways since I've arrived to Vanham," RJ explained. "Loading and unloading supplies, and explaining important things to me. From my experience, he's bright and hard working. I believe he'd make a fine employee."

"Bright?" Pa balked, and Olive shut him down with a look.

"When do you want him to start work?" she asked.

"Well, that's up to Woody, of course," RJ said. "But my truck up and quit on me, so the sooner the better. Woody's already told me how much he knows about Model AA engines."

Woody whipped off his apron and said "hot damn," and Olive scolded him for his language, smiling all the while. Mr. Parker was two steps behind, still trying to wrap his mind around any of it.

"Pa, you get on back to your butchering," Olive directed. "And Woody, you go get yourself washed up. I'll hitch up the wagon and take you and Miss Evans on over to her soil science station place so you can fix her truck."

The men hustled off as they were told, and RJ thanked Olive for offering a ride.

Olive's eyes teared up. She cleared her throat to compose herself. "Oh no, Miss Evans, thank *you.*"

Paying work was scarce. Time seemed to stand still. What better way to pass the day than to loiter at Ethel's with your pals and commiserate? The men occupied their usual spot, filling the three tables in the back corner of the diner. They smoked and nattered and played Spades.

Frank Cobb sat with his chair leaned back on two legs, his feet propped up on the table, perusing the newspaper. He shook out the pages and folded the paper backward to read the editorial section. After a moment or two, he thumped the page with the back of his hand and said, "Damn straight."

"What's that, Frank?" one of the other fellas said.

"I'm just reading this here editorial by some college professor in New York, talking about how to fix the unemployment and end the Depression."

"That right? What's it say?"

"Well, it's real simple," Frank continued. "Says here we got about ten million people out of work right now. But it says there's also about ten million or more women working. He says we just need to fire the women, who shouldn't be working anyhow, and hire the men for them jobs. And bingo! No more unemployment. No more relief rolls. No more Depression."

The men sang out in a chorus of "there you go" and "damn right."

"Y'all are full of beans." Ethel strode over to their tables carrying a coffee pot.

The men exchanged looks as she maneuvered around their chairs, filling their mugs.

"Most of the jobs women are working, none of you'd be caught dead doing and you know it. Teaching school kids, emptying bedpans at the hospital. Any of you all willing to do that work? How about washing and ironing laundry?"

The group mumbled and shifted in their seats.

"Uh-huh, that's what I thought," Ethel said.

She crossed her arms over her chest, the empty coffee pot dangling from her dishwater-chafed fingers. She shifted her weight onto one hip and stared directly down at Frank until he sheepishly removed his dirty boots from her table and sat up proper in his chair.

"And what about my job?" she asked. "Running this diner by myself since my Ed dropped dead from his burst appendix five years ago. Y'all want to fire *me*, take over my business, see to it I starve?"

The men were silent. Ethel shook her head at them and retreated back into the kitchen. They stayed quiet for a little while, examining their ragged cuticles, lighting up cigarettes, shuffling cards. Frank continued reading the newspaper to himself. After a bit he spoke up again, though softer this time. "What about that Evans gal having that fancy government job?"

"And hiring Woody to boot," another guy chimed in at half a whisper, glancing back over his shoulder toward the kitchen door.

"That's right," someone else said. "There's two good jobs that should go to able-bodied men, instead of a woman and a half-wit."

"Damn straight."

~~~

RJ knelt in the field to scoop a spade of dirt into a small canning jar. The morning's duster had finally subsided, and she
~~~

wanted to get fresh soil samples to see what the wind had blown in. It had roared in from the south, bringing with it what appeared to be a gritty layer of red earth from Oklahoma. She jotted a number on the canning lid with a grease pencil.

"Hand me the measuring stick," she directed Woody, trading him the stick for the jar, which he tucked into the duffle bag slung over his shoulder. She inserted the stick into the loose earth until it struck solid ground, then she noted the soil's depth in her journal. RJ stood, and the two began walking across the field.

"Have you ever felt the earth move?" Woody asked after a minute or two.

RJ turned her head to look at him. As usual, he was looking elsewhere, at some unknown, faraway place.

"What do you mean, like falling in love?"

Woody looked at her now, an expression of both horror and confusion on his face. "No! That ain't what I meant. Why would you say that?"

RJ laughed. "It's an expression, Woody. Haven't you ever heard of it? When you fall in love and it shakes you up. It's like you're feeling the earth move."

"Pfft." Woody winced. "Well, that *ain't* what I meant."

They walked a bit further, both quiet. RJ stopped again and knelt in the dirt. Woody handed her an empty jar, and she scooped up another sample. They traded jar for measuring stick. She jotted the depth in her journal. He tucked the jar in his duffle.

RJ looked up at him, squinting into the afternoon sun behind his head. "Well, what *did* you mean?"

"I meant have you ever felt the earth move?"

"Literally? Like an earthquake?"

"Yes," he said. "But not so big as an earthquake like you read about them having in California and such. I mean the everyday movement, as the earth rotates on its axis."

RJ stood up and grinned at him. "No, Woody, I can't say that I have."

They walked on for a bit, and then Woody stopped. "Have you ever tried?"

"Tried to feel the earth move? No, I don't suppose I've ever tried."

"I have," Woody said. "Lots of times."

RJ studied him a moment. And Woody didn't mind. It was one of the many things she appreciated about their friendship. What would have been awkward silence with anyone else was merely quiet reflection with Woody.

"Well?" she finally asked. "Did you feel it?"

"Yep."

"Truly?"

"You should try sometime," he said.

RJ raised her eyebrows, considering the possibility. She began to walk again, and Woody fell in stride. Then, he commenced one of his lengthy narratives, which RJ had already come to expect.

"Morning is my favorite time to start, after breakfast and chores," he said. I like to stand out back of the house, by Ma's clothes lines. The ground is hard and smooth right there. I take off my shoes and socks and stand with my bare feet planted on the ground. You gotta focus real hard and think about making your feet as flat as they can be, and spread your toes, and stand real tall and straight, so your whole body is planted strong. And you gotta close your eyes.

Woody stopped and stood arrow straight, eyes closed, demonstrating the correct stance for feeling the earth move. RJ watched him. Then, she closed her eyes and clutched her journal to her chest and stood as still as she could manage with the wind at her back. Woody opened his eyes and smiled with a gaping mouth when he saw RJ going along.

"There you go! Now, focus on the vibration of the earth. Your mind is the clear open sky, and your feet are part of the earth. Breathe nice and slow. Just make your feet as sensitive as you can, so you can feel the vibration."

They stood quietly for another minute or two. RJ slowed her breathing and focused. She felt the sun on her face, heard the wind murmuring across the earth, felt the solitude of the soil beneath her feet.

She opened her eyes, and Woody was staring intently at her face. She smiled.

"Did you feel it?"

She shook her head.

Woody shrugged, and they began walking again.

"You really should be barefoot. Cain't feel the vibrations through them boots. And early mornings is better, too. Like I said. And sometimes you have to wait a long time to feel it. I've been practicing since I was a kid. Sometimes I stand out back until the sun goes down and Ma calls me in for supper."

"Woody, really." RJ was shocked, and then she wasn't. She softened her tone. "Do you mean to tell me you sometimes stand barefoot in your yard all day? And Olive lets you be until supper time?"

"Oh, don't get me wrong, it used to drive Ma batty. Pa, too. They'd shout, 'What's the matter with you, boy?' And then I'd get all scared and mad at 'em for shouting. And I'd run off. But now they pretty much let me be. They just whisper to each other, 'What's the matter with that boy?' And it don't make me mad no more, because they ain't yelling it."

They walked a bit further. RJ stopped again and knelt down. Woody handed her an empty jar, and she scooped up a sample. They traded jar for measuring stick. She jotted the depth in her journal. He tucked the jar in his duffle.

"I'd like to try my hand at plowing the north field into ridges, to help keep the soil from blowing in the next storm," RJ said, while Woody opened a can of Van Camp's beans for their noon meal.

"Ridges? How come?"

RJ explained the dynamics of wind, how it moves across the land, how tall ridges of dirt, spaced properly, would help block the wind and prevent the soil between the ridges from taking to the air. "I'll drill some African buffel grass along the ridges, too."

Woody looked perplexed, as he poured the beans into a pan and lit the stove. "Who's gonna eat grass?"

"The grass wouldn't be for eating," RJ said. "It would help fight erosion. The native grass was here long before we ever were. Buffalo grass, little bluestem, curly mesquite, needle grass. That's what held the soil in place for centuries, even during the worst droughts and the worst winds."

RJ stirred the beans in the pot. "If we can get enough rain for the seed to take, the grass will also help block the wind and hold the earth in place. In the spring, we can plant some wheat or corn between the ridges, and the crops just might have a fighting chance."

"We call that strip cropping, planting two different things in one field," Woody said as he sliced two fat pieces of bread from a fresh loaf RJ had brought home from Ethel's. "But we sow wheat and sorghum, something like that. Never planted plain old grass. You really think that'll work?"

"That's why I'm here. To conduct experiments and see what happens." She stopped stirring the beans a moment and looked over at Woody. Then she gave a quick, decisive nod. "Yes. I believe it will work."

"Golly," Woody said. "An honest to goodness scientific experiment. Who'da thought I'd ever get to help out with something like that!"

RJ soaked up his smile. She was excited about the work, too. Having a friend who shared her enthusiasm was more than she had hoped for.

"I still don't know about grass, though," Woody added.

He set the bread on the table. RJ served up two bowls of beans, and they sat down to eat. RJ explained that African grasses were like Kansas' native grasses, with root systems that go down six to eight feet. They can be dormant for years and spring back to life with even the smallest amount of rain.

"That root system is what held the soil in place on the plains for centuries, until people came along to farm and dug it all up, acre after acre," she said.

Woody scratched the stubble on his chin. A light of understanding seemed to flicker in his eyes. "I'll be darned. That sure makes sense to me now. We've probably lost a good eight feet of top soil in the past three years."

"Well, that estimate is a bit extreme, but you've got the right idea," she replied.

Woody stared her square in the eye. RJ looked up at him and her hand froze midair on the way to her mouth with a spoonful of beans. The unusual directness of his gaze threw RJ off balance inside.

"You ain't been out to the cemetery to see your folks yet, have you?"

His question made her feel shaky, as if she hadn't eaten for days. RJ slowly lowered the spoon back into her bowl. She dropped her eyes and shook her head, too embarrassed to say the word. No.

"You should go," he said softly. "See your folks, and you'll also see how much topsoil we've lost."

RJ nodded her acknowledgment.

They sat quietly for a few minutes. Woody continued eating, and RJ drew circles with her spoon in the bowl of beans.

"You mad at me?" Woody finally asked.

"No. Of course not."

"Then why did you stop talking?" he pressed.

RJ let out a heavy sigh. She didn't want to tell him it was because she felt embarrassed. She knew he would then ask her *why* she felt that way. And what could she say? She was embarrassed because she hadn't yet paid her respects to her parents? Or because, deep down, she was terrified to go see their graves?

"I don't know, Woody. I just can't put my finger on it."

"You can't?"

RJ shook her head again.

"Well, what are you trying to put your finger on? Maybe I can do it for you," Woody said, extending his index finger in the air.

RJ chuckled. *Dear Woody.*

"Not literally," she said. "It's an expression. It means I can't quite pinpoint how I'm feeling."

Woody processed her explanation for a moment. Then, he drew his hand into a fist and hit his forehead with the heel of his palm, again and again. RJ sprung from her chair and ran to him. She took hold of his wrist to prevent him from striking himself again, so Woody balled up his other hand and hit himself again.

"I'm stupid," he said.

"No, Woody. You're not." RJ took hold of his other wrist and the two struggled for a moment. Woody was strong, but RJ was able to impede the worst of the blows. She pleaded with him to stop. "You're not stupid. Don't say that. Don't even think it."

They struggled a bit more. Woody finally let his arms drop, and RJ released her grip. Woody took in several big gulps of air, and RJ gave him the time he needed to pull himself together. She knelt on the floor in front of him with her hands in her lap. After a bit, she looked up at him.

"What was all that about?" she asked.

Woody didn't look up at her. He didn't speak.

"What's the matter? Can't put your finger on it?" RJ smiled.

Woody chuckled through his teeth, emitting a gush of air like a pressure cooker releasing its steam. He smiled and looked at RJ, making eye contact for a heartbeat before looking up and away. RJ waited again for him to speak.

"It's just," he began, hesitating before starting again. "It's just that, well, I do that all the time. Somebody says something, and I get it all wrong. And then everybody laughs. But I don't know why they're laughing. Sometimes they smile and say 'Oh, Woody.' Other times they shake their heads and call me stupid or dim-witted."

"That's awful," RJ said. "And it's flat out wrong, Woody. You're brilliant."

"No, I ain't."

"You are," RJ pressed. "I wouldn't have hired a dim-wit, I assure you. You just take things too literally, that's all."

She thought for a moment, then snapped her fingers as she rose to her feet and walked to her bookshelf. She scanned the books, pulled a thick text from the shelf, and blew the dust off the top.

"Maybe this will help," she said, opening the book and flipping through the pages. "It's one of my English books from school. It explains different parts of speech and how they are used."

She set it on the table, thumped the cover and sat back down to her meal. "Take that home with you and bring it back when you're done with it. You can borrow any of my other books, too, Woody. Anytime you want."

Woody looked down at the book and ran his fingers over the embossed title.

"Thanks, RJ."

"You're welcome."

They finished the rest of their meal in silence. Only this time, the silence was comfortable. Woody had bared a little piece of his soul, and it had brought them closer. It had erased any need for idle chitchat. When their bowls were empty, RJ rose to clear the table and Woody followed suit.

"We'll need to get the tractor cleaned up," he spoke up, returning to their earlier topic. "No way it'll run after sitting for so long in the barn."

RJ had learned from Woody that keeping an engine running in this environment was a significant project unto itself. He had shown her how to clean the air filter on the Ford and stressed that it should be among her daily chores. After each storm, she was to brush out the engine with a broom, flush it with water and add fresh grease to the bearings. As for the tractor, it had been sitting in the barn for Lord knows how long. It would have to be completely disassembled and cleaned. And who knew if that would be enough. Odds were it would require new parts and repairs after its extended neglect.

"Do you think we'll be able to get it running again, Woody?"

"Sure we can. I know everything about engines."

Woody, it seemed to her, knew everything about everything. Having him around fueled her optimism.

"We'll need help though," he said. "Taking an engine apart is a big job. You gotta have a lot of hands and muscle."

She looked out the kitchen window at the hazy brown sky. "Do you have someone in mind?"

"Harvey Clay," Woody said. "He knows engines like nobody else. Besides me, that is."

"Harvey?" she said. She turned to look at Woody again, scrunching up her face. "I don't know, Woody. You think he'd have time to help? You think he'd even be willing to help if he *did* have the time? Gosh, I don't know. Maybe if *you* asked him..."

Woody grinned wide. "I already did. He said he'd come out day after tomorrow."

Olive handed the last of the supper plates to Alice to wipe dry. The girl set it upside down on the stack on the shelf beside the coffee mugs, also turned upside down until the moment they would be used. Then, she draped her damp towel over them all, one last attempt to keep the dust at bay.

Pa sat in his chair by the window, gleaning the last fleeting rays of sunlight to reread the Crop and Business Conditions pages of his *Farmer's Almanac*. Wheat, buckwheat, corn, rye, barley, tobacco, cotton. Average bushel yields from 1926 to 1930. Estimated yields from 1933. Ten-year averages. Projected yield for the coming year. He shook his head, jotted a few notes in the margins.

"Shoulda drilled barley and rye in the spring," he muttered.

"What's that, Pa?" Olive asked.

He set the booklet in his lap, looked up at her, the creases in his forehead sinking deep as his eyebrows drew together. "Says in here the Department of Agriculture expects a big demand for rye and barley since they repealed prohibition. I shoulda drilled them instead of wheat last spring. We'd get a better price at harvest."

"You done all you could, Pa," she said. "Don't matter what you drilled without a drop of rain all summer. Don't matter what the demand is, without a harvest."

Pa turned to watch the sun sink deeper in the hazy sky. *Gonna drill rye and barley next spring*, he thought. *To hell with wheat.*

Olive dried her hands on her apron. *We'll try rye and barely next spring*, she thought. She turned her attention to Woody, who sat at the table immersed in a thick book bound in black leather. Olive took a step closer and peered at the pages of tiny print.

"What have you got there, Woody? Did the library get in some new books?"

Woody scrunched up his face. "Naw. The library ain't got nothin' new in for three years. Still only got the same 1,862 books I already read a million times."

"A million?"

Woody laughed. "That's *hyperbole*, Ma. An exaggeration."

He held up the book, so Olive could see the cover. "It's in this here book RJ lent me, from one of her college classes."

Olive took the book from him, felt the heft in her hands, flipped through a page or two. She wondered how much a book like that must cost. Three, four dollars? Maybe more?

"I really only read most of them books at the library one time, except for the Tarzan books which I read two times each and all the Sherlock Holmes books which I been working on reading for the third time now."

"And Miss Evans just gave you this book to read? You didn't ask her for it?"

"Oh no, Ma. I know my manners. I wouldn't of asked her for it. But, golly, does she have a lot of books. I helped her get 'em all unpacked the other day and dusted and put on her shelves. She said I could borrow any of them I wanted, anytime.

"She picked this one out, special for me. RJ says I take things too literal sometimes, figures of speech and jokes and whatnot. Maybe if I learned about stuff like metaphors and analogies and the other things in this book, it might be easier on me when I'm talking to folks. So they won't laugh at me or think I'm stupid."

Olive's stomach tumbled. She felt an old familiar sting in her eyes. She looked down at the book again. She'd had no idea you could buy such a book, one that could teach Woody those things that she'd been trying to teach him for some twenty years, things that everybody else on God's green earth seemed to just *know*. She sniffed and handed the book back to her son.

"You take good care of that, now, Woody. It was mighty generous of Miss Evans to loan you such an expensive book."

"Yes, ma'am."

Woody opened the book again to the place where he'd been reading, examined the words more intently in the dim twilight. Pa walked over to the table and lit the Alladin lamp in the center. Olive let a peep escape her lips. With kerosene at thirteen cents a gallon, Pa almost never lit the lamps after supper. He looked at his wife with moist eyes and a tight-lipped half-smile, eyebrows raised.

Alice clapped her hands and darted to her small bedroom. "If we're gonna have the lamp going tonight, I'm getting my sewing basket!"

"Get mine, too, child," Olive said, her voice breaking just a bit.

RJ dug her fingers into the kitchen sink drain to clear it of mud. She smeared a glob of gritty sludge onto a rag and plunged back in for more. If she couldn't figure a way to keep the dirt out of the pipes, the luxury of indoor plumbing would soon vanish.

The rumble of tires in the distance drew her eyes to the window. A thick plume of dust, even thicker than the dust already hovering across the landscape, billowed in the wake of Harvey's truck as it made its way up her drive.

Woody bounded from the truck before it even came to a complete stop and ran up to the house.

"Mornin', RJ!"

RJ smiled as Woody rushed into the kitchen when she opened the door. Mornings were his best time, before the stress of the day began to take its toll and work his nerves raw, after which his emotions were more easily set off.

She watched Harvey stroll across the windswept yard, starting his morning with a more subdued style, relaxed and easygoing.

"Good morning, Rosa Jean." He removed his hat as he stepped inside.

"Good morning, Harvey. I can't thank you enough for coming out to help with the tractor," she said. "I just opened a tin of biscuits, if you'd like a bite to eat before we get to work."

They settled around the table and shared a bit of small talk, on the weather and how a baseball player named Lou Gehrig had just "hit for the cycle" beating the White Sox, thirteen to two.

"Mr. Gehrig got himself a single, double, triple and homer all in one game," Woody explained to RJ. "Ain't that something?"

Then, Woody gave a long oration on baseball records held by the New York Yankees and what all the sports journalists were saying about Gehrig. When he'd finished, a quiet fell upon the threesome. RJ nibbled on a biscuit, searched her mind desperately for another topic of conversation. She came up empty.

"Say," Harvey said, motioning in the direction of the road. "What are all those flags for out there along your drive?"

"Oh," RJ brightened. "They're distance markers. Woody helped me place them at twenty-five-yard intervals, down the road and across the east field, to measure visibility. I record the visibility distance at specific times throughout the day and, of course, during any storms, for my weekly reports to Washington."

Harvey scrunched his eyebrows together. "And what does that do? Keeping track of something like that?"

RJ paused. She couldn't tell if he was truly interested or if he was mocking her work.

"Well," she said, then paused again. "It helps the scientists at the Department of Agriculture, the Soil Erosion Service team in Washington, to understand the challenges we're facing here. To understand the effects of the dust and help figure out ways to mitigate it."

She sighed, looked out the kitchen window. "It's hard to comprehend without being here, without living it every day."

"Yes," Harvey said. "I suppose that's true."

He popped the last of his biscuit in his mouth and stood up. "Well Woody, speaking of visibility, we better tackle that engine before the air gets any thicker out there."

"Already like pea soup," Woody said. "That's a *simile*."

"I'll just get the kitchen straightened up quick, and then I'll join you out in the barn," RJ said, clearing the table.

"Join us? What for?" Harvey laughed. "We don't need a cheering section, Rosa Jean."

RJ looked at him with the calm restraint she'd perfected in school. She remained mute for a moment.

"Woody said cleaning that engine would be a big job and take a lot of hands." RJ kept her voice steady. "That's why we asked you to come out and *help*. Because it was more than Woody and I could manage, just the two of us."

"Well, sure, but it won't be more than Woody and *I* can manage."

With that, Woody threw his hands over his ears. "Don't argue. I don't like arguing." He began to pace the kitchen.

"It's okay, Woody," RJ said, crossing her arms, careful not to raise her voice. "There isn't going to be any argument."

Harvey shook his head. He looked down at his feet a moment, smiling.

"Suit yourself, Miss Evans." He put on his hat and headed for the door. "Come on now, Woody, pull yourself together and let's get to work. This'll be heaps of fun. We'll be the Three Musketeers. How do you like that simile?"

RJ watched the men leave the house and trudge across the yard toward the barn, while Woody lectured Harvey on why what Harvey had said wasn't, in fact, a simile and was actually a metaphor. She couldn't help but laugh, despite her irritation. She should be wearing tap shoes, she thought, with all the dancing around she always had to do.

~

By the time RJ made it out to the barn, both men had their shirts off and were elbow deep in grease. She stepped in close, looking over the assembly of parts, and began rolling up her sleeves.

"Now, hyperbole," Woody said, "that's something else altogether. That's a figure of speech that uses exaggeration to make a point. Like saying this engine weighs a ton. See, because it's mighty heavy, but it don't really weigh a whole ton."

Harvey stopped working the bolt he was trying to break loose. He looked up at Woody, then over at RJ. Then, he dropped his head. "Lord, help me."

"How is it looking?" RJ asked. "Woody warned me we might need to replace the oil pump if there was too much dirt in there clogging things up."

"Come have a look," Harvey said, motioning for her to come closer.

He showed her how they had already removed the hood and side panels, and the radiator panels and grill. "Those all need to come off so you can get to the engine and get a good look around."

RJ leaned over him from behind while he pointed to the various parts of the engine and reported on their condition. She couldn't help but notice the taut muscles of his back beneath his suspenders, the name of his little sister tattooed on his bicep. She'd never been one to swoon over the muscular boys at school. She'd always been more partial to the brainy ones, with their noses buried in books at the library. Still, she had to admit, Harvey was quite a strapping fellow and it was difficult not to admire his form.

He turned and caught her watching him. She looked up quickly, nodding as though she were rapt with his engineering knowledge, but it was too late. He raised his eyebrows and gave her a sly smile. Her face blazed. She stepped away to look out the barn door and give her cheeks a chance to cool.

"My goodness," she said. "Are those rain clouds?"

Harvey and Woody moved quickly beside her to survey the horizon.

"Wrong color," Woody said. "That's a duster. A big one."

RJ silently chided herself for not being able to recognize the difference yet.

Harvey looked out around the barn and over to the house. "Where's your wire?"

"Wire for what?" RJ asked.

"Oh, for Pete's sake," Harvey said, wiping his greasy hand on a rag with an urgency that made her anxious. "You should have a wire running from the barn to the house."

He tossed the rag down onto the engine and began to mutter under his breath. "She's got pretty little flags from here to next Tuesday to measure *visibility*, but she ain't got no doggone wire running to the house."

"What did you just say?" RJ swirled to face him now, hands planted on her hips. "If you have something on your mind, be man enough to say it to me directly."

"Easy there, bulldog. I meant no offense." Harvey threw his hands up in the air. "I'm just surprised you don't have a wire."

RJ threw her hands up right back at him, mirroring his frustration. The bellow of the wind was increasing, and the two found themselves shouting at each other. "What do I need a blessed wire for?"

Harvey ran his dirty hands through his hair and closed his eyes.

"So you can find your way to the house if you get caught out here in a storm," he said. He was still shouting to be heard above the din, but his tone had mellowed. "You lived in Wisconsin. You probably heard stories about folks getting caught in a blizzard and freezing to death twenty feet from their own front door because they couldn't see. Dusters can be just as bad as that, just as dangerous."

The barn doors slammed shut in a sudden gust of wind, closing them off from what dim light there was outside. Woody ran to the door, pushing it open with his lanky body. The wind roared through the barn. The rafters rattled and shook.

Harvey took RJ by the elbow. "We have to get back to the house!"

Woody pushed on ahead, and RJ followed, her head down, Harvey's broad hand bracing her lower back. She pushed against the wind with all her strength, blinded by the driving dust.

Another gust whipped up and blew her backward into Harvey's arms. They stopped for a second, to regain their footing and keep from toppling over entirely, and then he gave her a steady push forward toward the house.

She could taste the dust in the back of her throat, feel it scratching deep in her lungs as she gasped for air. She tried pulling her shirt collar over her mouth and nose as a filter, but it did little good. By the time they reached the porch, she was overcome with a retching cough that brought her to her knees. Woody opened the door, and Harvey picked her up from under her arms and swept her inside. They stood hunched over in the kitchen, coughing and spitting up mud. Once she had regained some composure, RJ stumbled to the sink and pumped up water into a dish towel, wrung it out and handed it to Woody. She got another for Harvey and one for herself. And they all dabbed away the mud from their eyes, wiped the grit from their faces.

"Son of a bitch," RJ said, breaking from any decorum her Aunt May had taught her. But then, this situation was unlike any her Aunt May could have imagined. Unlike any RJ would even have believed, if she weren't living through it herself.

If Harvey and Woody heard her foul declaration, they ignored it.

"We better get this place stowed," Harvey said, gathering his wits faster than RJ. He pulled the curtains shut over the sink and turned for the other windows. Woody followed suit.

RJ looked around the room frantically, in the corners, under the desk. She ran to the bedroom and looked under the bed. Then, she rushed back out into the main room, wild-eyed.

"I can't find Stormy."

She looked at Woody. He turned and looked at the door, took a step.

"Oh, no, no," Harvey said. "Don't you even think about going back out there."

"It's okay. I know where to find her."

Woody took another step toward the door. Harvey grabbed hold of Woody's arm, and Woody shook him off fiercely. "Don't touch me!"

Harvey took a step back and threw his palms up in surrender.

"Just calm down, Woody. I won't touch you again, I promise. But you can't go out there. Don't be stupid."

"Don't call me stupid, Harvey!"

"All right, I'm sorry. That wasn't nice of me to say," Harvey stopped. RJ could see how he struggled to find the right words, the right demeanor to keep Woody from going over the edge and out the door. Harvey began again, more steady, more composed. "But I can't let you go out there looking for some dog. It just ain't safe, son. You should know better."

"Don't call me son, neither," Woody fired back. "I'm a grown man, and I'll do what I want. Plus, I'm smarter than you. That ain't an insult, Harv. It's just the truth. And it ain't just some dog. It's Stormy, and I love her and she loves me. And I know how to find her and bring her back, and you can't stop me."

Woody seized his work goggles from the hook and stretched the strap over his head. He pulled his bandanna from his back pocket and soaked it under the tap.

"Rosa Jean, talk some sense into him before he goes out and gets himself killed."

Woody pointed at RJ. "You can't stop me neither."

RJ bit her lower lip. She weighed the options in her mind, racing through the facts, desperate to deduce an answer to the problem. But her heart kept interrupting. This wasn't some theory to be tested in the safety of her lab. This was real life – the life of her beloved pet and the life of her friend. Her only friend.

"You're right, Woody," she said. "I can't stop you. But I also can't bear the thought of losing you. Help me understand what you're planning to do. How can you be sure you can find her and then make your way back?"

"It's already darker than two midnights in a jug out there," Harvey chimed in, waving his hand toward the door.

RJ shot him a stern look that said to shut his trap. She placed her hand on Woody's shoulder. "Please, Woody. Talk to me."

Woody shook off her hand, though less fiercely than he had with Harvey.

"Stormy has herself a hole out back of the barn, by the old chicken coop," he said, adjusting his goggles. "She sleeps there when it's hot. Sometimes I sit in there with her. She don't mind. It's eighty-five paces walking perpendicular from the east-side porch railing to the garden fence. Nine fence posts to the left puts you square in front of the barn door. It's another two-hundred-thirty-three paces from the fence to the barn. I'll feel my way around the barn from there, get Stormy and come back the same way. Work my way around to the barn door. Two-hundred-thirty-three paces to the fence. Nine fence posts along the garden. Eighty-five paces to the porch."

RJ couldn't help but smile at his detail, his certainty. She looked to Harvey, searched his face, but she couldn't read him. After a moment, Harvey slumped in defeat.

"Well, at least run yourself a rope from the porch to the fence and the fence to the barn," he said. "In case you lose track of your paces or direction, so you can feel your way back."

"Good thinking," Woody said.

"I'm going with you," RJ said and pulled a bandanna from her pocket.

"No, you're not," Woody and Harvey said in unison.

RJ felt her face flush with anger. She grabbed her goggles from the hook. "Oh yes, I am!"

Harvey slapped his forehead with the palm of his hand. Woody placed his hands on RJ's arms and looked her in the eye though his smudgy goggles. "Stay here, RJ. I'll find my way faster if I'm by myself. That's all there is to it."

And before she could argue, Woody tied his bandanna over his face and slipped out the door in a blast of piercing dust.

RJ and Harvey stood motionless for some time, still in shock that Woody had just charged back out into the storm and that they had let him. RJ's arms tingled from the memory of Woody's rare touch. The dark closed in around them as the mountain of dust rumbled over the house and across the fields.

"I should get a lamp lit." Harvey finally broke the spell.

"Yes. Good," RJ said. She felt her anger evaporate into worry.

He felt his way in the dark, until the dim flame of the oil lamp created a halo of red light in the dusty air. It was enough light to keep from bumping into things, but not enough to read a book or even the expression on one another's face. RJ paced between the stove and the door, arms crossed, hugging herself.

Harvey sat down and pulled a wad of string from his pocket. He set his elbows on the table and stretched the string out in a loop between his hands. His calloused fingers wove one way and then the other, creating a web between his hands. "Cat's cradle?"

RJ stopped and stared in his direction for a moment. She looked back at the door.

"How can you play a game at a time like this?" she said. "Aren't you the least bit worried about Woody?"

"Sure, I am. But what good does worrying do? We let him go out there, Rosa Jean, and now all we can do is wait for him to come back. Might as well occupy ourselves in the meantime."

RJ wiped her sweaty palms on the front of her overalls and slipped hesitantly into the chair opposite Harvey. He looped the string over his hands again, threaded it one way, then the other.

"I haven't played this since I was a child," RJ said, contemplating the pattern of the string.

Harvey waited.

Finally, RJ leaned forward and grasped the crossed strings at the top between her right thumb and forefinger.

"There you go," Harvey said.

She grasped the crossed strings at the bottom in her left thumb and forefinger, and pulled her hands slowly apart. Her hands were shaking, and she hoped Harvey couldn't feel it in the vibrations of the string. She glanced back toward the front door.

"Now bring 'em up and around," Harvey pulled her back to the game, and she did as he said. He eased his fingers from the string, passing the diamond-shaped web from his hands to hers. When the transfer was complete, their eyes met in the hazy light.

"They'll be okay," Harvey said.

~~

Woody charged out into the inky blackness from the east side of the porch. *Two midnights in a jug*, he said to himself. *What do I care? I ain't afraid of the dark.* He counted out his paces as he pressed his full weight into the fierce current of air.

The wind howled. Now, that. That deafening roar set his nerves on fire. Dirt began to pack in his ears like cotton, and he was grateful. It helped to quiet the howl.

He was halfway to the barn when he realized he'd forgotten to run a rope behind him. Panic turned his feet to lead, unmovable. He fell to his hands and knees. Self-doubt and worry rushed through his mind, faster than the wind drove the soil across the landscape. *What if I can't find Stormy? What if I can't find my way back to the house? I'm gonna be buried alive. No one will ever find me.* The hurling grit bore into the little bits of his skin that were exposed – his forehead, his hands, his neck. His heart sputtered off rhythm, halted for an eternity, resumed erratically. Lub-dub-dub... Lub... dub... Lub-dub-dub-dub. Woody tried to take a deep breath, but the bandanna and the dust and the wind and the roar denied him oxygen.

My paces? How many paces have I gone? Woody's question to himself brought him a type of oxygen. It brought him a number. Thinking about numbers relaxed his mind, soothed his nerves.

Seventy-two. He had gone seventy-two paces.

Woody crawled forward, still blind, pressing on against the assault of wind and earth. In his mind, he estimated the distance of crawling hand to knee compared to a full stride upright. Seventy-three. Seventy-four. The sequence of numbers steadied his heartbeat. He persisted forward. Seventy-nine. Eighty. Finally, at eight-five, he reached out and grasped the garden fence.

Nine fence posts to the left. Two-hundred-thirty-three paces to the barn. Around the barn.

Reaching the chicken coop brought him little joy. His hands groped over the weather-beaten wood, through the dune that had already collected around the structure. He dug furiously beneath the coop until, thank God, his hands collided with the dog's trembling body.

Woody tugged at the dog, but she refused to come to him. He tried calling to her, reassuring her with his voice, but the wind shouted over him. With no other option, Woody grasped tightly to Stormy's collar and dragged her toward him. The terrified animal twisted and nipped at his arms as he pulled her to his chest. Woody leaned his back to the coop, cradled Stormy between his arms and chest, stroked her head until she stopped fighting him. Then he rose to his feet and worked his way back around the barn, out to the garden fence. Two-hundred-thirty-three paces. Nine fence posts.

The muscles in Woody's arms and legs quivered under the strain. His lungs burned. His eyes remained useless.

"Just eighty-five paces," he shouted to Stormy. Just eighty-five more paces back to the house. And he began to count.

~~~

The front door flew open in an explosion of air and earth. RJ and Harvey jumped out of their seats in a tangle of string. Woody's hulking silhouette loomed in the doorframe just before the blast extinguished the lamp.

RJ stumbled toward the door, reaching out to take hold of Woody's arm and pull him inside. She leaned her full weight into the door, pressing with all her strength to push back the storm and secure the lock. Harvey fumbled at the table to relight the lamp.

Woody fell to his knees, clutching Stormy to his chest. RJ dropped next to him and embraced them both.

"Oh Woody, thank God you're safe." She eased his goggles up and off his head and untied the bandanna from his face. She pushed his unruly hair back from his forehead and cradled his cheeks in her hands. "Are you okay? Can you breathe? You're not hurt anywhere, are you?"

Woody couldn't speak. He coughed roughly and wiped a glob of mud from his mouth with his shoulder. RJ sprang to her feet to get him a cup of water. Harvey eased the dog from Woody's grasp and laid her down on the rug.

"Drink this." RJ handed Woody the cup with one hand and stroked his hair again with the other. He jerked his head away from her touch. Then, he gave her an apologetic, tight-lipped smile. He knew women liked being "touchy," and he didn't want RJ's feelings to be hurt by his aversion to it.

"Quit messing with his hair," Harvey said. "Woody don't like that."

RJ shot him a fierce look. Then she folded her hands in her lap, watched Woody as he gulped down the water. After a moment, she gave Woody's arm a quick, gentle squeeze.
~~~

"It's freezing in here," she said over her shoulder to Harvey. He said nothing more, went to the woodstove to build up the fire.

Woody lumbered up into one of the kitchen chairs, and RJ hopped to her feet. First, she retrieved the quilt from her bed and draped it around his shoulders. Next, she pulled her old wool blanket from the trunk and spread it over Stormy. RJ stroked the dog's head and ears. Stormy trembled and wheezed, but she did not stir. RJ washed the dirt from the dog's eyes, nose and ears with a wet rag.

"Damn this infernal dust," RJ said, half to herself, half out loud.

Harvey nodded in silent agreement. It was one of the few things on which they seemed to agree. He watched her for a moment as she massaged the dog through the blanket, bringing warmth and life back into the tiny animal. He shuddered, despite being warmed by the fire.

~~~

The storm raged on into the night. Woody slept slumped over at the kitchen table, wrapped in RJ's quilt, his forehead resting on his folded arms. Harvey had fallen asleep in the chair across from him. The farmer's long legs extended out under the table, crossed at the ankles; his meaty arms folded over his chest, and his head hung back.

RJ had curled up on the rug with the dog, beneath the wool blanket, but she only slept in fits. It took her back to that first duster, and how Stormy's warm body and steady pant had helped get her through the night.

How many storms had they endured since then? Too many, already, to count. And yet, she did count them. RJ tallied each storm in her logbook, noting its duration, its wind direction and speed, its after effects. It all went into her reports to Washington, along with accounts of what she and her neighbors had done to fight back, before and after the storms – hanging wet sheets over
~~~

the windows inside the house to catch the dust, climbing out the window when the storm had passed to shovel the dust piles away from the door. It was useful data, her superiors assured her, and she wanted to believe that. But it was times like this that tested her faith in science. Despite all their data, despite all their knowledge, they couldn't make the wind stop blowing or make the sky open up with rain. And without rain and the life it brought, it seemed there was no way to defeat the beast.

RJ lay on her side, one arm folded beneath her head, the other draped over the dog. She listened to the steady roar of the wind, to the dry rain of dirt pelting the house, to the earth getting its revenge upon them for not appreciating what they had, for taking too much. In the faint orange glow of the woodstove, RJ watched serpents of dust slither beneath the door and slink across the wood floor toward them.

"You stay away from us," she hissed, pulling Stormy closer. "Stay away."

"*You ain't been out to the cemetery to see your folks yet, have you?*"

Woody's question haunted RJ until she could no longer put off the visit.

The Ford rolled to a stop in front of the cemetery entrance. RJ emerged slowly. The wind had quieted. The air was relatively clear of dust. And yet, she couldn't seem to activate her lungs. It was like the time she'd fallen out of the mulberry tree in Uncle Lou's fruit orchard and landed flat onto her back, knocking the wind clean out of her. She had thought she might die as her lungs seized, and she struggled to take in air. At this moment, that memory was child's play.

RJ had been to the cemetery in Wisconsin as a teenager, when her granddad died. The hills there moseyed over and around, brilliant green with neatly manicured grass, evenly stitched with rows of headstones. It was a lovely place to sit on the ground and chat with him, leaning back against the smooth marble grave marker. Old maples lined the main road, and gravel walkways stretched like a pianist's slender fingers into the depths of the grounds. The mausoleum rose tall in the background, noble and brilliant with its white marble columns and black pitched roof.

The Vanham cemetery was not like that. Not at all. RJ had known a small town cemetery would not be as grand as the one in which her granddad had been laid to rest. Still, she hadn't been prepared for the scene stretched out before her. A wasteland of sand dunes and dead trees. Caskets, once buried six feet beneath the sod now half-exposed to the world again, unearthed by drought and unrelenting wind. RJ wasn't prone to believe in ghost tales, but if the souls of the dead were ever doomed to walk the earth in despair, this would be the right place.

She exhaled something between a cough and a sob, and pressed her palms against her forehead, as if to keep herself from doubling over. She tested her footing, took a wobbly step away from the truck and toward the cemetery gate. Her arms dropped to her sides, and she took another step forward, and then another, until she reached the entrance.

Someone behind her cleared his throat, and RJ spun around.

"Sorry," the man said, looking at his feet. "Don't mean to intrude. It's a shock to see, I know."

"Uh huh." RJ looked back toward the cemetery.

"You, uh, you need help finding someone?"

"Are you the caretaker?"

"Yap, that's me." He pulled a square of yellowed paper from his coat pocket, carefully unfolded it.

"Had to remove the headstones a ways back. Lost so much dirt, they was tumbling all over." He sniffed, knitted his eyebrows. "Store the markers over there, in the shed. But first, I made a map, you see, to keep track of where everyone is."

"Oh," RJ said, regaining her composure, looking over at the shed. "That was sensible of you. And kind."

The man scrunched up his face.

"Just making do, best I can. Like everybody else, I reckon." He looked at RJ with gentle regard and asked, "So who're you looking for?"

"My parents. Uh, Evans. Their name is Evans."

"Ah, sure. You must be Rosa Jean," he said, scanning the map. "I heard you was back in town. Figured you'd be around sooner or later."

RJ crossed her arms around her stomach, hugged herself, fought back the urge clawing at her insides to sprint back to her truck and speed away.

The caretaker looked up, studied her for a moment. "I'll walk you over to 'em."

He led the way across the grounds, along what must have been a walkway at one time. RJ followed without speaking. He stopped and pointed to two caskets, their corners jutting from the earth, the rough-hewn lids showing the effects of sun and wind they were never intended to see again.

"They're buried in order of age," he said. "Mr. Evans being the oldest, he's right there, and then Mrs. Evans is the next one over."

RJ meant to say thank you, but her voice was cowering somewhere inside her. The caretaker turned and walked off.

When the man was out of sight, RJ dropped to her knees between her parents' graves. She leaned over and pressed her ear to her father's casket, listened to the silence roaring within it.

What had their funeral been like, she wondered. Who might have been there to watch, and to cry, as the caskets were lowered deep into the ground? RJ hadn't been allowed to come home for the funeral, and that reality had nestled in her gut like a hot stone for fifteen years. Searing, jagged, indigestible. She straightened back up and flicked a tear from her cheek.

RJ clenched her jaw to hold in the emotion, and her teeth began to ache.

"I never even got to say good-bye to you," she whispered and placed her hand on her mother's coffin, squeezed her eyes shut.

The sun's warmth radiated up from the splintered wood. The heat coursed through RJ's fingertips, into her veins, through her bowels, her lungs, her heart, until it broke free from beneath her lashes in a fiery torrent of tears that burned its way down her cheeks. A single sob erupted from deep in her gut, and she collapsed in surrender onto her mother's unearthed resting place.

November 1934

Stormy whimpered as RJ cleaned the crusted gunk from her eyelashes with a wet cloth. It had become their morning ritual. RJ did her best to be gentle, and the dog did her best to sit still. After the first time RJ woke up with her own lashes glued shut over her red, swollen eyes, she began sleeping in her goggles.

"I'd get you a pair of goggles, too, if I thought you'd wear them," RJ said, then gave the dog a kiss on the forehead. Stormy returned the kiss on RJ's nose and bounded out of the bedroom.

"There ought to be a law against waking up at 4:30 on a Sunday morning," RJ muttered. A full night's sleep seemed impossible to wrangle from the restive wind and oppressive dust.

RJ turned her boots upside down and pounded them together. Two centipedes fell to the floor and scurried beneath the baseboard, into the wall. RJ shuddered. *I wonder how many of those critters are crawling around in there?* With so many birds suffocating or dropping dead of exhaustion in the dusters, insects were taking over the landscape. RJ gave her boots one more hardy shake for good measure, then pulled them on and stepped out to the front porch with Stormy close at her heels.

The morning air had a bite to it that reminded RJ of camping. It had been too long, she decided, since she'd slept outdoors and watched the sunrise. Just the idea of it infused new energy into her step.

She built a fire in the pit using the spindly Russian thistle bushes that had piled up at her garden fence from the wind. The twigs began to crackle and spit in no time. RJ held out her hands a moment to take in the warmth, then retreated to the house to gather the fixings for coffee and grab her old wool blanket from the chest. She paused a moment before heading back outside. It would be more sensible to sip hot coffee in the comfort and shelter of her kitchen, wouldn't it? More ladylike?

"Pfft." *What could possibly be more sensible than a front row seat at sunrise?*

RJ sat on the hard-packed ground, her back to the porch railing, her outstretched legs bundled in the blanket. She drank her coffee, felt it warm her chest. She stared into the flickering flames and into the darkness beyond it, lost in the quiet, waiting for the sun to break.

Her mind drifted. She was a little girl again, waking to the sound of her mother pumping water out at the well, lighting the kitchen fire. Her father was out in the barn milking, then in the coop collecting eggs. All before the break of dawn. Just like all the other homesteaders and farmers scattered across the plains, all those years ago. And this morning.

The giant glowing orb peeked up from the horizon, illuminating the wine-dark sky, the dormant landscape. Centipedes, hordes of them, too many to count, scurried for cover from the breaking light, below ground, into the cracks and crevices of the house, under the well pump.

Stormy's ears went flat. She emitted a low, menacing growl.

"I know, girl," RJ said, a shiver running up her spine. "They're creepy. But they should die off when the weather turns really cold next month."

The fire crackled, flames shrinking, embers losing their glow as the sun showed its superiority.

Sunday, when RJ was a little girl, had been the one day her mother would let her sleep in a bit. Then, they'd eat fried eggs and pancakes and get dressed for church. After, they might load the picnic basket with fried chicken and potato salad and pie, and head down to the Cimarron River. *Family day.* That's what her mother had called it.

RJ swallowed hard, blinked away the stinging in her eyes. She pulled back the blanket, rose to her feet. Stormy stood, too, shook the dust from her coat.

"Come on, pup. I'm making pancakes, then we'll go for a ride." RJ paused to scratch behind the dog's ears. "It's time for a family day."

~~~

Olive sat in her chair by the window stitching piecework for a quilt when she heard a truck rumble up. She set down her sewing and rose to open the door.

"Hiya, Olive. I hope you don't mind me coming by unannounced." RJ held out a tin of cookies.

"Not at all, dear. Come on in." Olive gave RJ a warm smile and thanked her for the goodies.

Inside, the women settled at the kitchen table. RJ noted that Olive appeared to have the house to herself. Alice was out searching for buried treasure around the yard, Olive said. The men were making the rounds to the neighbors, trading odds and ends for supplies to build a chicken coop.

"I decided we need to start keeping chickens," Olive said. "The eggs will do us good, and we can sell what we don't eat."

"That's a great idea," RJ said.
~~~

"Pa thinks it was all his idea," Olive said. "So just go along if he brings it up with you."

RJ chuckled. Then, she realized Olive was serious, and she laughed even harder.

"That's how it is with men," Olive said. "A woman's gotta plant the seed. Give it a bit of water, a bit of sunlight. And before you know it, the idea's all his, full grown and full of fruit."

Olive laughed then, warm and loving, not hard. She rose to retrieve her piecework and sat back down at the table. "You know what I mean."

RJ raised her eyebrows and shook her head in awe. *I have no idea,* she thought. But it would sure be nice to know. She had a whole herd of men she needed to persuade to adopt conservation farming as their own brilliant idea. She chuckled again softly and reached for a cookie from the tin.

They fell into a comfortable silence for a moment. RJ watched Olive as she pierced her needle through the small segments of fabric, creating neat, even stitches. She marveled at all the skills Woody's mother had, yet the woman never boasted.

"So, after our last cow died, I told Pa we should raise chickens," Olive began laying out the story. "Of course, he pooped on the idea right off the bat."

RJ nodded stoically. She understood that experience all too well.

"He's got his hands full already, he says, with keeping the fields plowed and the tractor running. Last thing he needs around here, he says, is animals drinking our water and eating our corn."

Olive paused to break a thread with her teeth. She set the completed block in her lap and smoothed over it with her hands.

"So I let it go," she continued, placing the block in her basket and reaching for a new set of pieces. "Then, a few days later, he says it *would* be nice to have fresh eggs in his belly before he went out to plow in the mornings. I said it sure would, but he shouldn't have to take on more work. Let's just not even bring it up again."

RJ leaned forward a bit. Her skin almost tingled as she waited for Olive to continue. The woman stretched out a length of thread, wet the end with her lips and eased it through the eye of the needle.

Another week had gone by, Olive said, and Pa wondered again about nice, fresh eggs. "That's when I said, 'I suppose if you really have a hankering for eggs, me and Alice could take on caring for the chickens. Lord knows you don't need the extra chores.' And I said it might be a good time for the girl to take on a responsibility like that, anyhow, now that she's grown a bit."

It wasn't much longer before Pa had started talking about how it might be nice to make a dime or two selling the extra eggs, how it was getting to be time for Alice to have a responsibility she could call her own, how it really wouldn't take much for him to build a coop out back. And, of course, Olive told him that made a lot of sense to her. It was a grand idea, really.

"Men act all big and tough, you see," Olive said. "But they're a cautious bunch. They want to do right by their family, so they keep their heads down and work hard at what they know. So if you want them to try something new, you have to plant the idea, and then you've got to gently pull them along until it feels right to 'em."

Olive smiled sweetly, never even looking up from her piecework.

"That's brilliant," RJ marveled. She leaned back in her chair and folded her arms across her chest. She sniggered softly through her nostrils and shook her head. Why hadn't she thought of that? Her mind jumped back to her childhood and the numerous times she'd seen her Aunt May apply the same technique with Uncle Lou. In hindsight, it was so obvious. She speculated that was how Uncle Lou agreed to take in their orphaned niece in the first place.

Just then, the front door flew open, and Alice dashed into the house. She said a hasty hello to RJ and emptied the contents of her drawn-up apron onto the kitchen table.

"Dandelions, Ma! I found a patch of 'em in the sand piled up behind the barn."

Olive pressed her fingers to her smiling lips and shook her head in disbelief. "Those darn weeds seem to grow without a drop of water."

They admired the wilted pile of prickly green leaves for a moment. Alice could scarcely contain her glee. She hopped up and down tugging at her mother's blouse.

"Are there more?" Olive asked, eyebrows raised.

"Yes! That many more, and then some. I couldn't get 'em all in my apron."

"All right then," Olive said, grabbing up a basket usually reserved for harvesting the family vegetable garden. "Let's go get us what's left. We'll set some aside to cook up with pork fat for supper tonight, and we'll spend the afternoon canning the rest."

In that fleeting moment, RJ thought perhaps it would be best if she headed on home, so she wouldn't be in the way. But Alice clapped and grabbed RJ's hand to pull her along, and RJ was instantly swept up in the excitement. They all hurried out the door and toward the barn.

"Won't Woody and Pa be surprised when they see us puttin' up greens?" Alice tittered. "How long has it been since we put up greens, Ma?"

"Too long, honey. Too long."

Storefront lights along Main Street and throughout town clicked off one by one as the sleepy town of Vanham surrendered itself once again to the need for rest. The lights inside Ethel's restaurant, however, burned long into the night. Dusty shelves in the shoe store and the Nickel & Dime or gritty counters at the post office and the service station were all fine and good. Dust and grit in a place serving up meals? No way, no how. Not in Ethel's place, not while she still had an ounce of energy left in her old bones to fight it.

From the wireless radio behind the lunch counter, The Foursome crooned their latest hit.

Ethel sang along as she picked up a pile of clean, empty sugar sacks from the counter and carried them over to a table by the window. Already set out on the table was a bowl of water, her sewing shears and a canister of flour. She settled into a chair and set about the task of tearing the sacks into strips.

Snip, snip, rip.

Snip, snip, rip.

One sack at a time, she worked her way through the pile. Every now and then, she'd stop to rub at her knuckles, work out the cramps in her fingers. Then, she'd return to work.

Snip, snip, rip.

Snip, snip, rip.

After a bit, after the pile of sacks was reduced to shreds, Ethel stood, stretched her arms up over her head. She tilted her head to the left, then to the right. The bones in her neck popped and cracked. She pushed her eyeglasses up onto her forehead and pressed her fingertips against her eyes, yawned.

She shuffled behind the lunch counter and grabbed the coffee pot from the hot plate.

"Hello there, Joe. We have to stop meetin' like this," she said, chuckling at her own joke, pouring the black coffee. She raised the cup to her lips, blew away the steam and took a sip.

The music stopped and four bells chimed from the radio.

"Ladies and gentlemen, with this musical presentation we are concluding today's broadcasting activities of WIBW, owned and operated by the Topeka Broadcasting Company, Topeka, Kansas, the United States of America," the soothing radio voice said. "Speaking on behalf of the entire staff of WIBW, the nation's station, may I bid you a pleasant good evening and good morning."

The bells chimed again, and then static crackled from the speaker.

Ethel waited a moment, listened to the static. She reached over and clicked off the radio.

Quiet descended on the restaurant like dust. Thick, suffocating.

She trained her ears on the steady tick-tick of the wall clock, the soft hum of the light bulbs overhead, the whistle of the never-ending wind outside – the faint sounds that helped her to press on with her work while everyone in his or her right mind was tucked in bed.

Back at the table, she scooped a cup of flour into the bowl of water, mixed it up into a thick paste. She picked up a strip of fabric, submerged it in the bowl. She pulled the strip out of the thick paste when it was good and coated, held it up and ran her thumb and forefinger down the length of it to squeeze away the excess goop. She carefully placed the strip along the window sill, sealing the hair-thin gap between glass and wood.

She picked up another fabric strip from the pile and began again.

Mr. Cline called the Farm Labor Union meeting to order and announced a second request from Miss Evans to address the quorum. The room erupted in a chorus of comments ranging from disgust and disbelief to annoyance and awe.

"Back to waste more of our time."

"Little Miss Know-it-all is at it again."

"That government broad sure has a lot of nerve, I'll give her that."

A hush fell as RJ rose from her seat and walked to the front of the room.

"You said you'd be happy if I brought the rain," she said, picking up the pitcher of water beside Mr. Cline's gavel. She filled a glass and raised it for the crowd to see. "Well, here you go. Here's your rain."

She slowly tipped her hand over the table, letting the water pour out onto the dusty wood, roll across the surface and trickle down onto the floor. After she'd emptied the glass, RJ looked out at the farmers, taking a moment to look eye to eye with one and then another and another.

"What good is the rain if the soil is gone?"

Folks fidgeted in their folding chairs, shuffled their boots on the gritty floorboards. She let silence linger in the air.

"Erosion is the most serious threat our great nation faces today. Soil is our most valuable natural resource. You all know that better than anyone. And yet it cannot be mined. It cannot be grown."

RJ withdrew a fistful of soil from her pocket, extended her palm in front of her face and blew the dust from her hand. Then, she swept her empty hand in front of her.

"Once it takes to the wind, there's no getting it back. It's gone forever. And you can't get wheat or anything else from the hard-packed earth." She knocked on the table.

A man in the front row crossed his ankle over his knee and leaned back in his chair with folded arms. "You can't make it rain, and you can't stop the wind from blowing," he barked. "So, what would you have *us* do?"

Others chimed in, voicing their agreement, expressing their exasperation, filling the air with their frustration. RJ let them go on. She stood silently while the room buzzed with conversation. After a bit, the crowd quieted and they turned, one by one, back to the front. All eyes fell back on RJ. She nodded her head slowly, stayed silent a moment more.

"You're right. We can't make the rain. Only God can do that. And we can't stop the wind. What *can* we do? Keep fighting the same losing battle? Give up altogether?"

She shook her head.

"My employer in Washington, D.C., Mr. Hugh Bennett, says soil erosion is a national menace, one that must be fought with every scientific method at our disposal. Contour plowing. Terracing. Ridge plowing. Strip cropping with native grass. Conservation farming, which nurtures the land, takes no more labor or equipment than other farming methods. And it just might stop further erosion. It just might hold the soil in place until the heavens open up again to bring the rain we need."

RJ pulled a stack of papers, journals and magazines from her satchel. She fanned the publications out on the table, which was already bone dry, and stacked the papers neatly at the corner.

"Mr. Bennett has published dozens of articles about soil erosion and conservation. *Country Gentleman*, *North American Review*, *Scientific Monthly*. You're welcome to borrow and read them if you'd like. President Roosevelt has. And he's authorized the Department of Agriculture to pay farmers to experiment with these conservation methods. I have applications here for anyone willing to give it a go. You've got nothing to lose if the experiments fail. And everything to gain if they succeed."

The room was still. Mr. Cline leaned forward from his seat behind the table, picked up a magazine. He stared at the cover for moment, then flipped it open to the dog-eared page. The other farmers watched, waited. One fellow jiggled a finger in his gritty ear. Another uncrossed his legs, re-crossed them the other way.

In the back row, Harvey rose from his seat and strode past his neighbors to the aisle. He walked to the front table, gave a nod to RJ and picked up an application. Her eyes met his, swimming with gratitude. She exhaled a quick, shallow breath of relief. A second man rose and came forward, and RJ's head felt light with pride. And hope.

Another man walked up, and another. One of the wives retrieved a magazine from the table. She asked how long she could borrow it, and RJ told her she could keep it as long as she'd like.

Folks moved about the room for a bit, chattering to one another, flipping through the magazines and journals. RJ's stomach fluttered as she took in the sight, enjoyed a warm flash of excitement at her apparent success. Then, one by one, the farmers began settling back into their seats.

"Hey there, Miss Evans," Mr. Tugwell spoke up. "I'm willing to try anything to get a better harvest. But how's changing the way I plow supposed to do me any good?"

"That's a great question," RJ said. She explained that, with contour plowing for example, one would plow across the land's natural slope following its elevation contour. That way, the ruts from the plow run perpendicular to slopes rather than parallel, creating level furrows that curve around the land. "So, when we do finally get some rain, the rows produce slower water runoff to prevent soil erosion and allow the water time to settle into the soil."

Mr. Tugwell nodded slowly, scrunching his eyebrows, digesting her answer.

"I'll be at the Feed & Seed tomorrow," RJ said, "and will be happy to answer any more questions, and to collect applications."

"Very good," Mr. Cline said, and then made a motion to adjourn the meeting. Someone else seconded the motion, and the meeting was called to a close. The crowed emptied into the street in a chatter of conversation. RJ remained alone at the front of the room to gather her materials.

"That went pretty well."

She knew Harvey's voice. RJ sensed him close behind her, fought the urge to quickly turn to him. "Yes, I think so," she said, and continued packing papers into her satchel.

"Pouring the water was a nice touch."

"Thank you," she said, smiling. "But I can't take credit for the idea. I read about Mr. Bennett doing the exact same thing during a meeting before the Congress last year. Worked for him. Figured I'd give it a try myself."

He took a half step closer. "You going to the potluck?"

She stopped a moment, then shook her head no.

"Yeah, me neither. How 'bout you let me buy you supper over at Ethel's?"

RJ turned now. She angled her head back a bit to look up at him. The subtle spicy scent of his aftershave made her want to reach out and touch his cheek. Instead, she reached up and tucked her hair behind her ear.

"I don't think it would be appropriate for you to buy my meal, Mr. Clay."

"Yes, you're probably right about that," he said. He scratched at his chin a moment, then stepped back and put on his fedora. "It'd be better if you bought mine."

Harvey walked to open the door and made a grand gesture with his arm. "Shall we, Miss Evans?"

"Woody! Quit your darn scratching at those windows and walk your sister to school."

Olive's patience was wearing treacherously thin. Last night's duster had added a fresh stack of chores onto her already heaping pile. She debated about whether to keep both her children home for the day, to help with the new onslaught of work and to avoid the risk of them getting isolated away from home if the storm kicked up again. But who could put things off for fear of another duster? Nothing needing done would ever get done that way. Besides, Woody had a job to get to, and that was a rare thing indeed.

"Yes, ma'am," Woody said, neatly stowing his art tools in the fabric bag Ma had made for him out of flour-sack remnants last Christmas. He liked the symmetrical blue-and-green triangle pattern. He took one last look at his window painting, a field of wildflowers under a sky of billowy clouds, and then stepped inside to get his orders.

"Alice honey, bring me your lunch bucket and go get your goggles."

Olive quickly assembled the girl's sandwich – a corn muffin with a slice of onion – and wrapped it in wax paper. She put it in the bucket with a small red apple, tucked it all in with a kitchen towel.

"You need a lunch today, Woody?"

"No, ma'am. Me and RJ usually fix something up."

Olive paused for a moment to look at Woody. She smiled and finished packing Alice's lunch.

"Alice, please, get your goggles, child. You'll be late for school. Woody, you walk your sister down to the schoolhouse and then hurry on into town before work. The Red Cross is handing out masks down at Doc Miller's office today. I want you to get a couple for each of us, before they run out. Alice, if the wind starts up again while you're walking to school, you hold Woody's hand. And you keep that rag tied over your face. Don't go taking it off. You hear?"

Alice's silence assured her compliance.

"The Red Cross masks will be more comfortable," Olive added, forcing herself to slow down a moment, smile, plant a kiss on her daughter's head.

The girl slid her goggles down off her forehead and into place. She bent over and gave each of her knee socks a tug to pull them up to the hem of her dress, which Olive had made from the same flour-sack fabric pattern that Woody liked. Olive liked it, too. It brought out the green flecks in her child's bright eyes, even through the dusty goggles.

~~~

The brother and sister walked hand in hand down the road toward the schoolhouse. Every now and then a gust of wind would overtake them, and the two would slow down their pace, stagger a bit, regain their balance, press on.

"Woody."

"Yes, Alice?"

"Thank you for holding my hand."

"You're welcome. Thank you for holding mine, too."

"You mean it, Woody?"

"Sure I do."
~~~

"Cause I know you don't like it when people get all touchy with you," Alice said.

"No, I don't. Especially when Ma gets all slobbery and kissy on top of it."

"Nobody likes that!" Alice giggled, then added, "Except maybe Pa."

"Alice! Ma'd wash your mouth with soap if she heard you talk like that."

Alice drew up her lips up tight and wrinkled her nose. "You won't tell, will ya?"

"Nah. I won't tell."

Alice peered up at him through her dusty goggles. Woody kept his watch trained straight ahead. They walked in lockstep down the road, continuing to hold hands. Another gust of wind pushed them off balance. Woody gave her hand a little squeeze after they regained their footing.

"I'm glad you're my brother, Woody."

"You mean it?" he said, stopping and turning to face her now.

"Sure I do."

"That's the nicest thing anybody's ever said to me, Alice."

His words caused an ache in her chest like she'd never felt. Alice threw her arms around his waist and held him tight.

"Aw shoot," Woody said, gritting his teeth.

After what seemed to Woody to be an eternity, Alice finally released him and stepped back. She sniffled and tucked her small hand back into his, and they resumed their sibling lockstep down the road to the schoolhouse.

"Thanks for your help with this engine again, Harv. Seems like it gets gummed up with grit the minute I turn it on. It's maddening." RJ gave the tractor tire a kick with her boot.

"We're all in the same boat," Harvey said.

Woody hauled the tools from the shed to the barn so the trio could work in the shade. RJ rolled up her shirt sleeves.

"The trick is to remove the oil pump after you're done plowing and flush out all the grit," Harvey said, picking up a wrench and adjusting the mouth. "Do that every time and it'll save your drive gear and the camshaft. Repairing an oil pump ain't cheap, on money or time."

RJ took the wrench from Harvey's hand. He rubbed his palm over his mouth and across his jowl, covering a grin. She leaned into the engine to get a good look. Harvey made room for her and pointed toward the pump.

"These bolts, here and there, hold the pump in place," he said. "Once we get it out, we can take the whole thing over to the workbench to take it apart and clean it."

RJ nodded and reached in to loosen the first bolt. She gripped the wrench with both hands and pulled. But the bolt wouldn't budge.

"Here," Harvey said, moving in. "Let me."

"No."

Harvey exhaled noisily, pushed his hat back a bit and scratched the top of his head. "Suit yourself." He walked over to where Woody had been standing. The men watched as RJ tried the bolt again with no luck.

RJ stepped away, leaving the wrench affixed to the bolt, and scanned the tool box and the barn. A two-foot piece of pipe lay in a scrap pile near the door. She picked it up and eyeballed the opening, then gave the makeshift tool her blessing. RJ crouched back beside the engine, slid the pipe onto the wrench handle and gave it a good hard pull. After a second or two, the bolt gave way.

Woody applauded, elbowed Harvey in the ribs. "That's called *leverage*."

RJ turned and smiled at the men. Harvey grinned back and tipped his hat to her as she turned back to remove the second bolt.

"What's next?" RJ asked.

"That there is what you call a worm gear," Harvey said, stepping closer in again to point. "So you'll have to turn the camshaft while you pull down on the pump."

RJ worked to loosen the camshaft. Beads of sweat gathered on her forehead. Maybe a little oil would help, she muttered. Harvey bobbled his head. She added the lubricant. The shaft still refused to budge.

"Try the pickle fork," Woody suggested.

RJ looked at him cross-eyed, and he quickly snatched up the tool and handed it to her. She thanked him and wiggled the serpent-tongued tool between the rods. She gritted her teeth and strained against the steel.

"Aw, hell. I can't get the damned thing to budge," she said. She wiped the sweat from her forehead with the back of her greasy hand and gave it another go, exhaling a loud groan of frustration. The bolt finally gave way in a sudden jolt that racked her knuckles into the wall of the backing plate. "Ow! Son of a..."

"RJ!"

Startled by Woody's shout, RJ looked over at the men. Woody's hand was pressed over his mouth, his eyes opened wide. Harvey was shaking his head. RJ raised her eyebrows and sucked on her skinned knuckle. "What?"

"Well, Miss Rosa Jean, this here job is making you cuss like a drunken sailor," Harvey said. "That's what."

"Oh." RJ's cheeks burned red hot. "I... I'm sorry. Sorry I upset you, Woody. It's just so irritating."

She shook her hand and then stuffed her bloody knuckle back in her mouth to ease the throbbing.

Woody shrugged one shoulder. "I don't really mind. Just never heard a girl swear like that, is all."

"Well, then, don't think of me as a girl."

RJ turned back to the engine determinedly. Harvey and Woody both scoffed at her suggestion, but she ignored their theatrics and got back to work.

The minutes marched on. Harvey described each step of overhauling the pump. Remove the oil pickup screen. Disconnect the tubes. Remove the plates and housing. RJ tackled the tasks with determination, refusing any physical help. Woody circled them both, watching and chattering in the background about tractors and farming and the history of both. From time to time, RJ would stop, wipe the grease from her hands and jot notes in her journal.

Outside, the wind changed direction. The temperature inside the barn began to rise. The dusty air became stifling. RJ removed a bandanna from the back pocket of her blue jeans and wiped the sweat from her forehead and the back of her neck. The cloth left greasy smudges behind.

Harvey watched RJ toil as she dismantled the pump. He studied the set of her brow, the quiver of her muscles, the droplets of sweat that trickled down the curve of her neck. He eyed the scabby scrapes on her knuckles and felt a sudden urge to take her tiny hands in his and lead her away from this grueling work.

"Don't you think so, too, Harvey?" Woody asked, tapping Harvey's shoulder.

Harvey jumped, clearly startled to realize Woody was still there with them, still chattering on about Lord knows what. "Huh? Don't I think what?"

RJ laughed. "He said don't you think Willa Cather's novel, *O Pioneers!*, is a lot like our lives here?"

Harvey shook his head as though he was trying to drive away flies. "Willa who? A novel? Do I look like the kind of fella who'd read some women's book?"

"It ain't a women's book," Woody said. "It's *literature*. It's a story about immigrants farming in the windy plains of Nebraska. About a Scandinavian girl named Alexandra, and her pa dies and she inherits his failing farm, and she has to figure out what to do, and has to raise her two little brothers all on her own, because her ma already died long before. And she has great success in her life, but she also makes great sacrifices. It's happy, and it's sad. It's a good book, Harvey. You should read it."

Harvey raised one eyebrow and sucked at his teeth. "I don't have time for make-believe."

"But it ain't all make-believe. That's was makes it so good to read. It's about *life*." Woody was almost winded. "That's why I asked you, don't you think *O Pioneers!* is a lot like our lives here. Gosh, Harvey. I learn a lot about things by reading books like that."

RJ kept at her work cleaning the grit and gunk from the oil pickup screen, but she smiled and acknowledged Woody as he spoke. Harvey watched her a moment. "I suppose you read that book, too," he said, accusingly.

"Yes," she said. "My first year in college. My botany professor actually recommended it, if you can believe that. It explores our relationship with the land – how people try to conquer it, how it sometimes conquers them instead, and how that changes them, for better or for worse."

Harvey picked up the wrench from the ground and set about wiping it clean with a rag. He had nothing to add to the conversation. Woody continued talking about the book, returning to the beginning of his monologue, as usual. RJ continued dismantling the pump and nodded along.

Woody said RJ reminded him of the book's main character, Alexandra. She was an orphan, too. She loved the land, respected it and feared it. She was a smart woman, too smart for most people's liking. And she always did precisely what she wanted to do. But she was also lonely.

RJ paused to wipe the grease from her hands, while she mulled over all that Woody had said.

"What makes you think I'm lonely?" she asked.

"Because you're alone," Woody said.

RJ froze for a moment, stunned by Woody's unvarnished reasoning. She looked up at him, and after a brief pause he continued with his book analysis.

Harvey was quiet, watching RJ intently. When she glanced over at him, he quickly looked away, fiddled with some tools on the worktable. RJ worked at the dirt under her jagged nails for a bit. Then, she looked up at Woody again.

"I don't mind being alone," RJ said.

Woody turned to her, and their eyes met. "I never said you minded being alone. I said you're lonely. There's a difference."

"Oh," RJ said.

Harvey looked from RJ to Woody and back again. He seemed to be waiting for her to dispute the hypothesis, to argue and debate with Woody the way she always seemed to do with him. But she only studied Woody in quiet thought.

"For Pete's sake," Harvey finally chimed in. "If you two keep jibber-jabbering, we'll never get this tractor running."

"Jibber-jabber means talking nonsense," Woody countered. "And that's not what we're doing. RJ and me are having a *philosophical discussion*."

"What's that?" Harvey asked, jiggling his finger in his ear. "A feather-socket-wrench discussion? Or did you say a pillow-sock-puppet discussion?"

Woody was on the verge of correcting Harvey again when he gave Woody a stone-serious look and said, "Jibber-jabber."

RJ roared with laughter. Woody knew RJ wouldn't laugh if Harvey was being mean, so he laughed, too. Harvey shot RJ a wink and a dimpled grin. She gave him a nod and turned back to her work.

The freshly-laundered sheets fluttering on the clothesline caused a wave of panic to wash over RJ as her truck rumbled up to the Tugwell farm. She contemplated backing up, but it was too late. The tires had already produced a swell of black dust that swirled in the air and clung to the wet sheets like metal shavings to a magnet.

"I'm so sorry, Mrs. Tugwell." RJ emerged from the truck, her face hot with embarrassment as she removed her Red Cross mask and goggles.

The old woman wiped her forehead with the back of her hand. "Cain't do nothing about this dust. Don't worry yourself over it."

The women scowled at the laundry.

"I'll just rinse 'em out again," Mrs. Tugwell said. She began removing the clothespins and gathering the sheets in her arms.

"Please, let me help," RJ pleaded, but Mrs. Tugwell waved her off.

"You got your own work to do," the old woman said and tilted her head toward the house. "Ernie's around back."

RJ retrieved her satchel from the truck and whistled for Stormy, who always rode shotgun when RJ made farm visits. They walked around the house to the south side, where Ernie was crouched on his haunches, drawing lines in the dirt with a stick. RJ approached him slowly, studying the ground. Ernie stood up and hiked his pants, and then removed his hat and extended his hand. "Mornin', Miss Evans."

"Good morning," she said and shook his hand enthusiastically. "I'm so happy you signed up for the program, Mr. Tugwell. I think you'll be really pleased with the results."

"Yap," Ernie said, and squatted back down in front of his dirt drawing.

RJ shifted her weight from one foot to the other. "Um, shall we go inside?"

"Nope."

RJ shifted again, moved her satchel from one shoulder to the other.

Ernie looked up at her, waited.

She looked back down at the old man's scratchings and realized it was a map of his property. RJ dropped her satchel off her shoulder and squatted down beside him. Stormy circled around behind them and lay down in the dirt facing the chicken coop.

"This is how my daddy always worked out his farmin' plans. And his daddy before him. Right here in the dirt, where the work's to be done anyhow."

Yes, RJ thought, here where the work is to be done. She preferred the elements of her job that took her out of the lab, that took her into the dirt. Just like *her* daddy.

Ernie began explaining his drawing, how his property was laid out, using the stick to point to different areas of his dirt map, indicating hills and landmarks, telling her what crops he'd planted in what fields and when. RJ pulled out her journal and began jotting notes, did her best to sketch a duplicate of his map. Every now and then, Ernie would pause and look up and out at his land, nod his head. RJ asked questions. What's this circle here? What would you say the elevation is on that rise in the north field?

"I think we should focus on the two northern-most fields first. Plow along the contour, this way and this way," she said, pointing with her finger. Ernie handed her the stick.

She continued, pointing with the stick. "We can plant those with broom corn, which has a better shot of holding ground through the winter if we get enough rain this December to get some sprouts. And we'll leave the fields just south of that fallow."

"Fallow?" Ernie said. "Why wouldn't we drill something there, too? What good does it do to leave a field bare?"

"It'll help the soil in those fields if we can let it rest a season, so it can regain some nutrients. But we don't want to lose it to the wind in the meantime. So we'll organize the fallow and planted areas in long, narrow parallel strips east and west against the northern winds to help minimize erosion in the bare fields. Next season, we'll switch."

Ernie's forehead wrinkled up as he scrutinized.

"It's called strip cropping," RJ added.

"Yap. I know what strip cropping is. I done it before, but with different seed. We never just left a field bare. Don't make sense the government'll be paying me not to plant nothing. Don't make no sense at all."

RJ blew her bangs out of her eyes and pressed on. She pointed to a section of land between the fields they had just been discussing and said, "I bet that little valley gets gutted by runoff when you get rain."

"Yap. Turns into a river of mud," Ernie confirmed.

"We're going to try and fix that by planting buffel grass," RJ said.

"Grass? Good God, Miss Evans. We spent years plowing all that under. And now you want me to put it back?" Ernie shook his head, surveying his map. "I don't know about that."

"It won't be much," RJ added quickly. "Maybe a strip about a hundred feet wide."

If they could can get a nice strip of grass to take root, she explained, it would take care of itself in time, year after year. That would slow down the runoff, saving the soil.

"And the roots will hold moisture deep below ground, too, which will help the adjoining fields," she concluded.

Ernie removed his hat and ruffled his thin gray hair back and forth. RJ noticed the line along his forehead dividing his tender pale scalp from his rough suntanned face. Her mind flashed to an image from her childhood of her father removing his hat, running his fingers through thick black hair. His forehead brandished the same dividing line between his pale head and his bronzed farmer face. RJ blinked hard.

"What do you think, Mr. Tugwell?" She coughed and tried to clear the lump from her throat. "Are you willing to give it a try?"

Ernie sniffed and situated his hat back in place. He stood and hiked up his pants. RJ stood up beside him, bobbed up and down a bit to work out the kinks in her knees.

"Yap," he said, working at the itchy dust in his nose with the back of his hand. "I'll give her a try."

"Oh, that's super, Mr. Tugwell. Thank you." RJ crouched back down to gather up her journal and satchel. She said she'd put in a seed order for him and would drive back out in a few days with a copy of her notes.

"Nah, don't bother with the notes," he said, waving his hand over the map in the dirt. "I'll remember what we talked about. It's too crazy to forget."

RJ wasn't sure how to interpret Ernie's comment. Did he believe her ideas would work and he was just having a little fun with her? Or were times so hard he was willing to give even her crazy scheme a shot, out of pure desperation?

Ernie hiked up his pants again, and RJ noticed his belt was cinched as tight as it would go, with several creases in the leather near the holes he'd previously used. She thanked him again and reached out to shake his hand for the second time that morning, this time feeling the bones beneath his loose, rough skin.

She made a mental note to ask for expedited checks for the farmers in the program when writing her next report to Washington that evening.

She called out to Stormy, who had drifted off to sleep watching the chickens scratch around the coop. The dog came running and leapt into the Ford when RJ opened the door. As they pulled out onto the road, heading to Harvey Clay's farm, RJ glanced in the rearview mirror at the darkening crimson sky to the south.

Harvey and RJ sat in his kitchen discussing plans for strip cropping his fields with African grasses. He asked the same questions as Ernie. Why grass, for Pete's sake? Why not some crop that could be harvested and sold if they were lucky enough to get a decent winter rain? RJ didn't mind explaining it all again. She was grateful to have a set of ears willing to listen.

They hadn't been at it for long before Stormy's bark from outside interrupted their conversation. Both seemed to realize at the same moment how dark the kitchen had become.

"What time is it?" RJ asked.

"Not *that* late," Harvey said, jumping to his feet. "Must be a duster rolling in."

They hustled out the side door and onto the small wooden deck. Stormy paced back and forth in the dirt. A churning mountain of menacing clouds roiled far in the distance. RJ's head flicked in the direction of home.

"Don't even think about it," Harvey said, touching her arm for a split-second. "You can't head out in this. Bring in the dog and lock down the shutters. I'll go pump some water. It could be a long night."

"I couldn't possibly stay the night," RJ balked. "It wouldn't be proper. "

Harvey shot her a sly grin and winked. "I'll be a perfect gentleman. I swear it on a stack o' Bibles."

"Oh, I, I...," RJ stuttered. "I didn't mean to suggest you'd be anything less. But won't people talk?"

"Nah," he said, starting off across the yard toward the well and shouting back over his shoulder. "People are more likely to talk if you pulled a scatterbrained stunt like driving into the face of that duster."

RJ looked out at the gluttonous brown mass devouring the landscape and growing skyward as it bore down on them. "Damn it," she muttered. Harvey was right.

~~~

After they had hustled through their storm preparations, RJ and Harvey settled back down at the kitchen table. She sat ramrod straight in the chair, hands folded in her lap. He sat across from her, fingers drumming the tabletop. The quiet hovered in the shadowy space between them, even as the wind howled outside.

"I have a rabbit in the Dutch oven." He looked toward the potbelly stove in the middle of the room. "Hope that'll be okay for supper."

"Sure, sure, that sounds delicious," RJ said. Even as the words came out, she scolded herself on the inside for trying too hard. They both knew nobody eats rabbit because they like it. They eat it because they have nothing else.

"It should taste all right. Got an onion and a potato in there with it." Harvey drummed his fingers on the table again.

Outside, something banged against the door, clattered along the wall, tumbling in the fierce wind. RJ flinched, her hand flying to her heart.

"That was probably just the chicken feed bucket," Harvey said. "I musta forgot to stow it away with the hens."

"Sure. It just startled me a bit."
~~~

"Sure," Harvey said. "Easy to get rattled when these dusters roll in."

"Sure," RJ said again. To keep her hands busy, she pulled her pack of Chesterfields from her purse and shook out a cigarette.

"I wish you wouldn't do that," Harvey said. "Ugly habit."

RJ looked down at the unlit cigarette in between her fingers.

"You smoke," she said.

"That's different."

She studied him, tapped the cigarette on the table a few times. She leaned back in her chair and crossed her arms over her chest. "Different because you smoke a *pipe*?"

Harvey's head flopped to the side and he rolled his eyes to the ceiling. She'd chased him right into a corner, like a hound hunting its prey.

"You know that's not what I meant, Rosa Jean."

"Oh, I see," she nodded in mock agreement. "It's different because I'm a *woman*."

"Yes. Women shouldn't smoke, and you know it. And that's exactly why you do smoke. Isn't it, Rosa Jean?" Harvey said, the temperature of his voice rising ever so slightly. "Because some *man* probably told you not to."

RJ smiled at him, a wicked smile that confirmed in an instant he'd said exactly the wrong thing. She struck a match along the table, put the cigarette to her lips, took a couple of quick puffs, and blew out the match with the smoke.

"Gee, Harvey, you're a man. You must be right."

Harvey dropped his head and took in a slow deep breath instead of responding. He exhaled slowly. Then, he pulled a tangle of string from his pocket, raised his eyebrows. "Truce?"

RJ thought for a moment, took another quick drag. It would be a better way to pass the time than arguing, she admitted to herself. She smiled at him, more amiably this time, and stubbed the cigarette out on the bottom of her boot. Harvey smiled, too.

They sat across the table from one another, their fingers quietly dancing in and around the string. The window shutters rattled in the brutal wind. Cat's cradle. Fish in a dish. Jacob's ladder.

Thumb here, ring finger there. Their eyes were dry and itchy from the dust hovering thick in the air around them. But they didn't stop the game to rub at their lashes. Pinkie here, index finger there. Witch's broom. Butterfly. Cup and saucer.

Their fingers felt their way through the loops in the expanding darkness. How long can two people play string games before their minds begin to unravel? An hour? Two?

Cat's whiskers. Eiffel Tower. Fish in a dish, again.

"Did you know string games date back to the fourth century?" Harvey asked, breaking the long silence. "The Greeks used to play this."

RJ's hands froze in midair. They both looked up from the string.

"Woody," they said in unison and busted up in laughter.

Harvey wadded up the string and stuffed it back in his pocket. "That's enough of that."

As their laughter died out, RJ's stomach tightened. "I hope Woody's doing all right. He probably got stuck at my place."

"He's a grown man. He'll be fine."

Harvey pushed his chair back from the table. He walked over to the potbelly, lifted the Dutch oven lid with the fire poker, jabbed at the rabbit with a fork, replaced the lid.

"I guess," RJ said. "It's just, well, he gets so anxious sometimes."

Harvey walked across the room to the oil lamp, struck a match, turned the knob to adjust the height of the flame. The light cast a dim ginger glow in the haze.

"I've been through plenty of dusters all by my lonesome," Harvey said. "Woody'll survive."

Even through the dusty darkness, RJ could see his posture had gone stiff. She heard the coolness in his voice. Why on earth did her concern for Woody make Harvey angry? He and Woody were friends. Could it be possible he was jealous of the attention? That was a rabbit hole RJ didn't care to explore for the time being. Her mind scrambled to change the subject.

"Is supper about ready?" she asked, thinking of rabbits. "I'm half starved."

"Should be. Pull your chair over to the stove," Harvey said. "We'll eat it out of the pot."

RJ stood reluctantly and moved her chair to the stove. Harvey pulled his chair up beside her at the potbelly, handed her a clean fork. She understood he was set pretty solid in his bachelor ways. Still, offering her a plate and a seat at the table would have been proper.

"This way we won't eat too much dirt," he said, lifting the lid just a bit.

Her mind flew back to the image of Woody's poor dairy cow, insides filled with mud. She glanced around the room, contemplated the dusty pall that surrounded them.

Harvey sunk his fork into the rabbit, tore off a piece of meat and stuffed it in his mouth. As he chewed, he motioned for her to dig in, too. RJ poked her fork into a chunk of potato and pulled it out from beneath the lid just before he dropped it back in place.

The savory root melted in her mouth, buttery and peppery with a hint of gamey tang.

"Try some of the rabbit," Harvey said, and he angled the lid open a couple of inches.

They both dug in at the same time, and RJ secured a shred of meat on her fork. She placed it in her mouth, let it sit on her tongue a moment. Then, she pushed the tender meat toward her cheek and chewed tentatively.

"Your first time eating rabbit?"

She offered a timid smile.

"Thought so."

"It tastes a little like chicken," she said, her scientific mind analyzing the specimen in her mouth. She swallowed, smacked her lips a couple of times. "But it's more buttery."

"It can cook up pretty dry if you're not careful, so I fix it with a mess of butter."

"I like it," RJ said, tearing off another chunk of meat as Harvey tipped the lid.

"My mom used to fry it with onions," he said, shaking his head. "Was like eating a mouthful of straw. You'd need a gallon of buttermilk to wash it down."

"Oh no!" RJ laughed.

He stuffed another piece of meat in his mouth and chewed, still shaking his head. "That woman was a saint, the way she put up with us kids, God rest her soul. But she was a terrible cook. Just terrible."

RJ ate another mouthful of meat as her smile faded. "I wish I could remember my mother's recipes, good or bad."

"I'm sorry, Rosa Jean. It ain't fair, the loss you had to bear at such a tender age."

It irked her that she felt jealous of all the happy memories he had, of all the love he'd received as a boy. She couldn't stand his pity, either. RJ was in dire need of another subject change. She motioned with her fork that she was ready for another bite, and Harvey tilted the lid open for her.

"You say you added onion, too?" she asked, stabbing another chunk of meat.

"Yes. Red onion," Harvey answered, easily taking the hint to drop the subject of RJ's childhood. "They're sweeter than the yellow, I think. Adds a nicer flavor to the stew."

"I agree," RJ said. "They do add a nice sweet flavor."

They ate until they were full, and Harvey carried the cast iron pot to the kitchen worktable. He quickly spooned the leftovers onto a sheet of wax paper, wrapped it up tight and popped the package into the icebox. Next, he wiped out the pot with a dishcloth, rinsed it with hot water from the kettle, and then dried it with a fresh towel. Finally, Harvey coated the pot with a thin layer of lard, draped it with a dry towel, and stowed it away in a sturdy wooden box.

"That was quite efficient," RJ marveled. He'd made such short order of the cleanup, she hadn't had a chance to offer any help.

Harvey took a bow, and RJ clapped.

"You learn a thing or two living on your own," he said. "But I don't guess I need to tell you that. You seem to manage pretty well by yourself."

He loosened the lid on a canning jar of water and handed it to her. She hesitated for just a moment before taking it.

"I can't tell if you're teasing me," she said.

"No, I mean it, Rosa Jean. You manage your place better than half the fellers I know."

"Even though I didn't have the sense to run a wire from my house to the barn?"

Harvey laughed out loud. "Geez Louise! How long you been carrying that thorn in your paw?"

RJ flipped her hair back, hoped he couldn't see the heat rising in her cheeks. "No, I'm just teasing you now," she said, hoping he would believe her.

"Don't be so hard on yourself," he said, settling back into the chair beside her. "Learning how to live out here takes time. Some folks never figure it out. I think you're catching on pretty damn quick, if you'll excuse my French."

He clinked his water jar against hers and then took a long drink before replacing the lid again.

"Thank you," she said, the tension in her muscles melting a bit. "I always was a quick study in school."

Harvey beamed at her. "I bet you were. What was that like? Going to school at a fancy college?"

"It feels kind of like a dream now, when I think back on it all. Almost like it never really happened. Or like it happened in a previous life."

Harvey unscrewed the lid to his water jar and took another quenching drink. The wind howled outside. He replaced the lid, waited for her to continue.

"I always loved school when I was a girl," she said finally. "And college was no different in that respect. I loved reading, taking notes while my professors talked about things I never knewn existed, never even could have imagined. But it was also hard. I always had to fight so hard."

"Fight?" Harvey set his water jar on the table, leaned back in his chair, his legs stretched out in front of him, his fingers laced together behind his head.

RJ watched him recline, marveled at his ease, while she sat up straight in her chair, her knees together, ankles crossed.

"It all would have been so much easier if I were a man." She had thought it many times, but she had never dared to say it out loud before. She certainly hadn't meant to say it then. Her stomach drew tight as a drum. She steeled herself for his reaction.

"Hmm." Harvey stood up and moved toward the sofa, the only other piece of furniture in the sparsely furnished room, motioned for her to join him. She hesitated. He sat down at one end, motioned again to the other side of the sofa.

"Tell me," he said, then flashed his trademark grin, all devil and dimples. "Come on now, Rosa Jean. I promise, I won't bite."

"It fell on me like a ton of bricks the moment I sat down in the registrar's office." RJ paused a moment, searching for the words to explain.

When she had first applied to the University of Wisconsin, RJ didn't know exactly what she wanted to do with her life. She only knew that she was on her own and that a college degree might help her stay that way.

The registrar had suggested an education in home economics, which the woman had said would "provide the widest possibilities for an independent career before homemaking comes to enrich your life." RJ had never had an interest in homemaking. She wanted to study science, to delve into the many wonders of the Earth, to unlock the mysteries she had marveled as a child. "To what end?" the registrar had balked, and RJ had had no answer. What use could such an education be to a woman, after all? After some discussion, they compromised on a degree in agriculture. That way, if RJ married a farmer, she would at least have skills he might find useful.

"I had no intention of ever marrying a farmer," RJ said, with perhaps a bit too much enthusiasm, and Harvey laughed out loud. She shifted in her seat, stymied for a moment.

"Don't worry, Rosa Jean, I ain't offended. I wouldn't want to marry a farmer either. We're an ornery lot."

Now it was RJ's turn to laugh. To her surprise, she felt herself lean back into the sofa cushions, relaxed.

"Well, as it turned out, the College of Agriculture was the perfect fit," she said, drifting on memory's breeze back to her first classes. They had been an ideal partnering between RJ's love of science and her love of the natural world. She had not only learned about the Earth and how it sustained itself, she had also learned about man's perception of the Earth and impact upon it.

She'd been mesmerized by Professor Leopold's lectures, by his bold declarations and philosophies. Civilization is not a state of domination over a stable and constant Earth, he had asserted in his unassuming, yet powerful, way. "It is a state of mutual and interdependent cooperation between human animals, other animals, plants and soils, which may be disrupted at any time by the failure of any of them," RJ quoted him.

Harvey rubbed at the dust collecting in his lashes.

"So that's what all this dust is then," he said. "A disruption caused by our failure to cooperate with nature."

"Why, yes. Yes, exactly."

He laughed out loud. "Don't sound so shocked, Miss Evans. I may be an uneducated farmer, but I'm not a complete idiot."

"No, I'm sorry," RJ blundered. "I didn't mean to imply..."

"Relax, Rosa Jean," Harvey said, laughing again. "I'm just ribbin' you. My goodness, it sure ain't hard to do."

RJ laughed at herself then. Uncle Lou always told her she took herself too seriously. Maybe he'd been right after all.

Their laughter quieted, and they sat for a moment, in a hush, avoiding eye contact. The dark was almost complete, even though it wasn't yet six o'clock.

"Maybe I should get another lamp lit," Harvey said abruptly.

"Yes, maybe," RJ said.

He rose and walked to the kitchen, moving with ease in the darkness, like a blind man familiar with his surroundings. RJ realized he must not indulge in the luxury of lighting the lamp often. "Thank you," she added quickly. "That's one thing I still haven't gotten accustomed to here. The dark. The utter completeness of it."

Harvey lit the lamp and turned toward her, backlit by the orange glow.

"I bet the city was bright all the time," he said. "Even at two in the morning."

RJ shrugged. "Well, I don't know about two in the morning. But yes, it was bright, generally, with a constant buzz in the air from the electric lights. It's more peaceful here, when the dusters aren't raging. That I do like better."

Harvey was quiet. RJ wondered if he had ever traveled beyond the fields of Kansas, if he'd ever even left Vanham city limits.

"Tell me more about college," he said finally, settling back on the sofa, just a bit closer to her than he'd been before. "How did you make do on your own? Did you have a job?"

She told him about the job she'd had washing beakers and test tubes in the lab at night, after classes and before homework. Come to think of it, she said, she often was awake at two in the morning, reading and studying and writing papers. But the little bit of money she earned working in the lab had helped pay for her meals.

"There was a place in town called the Brown Derby where they served chicken for the evening meal. A real swanky place," RJ said.

"No kidding," Harvey said. "And you made enough washing beakers to eat there?"

RJ laughed. "Oh, heavens no. They cooked the chicken early, in the upstairs kitchen. If you went up the back stairs at the right time of day, and you brought your own container, you could buy the chicken broth for five cents a quart.

"I'd take an empty coffee can to fill up, and they'd usually give me a day-old roll, too. I'd go back to my dorm, heat the broth on a Bunsen burner I borrowed from the lab, and crumble in the roll to thicken it up. It wasn't anything special, but it tasted okay and it kept my stomach from growling most nights."

"That's pretty creative," Harvey said after a moment, eyebrows raised, lower lip sticking out. "I hadn't really considered how tough it would be to get yourself fed every day without a kitchen or a garden or some chickens for eggs."

"Oh, I had a garden," RJ said, then grinned wide. "I had an old shoebox full of dirt sitting in my dorm room window."

Harvey laughed his approval.

"It wasn't easy, but I kept a little parsley growing most of the time. And some sad little basil plants. I'd tear up and sprinkle a few basil leaves into the soup some nights. Most times, I'd just munch on some parsley sprigs straight off the plant."

"Sounds delicious," Harvey mused.

"Oh, yes, it was. Believe me. Soup and a salad. Quite decadent."

They laughed again, and RJ shook her head, the memories swimming through her mind like a school of fish. The conversation came to a comfortable end, and they sat quietly for a while, listening to the howl of the wind, lost in their own thoughts. RJ yawned and sank back a little deeper into the couch.

~~~

RJ woke with a jolt, lost in the inky darkness that surrounded her. She shivered, and a soft whimper escaped from her lips, as she fought to get her bearings.

"It's okay, Rosa Jean. You're safe. I've got ya." Harvey's voice was barely above a whisper, yet strong, steady in the dark. She felt the couch cushions shift beneath her, as he moved closer and gently covered her with a soft quilt.

"Thank you," she whispered and repositioned herself on the couch, to lean into him.

Harvey put his arm around her as she tucked her head into the curve of his neck.
~~~

"I'm sorry," she whispered, almost inaudibly, not even sure why she was apologizing.

"Shhh, Rosa Jean. Go back to sleep."

~~~

The smell of coffee coaxed RJ awake. Bright sunlight streaming in through the lone window kissed her cheeks. She rolled over on the couch, realizing she had it and the quilt all to herself now.

"Good morning." Harvey stood in the kitchen, leaning back against the worktable. He raised his mug to her. "I put up some coffee. It's just a little past six."

"I should go," RJ croaked. She jumped up from the couch, coughed the dust from her lungs as she folded the quilt. "Thank you so much for your hospitality."

"No need to be so formal, Rosa Jean," he said. His face was animated with mischief. "We did just spend the night together, after all."

RJ twitched. She knew he was only teasing her, and yet. *That's precisely what people will think, isn't it?* She forced herself to laugh at his joke, though her stomach was in knots. She hustled to shake out her boots and then slipped them on her feet, fumbling with the laces.

"At least stay for a cup of joe," Harvey said.

"Thank you, again," RJ answered too quickly. "But I really should go. I have to get back to the lab and assess the damage from the storm, start cleaning up."

"Sure, sure," Harvey said. "I understand."

She hustled toward the door and he stepped in front of her to open it. RJ walked past him, stepped out onto the porch. She turned to thank him again, reaching out for a handshake.

Harvey gave her a small tight-lipped smile, just enough for the dimple in his cheek to flash at her. He took her hand and turned it
~~~

flat, covered it gently with his other hand. Her heart fluttered in her chest like a meadowlark enjoying a cool spring rain.

"I sure appreciated having some company during the storm, Rosa Jean," he said, looking down at her tiny hand for a moment. Then, he let go, stuffed his hands in his trouser pockets and took a step back.

RJ forced herself to breathe.

"Yes," she said. "So did I."

They stood facing each other for just a heartbeat more, and then RJ whistled to Stormy as she turned and headed toward her truck. As she strode away, she fought the urge to turn back for one more glimpse of him.

Mrs. Florence Meginnis settled down with her quilting circle in a quiet corner at Ethel's restaurant. The four women had gathered once a month, come rain or come shine, for nearly a decade to do their piecework together and escape from their daily chores and enjoy a few hours of friendly chatter. Now, of course, they met come dust or come shine. Rain hadn't been an issue for the quilting circle for nearly three years.

On this day, they were selecting fabrics for an undertaker's quilt they'd be piecing together for Marie's bed.

The undertaker from Dodge came to Vanham every few months to visit his daughter, and he'd bring clothes that people had gotten rid of when someone died. The women would sort through bags and pull out whatever material was usable for making blankets and other necessities. Some thought it was bad luck to sleep under a quilt made of a dead man's clothes. But when the temperature dropped below freezing and there was no coal or wood for the stove, these farm wives valued warmth over superstition.

"This is gonna come together real nice, Marie," said Florence, pulling a blue flannel shirt from the undertaker's bag, giving it the once over and setting it in Marie's pile. "I like that pretty new pattern you picked out. What did you call it again? Sunbonnet Sue?"

"Yes. Isn't it precious?" Marie asked, setting a faded yellow nightgown on her stack of fabrics. "I thought it might make the quilt more cheerful, considering. You know what I mean."

Flo and the others nodded in silent agreement.

"Did I tell y'all that Chet got his application for that Civilian Conservation Corps accepted?" Helen spoke up. "He'll be heading to a camp up in Colorado next week. Said he'll be digging holes and planting rows of trees. Supposed to help block the wind and dust from blowing across the plains."

"You think it will work?" Flo asked.

"Don't know if it will help stop the dust," Helen said. "But his monthly wage will sure help feed the family, I'll tell you that."

The friends echoed their agreement with a few amens and sure wills. Hazel said her boy Mikey wanted to sign up, too, but it's only for men eighteen to twenty-three years old. She hoped he'd get in next year. "He keeps going on about joining up with Roosevelt's tree army."

Helen snorted. "Yes, that's what Chet called it, too. From what I hear, they are pretty tight on the discipline at the camps. Glad to hear it, too. It'll be good for him. That boy has some sass."

"Too bad Mr. Meginnis is too old to join up," said Flo. "Talk about a man with sass. I'd ship him off in a heartbeat."

The women laughed heartily, no doubt musing about shipping off their own husbands to the CCC camps. Ethel came over to their table with a fresh pot of coffee and filled all their mugs. She pointed at a washed-out green polka-dot dress the women had set in the discard pile and remarked that it would be fine material for a set of handkerchiefs. Flo agreed and moved the dress to her own pile of fabrics.

Ethel sighed and turned back toward the kitchen. "Well, I got a sink full of dirty dishes calling my name. You gals know your way around. Just give a holler if you need something."

The woman said their thanks to Ethel, then quietly continued their sorting for a few minutes.

"It's a shame there ain't more work to be had right here in Vanham," Marie said, returning to their previous conversation. "Doesn't seem right we have to ship our men off to another state just to make do."

She added in a hushed voice, "I don't see why the government couldn't have hired a local to run that soil lab instead of bringing in some armchair farmer from the city. And a woman to boot."

Flo huffed. "I couldn't agree with you more."

"And ain't that little Miss Evans something else?" Hazel chimed in. She flicked her glance toward the kitchen to be sure Ethel was out of earshot. "Living alone, smoking, driving around paying visits to men. It ain't proper if you ask me."

No, Flo agreed. Ain't proper at all. Sinful really.

"She's out of place, that's for sure," Helen said. "But sinful? I don't know."

"Guess that depends on what sort of *work* her visits include," Hazel said. "You have to wonder."

Marie wrinkled up her nose, shifted in her chair a bit. "I don't know, Hazel. She's no friend of mine, but I can't believe Miss Evans is loose. If she were, she'd be in a family way by now."

Hazel rattled her head side to side, reluctantly agreeing with Marie's logic. Helen raised her eyebrows, nodded. Flo looked around the circle at her friends, then glanced over her shoulder to make sure their conversation was private.

"Bud over at the post office told me Miss Evans often gets packages delivered from overseas, wrapped in plain brown paper," she whispered. "I heard you can get rubbers through mail order from France. I bet you she's got boxes and boxes of 'em at her place."

"Flo!" Hazel cackled and Marie's face turned bright red – from the nape of her neck to the tips of her ears.

Helen looked from one woman to the other. "What's a rubber?"

Hazel crowed again, and Marie just shook her head. Flo smirked and went back to sorting and folding.

"What's a rubber?" Helen asked again, but none of the women could bring themselves to answer.

"I ain't looking for a handout." That's what Mr. Sharp had snapped at RJ when she suggested he sign up for the government conservation farming program.

None of the farmers she had talked with liked the idea of "going on relief." When you tell a farmer he'll be paid to leave his fields barren, the math doesn't add up in his mind. It means being paid to do nothing. Marion Sharp had been one of the most ornery and loudest of them all. And yet somehow RJ had convinced him to hear her out.

She pulled her truck into the Sharp farm and shut off the engine. She hesitated before slowly opening the door and stepping out. *You can do this, RJ.*

"You're late." Mr. Sharp appeared from around the side of the house, wiping his hands on a greasy rag.

"Good morning, Mr. Sharp. I'm sure sorry about that." RJ extended her hand to greet him. "That duster yesterday made a mess of the roads, and it took longer to get out here than I expected."

Mr. Sharp glanced at RJ's outstretched hand, continued to wipe his hands on the rag.

"Might as well talk, now that you're finally here." He turned and disappeared into the earth.

The Sharps lived in a sod dugout left over from homesteading days. RJ had seen the rugged structures from a distance, nestled into hills or half buried below ground. She had never set foot inside of one.

Most homesteaders used the dugouts to house their goats and other stock after they had had the time and money to build a more traditional home of wood or brick. Those who hadn't enjoyed such good fortune continued to live in their soddies, constructed of mud and grass, with splintered roofs and perhaps two or three small windows.

RJ gathered up her satchel and descended into the dark house. Mr. Sharp was already seated at the kitchen table. Mrs. Sharp stood at a wash basin rinsing out towels and rags. RJ smiled and said hello. His wife lifted her chin in RJ's direction and continued her chores.

Mr. Sharp told RJ to sit in the chair across from him. The muscles in her neck began to tighten. She hadn't expected tea and cookies, but they didn't have to be so rude either.

"Thank you," she said, taking a seat, replaying her Aunt May's advice in her mind. *You can catch more flies with honey than with vinegar, Rosa Jean.*

RJ smiled again as she pulled out her notes and began explaining the science behind contour plowing and strip cropping. The farmer sat back in his chair, stone silent and statue still as she spoke. She soldiered on with her sales pitch, talking about the benefits of planting grasses from the African plains, which were similar to the native grasses of the North American Great Plains. Then, RJ began to explain why he should leave several fields fallow.

"Hold on now," Sharp said, sitting up straight and placing both his palms on the table in front of him. "I thought you were coming out here to tell me ways I could get a better harvest when we finally get some rain. But all you're telling me is that my fields will come up with grass and a whole lot of nothing. What good'll that do me?"

RJ pressed forward and attempted to explain that the conservation techniques she had described would help fight erosion. It would replenish nutrients the soil needs to grow healthy crops in the future.

"What the soil *needs* is rain," he interrupted her again.

"That's true. But you can't make it rain," she snapped back. "So you might as well try something productive while you're waiting around for a miracle from the sky."

"If you was my daughter, I'd tan your hide for that kind of sass," Mr. Sharp said. His voice was low and steady. His hands, still on the table, tightened into fists. The hairs on the back of RJ's neck prickled.

Mrs. Sharp walked across the room to retrieve a basket of dirty socks. She shot her husband a look as she passed him, and he relaxed his fists.

"Mr. Sharp," RJ said, working to keep her voice pleasant and measured. "I'm merely trying to point out that the techniques I'm describing have been proven through scientific study to be effective. And I would think that you would want to do all you can to preserve your land for yourself and your children."

The farmer drummed his fingers on the table.

"I'm doing plenty," he said.

RJ said she'd love to hear about what he'd been doing. Mr. Sharp looked across the table at her, his eyes narrow, his chin protruding. RJ could almost see the wheels turning in his head, as the farmer debated in his mind whether to divulge his secrets.

"I've been working with a fella from Chicago," he finally said.

RJ raised her eyebrows, sat quietly to encourage him to continue.

"He's a *real* scientist," Mr. Sharp said. "And he's invented a way to make it rain. He's been traveling around the country helping folks out. A bunch of us are chipping in to pay him. For a hundred dollars, he'll come out here and make it rain."

A scoff escaped from RJ's lips. Mr. Sharp pounded his fist on the table.

"It works," he said, raising his voice. "He's done it a dozen times or more. He's got this contraption that shoots dynamite ten thousand feet into the air. When it explodes, a chain reaction creates storm clouds, and within two days, the skies open up with rain."

"Oh please, Mr. Sharp, you can't honestly *believe* that shooting dynamite into the sky somehow creates water?"

RJ regretted the crack the moment it left her tongue. The farmer stood up from the table, his fists clenched again. He paced around the kitchen. Mrs. Sharp dried her hands on her apron. Her eyes darted from her husband to RJ and back again.

"You government pen-pushers are all the same," Mr. Sharp said. "You think you're the only one who has any answers, the only one who can solve our problems."

RJ scrambled to backtrack and repair the damage she had done.

"Mr. Sharp, I'm sorry. I didn't mean to offend you. Please, sit back down."

"You need to learn some manners, little lady. You need to learn your place."

And there it was. RJ was on her feet now, too. Her diplomacy evaporated.

"My *place*? My place is working as a geologist for the United States government, trying to help pigheaded farmers who wouldn't know a good idea if it fell on their heads," she said.

She could see the heat rising in Mr. Sharp's face, the vein pulsing in his neck. She knew she should stop before she made things worse. But she couldn't hold her tongue.

"That man who's promising you rain is *not* a scientist," she said. "He's a charlatan. He's going to take your money, fire his dynamite into the sky and leave town on the next train. He'll be conning some other fool farmer out of his money in the next county before you even realize you've been had."

Mr. Sharp lunged forward and flipped the kitchen table on its side, sending RJ's papers flying. She jumped back with her hand on her chest, watched her pencil hit the floor and roll beneath the icebox.

"Get out of my house and stay the hell off of my land," he hissed through clenched teeth.

RJ held out her hands in surrender. "Mr. Sharp, please, calm down."

His fingers coiled back into hardened fists.

"You better git, girl" Mrs. Sharp warned RJ, stepping in and placing a hand on her husband's chest.

RJ crouched down to scoop up her belongings, keeping her eyes locked on the farmer. She backed toward the door, her satchel clutched to her chest. When she reached the exit, she turned quickly and bolted out of the house toward her truck.

Mr. Sharp shouted at her from the open doorway. "You and your Kraut dog better not set one foot on my land again, if you're so smart as you think you are."

RJ tumbled into the cab of the truck and fumbled with shaking hands to get the key in the ignition. Stormy jumped up to the passenger seat from her slumber on the cab floor. The hair along her spine rose, and she emitted a low growl out the window.

"It's okay, Stormy," RJ said, trying to reassure herself as much as the dog. "We're okay."

The engine sputtered and roared to life, and RJ sped down the drive through a shroud of dust.

The chill of late fall nipped at RJ's ears as she walked down the sidewalk in town, past Ethel's place, toward the Feed & Seed lot. The brisk breeze made her brown tartan dress flutter, threatening to fly up and expose her knees. The casserole dish of corn pudding in her hands prevented her from reaching down to smooth the fabric and thwart any indiscretion. *Should have worn my damned overalls.* RJ shook her head and sighed, hoping the wind wouldn't catch her feathered pillbox hat next.

Ahead, men poured out of the Town Hall from the monthly union meeting, and further ahead still, the women folk were setting up tables for the potluck.

RJ slowed her pace. She scanned the crowd. She was still rattled from her visit to the Sharp farm the week before. What would she do if she ran into the Sharps at the potluck? *Can't believe I let Ethel talk me into this.* She shook her head again. RJ stopped walking, began to turn on her heels and hustle back in the direction from which she had come. But she caught sight of Harvey emerging from the hall, and she froze. He looked at the sky, then secured his fedora on his head and glanced up and down the street. His eyes fell on her, and he flashed a brief smile.

"No turning back now," she muttered. Harvey would never let her hear the end of it if she ran off. She smiled back at him and began walking again toward the farm wives.

The women spread out the tablecloths on the buffet tables in the feed store back lot and began arranging the dishes everyone had brought. Hamburger casserole, creamed peas and bread pudding. Spam loaf, baked beans and butterscotch pie. Scalloped tomatoes, creamed onions and applesauce cake. The women pinched pennies and scrimped on meals all month to put on such a spread. It was one thing the farm families could look forward to with certainty and excitement – the monthly feast.

RJ approached the table in a sudden rush.

"I've brought corn pudding," she almost shouted, and the women all looked up at her at once. Flo Meginnis turned away quickly, smothered a laugh. RJ felt her entire body go hot from the inside out. "It, it's my Aunt May's recipe."

"Isn't that lovely, dear," one of the wives said, taking the dish from RJ and scanning the table for an open spot. The woman placed the dish beside two others containing corn pudding, then she looked up and gave RJ a too-large smile. "It was mighty big of you to bring a dish."

One of the other wives snickered and shifted a platter of corn muffins.

RJ nodded at the woman, matching her facetious smile. Then, she turned and moved away from the table with an urgency that caused her to trip over her own feet and stumble as though she'd been taking nips at Ethel's bourbon. Laughter erupted behind her.

She stopped beside a Model A truck parked beside the open lot and placed one hand on the fender to steady herself. She assessed her surroundings, trying to determine her next move. Barefoot children of varying ages ran in circles around the tables, and mothers scolded them for kicking up dust. Men clumped together in small groups out of earshot of their wives, to talk and smoke and curse.

This potluck experiment was turning out to be even more difficult than RJ had anticipated. It was clear she couldn't mingle with the farm wives. She had no children to chase after and scold. She couldn't loiter with the men to discuss farming, either.

RJ scanned the area for a discreet exit. Her eyes landed on Woody and his family, settling in at one of the small tables. Olive smiled and waved her over.

RJ moved toward them, grateful for Olive's warmth.

"Are you sure there's room for me?" RJ asked, surveying the small table draped with a red-and-white gingham cloth.

"We'll make room," Olive said with an authoritative nod. "Pa, grab up another one of them folding chairs."

Woody and Alice hustled to get in line at the buffet table behind the men. RJ asked Mr. and Mrs. Parker if they were going to help themselves to the feast, and Pa said they'd wait until the buzzards were done swarming. Olive laughed and slapped his knee. A hundred-pound weight slipped off of RJ's back. She settled into a chair beside the Parkers and said she'd wait, too.

Pa commented on the weather, said he thought they might get some rain next week because his hip had been aching. Olive said his hip never lied. RJ drank in the small talk and watched the group mill about the buffet, heap their plates with casseroles, creamy vegetables and sweet treats.

Harvey stood leaning against the Feed & Seed doors, tapping tobacco into his pipe. Several young women crowded near him, laughing at something he'd said, shooting him furtive smiles. Olive noticed RJ watching and leaned over to whisper near her ear.

"Speaking of buzzards swarming," Olive said, and RJ let a small laugh escape her lips. Olive added, "Mr. Clay is Vanham's most eligible bachelor."

"Apparently," RJ said, and laughed again.

Her attention was pulled back toward the food tables. The mounds of foods were rapidly disappearing, yet she couldn't help but notice that her dish of corn pudding had not been touched. She watched one farmer pick up a spoon to scoop some up, and one of the union wives shook her head, leaned in to tell him something. The man replaced the spoon without helping himself and moved on to the next dish.

RJ scoffed quietly. *I should've known.*

She continued to watch the group fill their plates, and not one dipped into her dish. Woody and Alice fidgeted as they waited their turn. Harvey sauntered past them as a young woman in a blue dress with a big white collar motioned for him to get in line beside her.

RJ scoffed again. She willed herself to look away.

"You're prettier than her, Miss Evans," Olive whispered, looking away too.

"What?" RJ said and fiddled with the pin in her hat.

Olive simply raised her eyebrows, crossed her arms across her chest and toggled her head in the direction of Harvey and his female fan club.

RJ looked back at the food table just as Harvey reached the corn pudding. The union wife repeated her apparent secret warning, leaning in to divulge some dire information, pointing at RJ's dish. Harvey frowned and gave the woman an exaggerated nod. Then, he grinned, picked up the spoon and plopped a sizable helping of pudding onto his plate. The gal in the blue dress gasped, and Harvey threw his head back and laughed. He leaned back a bit and shouted down the line.

"Hey, Woody! Don't miss out on this here corn pudding Miss Evans brought. It's her aunt's recipe."

He punctuated his point by turning back to the buffet and scooping up one more spoonful.

Olive whooped out loud and quickly plastered her hand over her mouth. Pa shook his head and muttered, "Cluckity, cluck, cluck," which sent Olive into near hysterics. RJ watched eyes flick their way, heard a roar of whispers move through the union wives, felt the burning stares of the lovely young buzzards vying for Harvey's affections.

Harvey tipped his hat to the blue-dress gal and strode toward the Parker table.

"Y'all have room for one more?" he asked.

Olive beamed and Pa quickly jumped up to fetch another folding chair. A fresh round of whispers and rumbling moved through the crowd as Harvey took a seat beside RJ.

Alice and Woody joined the family at the table, Woody's plate heaped high with corn pudding. He smiled at RJ as broad as he ever had. She looked around the table at Harvey and Alice and Woody and Mr. and Mrs. Parker, and she suddenly was overcome with a feeling that made her heart skip and ache at the same time.

"Come on now," Olive said, jumping up from her seat. "We better get us some food before it's all gone."

RJ obediently fell in line behind Olive, like a duckling following its mother. They returned to the table with their plates piled high, just at Woody was headed back for seconds.

Pa repeated his prediction for rain and his reason for it, and Harvey agreed. They all ate and talked about the weather and the price of oil and the best time to sow the winter wheat. The sun began to sink lower in the sky and a pink light fell upon the gathering. A wind from the south kicked up a sheen of dust that swept across the Feed & Seed lot.

"Aw, shoot," said Olive. "Wouldn't you know it."

"Looks like a sandstorm," Pa said.

The gathering quickly broke into organized chaos, as the women hurried to cover and stow away the food and the men packed up the tables and chairs. Mothers rounded up their children and shop owners shuttered their windows.

RJ retrieved the empty corn pudding dish and asked Olive if there was anything she needed.

"No thank you, dear. I got Pa and Woody to put to work. You just get yourself on home now, before the worst of it hits."

"I'll walk you to your truck," Harvey said, taking RJ's elbow.

She smiled and allowed him to lead her, secretly pleased to realize he knew where she had parked. They made their way through town, leaning into the wind, their heads turned sideways to avoid the sting of dust on at least one side of their faces. When they reached the truck, RJ set her purse and casserole dish on the passenger seat.

"Do you need a ride?" she asked.

"Naw, my truck's just down the way a bit," he said. "You got your goggles in the glove box there?"

RJ nodded.

"And your Red Cross mask?"

RJ nodded again.

"Okay. Well, you mind the road. If the wind kicks up too bad, just pull in somewhere and wait it out."

"I'll be all right."

They stood facing one another as the wind whipped around them. All of a sudden, Harvey leaned in and planted a kiss on her cheek. RJ looked down, then tilted her head back up to look at him. He held her in his eyes.

"You be safe, Rosa Jean," he whispered.

"You, too, Harvey."

Then, he turned and strode away.

The sandstorm came and went. Two days later, there was another duster. And then another. They turned the fields into a scene from a picture book of the Sahara Desert, all smooth and rolling with fawn-colored dunes instead of neat rows of tilled black earth ready for winter wheat.

RJ was out in her fields, working to reverse the damage, plowing along the contour, creating deep furrows, hoping it would help preserve at least some of the soil when the next storm kicked through.

The tractor rumbled and coughed as she worked her way up and down the north field. Woody had helped her attach the lister plow, then he went inside to clean the typewriter and wash flasks. They'd agreed early on which tasks would be Woody's responsibility, and plowing had not been one of them. The roar and vibration of the giant tractor was more than his nerves could tolerate.

RJ, on the other hand, loved the power the behemoth gave her over the land. Even as she tilled the dry, dead earth and lamented the damage over-farming and over-plowing had done to the grasslands, there was a part of her that understood how that had come to be. She could identify with the desire to make something out of nothing, to be in control of one's own destiny. She understood the ambition that farmers must have had to plow under more and more acres of land, as the rains came every season and the wheat grew plentiful as far as the eye could see.

She approached the end of the field and made a wide semicircle, leaving a good twenty yards between the row she had just tilled and the one she would till on the way back. The tawny dust hovered over the field like smoke, thick, suffocating. RJ killed the engine. She pulled her Red Cross mask down to her chin and took a long drink from her canteen. She gaped at the horizon, where a dark cloud was forming.

"Oh for Pete's sake," she said, pulling off her hat and goggles to get a better look. "Not another damn duster."

Just then the wind shifted, and she felt the gentle caress of something different in the air. Something fresh, clean, life-giving. The aroma danced through her nostrils as she inhaled deeply. Rain.

RJ shouted out loud and sprang up from the tractor seat, leapt down to the ground. For a moment, she wondered if she were losing her mind, if it were only a dream. She breathed in deep again, letting the fresh smell fill her head, settle on the back of her tongue.

The pewter clouds rolled along, bulbous and ripe, sweeping over the land in the distance. And then she saw it – a silver sheet of rain, breaking free from the clouds and falling gently, gracefully to the earth. RJ closed her eyes and spread her arms out wide, waited for the shower to reach her. She listened to the patter of the drops hitting the bone-dry land and almost heard the Earth sigh in relief.

Eyes wide open again, RJ watched, mesmerized. The water poured from the heavens in a steady shower. So simple, so ordinary, and yet, a miracle. She felt a drop roll down her cheek and fall from her chin. But the rain hadn't reached her yet. She allowed a joyous sob to escape from her lips, and more tears to wet her lashes, washing the dust from her face. Her heart swelled, a hot-air balloon lifting her up to kiss the rain clouds.

And then the cascade came to her, clean and sweet and pure, caressing her bare face and arms with the gentle fingertips of a mother's love. She wondered where Harvey was at that very moment, and Woody, and Ethel, and all the rest of the folks in Vanham. She smiled wide, imagining their reaction to the rain. The tears continued to flow, tears of joy and gratitude and relief.

~~~

Ethel plunged her hands into the sudsy water and retrieved a plate from the sink. She scrubbed it clean with the dishcloth, wiping away the remnants of egg yolk from the morning's Blue Plate Special. From the wireless, Rudy Vallee intoned about hard times, singing, "Brother, can you spare a dime?"

Somewhere outside, voices rose up. Ethel paused her work to listen. She set the plate in the bin of rinse water and dried her hands on her apron. The voices grew louder, shrieks and hollers and laughter mingled with something else, something Ethel couldn't quite put her finger on. She clicked off the wireless and pushed aside the curtain in the doorway leading from the kitchen to the diner.

The commotion grew clearer. Through the giant diner window, Ethel saw what was happening. Everyone was out in the street – her friends, neighbors, customers – reveling, dancing, laughing. In the rain. Ethel gasped and ran toward the door like a schoolgirl when the teacher rings the lunch bell.

She ran into the center of the street, joining in the laughter, feeling the cool, fresh shower soak through her cotton dress and kiss her skin. Ernie Tugwell grabbed her by both hands and spun her around. Folks started clapping in time, and others paired off. Mr. Meginnis started calling familiar square dance moves, and everyone seemed to fall into joyful step. And they spun and skipped and do-si-do'd, around and around, arm to arm, hand to hand, in the glorious, miraculous rain.

~~~

"Harvey!" RJ spotted him in town the day after the rain. She waved, sure he must have seen her, must have heard her call out, but he continued his trudge up the sidewalk toward the feed lot.

RJ broke into a trot and called to him again. Harvey's body stiffened. He stopped walking so she could join up, though he didn't turn around. When she finally caught up, he gave her a tight-lipped smile. "Mornin', Rosa Jean."

"Good morning," she blurted, panting after the short jog. Her exhilaration from the day before hadn't waned. The morning air felt washed clean and tingly in her lungs. "Wasn't that rain yesterday the bee's knees? Oh, Harv, I measured nearly a quarter inch!"

Harvey resumed his walk. "That's great, Rosa Jean."

RJ had to skip alongside him to keep up with his long, quick strides. "How much do you think you got up at your place?"

Harvey paused in his stride, almost imperceptibly. He kept his eyes cast to the ground in front of him as he walked. "Not a drop."

"Not a drop?" RJ was incredulous. She stopped skipping along and grabbed hold of his arm to stop him, too. She shook her head, questioning. "What do you mean? You must have gotten at least a little bit your way."

His eyes darkened, and the muscles in his neck bulged under his clenched jaw. "It's the damned hogback, Rosa Jean. It does me in nearly every time."

"The hogback?"

Harvey huffed wearily. He pulled off his hat, scratched at his head a bit, and then used both hands to secure the hat back in place. RJ waited. He looked down at her. They both knew she wasn't about to walk away without an explanation, and he huffed again.

"You know that rise of land a couple miles to the west of my lot? That ridge? It runs maybe three and a half, four miles long, probably three-hundred feet high. It's called a hogback."

He used his hands to help tell his story. RJ watched and listened.

"Well," Harvey continued, "when the rain clouds come in, they usually come from the northwest. Just like they did yesterday. I can't tell you how many times that damned hogback stole my rain. Stole it right out from under my nose."

His gestures grew larger, as he drew pictures in the air of the ridge of land and the dark rain clouds approaching from afar.

"I could see it, Rosa Jean. I could see the rain coming down heavy in the distance, a sheet of gray, flashes of lightning firing up the sky. I could hear the thunder crackin' and feel the cool in the air. I could smell it."

He closed his eyes. "My God, the smell of it."

He paused a moment, drew in a jagged, weary breath. Then, he opened his eyes again and spread his hands apart in front of him.

"And then the clouds hit that hogback, and split in two, one part heading south, the other part heading to the east, and it all just passed me by. Again."

He stopped and squeezed his stomach, and RJ worried he might become physically sick. Her mind flashed back to the smell of the rain, to the cool drops on her skin. And a blunt pain gathered in her own gut, a dull ache for what he'd missed.

"Oh, Harvey." She put her hand on his forearm, gave it a gentle squeeze. "I'm so sorry."

He jerked his arm away. "I don't need your pity, Rosa Jean."

"No. That's not..."

She couldn't find the right words. And he didn't give her much of a chance. He stuffed his hands into his pockets, turned back toward the Feed & Seed, and charged off with swift, formidable strides.

The bell above the post office door jingled as RJ made her weekly visit. After a moment, Bud emerged from the back room.

"Hiya, Miss Evans."

"Hiya, Bud," she said, handing him the large manila envelope addressed to the Soil Conservation Service in Washington, D.C. "Could you post this for me? And please, I wish you'd call me RJ."

The tips of his ears turned crimson. He grimaced. "Aw shoot, I don't know."

RJ smiled. "Don't know what? If you'll post the letter or if you'll call me RJ?"

Bud let out a gush of air that sounded like a tire going flat, and the rest of his face lit up to match the color of his ears.

"I'll post your letter, Miss Evans. And there's a package here for you, too." Bud disappeared into the back room for a moment, then re-emerged with a box wrapped in brown paper. "You get some mail order from that Sears & Roebuck, did you?"

RJ simply thanked him for the package and left, refusing to indulge his nosiness.

On the walk, RJ saw Harvey approaching. He had his fedora tipped low on his forehead and the collar of his wool Navy peacoat popped up to block against the frigid wind. His hands were stuffed, as they most often were, in his pants' pockets.

"Good morning, Rosa Jean," he said, flashing his tight-lipped smile and dimples. "Cold enough for ya today?"

"Good morning. Boy, I'll say. Plenty cold enough," she said, crossing her arms over her torso to emphasize her point.

They smiled at one another for a moment. RJ bounced on her heels a bit to shake off the cold and the silence that hung in the air.

"I'm glad I ran into you," he said.

"Oh?"

"Yeah, yeah. See, I was wanting to apologize for being short with you the other day, about the rain and all."

"Oh gee, Harv, you don't need to apologize." RJ waved his words away. "I'd already forgotten all about it."

He bobbled his head, smiled down at the ground. The wind kicked up again. RJ shivered and tugged her knit cap down over her ears.

"Say," Harvey said. "Would you like to go to the picture show with me Saturday night?"

RJ was at a loss for words.

"That new Shirley Temple movie is playing," he added.

She wasn't sure how to answer. The fall frost fueled the awkward pause in their conversation, made her response feel chillier than she intended.

"What would people say?" RJ asked, glancing around. She'd heard the whispers and snickers. She had a good idea of the rumors being spread. She glanced down the street, started formulating in her mind a polite way to dodge his question and get on with her errands. Harvey could sense she was about to flee.

"Well," he said. "If they have any brains, they'd say, 'Look how lucky that Rosa Jean is, going to the picture show with the handsomest feller in town.'"

RJ laughed out loud. "Yes, if they had any brains."

He smiled at her, nodding decisively.

"I'll pick you up Saturday at six. Okay?"

"Okay," she said. "See you then. I better run now before my shoes freeze to the walk."

"You sure better run, Rosa Jean. Last thing I want is you getting cold feet." Harvey shot her his trademark wink and hustled past her down the street.

~~~

RJ moved down the walk with a little extra hop in her step, her cheeks a bit rosier than they'd been earlier.

She headed straight for Ethel's, to grab a bite to eat and maybe get a little advice about her upcoming date with Harvey. Through the window, RJ could see Ethel sitting alone, elbows on the counter. She tugged at the door to go in, but it was locked.

RJ pulled out her pocket watch to double check the time. Ethel was always open for breakfast unless there was a duster blowing. She knocked on the window. Ethel flinched, then slowly swiveled to face the front. RJ waved, grinning wide. After an almost imperceptible pause, Ethel rose to open the door.

"Hiya Ethel," RJ said, easing through the door and taking in the empty diner with a quick sweep of her eyes. "Is everything okay? It's not like you to open late."

Ethel smiled, but the usual glint in her eyes was absent. She pushed her hair back from her face. "Oh sure, hon. Everything's fine."

She shuffled behind the counter, and that's when RJ noticed Ethel was still in her slippers. Her thick, salt-and-pepper hair tumbled around her face and shoulders, down her back. RJ sat down sat at the counter, noticed the handprints in the dust where Ethel had hoisted herself up to answer the door.

"That was some duster last night," RJ said.

"Suppose so," Ethel said, dragging a finger along the counter, leaving a swerving line in the dust. "Slipped in and out of here like a damned prowler in the night. I slept right through it."
~~~

"Me, too," RJ said. "Slept right through it, and woke up buried in dust."

Ethel tapped a cigarette from its pack, set it between her lips and leaned over the hot plate to light it up. She pulled in a lungful of smoke, held it in a moment, and then let it go slowly to comingle with the dust in the air. "Sure felt good to finally sleep."

"Oh?" RJ said. "You been having trouble sleeping?"

Ethel didn't answer, just tapped out another cigarette for RJ. The women smoked silently, while the wall clock ticked off the minutes. RJ studied Ethel's tussled hair, wondering if she had ever seen it other than pulled back in a thick neat knot. She looked at the dark puffy bags beneath Ethel's eyes.

"Let's finish our smokes, and then I'll help you clean up," RJ said.

Ethel shook her head. "Aren't you a dear. You don't need to help me, RJ. I'll manage just fine. You've got your own work to do."

"I've finished with my errands. And I've got Woody cleaning up back at the lab. I'm happy to give you a hand, Ethel. It'll go faster with two instead of one."

RJ sprung to her feet, ready to work.

"No, honey, you run along and help Woody. I'll take care of this mess myself."

RJ studied her friend again. Ethel leaned her hip against the counter and smashed her cigarette into a ceramic ashtray.

"Are you sure?" RJ asked.

"Sure, I'm sure," Ethel said.

"Okay, then, I guess I'll get going," RJ said, hesitating a moment before walking slowly toward the door. It didn't feel right to leave, but it also didn't feel right to question her any further. Ethel wasn't the kind of person to hold back. If she needed help, she would ask. Wouldn't she?

Ethel waved good-bye, and RJ slipped out the door, looking back over her shoulder before climbing into the Ford. She rested her hands on the steering wheel and watched Ethel a moment through the filthy diner windows. Ethel waved again, and RJ revved up the truck and pulled out down the road.

When the young woman was out of sight, Ethel shuffled back to the door, turned the lock and leaned her forehead against the cold glass of the window.

February 1935

Ernie Tugwell rolled out of bed and then turned around to help his wife to her feet. With the New Year, winter had turned bitter cold, and Minnie's old bones weren't happy about it. Ernie held onto her hands until he was sure she wouldn't topple over. She nodded to let him know she was "just fine," then she brushed away the dust that had settled in his wiry hair overnight.

They shuffled into the kitchen where Ernie lit the potbelly stove and Minnie pumped water into a kettle. Woody rustled about on the makeshift pallet Minnie had set up for him on the floor the night before. He'd come over to help Mr. Tugwell work on the tractor, and had been laid over by a duster.

"Morning, Mr. and Mrs. Tugwell," Woody mumbled. He sat up and rubbed at the crust in his eyes with his knuckles. The Tugwells offered up their "morning" in unison and continued about their business.

"Going out to the barn," Ernie said.

"Button your coat," Minnie said.

She braced herself against the cold blast of air Ernie let in the house as he hurried outside. Thank goodness the stove was already kicking off good heat. Minnie thanked the Good Lord they still had their cows, which provided fuel for the fire, as well as milk for their bellies. When was the last time they'd had money to spare for coal or wood? She couldn't remember. No matter. Cow patties didn't smell pretty burning in the stove, but they warmed her aching joints and didn't cost a darn penny. That was good enough for her.

"Think we'll get snow?" Woody asked, while he rolled up the blankets and mat that had been his bed.

"Might," Minnie said. A few winter storms had already browbeaten the small farming town – fierce, bitter, unforgiving. But there had been no snow. Just the possibility of it made the dull pain in her bones more tolerable. Snow cover helped protect the dormant seedlings in the winter months and provided moisture with the spring melt. Maybe this would be their year.

When Ernie returned to the house, Minnie had hot corn mush waiting on the potbelly. A gust of frigid air assaulted the kitchen when he slipped in from outside.

"Lordy!" Minnie exclaimed. "Almost seems colder now than when you went out."

"Yap," Ernie said, rubbing his hands together to get the blood flowing in his knobby fingers. "Lookin' like snow."

"It'd be a blessing," Minnie said.

"A blessing," Woody echoed.

They opened the curtains wide to watch the dense gray clouds in the distance move their way while they ate. After breakfast, Minnie sat in her rocking chair and got to work on the pile of clothes in her darning basket. Ernie and Woody sat down at the kitchen table to tinker with the old wireless radio Ernie liked to keep in the barn. The electric buzz in the air from a recent duster had zapped it, and he hoped to bring it back to life.

By ten o'clock, Ernie had to light the lamp. He moved to the window and peered at the sky.

"It's getting too dark."

Minnie tucked her afghan around her knees. "Sure hope you're wrong."

Woody looked up from the radio and out the window. He pushed his chair back from the table and stood. He crossed and uncrossed his fingers on both hands, alternating from one pair of digits to another.

"Yap, I could be wrong," Ernie said. But his expression grew darker, a reflection of the inky clouds overhead. "All the same, maybe I ought to stow the chickens."

Minnie rose from her chair and moved beside him at the window. She eyed the angry rumbling sky. "Yap. You'd better."

Before Ernie could move, lightning lit up the room and a piercing crack of thunder broke open the heavens. Woody yelped and sprang back toward the corner of the room, hands pressed tightly over his ears, eyes squeezed shut. Ernie pulled his wife back away from the window.

Jagged chunks of hail plummeted to the earth, bouncing and vaulting back up after colliding with the hard ground. Another bolt of lightning fractured the sky, and a thunder boom shook the walls. Misshapen lumps of ice, some the size of baseballs, rocketed from the black abyss above them. The windshield of Ernie's old truck shattered. The fenders and roof and hood became warped by deep craters.

"The chickens," Minnie cried.

Ernie shook his head and pulled the heavy curtains closed. He took off his glasses and wiped the lenses with his handkerchief.

"The chicks'll be all right, Ma."

"Don't you coddle me, Ernest Tugwell." Minnie returned to her rocking chair, eased herself down and pulled the afghan up around her shoulders good and tight. She stared down at the heap of tattered socks in her darning basket. If only everything in life was as easy to mend.

The hail storm ended as abruptly as it began. Once the din had stopped, and light broke through the clouds, Ernie and Minnie ventured outside to assess the damage. Woody lingered in the open doorway, twisting a lock of his unruly hair around and around on his finger. Bits of splintered wood and roof shingles littered the area. Ice shards and matted feathers covered the yard, glittering and white under the sunbeams coming down. Almost like snow.

Minnie spotted a few of her prized hens amongst the debris. There wasn't much left of them to spot.

"The garden fence'll need to be rebuilt," she said.

"Yap," Ernie said.

Out in the field, pebbles of ice blanketed the terraces and contours Ernie had plowed. The grass seedlings were beaten down, destroyed.

"The ice melt will help come spring," Minnie said.

"Yap."

Ernie sniffed and rubbed his nose with the back of his hand. They stood a moment more, surveying the land. Then, he put his arm around Minnie's shoulders and led her back into the warmth of the house.

A sliver of sunlight peeked through the small dusty window of Ethel's basement bedroom. It whispered in her ear. *You missed the breakfast crowd again.*

She lay in bed staring at the ceiling. The clock on her nightstand was silent. She had neglected to wind it, so its methodic tick-tock had ceased during the night. But Ethel didn't need an alarm clock to tell her it was time to get up. She knew it was time. Past time. And yet, she couldn't will her limbs to move.

Ethel rolled onto her side and hugged her pillow. Just a bit more sleep, perhaps, and then she'd get ready for the lunch crowd.

~~~

The telephone rang out through the empty diner. Two shorts and one long, which was Ethel's designated ring on the party line she shared with the other businesses nearby. A few minutes passed, and the phone rang again.

"Oh, for the love of Pete," Ethel muttered and rolled over in her bed. Tears streamed silently down her cheeks as she pushed back the sunflower quilt and set her bare feet on the cold gritty floor. The phone rang again. "I'm coming, for crying out loud," she shouted at the phone, then repeated softly, "I'm coming."
~~~

Ethel shuffled up the narrow stairs and emerged into the bright, empty diner, retrieved the earpiece from the phone on the wall. "Hello?" she puffed.

"Ethel, honey, that you?" Marjorie asked.

"Who else in blazes would it be?" Ethel shot back, wiping tears from her face with the back of her hand.

"Well, of course it's you, honey. I'm worried, is all. Is everything okay? You feeling all right?"

"I'm fine, Marge." A fresh batch of fat tears pooled behind her gray lashes.

Silence hung in the air, along the telephone line. Ethel wondered how many other people were quietly listening in on their conversation. Everyone on the party line knew everyone else's specific ring. Common courtesy meant you didn't pick up and listen in if it wasn't yours. Still, some folks couldn't help themselves. It was a small town, after all.

"It ain't like you to miss opening up for breakfast and lunch."

Ethel's eyes shot to the clock above the counter. The hands ticked just past two. She swallowed hard.

"You ain't coming down with the dust pneumonia are you, dear?" Marjorie asked.

"No," Ethel answered slowly. "No, I ain't sick. Feeling a little tired is all."

"Do you want me to come over?"

"No," Ethel said. She rubbed her temple. "No need for you to come over. I'm perfectly fine, Marge. Sorry I worried you, hon."

"You're sure?"

"Yes, I'm sure. Why don't you stop on in for supper? I'll fix you up a Blue Plate and you can see for yourself that I'm just fine."

Ethel had forced the familiar tone of assuredness into her voice, its familiar strength. Her old friend seemed appeased. "Okay, dear. I'll stop on in after my shift."

Ethel said good-bye and placed the phone back on the cradle. She sighed another heavy lungful of air and looked around the restaurant, at the dust that obscured her windows and cast a pink haze about the room, at the brown film that coated her Formica lunch counter and the tables and the chairs and the floor. She leaned her back against the wall, sunk slowly down to the cool tile and buried her face in her hands as quiet sobs erupted from deep within her gut.

How do you let a man know you're ready to be kissed good and hard?

That was the question plaguing RJ's mind ever since she and Harvey had gone to the picture show. He'd been a perfect gentleman all evening, which is precisely what she'd expected. The date had ended with one brief, tender peck on the lips. Then, Harvey had tipped his hat and left, while RJ imagined grabbing hold of his shirt collar and pulling him back for a little something more.

Tonight, Harvey had invited RJ to his place for dinner. Out of the corner of her eye, she watched him work in the kitchen with his shirtsleeves rolled up to his elbows. She spread a cloth across the table and smoothed out the creases with her hands.

"It's nice of you to cook dinner," she said.

"Yes, it is." He winked at her and pulled a bread pan from the icebox.

RJ walked across the room and stood beside him. She gave his bare forearm a quick, light squeeze. She wondered if that brief touch made his heartbeat quicken the way it did hers.

"I hope you like fried corn mush," he said, nodding toward the bread pan. "Had some left over from breakfast. I was planning to slice it and cook it up in some pork fat."

"That's creative," RJ said. She put one hand on her hip and leaned against the sink basin.

"You teasing me? Haven't you ever had fried corn mush?"

"No," she laughed. "Not teasing and never had it. I've always been impressed with your cooking skills."

Harvey lit the stove and set the skillet on the burner. "Just farm cookin'. Nothing special about it."

He dug a spoonful of pork fat from the jar on the counter and plopped the gooey mass into the pan where it sizzled and popped and began to melt. He turned the bread pan out onto the worktable and gently shook out the cold, solid loaf of corn mush. RJ watched him closely.

"Farm cooking class," she said. "Taught by Professor Harvey Clay."

"Watch and learn, little lady. Watch and learn."

RJ wondered if she could teach *him* a thing or two. She wasn't what you'd call loose, but after six years on her own at the university, she'd been out with a rascal or two. Would Harvey balk if she told him she wasn't as innocent as he probably believed? Did she dare say she wanted more from him than his chivalrous manner had allowed so far?

Harvey cut the moist corn mush into even slices and dipped them into a shallow plate of flour, coating all the edges. He set them one by one into the skillet bubbling with grease. A toasty scent rose in the steam from the pan. RJ inhaled deeply and smiled.

"There's a jar of corn syrup on the shelf there," Harvey said. "By the icebox."

When the mush was crisp and golden brown at the edges, Harvey picked up the spatula and expertly turned the slices over in the pan. RJ set the table. They moved smoothly together through their chores, needing few words, in perfect sync, like an old married couple.

"Mush is ready," Harvey said, turning off the flame of the stove and transferring the mush from the pan to the plates.

"We make a good team," RJ said, as Harvey pulled out a chair for her.

He smiled and sat down across from her. He poured some corn syrup over her mush slices, then did the same to his own. "Dig in."

RJ picked up her fork and cut into the crispy serving on her plate. She delivered a piece into her mouth. The salty bite of the pork fat blended with the sweet tang of the corn syrup in perfect harmony. She bit through the crusty outer layer and into the warm soft corn mush. The concoction all but melted in her mouth.

"Oh my goodness," she said, shaking her head in near disbelief at how such a simple recipe could taste so delicious.

"I knew you'd like it," Harvey grinned. "I grew up on this. It's always been one of my favorites."

RJ scooped up another mouthful. They finished their meal without talking, savoring the food and the comfortable quiet of each other's company. Then, they rose from the table, stacked the plates, and cleaned the kitchen together in their already familiar way.

"Shall we play cards?" Harvey asked. "Has Ethel taught you any new games?"

"She taught me German whist," RJ said. "But I don't feel like sitting. How about we turn on the wireless and dance?"

"Dance?" Harvey laughed and then coughed and scratched the top of his head. "I don't know, Rosa Jean. I ain't much of a dancer."

RJ clicked on the radio and fiddled with the dial to reduce the static. She was pleased to hear Greta Keller's sultry Austrian accent floating from the speakers.

"Come here," RJ said, starting to sway to the rhythm of Blue Moon. "Dancing is about the easiest thing in the world. Let me show you."

She stepped close to him, took his right hand and placed it on the small of her back. She took hold of the thumb on his left hand, and he instinctively wrapped his fingers around her tiny hand. She moved closer and rested her head against his chest. They swayed slowly in rhythm to the music.

Harvey kissed RJ's fingers and then pressed their entwined hands against his chest. RJ moved her other hand further across his back. They embraced a bit tighter. She could feel Harvey's heart pounding beneath his solid chest, and the sensation made her stomach grow taut. His hand moved slowly, gently, down her back to her tailbone. He lowered his chin and inhaled the delicate scent of her hair.

The song ended. A broadcaster with a nasal voice began rattling off the weather forecast and crop reports. But the music had already cast its spell on the young couple; they continued to cling to one another and sway rhythmically to the pulse of their breath.

RJ turned her head and nuzzled the curve of Harvey's neck. He sighed. Encouraged, she slid her lips lower and kissed his chest just below the collarbone. This made him shudder, almost imperceptibly. The response made RJ dig her short nails into his back. Harvey moaned.

"Rosa Jean, we better stop." His voice was soft, yet urgent. He took a halfstep back and gently pushed her away. RJ resisted. Not as much as she wanted; just enough to let him know she didn't want to stop.

She placed her palms on his heaving chest and leaned her forehead against his heart. Harvey stuffed his hands in his pants' pockets and let his head drop backwards. He closed his eyes and tried to catch his breath, like he'd just run a race and stopped short of the finish line.

"I should go," RJ said.

"No, you don't have to leave, Rosa Jean. Just… just give me a minute."

"No," she said. "I have to go."

She grabbed hold of his shirt and pulled him toward her. He surrendered. RJ kissed him hard on the lips, her mouth open just a bit. Harvey kept his hands in his pockets, but he allowed his tongue a small taste. RJ parted her lips wider and took him in as much as he would let her.

Harvey pulled back abruptly. She touched her fingertips to her wet mouth and smiled at him. Then, she grabbed her purse and goggles from the peg by the door and dashed out.

Mr. Meginnis sat on the tall stool outside the Seed & Feed, digging the dirt out from under his nails with a pocket knife. His son George slouched beside him, his hands buried deep in his pockets.

"Geez, Pa. All's I'm saying is that leaflet I saw sounded pretty darn good," the boy said.

"Nope," Mr. Meginnis said. George shook his head and kicked at the dirt.

Mr. Sharp was sitting on the running board of his truck, parked nearby, flipping through the *Farmer's Almanac*. He stood and walked over to the man and his son.

"What's this your boy's grumbling about, Meginnis?" he asked.

Mr. Meginnis extended his hand to inspect his jagged nails, shaking his head. He folded his knife and tucked it into the front pocket of his overalls. Some fella was over at the Union Hall the other day, he explained, handing out leaflets about field jobs in California. Said you could spend your days harvesting peaches and grapes and whatnot in the sunshine under a clear blue sky, then sleep in a soft bed in a cabin right there at the farms. Said they're looking to hire five thousand men.

He'd heard some of the other fellas talking about that, Mr. Sharp said. "Sounds too good to be true."

"That's what I told the boy." Mr. Meginnis said and threw his hands up in the air.

"Oh, I don't know about that," Frank Cobb spoke up, stepping into the conversation. "It ain't like I just fell off the turnip truck, but I been thinking about taking my family out there. Even if it's only half as good as they say, it'd be ten times better than what we got here now."

A few other farmers moseyed over to join the debate.

"Maybe it would be for the best," another said, "to start fresh."

"Naw," Mr. Meginnis huffed. "Start fresh doing what? To be at the mercy of the land and sky a thousand miles away from your roots? What guarantee do you have the farming will be any better there than it is here?"

"I heard lots of folks are making the trip out there, living the good life now," young George chimed in.

Mr. Meginnis shook his head at his son and spit in the dirt. "And who'd you hear that from? The feller handing out the leaflets?"

Mr. Sharp snickered. He took a pack of Chesterfields from his overalls and tapped out a cigarette. The group was quiet. They watched him strike a match, light his cigarette, take a long slow drag and blow the smoke up into the brown air.

"Welp," Mr. Cline said, "I don't want to give up my farm and move a thousand miles away, but I do need to figure out a way to get by until the next harvest."

The men all agreed. Too bad the CCC only accepts single fellas, one said. Yap, the others concurred. Seemed like all the federal work programs were only for young, unmarried men. What about men with families to feed?

All through the debate, Harvey stood on the sideline and kept silent. He leaned his back against the Seed & Feed wall, shifting his pipe between his teeth. He'd used up the last of his tobacco the week before, but even an empty pipe provided some comfort.

"My boy Walter's heading up to Wichita at the end of the month," Mr. Cobb said. "Got a friend of a friend says he can get him a spot at the Stearman factory."

Harvey knew the friend to whom Mr. Cobb referred. It was Harvey's brother, Ben. He'd made the same job offer to Harvey, too. A few times.

Walter would send home half his paycheck every month, Mr. Cobb continued. Then, once Vanham got some decent rain, he'd come back home and help with the harvest. The other farmers agreed it was a sensible plan.

Harvey remained silent. He gnawed at his pipe, while the idea of moving to the city gnawed at him.

Stormy ran to the front door, tail buzzing, and let out her single "Woody's here" bark. RJ rushed to greet him.

"Happy Birthday!"

RJ threw her arms around her friend, who stood stiffly, grimacing, arms pinned at his sides beneath her embrace.

"Shucks, RJ," he said, wriggling free. "You know I don't like getting hugged."

"I know. I know, Woody. I'm sorry."

Her smile gave away the insincerity of the apology, but Woody only heard her words.

"Okay," he said. "I forgive you."

RJ retrieved a package from her desk, wrapped in brown paper and tied with a piece of packing string she had dyed purple with beet juice. She held it out to him, beaming. "I got you something."

Woody's eyes opened wide. "A present? I ain't got a birthday present from anybody in probably ten years."

"Well then you're sorely overdue," she said. "Go on, now. Open it."

Woody sat down at the kitchen table and untied the string. He slipped his finger under the small strip of cellophane tape, using care not to tear the wrapping. Folded within the paper was an artist's sketch pad and a small tin box of charcoal sticks. Woody stared at the items in his lap for moment. The excitement drained from his face.

"It's for drawing," RJ offered. She sat down beside him at the table. Woody didn't move.

RJ took the items from him and spread them out on the table, opening the box of charcoals and lifting the cover of the sketch pad.

"I don't know how to draw," he said.

"Of course you do, Woody. It's just like your wonderful window paintings. Except your sketches on paper will last forever. We can frame them, hang them on the walls."

Woody sat with his back ramrod straight. "But I don't know *how* to draw."

"Just give it a try."

"I said I don't know how to draw!" Woody sprang up from his chair, all arms and legs, in a flourish that jarred the table and sent the charcoals clattering to the floor. He ran to the door, flung it open and charged outside.

"Woody, wait!"

RJ gathered herself up and ran after him, Stormy close at her heels. When they reached the edge of the porch, she looked around to see which direction Woody had gone. Stormy barked and took off across the yard toward the barn, and this time it was RJ who followed.

They found Woody sitting on the ground behind the empty chicken coop, hugging his knees, rocking back and forth. RJ knelt down in front of him, though not too close. Stormy laid down beside him. The three sat together in silence. Several minutes ticked by. Woody finally stopped rocking. He crossed his legs, and Stormy rested her head on his lap. He began absently stroking her ears.

"Please don't be mad at me," he whispered.

"Oh, Woody," RJ sighed. "I'm not mad at you. Not one single bit."

She let another minute pass. "I just don't understand why my gift upset you. I don't understand why you say you can't draw."

Woody shrugged. RJ was beginning to understand that shrug of his. It said so many things about him – his modesty, his frustrations, his fears – without him speaking a single word.

"Your window paintings are the most amazing creations I've ever seen," she said.

"That's different."

"How? Help me to understand, Woody."

He looked up and off into the distance. He sucked in a lungful of air and puffed out his cheeks as he exhaled. Then, he did it again. RJ sat back into the dirt and crossed her legs. She waited for her friend to collect himself, to find his words.

"I saw the angel in the marble and carved until I set him free," he said.

RJ stayed quiet. She waited for more.

"Michelangelo said that. You heard of him?" Woody said. "He was that Italian fella during the Renaissance who did all those big sculptures, the one of David, and the one of Mary and Jesus. That's what he said when somebody asked him how he did it. He said he saw the angel in the marble and carved until he set it free."

He looked at RJ then, intently, his eyes pleading for understanding.

"And?" RJ prodded.

"And when I paint the windows, I see things in the dust, and then I scratch away the dust until I set them free."

"And drawing on paper is different?" she asked.

"Drawing is backwards. It's all blank. There's nothing to carve away. You have to make the picture yourself, and I don't know how to do that." Woody shrugged again. "You probably don't understand. Most people don't understand the way I do things."

RJ reached out and took his hand in hers. He flinched a little, then sat statue still.

"I think I do understand, Woody. You explained it the same way my Aunt May explains happiness." She paused to breathe, to reflect. "I was always so sad when I was little, after my parents died, and my Uncle Lou used to try everything to make me happy. He'd juggle apples, or pretend to trip and fall over. But nothing seemed to work and then he'd get frustrated with me for still being sad. He said maybe I just didn't want to be happy."

Woody nodded, while slipping his hand away from hers. This time it was RJ who flinched. She wanted to cling to him, but she let go. She was finally beginning to understand a touch just didn't comfort him the same way it did most people.

"So, my Aunt May said, 'Lou, you can't force her to be happy. Happiness isn't something you can wrap in a bow and give somebody. It's more like a buried treasure they have to discover on their own.'"

Woody smiled. "Happiness is inside the marble."

"Yes," RJ said. "And hidden in the dust."

They sat quietly, reflecting. After a minute or two, Woody reached over and gave RJ's hand a quick squeeze. Then, he folded his hands back in his lap.

"You're my best friend, RJ."

"You're my best friend, too, Woody."

"The job of creating a program for the nation's welfare is, in some respects, like the building of a ship," President Roosevelt said during his weekly fireside chat. "At different points on the coast where I often visit, they build great seagoing ships. When one of these ships is under construction and the steel frames have been set in the keel, it is difficult for a person who does not know ships to tell how it will finally look when it is sailing the high seas."

RJ and Harvey sat on opposite sides of the kitchen table, their left arms reaching diagonally across the distance so they could hold hands. RJ rested her right elbow on the table and her chin in her palm, looking intently at the crisscross pattern of the radio speaker. Harvey sat up straight, taking occasional swallows of coffee from the mug he cradled in his other hand.

All across the United States, couples and families, rich folk and poor folk, farmers and financiers gathered around the radio on Sundays to hear the president speak, hoping to hear words of wisdom, confidence, clarity.

Roosevelt detailed a vast program of projects that would provide employment to men and women currently on the relief rolls. He spoke of enacting measures to relieve unemployment. He outlined details for a social security program to make provisions for the future. Finally, the president spoke of re-establishing public confidence in the nation's private banks through improving and expanding regulation by the Federal Reserve.

"Never since my inauguration in March, 1933, have I felt so unmistakably the atmosphere of recovery. But it is more than the recovery of the material basis of our individual lives. It is the recovery of confidence in our democratic processes and institutions."

As the president neared the end of his address, his voice took on an increasing timbre.

"We have survived all of the arduous burdens and the threatening dangers of a great economic calamity," he said. "We have in the darkest moments of our national trials retained our faith in our own ability to master our destiny. Fear is vanishing and confidence is growing on every side, renewed faith in the vast possibilities of human beings to improve their material and spiritual status through the instrumentality of the democratic form of government. That faith is receiving its just reward. For that we can be thankful to the God who watches over America."

RJ rose from the table and turned off the radio. She stood in the quiet for a moment. The wind spoke its own public address outside, bellowed its own advice and plans for the American people. She sat back down across from Harvey and drummed her fingers on the table in a slow staccato.

"Penny for your thoughts," Harvey said.

"I'm just thinking about what the president said." RJ shook her head. "He sounded so hopeful, so positive. But everything here is still such a mess."

Harvey couldn't argue with that. He took a final swallow of his coffee.

"Do you think he even really knows or understands," RJ asked after a moment, "how bad things are here?"

She massaged her forehead with the tips of her fingers. Stormy's rhythmic snore floated up from her spot on the rug beside RJ's desk.

"Sometimes I think about moving on," Harvey said. His eyes were set on the window. "Moving to the city, I mean. Getting a job at a factory, earning a steady wage."

He turned his face toward RJ. She was studying him, her lips pursed, her eyebrows drawn together.

"The city? Wouldn't you miss the wide open land and sky? Working the soil? The smell of wheat in the air at harvest?"

Harvey smiled for a second. Then, his face got hard.

"Sure, I would," he said. "But I miss all that now. I keep saying maybe next year things will get better. Then another year drags by, and I've got nothing to show for it."

RJ reached across the table for his hand. He set down his mug and sandwiched her small hand between his. *Don't give up*, she wanted to say, but the words seemed trite. So she simply smiled at him. They sat quietly for a moment, listening to the dog snuffle in and out.

"You know the Cobbs are moving?" He broke the silence. "Heading to Wichita, I think they said."

RJ's heart thundered in her chest. Last time she'd been in town, Ethel had told her the Cobbs lost their youngest child. The girl had taken sick with a cough and fever. Within a couple of weeks, the poor thing could hardly breathe. She lay in bed all day and night, wheezing and sweating and trembling. Another week passed, and she slipped away in the middle of the night.

Hundreds of children and older folks had taken ill like that in the past year throughout the Plains. It was in all of the newspapers. The doctors called it dust pneumonia.

"I suppose it's hard for them to live in the same house where their child died," RJ said.

"Suppose they want to get the hell out of here before another one does," Harvey said.

RJ's eyes were stinging and she blinked hard a few times to push the feeling away. She rose from the table and moved around behind Harvey's chair. She leaned forward and wrapped her arms around him. Harvey rested his head back against her shoulder and touched his cheek to hers.

“Things’ll get better,” she whispered and squeezed him tighter around the chest.

Harvey put his hand on her forearm and stroked it gently with his calloused thumb.

“Sure they will,” he said. “Maybe next year.”

Woody walked beside RJ as she hiked her usual route through the test fields surrounding the lab. She was absorbed in her work, taking measurements, making observations, jotting notes. The last sandstorm had made another mess of the fields.

"Hey, RJ?"

"Yes, Woody," RJ responded absently, scribbling in her journal.

"Do you believe in God?"

RJ stopped then, looked up at him. Her answer didn't come quickly. She rolled the idea over in her mind. Woody waited.

"Yes," she said, finally. "I do."

"A lot of scientists don't."

"That's true. They want proof, I suppose. But I'm learning proof is hard to come by in life, even in science sometimes."

"I go back and forth," Woody said.

"Tell me." RJ motioned for them to carry on with their trek, knowing Woody would elaborate on his thoughts while they continued their work.

"When I was little," Woody said, "Ma always preached about the Good Lord, always loaded up the family in the wagon on Sundays to head to church. I didn't like wearing church clothes, all buttoned up and tight, and pinchy and scratchy. But I liked listening to the preacher man talk about grace and faith and the good works of God. Then, we'd ride home, me dangling my bare feet over the edge of the wagon, bumping down the dirt road, past the fields of green baby wheat blowing in the wind. It's easy to believe in God when you're taking in a sight like that."

RJ replayed a similar scene in her mind from her own childhood in Vanham. She saw herself fidgeting on the church bench beside her parents. She remembered plucking tender grass from the side of the road and chewing it between her teeth on the way home.

"Then the rain stopped," Woody continued. And everything dried up. And the dusters started. The first time we got a duster it was kind of exciting. Never seen nothing like it. But then we got another, and another, and another. And it wasn't exciting no more. It was exhausting and scary and frustrating. And Ma stopped talking about the Good Lord.

RJ nodded, looking to the horizon, wondering if tonight would be the night another duster would rumble through. She'd only been back in Vanham for nine months, and she was already sick to death of them.

"After a while," Woody continued, "whenever I'd see a duster coming, and we'd have to hunker down for hours on end, I'd think, nope, there ain't a God after all. No way God would do this to us. Why would He?"

"It's hard to understand it," RJ said. "That's for sure."

RJ adjusted her Red Cross mask, finding little comfort from the warm, stagnant air ricocheting off the moist, gritty cloth.

"Gee, Woody, I wish we could talk about this with Dr. Leopold," she said, finally pulling her mask down below her chin. "He was my favorite professor. You'd like him a lot. He's amazing, his ideas about religion and science and the laws of nature, the balance of things."

"Like what?" Woody asked. "What kind of stuff did he say?"

"Well," RJ searched her mind to find the right words to do justice to her beloved professor's ideas. "For one thing, he believes there's a mystical supreme power that guides the universe. But that power might not necessarily be as specific as the God you and I learned about in church. The power he believes in is more like, well, like the laws of nature that tie us all together. So his beliefs don't quite include a defined notion of God, but they don't necessarily rule out the idea either."

RJ watched Woody digest what she had just said. She wondered, as she often did, how the people of this town could talk with Woody and actually believe he was dim-witted. Couldn't they see what she saw? He was brilliant.

"So what *are* the laws of nature?" Woody asked. "How does your professor think we're all tied together by them?"

RJ's skin prickled with the thrill of a philosophical discussion about science and nature. And she felt an ache in her heart knowing Woody had never even had the chance to finish high school, much less go to college.

"His field of study is ecology," she said. "And Professor Leopold defines ecology as the *science of communities*. He would say, 'a thing is right only when it preserves the integrity, stability and beauty of the community,' and that that community doesn't just include people, but also animals and plants. Even soil and water."

The wind changed direction, and the dust drifting along the landscape swirled and turned back on itself. RJ and Woody turned their backs to the wind, cleared the grit from their eyes, looked out over the barren fields of hardscrabble earth where life once flourished.

"So...," Woody said, slowly raising his eyebrows, "farming this land is only the right thing to do if it preserves the integrity and stability and beauty of the *whole* community, not just produces food for people. Is that what you're getting at?"

"Gosh, Woody. I actually hadn't thought of it in quite that way before. But, yes. Maybe that is what I'm getting at, or at least maybe that's what Professor Leopold was getting at."

She shook her head and sighed. "I mean, if we're going to keep farming this land, we've *got* to figure out a different way to go about it, a way that doesn't destroy it forever."

Woody looked up to the sky. "That goes back to what I was saying, about how I go back and forth on God.

"One day this big old duster came barreling down. And Pa gathered up everybody and told us to get into the storm cellar. But I couldn't do it. I just couldn't go down there again. So I stood in the yard, and I let the dust blow over me, let it cut into my skin, clog my throat. I could hear Ma crying out to me through the storm, to come inside, for God's sake, come inside. For God's sake, Woody. And I remembered my Sunday school lessons about the dust storms, and the locusts and all that. Then I thought, yessir, there's a God all right, and He's at it again."

They'd stopped walking then, Woody looked up at the sky as he spoke. RJ watched him, soaked in his words.

"So maybe it's both," Woody said, nodding slowly. "Maybe there is a God and maybe He's trying tell us something about the laws of nature, trying to get us to pay better attention to what we're doing. And maybe He wants to make sure we really take notice. No forty days and forty nights of rain this time around. No sir. No rain at all... maybe there'd be too much hope in rain."

Woody looked down at RJ and shrugged one shoulder. She smiled and clutched her notepad to her chest. The desire to reach out to him seized her, to put her arm around his shoulder or maybe take hold of his hand. She fought back the feeling. Not because Woody would pull away, but because even the lightest touch would be too intense – for her – after what they'd just shared.

The diner hummed with the clatter and chatter of a full supper crowd. Forks and knives clinked against porcelain plates. Music wafted from the wireless radio. Talk of spring warmth and the hope for rain rose above the din. Ethel smiled and gossiped with her patrons as she sashayed about the dining room delivering meals and clearing empty plates.

It had been nearly a week since the last duster. Ethel had given the restaurant a good spring cleaning. It was starting to feel like old times.

She walked over to the table by the window where Flo Meginnis and the other wives from the quilting circle were enjoying coffee and dessert.

"Another cuppa, gals?" Ethel asked, pouring the steaming hot brew into their mugs.

They thanked her and complimented her buttermilk pie. Ethel thanked them in return.

"So, the insurance fella come out to our place the other day," Flo said, out of the blue. The women turned their attention to her. "He's filling out papers and he says to me, 'Lady, is there any insanity in your family?' And I says to him, no, except my husband often imagines he's the head of the house."

She punctuated her joke with a snort. Her friends roared. Ethel gave her a wink. "Aw shoot, Flo. That's a good one."

Across the room, RJ and Harvey sat at a table in the corner. They spoke softly over their Blue Plate Specials. Harvey reached across the table and stroked the back of RJ's hand. She smiled and opened her palm, laced her fingers between his. They were an item now, and RJ didn't care who knew.

"Your hands are so teeny," he mused, a glint in his eye. RJ giggled.

"All right you two, break it up," Ethel teased as she approached with the coffee pot. "Let me warm your cups. Although maybe I ought to bring you some ice water instead, to cool you off."

"Ethel, hush!" RJ's cheeks turned deep crimson.

Harvey laughed out loud and said Ethel just may be right. Ethel laughed, too, and gave his shoulder a little shove as she moved to the next table.

The bell above the door jingled and the boy from the General Store rushed in the diner.

"Sorry to spoil supper, y'all. But we got a sandstorm heading in from the west. Looks like a big one."

As if on cue, everyone took to their feet. They thanked the boy for the warning, dropped coins onto their tables, gulped down their last swigs of coffee. Ethel wilted. She watched as her patrons made for the exit one by one, darting off in different directions down the street.

Harvey stood and tossed two quarters on the table. He took hold of RJ's hand.

"My place is closer," he said. "You better come home with me, just to be safe. We don't know how fast that storm is moving."

RJ looked over at Ethel. The woman was still standing in the middle of the room, coffee pot in hand, dazed. Everyone else had left. A melancholy tune drifted from the wireless.

"I think I'd better stay and help Ethel," RJ said, giving Harvey's hand a squeeze. He looked over at Ethel, studied her for a second or two.

“All right then,” he said. “I’ll run outside and get Stormy for you.”

RJ walked over to Ethel and placed a hand on the woman’s shoulder.

“Ethel? Shall we clear these dishes and start battening down?”

Ethel blinked to life. She mumbled something about RJ being right, lots of work to do. Harvey came back in from outside, and Stormy bolted past him, headed for the stairs to Ethel’s room.

“Going straight under the bed,” RJ said.

Harvey chuckled, but the glint in his eye had disappeared.

“Drive safe,” RJ said and placed her palm on his cheek. “We’ll be all right here.”

He stole a quick kiss, then bolted back out the door.

April 1935

RJ ran to her front door, flung it open wide and rushed out to the porch. She gripped the handrail in front of her with both hands and leaned forward. Instead of the usual brown haze that greeted her each morning, the golden sun smiled at her from a soft blue sky. She drew pure oxygen in through her nostrils and exhaled through her mouth, as though she were cleansing a year's worth of dust from her lungs.

"Jeepers! What a gorgeous day."

Stormy sauntered out onto the porch and stretched her front feet out far in front of her. She yawned and shook from her head all the way down to the tip of her stubby tail.

"Isn't it just the most beautiful day you've ever seen?" RJ asked, almost breathless.

The dog barked in agreement and scampered off the porch into the front yard, leaping and bounding like a deer.

It was the first time RJ had seen blue skies in Vanham since she and Stormy had rolled into town ten months before. The first time the air had been dust-free. It was too perfect a day to squander. Her mind landed on Harvey. A Sunday picnic!

RJ hurried back inside to pack a basket – a can of brown bread, jar of preserves, four hard-boiled eggs and two large canning jars of water. She tucked it all in with a couple of kitchen towels.

Maybe they could drive down to the Cimarron River, like her family had done when she was a child. The river was dry now, but there might be a few shade trees still standing along the banks.

RJ set the basket on the passenger side floor of the truck and whistled to Stormy to come along. She set off down the road, windows rolled down. Her goggles and Red Cross mask were tucked away in the glove compartment. She sang a snappy tune as the truck bumped along the rutted road toward Harvey's place.

Stormy whimpered.

"What's the matter, girl? I thought you liked my singing."

The dog circled in the passenger seat a couple of times and then crouched low, ears flat against her head. RJ glanced at Stormy, her eyebrows knit with concern.

A flutter of movement in the field to her left caught RJ's eye. She looked over to see a drove of jackrabbits racing across the flat brown plain toward the road. RJ slammed her foot on the brake pedal just as the mass of animals leapt and zipped past the truck on all sides.

"Lordy," RJ exclaimed. "What do you suppose has gotten into them?"

Stormy continued to whine and whimper.

Just as the ruckus from the rabbits died down, RJ heard a low rumble in the distance. She looked and saw what had spooked the critters. A duster was approaching from the northwest. Approaching fast.

The colossal black cloud rolled and tumbled along the earth, like a living breathing mountain range on the horizon, towering thousands of feet into the sky. It churned over the land, devouring everything in its path, blacking out the sun in its wake.

"Holy Mary, mother of God." RJ couldn't look away from the approaching beast. It was bigger than anything she'd seen yet.

A flock of birds flew screeching overhead in a blind, panicked flight of their life to somehow escape the rumbling mountain of dust. Stormy howled.

The dog's anguished cry snapped RJ out of her trance. They had to find shelter. If they turned back, they'd never reach home in time. Crawling beneath the truck wouldn't protect them from this aberration. They'd be buried alive.

RJ looked around to get her bearings. The Sharp farm was just a half mile up the road. RJ's stomach seized. Her mind flashed back to the angry farmer telling her to stay off his land, or she and her Kraut dog would regret it.

She turned back to watch the black blizzard bearing down on them. She had no choice. RJ put the truck in gear and sped down the road toward the Sharps' earthen haven.

The wind picked up, pushing a wall of sand across their path. RJ gripped the steering wheel, struggling to keep the truck on the road. The hairs on her arms and the back of her neck prickled from the buildup of electricity in the air.

She turned onto the drive, the wind at their back now and pulled up to the Sharp house. Mr. Sharp stood halfway between the house and barn, staggering against the wind. He stomped toward her.

"What the hell are you doing here?"

RJ jumped from the cab. She could barely hear him shout above the roaring wind. But his body language told her all she needed to know.

"I'm sorry," she shouted, then looked back toward the approaching storm.

"Just get in the house," he said. "Go on!"

Stormy huddled in the truck, frozen with fear. RJ scooped the dog into her arms, grabbed hold of the picnic basket and hurried toward the house. She burst through the door and Stormy leapt from her arms, scrambling beneath the nearest piece of furniture. The three young Sharp children sat huddled together on the couch wailing. Tears and snot ran down their faces.

Mrs. Sharp was hastily taking stock of her supplies, concern etched on her face. She looked at RJ, and recognition drifted into her expression. Her face turned hard. Her eyes were dark.

"I, I'm so sorry," RJ stammered. "We were on the road. The storm. I had nowhere else to go."

The woman shook her head quickly. There was no time to argue. No time to indulge in anger.

"Go back out and lock down the shutters," the woman shouted.

RJ obeyed. She hurried around the dugout, straining against the fierce wind and biting dust, fighting with all her strength to pull the shutters together. She cursed herself for leaving her goggles and mask in the truck.

When the shutters were all secure, she decided to make a run for the vehicle to retrieve her safety gear. She tipped her head down and pressed into the wind. She heard the chickens shrieking and squawking as Mr. Sharp and his oldest boy scrambled to round up the birds and secure them in the coop.

The barbed wire fence leading to the barn crackled with blue flames, set ablaze by the frenetic dust barreling through the atmosphere.

RJ made it to the truck and placed her hand on the door handle. A jolt shook her to her core, the door flew open wide and RJ fell back onto the ground. The oxygen was knocked from her lungs, and she struggled to re-inflate them, gasping and choking on the dust-filled air. Her hand throbbed. She crawled back to the truck, carefully stood and leaned in to open the glove compartment. She hesitated a moment, knowing she was in for another shock. RJ rooted her feet beneath her and reached for the latch. The jolt rattled her, but she remained standing this time. She quickly put on the goggles and mask and turned back toward the house.

The black cloud overtook her. The gale knocked her to her hands and knees. The darkness was so complete RJ couldn't see the ground that was only inches from her face. The wind roared in her ears, until they filled with dust and then there was quiet. She dropped to her stomach and scuttled like an infantry solider along the ground in the direction of the house. Blind and deaf, she struggled forward, inch by inch. Her muscles began to tremble.

RJ willed herself to reach forward just one more time, and then another, and another until she felt the incline leading to the door of the sod dugout. With her last burst of strength, she crawled forward, reached up to twist the doorknob with her burned hand, and tumbled in across the stoop as the door flew open.

Mr. Sharp grabbed hold of RJ by the seat of her overalls and pulled her the rest of the way inside. Mrs. Sharp and her son leaned their bodies into the door to push it closed against the wind and dust.

The oil lamp on the kitchen table cast a faint orange glow through the dusty air still swirling inside the house. RJ remained on the floor, lungs burning as she coughed and spit mud, head reeling as she shook the dirt from her ears like a dog. The Sharps were shadowy figures scattered about the room, still as death in the darkness. The roof and windows rattled with a fierceness that RJ had never experienced.

"It's the Judgment Day," Mrs. Sharp said.

No one had the nerve to confirm or dispute her declaration.

The shutters on the small kitchen window knocked and thrashed. The lock gave way and they banged against the glass. The window shattered, sending a spray of shards and dust into the room. Mrs. Sharp shielded the children who shrieked in terror.

"Find something to cover it!" Mr. Sharp bellowed into the wind and onslaught of dust.

His son, the oldest child, grabbed up an empty canvas sack and stretched to hold it over the gaping window. Mr. Sharp snatched a handful of pencils, butter knives, a screw driver. Anything sturdy enough to poke through the flapping canvas and into the mud wall to hold the covering in place. After they'd done their best to secure the canvas, Mr. Sharp and his son upended the kitchen table and pushed it up against the wall to further secure the window.

RJ got her wits about her and scrambled to clear away the broken glass before anyone could be cut. She took up the broom leaning beside the door and swept the shards into the corner.

With the small catastrophe in hand, the group gathered together back in the living area, away from the other two small windows. They stood petrified, mute, as the wind raged. The house shook. The dust swirled in the air around them.

"We best pray," Mr. Sharp said.

"Come children, on your knees," Mrs. Sharp said, and the family knelt on the floor, hands clasped tightly.

"Our Father which art in heaven," Mr. Sharp began. The rest of the family joined in, "Hallowed be thy name."

RJ swallowed hard. It had been years since she'd said the Lord's Prayer. A loud crash against the front door made everyone flinch, momentarily halting their plea.

"Thy kingdom come, Thy will be done," RJ continued and dropped to her knees.

The black blizzard waged its war on Vanham all through the day and the night. Mr. Sharp worried about their stock of oil, so he extinguished the lamp after a few hours. It was relit for the evening meal, then extinguished again. In the morning, he awoke at four o'clock, as he always did, and struck a match to check the time. He sat in the dark two more hours, as his family slept scattered about the room. The littlest children had piled together on their parents' bed in the corner. Mrs. Sharp slept on the couch. RJ and the teenage boy had taken blankets to the floor.

When he could sit still no more, Mr. Sharp lit the lamp again.

"What time is it, Pa?" His youngest pulled the goggles from her face and pawed at her eyes with her miniature fists.

"Six," Mr. Sharp said. "In the morning. Put your goggles back on."

The room was just as dark, the air just as thick with dust as it had been the day before. The wind continued to bellow. The house moaned and creaked. Stormy had slinked out from beneath the couch sometime during the night and was curled up on the floor beside RJ.

"How long you think this can last?" Mrs. Sharp asked.

No one responded. RJ glanced about the room and realized the entire family was looking at her for an answer. The scientist. The know-it-all.

"I don't know," she said.

They all sat quietly for a moment or two.

One of the little ones whispered to her mama that she needed to pee. There was no way they could go to the outhouse. Mr. Sharp hung a blanket from the ceiling in the corner of the room and set a bucket behind it. Everyone took turns doing their business. Stormy paced and whimpered at the front door. When she couldn't hold out any longer, the dog squatted and relieved herself on the rough wood floor.

"Oh!" RJ jumped up. "I'm so sorry. I'll clean that up right away."

Mrs. Sharp handed RJ a rag and crossed her arms over her chest.

Not long after, the children started whining for breakfast.

"I'll mix up some corn mush," Mrs. Sharp said.

"We had corn mush for breakfast yesterday," said the youngest.

"And for supper," said the oldest.

"Don't you sass your ma," Mr. Sharp scolded.

The children pouted quietly in the dim light, and Mrs. Sharp headed toward the kitchen shelves. RJ remembered her picnic basket. She debated in her mind about whether to offer up the meal. Certainly, the children would enjoy the change of menu. But the Sharps might take offense if she undermined their authority.

"If you'd like, Mrs. Sharp," RJ spoke up. "You can see if there's anything in my basket you might see fit to serve."

Mr. and Mrs. Sharp exchanged looks. The children fidgeted. RJ felt a trickle of sweat run down the side of her rib cage. After what seemed to RJ to be an eternity, Mrs. Sharp finally walked over to the basket on the kitchen table and looked inside. She shifted the towels packed between the items. She raised her eyebrows and shook her head.

"Hard-cooked eggs and canned brown bread."

The children clapped and whooped. The parents exchanged another look. Mrs. Sharp set about opening the B&M bread and slicing it along the even grooves created by the can. The children each peeled the shell from an egg. The moist eggs attracted the dust from the air, becoming muddy globs. The children gobbled them down, dirt and all.

When the meal was finished, a hush fell upon the family again. How long *will* this storm last? Certainly, they all still wondered about it. None had the courage to voice the question out loud again.

"You know, you could make ten loaves of brown bread for what that one cost you," Mrs. Sharp said.

"I know," RJ said. "But I'd have to use them to pave my garden instead of eat them."

The children giggled.

"Didn't no one ever teach you how to bake?"

"I get by with canned goods from the market," RJ said.

"Don't see how," Mrs. Sharp replied. RJ thought the woman was going to say something more, but she did not.

Painful silence again descended upon the group. After a bit, the children huddled on the floor to play a game of marbles. Mrs. Sharp settled in the corner chair to knit, her fingers expertly working the yarn and needles though she was nearly blind in the dusty darkness.

RJ retrieved a deck of playing cards from the pocket of her overalls. She pulled a kitchen chair up beside a small nightstand, took a seat and dealt a hand of solitaire. Staring through her goggles in the weak glow of the oil lamp, she could barely make out the cards. At least the act of playing kept her hands busy.

When she'd exhausted her options for the hand, RJ scooped all the cards into a pile and straightened them into a neat rectangle. She spilt the deck and attempted to riffle the two halves together. The burn on her right palm objected with a fierce stab. RJ cringed and grunted as the cards sputtered into the air and scattered onto the table and floor.

Mrs. Sharp looked up from her knitting, watched RJ gingerly collect the cards and switch to an overhand shuffle.

"What's wrong with your hand?" Mrs. Sharp asked.

"Just a little burn from grabbing the truck handle in the storm. I'm fine."

Mrs. Sharp set aside her yarn and walked over to RJ. "Let me have a look."

"It's fine."

After birthing and caring for four children, the woman couldn't just turn off mothering like it was a water spigot. She repeated her command to have a look, and RJ obeyed. Mrs. Sharp held RJ's hand gently in hers and gave the young woman a tsk-tsk as she eyed the scarlet blistering skin. "You should've said something."

Mrs. Sharp retrieved a white metal box from a drawer in the kitchen, a small towel and bowl of water. She pulled up a chair beside RJ and snapped open the box, which was painted with a red cross and "Johnson's Housekit for First Aid." She gently washed RJ's wound with the towel and water, then she dabbed it with a glob of clear ointment she squeezed from a tube of Joncolia.

The cool water and analgesic ointment soothed RJ's burn. Yet Mrs. Sharp's gentle touch hurt her in a different way. RJ had no memory of her own mother tending a cut finger or scraped knee.

"Thank you," RJ said, barely above a whisper.

Mrs. Sharp only nodded in acknowledgment, as she gently wrapped RJ's hand with a thin Red Cross bandage from a roll. She snipped the bandage with a small pair of scissors from the kit and tied a knot at the back of RJ's hand. Without saying a word, she packed up her kit, put away her supplies and returned to her chair.

~

The minutes turned to hours. The hours piled on through the day and into the evening once again. Outside the wind roared and pounded, showing no signs of easing. Mr. Sharp had taken to pacing the floor. Tension charged the air even more than the static electricity from the spiraling particles of dust that kept everyone's arm hairs standing on end.

The littlest Sharp crawled into her mother's lap and began to weep again. Mrs. Sharp exhaled noisily through her Red Cross mask and stroked the child's head.

RJ shuffled her playing cards again and again. She set the deck on the table and sunk to the floor with Stormy. The dog shifted closer, laid her head in RJ's lap. RJ used her thumb to clear a glob of muddy gunk from the corner of Stormy's eye. It reminded her of their first day together, after RJ's first duster, after the sun returned. Stormy whimpered and snuggled in even closer.

"Forget your troubles, c'mon on get happy," RJ began to sing, slowly, softly to the dog. "You better chase all your cares away."

One by one the Sharps looked at her.

RJ hesitated a moment. "Shout hallelujah, c'mon get happy."

She paused again.

"Get ready for the Judgment Day," Mrs. Sharp sang.

RJ smiled at her through the gloomy haze.

"The sun is shinin', c'mon get happy," the women continued in unison, picking up the pace a bit. "The Lord is waiting to take your hand."

Mr. Sharp began to clap and the children took to their feet.

"Shout hallelujah, c'mon get happy," they all sang. "We're going to the Promise Land."

The little ones linked arms and spun around, skipping, singing. Verse after verse, the motley crew sang. And verse after verse, a bit of their tension melted away. Stormy cocked her head to one side and then the other. Then, she joined in the chorus with a howl. The youngest child took hold of the dog's front paws, and the two danced about the living room. When the song ended, the children fell on top of one another on the floor, a giggling mass while Stormy licked their dirty faces. Mrs. Sharp clasped her hands together in silent prayer.

RJ reveled in the moment. Mr. Sharp walked past her, patted her two times on the back of the shoulder, then went to sit on the couch beside his wife. A lump formed in RJ's throat. She said a silent prayer of thanks that this family had given her a second chance. Despite the utter darkness that engulfed them, it was as though she and the Sharps had actually seen each other for the first time.

~~~

By the second morning, the group had used up all of the fresh water in the house. And the stench from the latrine bucket was overwhelming. The storm continued, but the wind had eased. Mr. Sharp announced he would go out to get fresh water from the well. If all went well, he'd head back out to empty the waste bucket into the outhouse.

"You sure it's safe?" Mrs. Sharp twisted her apron.

"The children need water," he said.

Mrs. Sharp asked that he at least take a peek through the front door eyehole, to assess the storm before heading out. He strode to the front door and slid open the small flap. Dirt began pouring in through the hole. Mr. Sharp fumbled and forced the flap back in place.

"Pa?"

Mr. Sharp shook his head. He couldn't form the words. He didn't have to. It was clear to all, even the youngest among them, that the door was blocked. Mrs. Sharp took a shaky step back and sunk into her chair.

"We're trapped!" The middle daughter wailed, ran to the door in hysterics. Mr. Sharp caught her by the arms before she had a chance to pull the door open wide. She screamed and flailed and fought him to break free. Mr. Sharp slapped her across the face and she froze. The room was dead silent for a heartbeat, and then she and the other children began to howl.
~~~

"The wind was blowing from the north." RJ spoke above the din of wailing children.

Mr. Sharp looked at her with confusion at first, and then he understood. The other sides of the house wouldn't be buried as deep. He and RJ moved to the tiny kitchen window that had been shattered. They carefully pulled away the table and the canvas. The dim light of day broke through the opening.

He sighed with relief. Then his face went dark again. "I'll never be able to squeeze through."

The Sharp boy stepped forward and his pa quickly sized him up, shook his head. RJ looked about the room. She was the only one, aside from the little children, who was petite enough.

"I'll go," she said, adjusting her goggles and mask. "But I'll need a boost."

Mr. Sharp crouched down. RJ placed one hand on his shoulder and the other in the window frame. She stepped onto his bent thigh and hoisted herself up. She tucked her head and arms through the small window and wiggled to grab hold of some support on the outside to help pull herself through. The boy rushed forward to help, grabbing hold of RJ's legs and giving her a shove.

"Easy," Mr. Sharp shouted. "Easy now."

RJ couldn't help but laugh.

"I did say I'd need a boost," she said.

She eased herself the rest of the way through the window, coming to her hands and knees as she rolled out into the soft dirt just a few inches below the window. The air outside was a billowy mass of particles, glowing iridescent pink in the morning sunlight. The wind was ever present, but it blew gently. The worst of the storm seemed to have passed.

"Hand me the shovel," RJ said.

She took hold of the handle as Mr. Sharp handed it out to her through the window. He held on for a moment. RJ looked at him, and his eyes spoke a thousand unsaid words to her – regret for their rough beginnings, respect for her quick thinking, thanks for helping his family. She gave him a tight-lipped smile from behind her dust mask and a couple of quick nods. He returned the nods and released his grip on the shovel.

RJ trudged through the soft dirt, sinking down to her ankles. Her mind flashed to the holes she'd dug in her uncle's yard as a child, to her longtime fixation with her parents being buried alive. As she worked her way around to the front of the house, the irony struck her. She had returned to her childhood home and literally been swallowed up by the earth. And she somehow felt stronger because of it.

When she got to where she guessed the door should have been, RJ began to dig.

All across Vanham – in town, in the surrounding farms – folks dug their way out of the dust, emerged from the darkness to see the sun. Some thanked God for giving them another day. Others cursed Him, wondered what they'd done to deserve His wrath. Still others took in the devastation around them, nodded their heads knowingly, told themselves there must be no God after all.

What they did not yet know was that the storm had not been their misery alone. It had come down from Wyoming and the Dakotas, picked up earth from Colorado and Nebraska, rumbled and rolled across a thousand miles of plains, south and east, fueling its anger as it swept over the land. It blanketed small towns and big cities, family farms and cattle ranches.

Four days strong, the dust storm eclipsed the sun in Washington D.C., blackened the White House. Then, it roared two-hundred miles out to the Atlantic.

Earth from the American heartland, thousands of years in the making, settled upon the ocean and sank beneath the frothy blue-green surface, to the depths of the dark water forever.

Still, the plains folks got the worst of it.

"What'll we do with 'em, Pa?" asked a tiny girl with blackened bare feet, as she and her family looked over their last few dozen heads of cattle. The ones that had not already died of starvation or thirst. The ones that, instead, were overcome by the storm and lay scattered among the fresh dunes, unmoving, necks contorted in unnatural ways, half covered by the earth, mouths gaping, eyes and noses and ears packed with dirt.

"Finish burying them, I reckon."

The girl dropped to her knees in the dirt and buried her face in her hands. Her pa watched her weep. He thought hard about dropping to his knees right beside her. Instead, he wiped the snot from his nose with the back of his sleeve, and turned and wandered away toward the barn.

Throughout the plains, farmers and ranchers dug trenches, deep and wide. Used tractors and plows to drag and pull the carcasses to their graves – cows, dogs, horses, hogs. Covered the bodies with fresh dirt, and prayed the next duster would not unearth them. Chickens that had suffocated in their coops were shoveled into wheelbarrows, dumped into pits, burned.

Meanwhile, many families – too many families – laid to rest their own. Babies whose tiny lungs couldn't tolerate the onslaught of dust. Grandparents whose hearts couldn't withstand the terror of the storm. Men who'd died on the road – buried in and beneath their cars and trucks, or crushed by mangled steel from steering blind into walls, trees, other vehicles.

Vanham was a virtual ghost town. Stores and businesses remained shuttered. Parents kept their children home from school. Farmers were afraid to venture too far from shelter. Power lines and telephone wires were down for miles and miles, charred beyond repair by the storm's electrical charge, knocked to the ground, covered by the earth. Roads and rail tracks lay hidden beneath sandy dunes. The air was thick with dust, black smoke, the smell of death, fear.

~

The days rolled into weeks. With each new day, folks worked at putting things back together, double checked their emergency supplies, and waited. Waited for things to return to normal. Waited for the next duster.

And another duster did come. Compared to the last, it was child's play.

Things might not have returned to normal, per se, but things had eased back to life. Folks began venturing out a little further from home, even into town. They'd gotten blocked roads cleared and broken windows replaced. Vanham shopkeepers began opening for business again, at least partial hours. Ethel welcomed back her old lunch crowd with whatever meals she could pull together.

"What's the paper say?" she asked Ernie, while serving up powdered eggs with canned tomatoes and corned beef.

The old man shook the newspaper open wide in front of him, folded the pages back, then in half again.

"Welp," he said, scanning the front page. "They're calling it Black Sunday now."

Accounts of the storm had made their way back and forth across the country, and journalists were all putting their own compelling spin on the news, creating their own tantalizing catchphrases. One Associated Press reporter and his photographer had been in Oklahoma covering another story when they'd received word of a big storm on the way. The men later offered the nation a dramatic, first-hand account of the black blizzard in a series of reports, complete with before and after photos of the ruin.

"This reporter feller, Robert Geiger, been traveling around and talking to farmers," Ernie continued. "Listen here to what he wrote… 'Three little words achingly familiar on a Western farmer's tongue rule life in the dust bowl of the continent – *if it rains.*'"

Ethel set the coffee pot on the counter, looked at Ernie. "Life in the dust bowl?"

"Yap. That's what he wrote."

Ethel turned her head toward the brown-tinted diner window. She lit a cigarette and leaned back against the cash register, still looking out.

Ernie went back to reading the paper to himself, leaving Ethel to her own thoughts. She took a deliberate draw on her Chesterfield. Then, she blew the smoke out in a platinum ring that expanded as it drifted up toward the ceiling. She watched the ring until it vanished, then looked back out the front window.

"The Dust Bowl," she whispered.

After a simple Sunday dinner at her place, RJ walked Harvey out to his truck to say good night.

"I don't have to leave just yet, Rosa Jean. It's still early. We could play cards if you'd like."

RJ raised on her tiptoes to give Harvey a kiss. She placed her hands on his chest and tilted her head like a robin.

"That's sweet of you," she said. "But I'm bushed, and I have a long day tomorrow cleaning the gunk out of the well pump."

"Have Woody clean the pump," Harvey said.

"Woody's going to have his hands full working on the tractor."

Harvey nodded broodingly. He draped his arms around her, and clasped his hands at the small of her back. "How 'bout I come back over in the morning and take care of the pump?"

RJ sighed. "I don't need your help."

"I know. I know," Harvey admitted. "You can clean that pump yourself, and you'd probably do a damned better job at it than I would. You don't need me to do it."

They stood quietly, though Harvey's face was etched with more he wanted to say. RJ studied him. She couldn't decipher his expression. "But…?" she prodded him after a moment.

"But, there are different sorts of needs, Rosa Jean. Like maybe *I* need to help you with the pump. And maybe," he closed his eyes, "maybe you need to let me help you, even if you don't need the help."

RJ narrowed her eyes and tilted her head in the other direction. He opened his eyes again and gazed at her intently. It finally began to dawn on her that this wasn't about Harvey wanting to be stronger or superior or even chivalrous. It wasn't even about the well pump at all. She reached behind her back, took Harvey's hand and led him to the porch. She sat down on the step, pulled him down beside her.

"Go on," she said.

Harvey tugged at his ear and cleared his throat. Tiny beads of perspiration broke out on his forehead.

"Ever since Black Sunday hit, I've been thinking. I've been through a lot of storms, but that was different. I was scared, Rosa Jean. I mean, I was really and truly scared," he paused a moment, then continued. "But I wasn't scared for myself. I was scared thinking about you, scared you were in danger, scared I'd lose you."

"But I'm okay," she said and squeezed his hand. "I can take care of myself. You don't have to worry so much about me."

Harvey gave his familiar nod, *yes, I know*.

"You're a strong, smart, capable woman," he said.

"But…?" she prodded.

Harvey fished around in his shirt pocket and pulled out a dainty ring between his calloused fingers. RJ's hand flew to her mouth.

"It was my mother's," he said. "They call it rose gold."

"It's lovely," she whispered through her fingertips.

"Nothing would make me happier than to see you wear this ring, Rosa Jean."

RJ took in a jagged breath. She brought her hands together at her stomach.

"I know you don't *need* a husband to take care of you." He reached for her hands, gently unfolded them and placed the ring in her palm. "But wouldn't it be nice to have something you don't necessarily need? Wouldn't you be happy knowing you had someone you could count on, for better or for worse?"

She eyed the slender pink band, turned it over with her fingers. It was etched with a delicate pattern of curling vines, though the etching had been worn smooth in spots from years of wear and farm work. RJ tried to remember Harvey's mother, how the ring might have looked on the woman's hand as she cooked and scrubbed and sewed all those years.

Harvey's eyes pierced RJ, searching for an answer. Yet she couldn't speak. She leaned back, seeking some sort of comfort, or maybe a way to escape. She wished she could slither down between the crevices of the porch and hide in the cool dark shadows until she could figure out how to make words come out of her mouth.

"Marry me, Rosa Jean. We make a good team. You said so yourself."

She nodded.

"Do you love me?"

"Oh, Harvey, of course I do." She paused and shook her head. "I, I just don't know what to say."

"Say you'll *marry me*."

She opened her mouth, but the words would not flow. She felt Harvey stiffen. The air between them seemed to grow cold. She saw the muscles of his jaw tighten, as her mind raced for something, anything, to say.

"It's just so unexpected." RJ could feel the oxygen catching in her chest, as if her lungs refused to accept any air unless she accepted the ring. Her hands grew clammy and moist, and she wanted to pull them from Harvey's grasp, to wipe them dry on her overalls, but she didn't want to hurt him more than she already had with her silence. She forced another breath in and out, even as she felt her throat constricting. Her heart seemed to thrash against her rib cage.

"Getting married would change everything," she whispered.

Harvey's grip relaxed. The tension retreated from his face, and he smiled. "It would change for the better."

He moved closer to her on the step, leaned forward and pressed his lips to her forehead. RJ shut her eyes and allowed herself to surrender to his kiss.

"Just think about it," Harvey said, barely removing his lips from her skin. He turned his head and brushed his cheek against her hair.

"I will," RJ whispered. "I'll think about it."

RJ sat across from Ethel, tallying the green speckles on the Formica countertop. She had driven to town first thing in the morning after Harvey's proposal and was happy to see the diner hadn't opened for breakfast yet.

Business had been slow, Ethel said. She hadn't yet changed out of her housecoat, and her long hair tumbled in loose waves down her back.

"I'm sorry Ethel," RJ said. "It's selfish of me, I know, but I'm glad you're not open. I really need to talk to you. And I don't need any gossipy busybodies listening over my shoulder."

Ethel scrunched up her eyebrows in concern. She settled into the stool behind the counter. "What is it, hon?"

RJ retrieved the ring from her overall pocket and dropped it on the counter. It clinked when it hit the Formica. Ethel's eyebrows raised. She picked up the ring between her thumb and forefinger and inspected it.

"Ida's wedding ring," Ethel said. "And I'm guessing you haven't given him an answer yet?"

RJ shook her head.

Ethel whistled softly and set the ring back down on the lunch counter.

"Are you wanting me to tell you whether or not to marry the man?"

RJ raised her eyebrows just a bit and titled her head.

"Well, for Pete's sake, RJ. Cat got your tongue? How am I supposed to help if you won't talk to me?"

"I thought you always said I'm an open book," RJ tried to joke.

Ethel looked at RJ sideways. She swept her long hair back into a ponytail, twisted it up into a bun at the top of her head and stuck a pencil through it to hold it in place. She looked sideways at RJ again, waiting.

RJ groaned. "It's complicated."

"Go on," Ethel said.

Getting married would change everything, RJ explained. Harvey wouldn't want to give up his farm. She'd have to move out to his place. That would make her daily work at the lab so much more difficult. And what if she got pregnant? How on earth would she continue her work at the lab, tend a home and raise a child? It would be impossible.

The thought of losing all she had worked for in school and her job created a sour taste in the back of her throat. Then again, if she turned down Harvey's proposal, she would surely lose him. And that thought made it hard to breathe.

"Things change, RJ. That's just the way of the world. People come and go from our lives all the time. Sometimes there's nothing we can do about it, like when my Edward passed. Other times, we have a choice. The question is which will pain you more, keeping him in your life or losing him?"

RJ shook her head. "I understand what you're saying. But it's not that simple."

Ethel stood up and collected their empty cups. "Sure it is, honey. Maybe it ain't easy. But it *is* simple."

RJ propped her elbows on the counter and rested her head in her hands. She had been up most of the night. Her head was throbbing. Ethel let her be for a bit, filled the time by wiping down the counter, dusting off the salt and pepper shakers.

Finally, Ethel spoke up again. “You should talk to Harvey. Maybe he would understand. Maybe he wouldn’t want you to give up anything?”

RJ shook her head slowly.

“I don’t think so,” she said, her voice spilling over with skepticism. “He’s pretty set in his ways. He’ll want me to quit working and have a litter of children. Shoot, he didn’t even really *ask* me to be his wife. He just said, ‘Marry me, Rosa Jean.’”

Ethel was deep in thought. She dunked her towel in a basin of soapy water and rung it out. She picked up another pepper shaker from the counter and wiped it clean.

“You think you’ll *ever* want to be married, have a family?” she asked.

“Sure I will. Of course I will. Just... not quite yet.”

“Well then, tell Harvey that. If he loves you, he’ll wait a bit, give you time to figure things out.”

RJ angled her head thoughtfully. “You think so?”

“He’s a good man.”

“You’re sure right about that,” RJ said, allowing herself to smile for the first time all morning. “He’s a damned good man.”

RJ stood up on the rung of her stool, leaned across the counter and gave Ethel a hug. She had known her friend would say all the right things. She’d just known it. It was settled, then. RJ would talk to Harvey that night. She would accept his proposal, but she would ask for time. Nothing had to change just yet.

“This calls for a celebration,” Ethel said, pulling out a tin of snickerdoodles.

“Yes.” RJ clapped. “But no bourbon!”

The sun hung low in the sky, a blazing ball of light waiting to dip below the western horizon for its nightly slumber. Ethel stood in her slippers and nightgown, her eyes on the eastern skies, watching the black cloud of dust that was tumbling and churning its way toward Vanham.

She never had opened up the diner after RJ left that day. She'd meant to, after just one more cigarette. She had meant to wipe all the tables clean and sweep the floors. She had meant to shake out the tablecloths and dust the chairs. She had meant to put a batch of biscuits in the oven and put a pot of stew on the stove. But she never had.

Instead, she'd settled into a chair back in the kitchen, and drifted off to sleep. Every now and again, she'd hear the bell over the entrance jingle as someone pulled at the locked door. A few people tapped on the window, might have even pressed their faces against the glass to peek inside, look for her.

"Where do you suppose Ethel is?" they may have wondered. She wondered that herself.

Ethel watched out the front windows as the shopkeepers and others up and down the street pulled the shutters down over their windows, braced themselves for the coming storm. Mabel, at the shoe store, forgot to bring in her flag. Ethel watched it thrash in the wind.

She looked back toward the approaching storm. The dark eased its way down the road, the thick tumble of dust rolled past her window, higher than she could see, like a giant mythological beast lumbering through town. Tumbleweeds and debris scattered before it, as the monster snorted and puffed and roared with dark, dusty breath. The wind was its tail, sweeping along behind, causing further destruction in its wake.

The air around her crackled and made her scalp tingle. The lights in the diner flickered and hummed and died. The dark didn't bother her. Been living under a black cloud for years, she thought as she felt her way along the hall and down the stairs to her bedroom. Exhausted from her day full of nothing, Ethel lay down in bed, clutching her rosary beads to her chest.

Time seemed to stand still in the thick of the dust. Her body was tired. And yet, her mind raced. Sleep was elusive.

In the old days, she and Edward would go for long walks together after they closed up the diner for the night. The air would be crisp and fresh. The stars and moon would shine bright in the black velvet sky.

"Was it really all that long ago?" Ethel wondered aloud. *Yesterday? A lifetime ago?*

She sat up in the bed, pulled on her housecoat in the dark. She slowly made her way back upstairs, her rosary still clutched in her fist. She stood in the middle of the diner. The wind wailed through the windows. It called to her.

Ethel shuffled to the front door, turned the lock and gave the handle a tentative tug. The wind and the dust shoved its way into the diner, pushing the door open wide, rushing past her to consume the floor and tables and chairs and anything else in its path.

The dust assaulted her eyes. Blinded, she slipped out the doorway, stumbled to the center of the street, then stood facing west with the wind at her back. She fought to stay on her feet. The beast nudged her forward. Go ahead, it told her. Walk.

Tears welled in her lashes, then turned to mud in seconds. Dust clogged her lungs. And yet, she did as the wind bid her. She walked. Down the street, through the darkness. And the dust churned and tumbled and consumed everything in its path.

The rumble of an engine and the crush of dirt sent Stormy into a fit of anxious barking. RJ pulled back the kitchen curtain and saw Harvey emerge from his truck. A jolt of energy flooded her body. Last night's storm had derailed her plan. But this morning, she would tell him her decision.

She smoothed back her hair and ran her tongue over her dry lips. She opened the front door just as Harvey raised his fist to knock.

"Hiya, Harvey," she said and gave him a quick kiss. "I can't tell you how happy I am to see you."

Harvey removed his hat and stood rigid at the doorstep. The muscles in his jaw were taut.

RJ's stomach plunged. "What is it? What's wrong?"

Harvey stepped inside. RJ closed the door behind him, waited. The air around them felt thick, suffocating, even though it was mostly clear of dust. Stormy whimpered and scuttled to hide under the bed.

"It's about the storm last night," Harvey began. "There's been... I don't know, an accident, I guess."

"What kind of accident?"

"It's Ethel. Mr. Meginnis found her at the edge of town this morning."

RJ pressed her hands to her chest. She felt her heart pounding in her ears.

“Found her? I don’t understand. Is she hurt?”

“She’s gone, Rosa Jean.”

“Gone? What do you mean?”

“I’m so sorry.”

“No.” RJ sunk to her knees on the floor. *No, no, no.* Harvey dropped to his knees beside her.

“What happened? Why was she out in the storm?”

Harvey shook his head. He hardly had the strength to tell her anything more.

“Meginnis saw her foot sticking out of a sand dune this morning. She wasn’t wearing any shoes. He called to his boys and they dug her out right quick, but she was already…,” a lump caught in Harvey’s throat. “She was only wearing a nightgown and housecoat.”

RJ rattled her head, tried to make sense of it. She had just been with Ethel yesterday morning. *Why would Ethel go out like that?*

“It doesn’t make any sense,” she whispered.

Her mind flashed to the haggard woman in housecoat and slippers, with tousled, unkempt hair. RJ saw herself whining to Ethel about her own problems, as she so often had. Anger started to roil in her gut, like water in a tea kettle. If only she hadn’t been so self-absorbed. If only she had paid closer attention to her friend. If only.

Harvey slumped back to sit on the floor, his legs sprawled in front of him. “It’s this damned dust. Day in and day out. It wears at your mind. Makes you forget what you’re working so hard for. Makes you forget why any of it matters.”

RJ turned to look at him. His eyebrows were drawn together tight. His mouth was pinched in a scowl. He shook his head.

“It’s a wonder more of us haven’t gone down the path of a pistol in the mouth,” he said.

“Don’t say that,” RJ shouted. “Don’t you say that!”

She lunged at him, fists flying. She pounded at his chest, slapped his face. They tumbled backward on the floor. He grabbed hold of her wrists. Her legs flailed as she fought him. All the while she shouted. No! Don't say that! *No, no, no.*

Tears streamed down her face. Then, as quickly as the anger had overtaken her, it evaporated. She collapsed on top of Harvey, sobbing. Her whole body shook. Harvey wrapped his arms around her, blinked away the tears stinging his own eyes.

"I'm sorry, Rosa Jean. I'm so sorry."

Gradually, RJ's sobs quieted to silent mournful tears and stutter-breathed hiccups. Stormy peered out from the bedroom, her ears flat against her head. She crept toward the couple where they lay on the floor. The dog tucked in beside them, her ribs pressed against Harvey's, her chin rested on RJ's hip. RJ reached down and stroked the dog's head.

~~~

A memorial service was held two days later, though it was cut short when a duster rolled in from the north. The irony was not lost on the mourners.

The sheriff ruled her death an accident, allowing Ethel a Catholic burial as she would have wanted. But the windswept Vanham cemetery was in no condition to inter caskets. Ethel's sister in Ohio sent a telegram requesting that her casket be shipped there for burial. Everyone in Vanham chipped in whatever change they could spare to have her husband's casket removed from the cemetery and shipped along with Ethel's to Ohio. Mr. Meginnis had been the one to suggest it.

"They should rest together," he'd said, and everyone agreed.

RJ went to the train station the day the caskets were loaded. Edward's casket had the same weather-worn appearance that her parents' caskets had had the day she visited the cemetery, having been exposed to the sun by unrelenting wind and devastating erosion.
~~~

Ethel's casket rested beside his on the ground by the freight train, its polished russet wood and metal hinges glittering in the sun. RJ knelt down and placed her hand on the lid. The wind blew a flurry of dust across the train platform. *Why didn't you talk to me?*

RJ didn't want to be angry at her friend, but she was. Angry at Ethel for always being so encouraging and cheerful, for being so supportive and strong. Angry at Ethel for being so tightlipped about the deep sadness she had battled. Angry at her for giving up the fight. It was so clear to RJ now, just like Black Sunday had been so clear before the darkness consumed them all.

The freight loader stood silently behind her. RJ knew he wanted to load the caskets, keep the train on schedule. But it pained her to walk away from her friend, again, and for the final time. "I'm so sorry," she whispered.

"Miss Evans?" the young man finally spoke up. "We need to get these loaded now."

RJ stood and stepped back from the casket. The imprint of her hand remained in the sheen of dust that coated the wood.

"Hurry," she said, feeling a sudden sense of urgency for the caskets to be sealed in the freight car before the wind stole her handprint. She liked the idea of it staying with Ethel all the way to Ohio.

The men loaded the caskets and slid the freight car doors shut with a bang that made RJ jump. She took a few more steps back away from the tracks. After another minute or so, the whistle blew and the train lurched into motion.

Another gust of wind swept the platform. It was stronger than the last. It seemed to taunt RJ as the train disappeared into a cloud of dust down the line.

I told you, the wind snarled at her. It's too late. The damage has been done. The Earth is getting her revenge.

No. RJ shook her head at the wind. *I can fix this before anyone else is lost. It's not too late. It can't be too late.*

Spring danced into Vanham with warm breezes and a few light showers. After the terror of Black Sunday, it was as though Mother Earth was making amends.

Then, summer descended.

Once again, the farmers began to feel the Earth's wrath. The mercury soared. The clouds evaporated. Tender green sprouts that had begun to peek through the soil in May turned crisp and brown. The winds tore them from their homes and carried them far away.

Suffocating heat from a white hot sky pressed down on the land throughout the long days. The dark nights brought little relief. Folks moved their beds outside, or broke down and opened the windows they had carefully sealed to keep out the dust. They hoped a breeze might enable them to sleep, might justify the extra cleaning that would be required in the mornings. It didn't. They tossed and turned throughout the nights, sweating in the dust-filled air, and rose in the mornings exhausted and muddy.

Woody arrived at the lab in the morning as he always did, ready to work, if perhaps a bit less enthusiastically.

"Morning, RJ. Morning, Stormy," he said as he came in through the front door, his shirt already soaked through with sweat from the walk over.

"Morning," RJ said, without looking up from her work. She stood at the lab table hunched over several petri dishes of soil samples. With a dropper, she placed a small amount of water into one sample and mixed it with a flat, tapered metal rod. When the sample was pliable, she squeezed it between her thumb and forefinger to see if it would form a ribbon. She measured the length of the ribbon, and jotted some notes in her journal.

"Significant amount of clay," she muttered as she wrote. "Smooth feel. High silt content. No sand."

"Got any coffee?" Woody asked.

"On the stove."

There was no flame burning. The metal pot was cool to the touch.

"It's cold," Woody said.

"Oh? Sorry."

RJ wiped the mud from her fingers on the front of her overalls and moved on to examine the next soil sample. Woody watched her work another minute or two. He studied the dark puffy half-moons beneath her eyes.

"How long have you been up?" he asked.

"Huh? Oh, I don't know. A while, I guess." RJ glanced at him briefly, scratched at her gritty scalp, then turned back to her journal and scribbled a few more notes.

He set the cold coffee pot back down on the stove. His nose twinged at the ripeness of the room. Were those the same shirt and overalls she had been wearing yesterday?

"You look like you could use some sleep," Woody said. "Why don't you get cleaned up and rest for a bit while I wash the sample dishes and whatnot."

RJ shook her head, kept her bleary eyes trained on her work. "I'm not tired."

~~~

It went on like that for days.
~~~

RJ visited with the farmers, offering impassioned pleas for them to stick with the conservation techniques despite recent setbacks. She wrote lengthy reports to Washington, all but begging for more help in their all-out war against the dust. She stayed up late into the night scouring her old college textbooks and the latest science journals, searching for ideas, for answers.

Harvey called on her, but he couldn't pry her from her work. He didn't press her for an answer to his proposal, and she didn't bring it up. Take a break, he told her. Put on a pretty dress and come with me to the pictures, he said. After getting the brush-off a few times, he left her to her work. He shut the door with a bang on his way out, roared down the drive faster than he should have.

RJ took no notice. There was simply too much work to be done. Far too much to be goofing off at the pictures. Too much to bother with banalities like cooking or washing or sleeping.

Besides, work helped her to ignore how much she missed Ethel. It helped push back the shame she felt for not seeing how vulnerable her friend had been. Ethel had always seemed so wise, so strong. Invincible. In hindsight, RJ could see how Ethel's essence had been slowly worn away, just like the earth around them, until there was too little left to sustain her.

Woody understood. His sensitivity to numbers meant the slow destruction of life was thrust at him every day. From the millions of grains of dirt sailing away on the wind, to the pounds dropping from the frames of his neighbors, the constant decline pained him.

"Erosion takes its toll on more than just the land," he had said one day while they worked quietly in the lab. RJ had paused at her task, digesting his words. "Yes," she said after a moment, and then continued her report computations.

RJ needed to know that Ethel's death hadn't been for nothing. She came to believe the loss was a warning, a directive for her to work harder, to heal the land before anything else irreplaceable was lost forever.

And so Woody's patience with RJ's erratic behavior held out longer than Harvey's. But after he'd watched his friend survive on cold coffee and saltines for days on end, he could calculate the alarming toll it was taking on her. He pleaded with her once more to let him make her a hot supper, for her to take a cool bath and a long nap.

"Dammit, Woody, you work for me. Not the other way around."

Woody lurched backward as though he'd been struck. "Don't yell at me. I don't like it when people yell."

"If you don't like it, go home, Woody. I don't have time to baby you."

Woody's mouth drew tight. He retreated toward the door. RJ turned back to her work. Woody stared down at the floor for several minutes before he finally turned and left.

Harvey sat on the dead stump beside his porch until the sun dropped below the horizon and the sky turned dark. He looked up into the great beyond, straining to spot at least one star so he could make a wish, like he'd done when he was a boy. But the air was too thick with dust. The sky above was the same dark chocolate as the ground below.

When the wind began to blow and the dust began to pelt his skin, he went inside.

"I'm worried about RJ." That's what Woody had said to him earlier in the day. "She works too much."

Harvey had snorted and rolled his eyes. "Tell me something I don't already know."

So Woody had told him. "She never sleeps. She's always wearing the same clothes one day as she wore the day before. She ain't washed her hair or nothing in a week. And she hardly eats. Just drinks cold coffee all day long. A few times, I walked to her place in the middle of the night, 'cause I was worried, and her lamp was still burning in the lab. I saw her shadow moving past the window, so I know she didn't just fall asleep with it lit. When we're out gathering field samples, she can hardly catch her breath after walking a few hundred yards."

Harvey'd put up his hands in surrender then. He couldn't listen to any more of it. He sent Woody away with a promise he'd fix things.

I'm a damned fool, he'd thought after Woody left, and he'd been repeating that mantra in his head ever since. It pained him to think that Woody might be the better man. Harvey had been angry and hurt by RJ's behavior; he'd been sitting at home licking his wounds. And Woody had been nothing but worried about her.

"No wonder she didn't leap at the idea of marrying me," Harvey berated himself. He cursed himself for not swallowing his pride and going back over to see her days ago. Harvey paced the floor half the night, to come up with a plan to fix things like he'd said he would, to prove he was the better man.

In the morning, he drove to Dr. Miller's office.

"I need something that will knock her out, Doc. Something that will help her get some good solid sleep," Harvey said after explaining the situation.

Dr. Miller unlocked the medicine cabinet. He took out a bottle of barbital and poured a handful into a small envelope.

"Have Miss Evans take one of these about an hour before she goes to bed," he instructed.

"What if she won't take it?" Harvey asked.

The doctor studied him for a moment. No doubt Doc Miller had heard stories about the government woman – the bossy type, not the kind who readily did what she was told. "Best just break open a capsule and mix the powder in with her coffee. She'll be none the wiser and better off for it."

Harvey tucked the envelope in his shirt pocket and headed for RJ's place.

~~~

It had been more than a week since he'd seen RJ, and when she opened the door Harvey felt unsteady on his feet. It was as bad as Woody had warned, and then some.
~~~

"How's your work coming along, Rosa Jean?" Harvey asked and planted a kiss on her grimy cheek.

RJ didn't answer right away. She stood in the doorway, one hand still on the doorknob, the other on her hip. "You never ask me about my work."

Harvey looked down at his shoes.

"I know. I know, darlin', and I'm sorry for that," he said. "I've come to apologize."

RJ motioned for him to come in. She was quite busy, she said, typing up her recent notes to be sent off to D.C. She sat down behind her typewriter and began tapping away.

Harvey didn't want to disrupt her work, he assured, just wanted to spend some time with her. He offered to put up a fresh pot of coffee, and RJ said that'd be swell. A half hour later, she was slumped over her desk, out cold. Harvey carried her to her bed, removed her shoes, and peeled away her grimy overalls and cotton shirt.

He watched her, as she lay sleeping in her loose lacey bloomers and thin cotton brassiere, her chest gently rising and falling, a tiny pool of perspiration glistening in her navel. He stroked her cheek, then ran his fingers down her neck to her collarbone. He swallowed hard and then shook his head fiercely. *Behave yourself, Harvey*, his conscience told him.

Harvey retrieved a nightgown from RJ's trunk. He slipped it over her head, tucked in her arms and gently pulled the gown down over her torso and hips. Then, he gathered up her dirty clothes and headed to the wash basin.

~~~

RJ awoke eighteen hours later to the smell of canned ham and onions sizzling in the fry pan. She sat up in bed and swung her feet around to the freshly-swept floor. She fiddled with the hem of her nightgown. Her mind was a haze. When had she gone to bed? The
~~~

last thing she could remember was Harvey handing her a cup of coffee.

"How long was I asleep?" she asked as she emerged from the bedroom.

"As long as you needed to be, I reckon," Harvey said. "Have a seat. Breakfast is ready."

RJ rubbed at her sandpaper eyelids with her fingertips to work up some tears and get some relief. She still couldn't quite wrap her mind around what was happening, or what had happened. But there was one thing she knew for sure. She was ravenous.

When was the last time she'd eaten a decent meal? Not since Ethel had died, probably. RJ drank down the cup of canned milk Harvey had placed at her spot. She gobbled down the ham and onions and buttered toast.

The fog in her brain slowly started to lift. The events of the past few weeks began to flicker through her mind like a silent movie. Working all through the day without eating. Tossing and turning in bed, and getting back up to work through the night. Pushing Harvey away when he suggested the picture show. Snapping at poor Woody every time he urged her to take a break.

"It's good to see you eat, Rosa Jean." Harvey eased into conversation. "I've sure been worried about you."

RJ blew her bangs out of her eyes. She braced herself for the lecture she figured was coming next. She'd let him speak his mind, she decided. But she had no intention of allowing him to tell her how to do her job or live her life.

"You've been ornery as a mule," Harvey said. "More than usual, I mean."

"More than usual?" RJ couldn't help but chuckle. Some of the anxiety in her chest released. "That's pretty bad, I have to admit."

Harvey smiled at her, reached across the table and took her hand in his. He offered to refill her plate, get her more milk. She accepted. They sat quietly again, while RJ devoured her seconds.

Harvey drank his milk and watched her. After a bit, RJ wiped her mouth with a napkin and leaned back in her seat.

"What exactly happened last night?" she asked. "The last thing I can remember is you coming over and making coffee."

"That doesn't surprise me," he said. "You haven't been taking care of yourself."

Harvey told her he'd been worrying about her for weeks. He'd come over the day before to check in on her and she'd fallen asleep right at her typewriter while they were talking. So he'd tucked her into bed, did a little cleaning, and then slept on the couch so she wouldn't wake up alone. That's what he told her.

"And my clothes?" she asked.

"Yes," Harvey said. "I got you into your nightgown. Your clothes were a mess. I washed them for you, by the way."

RJ studied him for a moment. She inhaled deeply and let the air out slowly.

"I kept my eyes closed the whole time, Rosa Jean. I swear it."

She couldn't decide which was sillier – him lying about keeping his eyes closed, or her worrying about whether he'd seen her in her unmentionables. She rolled her eyes at him. The more she thought about it all, the more she softened. It really was sweet of him to take care of her.

"Thank you," she said, finally, and tucked her knees up beneath her nightgown. "You're a good man, Harvey Clay."

Harvey shook off the compliment and rose to clear the dishes from the table.

"It's true," she said. "Don't be modest about it. Nobody else stepped up the way you have to take care of me when I needed it most, even though I was at my worst."

He moved to the sink and tended to the remains of the meal. RJ moved beside him and planted a kiss on his cheek while he worked. Then, she returned to the bedroom to wash up and get dressed.

~~~

Harvey muttered at himself while he scrubbed the breakfast pan. Having RJ think of him as her knight in shining armor was a good thing. It's what he'd always wanted from her. Then why was he feeling prickles of guilt along the back of his neck. He'd walked the dishes to the sink, so she couldn't see the contradiction in his eyes when she'd said he was a good man.

Now he imagined himself in one of those short films he'd seen at the picture show. Harvey was a cartoon character with a tiny angel on one shoulder and a devil on the other.

Tell her it was Woody who knocked some sense into you, the angel told him. *He's the one she should be thanking.*

Bah, said the devil, *Woody didn't have the nerve to do what was best for her, what needed to be done. Don't tell her a damned thing.*
~~~

Woody sat at the kitchen table, preparing a snack of bread and jam, while his folks spoke in hushed tones in their bedroom. Little Alice had been sick for two weeks, and Doc Miller had just visited again. Woody strained his ears to make out bits and pieces of their conversation. And yet, a voice in his head was telling him he didn't want to know what they were saying.

The bedroom door opened, and Pa came out of the room, pulled the door shut behind him. Woody looked up. Pa gave him a strained smile.

"Woody, I need to talk with ya."

"Okay. I'm eating bread and jam. You want some?"

"Sure, son. Is that coffee on the stove still hot?"

Pa didn't wait for an answer. He poured himself a cup of cold coffee and pulled out the chair across from Woody to sit. He took a gulp of the bitter brew, puckered his lips as he swallowed it down. Then, he set the cup down on the table in front of him and stared into its shiny black surface.

"You know, your sister is mighty sick," he said, without looking up.

"I know."

Woody dipped a spoon into the jar of jam and removed a large glob of the raspberry sweetness. He plopped it onto a slice of bread, spreading it carefully and evenly to the edges with the back of the spoon. He handed the slice to Pa. "She gonna die?"

Pa looked up at Woody then, his eyes glassy. "No, Woody, she ain't gonna die. Your Ma and me won't let the happen."

He took the slice of bread from his son and took a giant bite.

Pa wasn't the type to make bold claims. He was a man of his word. If he said he wouldn't let Alice die, that was as good as gospel to Woody. The young man prepared another slice of bread for himself.

"Doc says she's got that dust pneumonia," Pa said.

Woody set down his bread. His faith took a stagger step back. Kids died when they got the dust pneumonia. Everybody knew that.

"What are you and Ma gonna do?"

"We've gotta get her away from this dust. It's her only chance."

Woody thought about that a moment. He took a bite of his bread.

"We're moving to Kansas City," Pa said. "There's no more point in fighting to hold on here, especially if it could cost us another child."

The creases along the farmer's forehead were softer than they'd been earlier. The taut muscles of his neck were slack. It was as if he was finally and truly resigned, and maybe a little bit at peace, with the idea of leaving the land his own pa had broken.

Woody remained quiet, chewed his bread and swallowed, took another bite.

"Your big sister says it's mighty nice up there in KC," Pa continued. "Says I can get me a job at that Fisher factory where her husband works. He's a manager there now. Does all the hiring."

"Fisher Body Corporation is owned by General Motors. GM bought sixty percent of Fisher in 1919 and the rest in 1926. That's when Fisher became a full in-house subsidiary of GM."

Pa took another drink of his cold coffee, set his mug down harder than he meant to. "Woody, please. I'm trying to tell you something here."

"Sorry," Woody said. "Just one more quick thing. The plant in KC makes integrated body parts, ones that can work on all different models of cars. Buicks. Even Cadillacs. Okay, that's all I got to say. Except, I still like Fords better. Okay, that's all. Sorry."

Pa let out a sigh. Smiled at his son, in spite of himself. Woody looked up and to the side the way he always did when he was trying to concentrate on what somebody else was saying.

"We'd like you to come with us, Woody. To KC."

"I don't like KC."

"You've never been," Pa said.

"That's the reason why I don't like it."

Pa chortled, shook his head a little. His son's response couldn't have been a surprise.

Woody dipped the spoon into the jam and prepared a second slice of bread. He pushed the back of the spoon to each corner and edge, right up to the crust, covering every spot of white with gooey red preserves. Pa watched.

"I know you don't like new things, son." Pa paused to collect his thoughts, bought some time by taking another drink of his cold coffee. "But you'd have your family with you in Kansas City. You wouldn't be alone. You'd get used to the place in no time."

Woody wrinkled up his nose, shook his head no. "No. I don't like the city."

The two sat in silence for some time. Pa finished up his coffee, sat staring into the empty mug. Woody ate the last of his bread, placed the lid back on the jar of jam.

"We have to go," Pa said. "You understand that, don't you? For Alice. Your ma and me, we have to."

"Sure, Pa. You have to do right by Alice. You have to go."

"What about you? Don't I have to do right by you, too? You're my only son. And I worry about you. I ain't ashamed to say it. I know you're a grown man."

Pa stopped to clear his throat. He rubbed at his burning eyes, then placed his palms down on the table. "I love you, Woody. You're strong and you've got a good heart. But I worry about you getting by."

Woody turned now and faced his father. The frank talk from a man who usually didn't go for big shows of emotion made his heart ache.

"I'll get by, Pa."

Pa looked Woody square in the eye. Even Woody could see the old man wanted to believe. His look seemed to plead, *tell me, son, tell me how*.

Woody looked up and away again, his mind running his entire life through like a projector at the picture show. When his life's story came to the past year or so, he smiled.

"I finally got me a job. A darn good one, too."

Pa nodded. Woody's job at the soil station probably paid better than the factory job Pa hoped to get.

"And I finally got me a friend," Woody added.

"A darn good one, too," Pa said.

Father and son smiled at one another. Then, their eyes parted ways. Pa looked down at his farmer hands resting on the table, studying the thick calluses and patent signs of age. Woody looked up at the dust particles hovering in the air, examining the golden flecks and spectral works of art.

Pa pushed his chair back away from the table and stood up. "I'll go tell Ma."

Harvey had come to RJ's place early Sunday morning, and she'd made him a hearty breakfast of biscuits and eggs. They needed extra energy to once again disassemble and clean the tractor engine.

Out in the barn, the air was already stifling hot. Harvey propped open the doors in the front and the window shutters at the back to create a cross breeze. But the air was uncharacteristically still.

"Don't that just figure." Harvey muttered as he wiped his dripping forehead with his handkerchief.

"What's that?" RJ asked.

"That damned wind seems to blow nonstop 'round here. Until you'd just about kill for a breeze. And then there's nothing."

RJ agreed. She rolled a red bandanna and tied it around her neck to sop up the sweat.

Harvey leaned over the tractor engine and pried loose a bolt. RJ handed him the gasket scraper. Her mind traveled back to the first time they had worked on the engine together. Somewhere along the line, she'd let go of her stubbornness, had come to appreciate the muscle he was eager to put into work like this. She watched him work and sweat, and her heart thumped harder in her chest.

"Hand me that wire brush, would you?" he said.

RJ stared at him a moment. Harvey turned his head to look at her. "Rosa Jean? The brush?"

She still didn't move.

"What's gotten into you?" he said, making a goofy face at her.

Harvey shook his head and reached for the brush himself. He began scrubbing the dirt and gunk from the gaskets and rods. RJ placed her hand on his to stop him, knelt down beside him.

"I love you so much," she said. Her voice cracked a bit and she swallowed hard. Harvey set down his tools, worry stitched across his brow.

"Is something wrong?" he asked, surprised by her uncharacteristic declaration.

"Not a thing." She smiled wide at him, her eyes brimming with tears. "Harvey, do you still want to marry me?"

"Well, that's a damned stupid question." Harvey pulled RJ to her feet so he could look her in the eye. "Of course I do."

"Then my answer is yes."

He hooted and picked RJ up, swung her around. She threw her head back and laughed. They wrapped their arms around each other. Harvey set her feet back on the ground and leaned in to kiss her square on the mouth, hard. They were winded, giddy. He pulled back a moment and smiled at her. Then, he leaned in again for another kiss, this time tender, intense.

All at once their giddiness shifted into something more serious, something instinctive, carnal. Harvey's kiss lingered. RJ parted her lips to accept his gently searching tongue. She reached her hands up behind his head, scrunched his hair up in her fingers. His lips moved from her mouth to her neck, his hands down her back. He pulled her hips tight against him, and RJ gasped with surprised delight. It was more than Harvey could stand.

He lowered her to the ground and laid her back into the soft dirt. His arms trembled slightly as he held his body above hers. RJ raised her lips to his again. He pressed his pelvis to hers, and they began to move in rhythm together, rocking as one through their dusty, sweaty layers of cotton and denim.

All at once, the ecstasy was too intense. RJ's body quivered and her stomach tightened. She bit her lip and cried out in gratification.

"Oh, Rosa Jean. Oh, God." Harvey moaned, pressed hard against her in one final thrust. He drew her body to him tight and shuddered.

They lay side by side on the dirt floor of the barn for several minutes, quietly relishing their rapture.

"Well," RJ said after a bit, "I guess it's official."

"If you think *that's* what makes it official, you're in for quite a pleasant surprise on our wedding night."

"Harvey!" RJ blushed and playfully hit his chest. Harvey laughed, pulled her close and sighed.

~~~

Later, after they'd cleaned and reassembled the tractor engine, RJ and Harvey washed up and prepared dinner. She was ravenous. But Harvey seemed to be hungry for things other than food. He spoke of their future together, words and ideas and plans pouring from him like grain from a silo, tumbling and piling up and amassing in a giant mountain. Getting hitched, adding a woman's touch to his place, having children, teaching sons to sow and reap, watching daughters learn to sew and cook. The larger Harvey's pile of plans became, the quieter RJ became, as though she were being smothered by the heft of its consequence.

Finally, Harvey took notice of RJ's detachment. He stopped talking, stopped eating, looked at her with concern.

"What's the matter, Rosa Jean?"

"Hmm? What? Nothing's the matter."

Harvey exhaled noisily. His shoulders slumped. He shook his head slowly. "You don't want to get married."
~~~

He dropped his knife and fork onto his plate, clasped his hands together in front of his face.

"No, Harvey. That's not it. Honestly. I do. I do want to get married."

She reached for his hands, pulled them toward her. Her mind reeled as she searched for words that would be simple, direct, logical. Words that wouldn't break Harvey's heart.

"But?" he said.

"Just not right away," she said. "So much is going to change once we're married, and I just need some time to get organized."

"What on earth do you need to organize?"

"Well..." she paused. "For one thing, I need to figure out how to do my work at the soil lab if I'm living at your place. Would I spend the week at the lab and go home on the weekends, or would I drive back and forth every day? Maybe I could bring my typewriter to your place and write up my reports there, to give us more time together."

Now RJ was the one whose words and ideas were charging forth, abundant and feral. Harvey pulled his hands from hers and leaned back in his chair.

"Why would you keep working at the lab? You don't think I'm capable of taking care of you, of supporting a family?" He hesitated, shook his head. "You don't believe in me."

Harvey was shrinking before her eyes, crumbling into himself as though she'd sucker punched him right in the gut. How could such a strong man be so easily hurt? So swiftly cut down by the woman he loved?

"Harvey, no. Sweetheart, that's not it. I *do* believe in you."

"Then, what in the hell are you talking about?" Heat tinged his voice now. He was no longer simply hurt. He was angry.

"It's just that... the work I'm doing is important to me. You know that. I'm not ready to give it up. There's still so much that needs to be done to make things right, to heal the land, to help get people like the Tugwells and the Sharps back on their feet."

RJ looked at him intently as she spoke, trying to inject her words deep into his veins, so her dreams could pulse through him the same way they pulsed through her.

He met her gaze. They were quiet for a moment.

"And that's more important to you than being my wife?"

"Can't it all be important to me? I shouldn't have to choose."

He stood and walked away from the table, slipped back to being more hurt than angry. RJ's stomach drew tight, knotted.

"I just need a little time." She spoke softer, stood and went to him. She placed her hands on his cheeks and leaned her body against his, her pelvis pressing into his.

Harvey looked at her, searched every feature of her face. He brought his hands to her hips, pulled her tighter against him. She raised up on her tiptoes and kissed him, tender at first, then hard. They embraced with new intensity.

"We'll figure all this out," RJ whispered in his ear. "I promise. We'll be together. And we'll be the happiest two people on Earth."

He buried his face in her freshly washed hair, inhaled deeply. Fear gripped him, fear that she might never truly be his, and so he gripped her tighter still.

The afternoon winds kicked up as they generally did, sweeping a suffocating cloud of dust along the fields and across the roads. RJ and Woody decided to stay indoors and tend to some paperwork they'd been neglecting.

RJ sat at her small desk, huddled over her typewriter, bleary-eyed in the faint light of the oil lamp. Her fingers flittered over the keys, click, click, clack, click, clack. Ding. Zip. Click, click, clack.

Woody worked in sync with the rhythm of RJ's typing, talking through the steps of his task as he put the carbon copies of the weekly reports in chronological order. March, April, June, he said. And this here is January. April, April. June. How'd these reports get so mixed up, anyhow? December, December, March.

When he'd gotten the reports in order, he tucked them into large manila envelopes, one quarter each. January, February, March, he said, and wrote Q1 1935 on the brown paper.

"I got all the reports in order," he said, addressing RJ, rather than just muttering to himself. She had become accustomed to the difference in his voice when he was speaking to her versus simply speaking.

"That was fast," she said. "Maybe tackle washing those beakers next?"

"Okay."

Woody pumped some water and put it on the stove to heat. He retrieved the wash basins from beneath the worktable, filled each a quarter of the way with water. One for washing. One for rinsing.

"Alice is sick," he said. "My family is moving to Kansas City."

He added soap to the first basin, then poured hot water from the stove into each, watched the steam rise and comingle with the dust in the air.

RJ was clacking away at the typewriter. She stopped, scrunched her eyebrows. "What did you just say?"

"Alice is sick. My family is moving to Kansas City."

"What?" RJ turned in her chair to face Woody at the sink. She was taken aback.

"Alice is sick," Woody began to repeat again.

"No, no, Woody. Stop. I heard you that time. I'm just surprised."

"Oh." Woody looked down at the sudsy water. Softly, he finished his statement. "My family is moving to Kansas City."

RJ rose from her chair and moved to stand beside him. Woody submerged the dirty beakers into the water, one at a time. RJ watched silently while he worked.

"What are you going to do?" she asked after a bit.

"Same thing I always do."

Woody swished the dishrag along the outside of a beaker, then gently pushed the rag inside the fragile glass and twisted it around and around. He dipped the beaker into the tub of rinse water, lifted it out and shook off the excess droplets. RJ handed him a clean dry towel. "Will you be moving, too?"

Woody shook his head. "I already told you, I'll be doing the same thing I always do. Living in Vanham. Working here with you."

RJ smiled with relief. The idea of losing another friend so soon after Ethel created a weight in her chest worse than running through a duster with no mask.

Then, it struck her how selfish she was being. Alice must be mighty sick for Woody's parents to up and move away, knowing their son likely wouldn't have the capacity to go with them.

"Your folks must be beside themselves with worry," RJ said.

"Yes. They say she's got that dust pneumonia. Getting her out of this damned dust is the only way she's got a shot. Ma said she won't lose another child, not while she's got a heart beating in her own chest and can do something to stop it."

RJ clenched her teeth. She could hear Olive saying those exact words, just as Woody had recited.

"Will you take on a hand to help with the house and land?" RJ asked.

"No. Bank's coming for all that any day anyhow. Pa said just let 'em take it. It don't matter no more."

That knocked the wind from RJ's lungs. Her mind returned to one of her first conversations with Woody, when he'd explained the locals' anger toward her at the penny auction. *Those banker sons-a-bitches.*

"Where will you live?"

Woody said he figured he'd rent a room in town. The motel was near always empty, so Mr. Rothstein would probably work a deal with him on a monthly rate.

RJ shook her head again. "You can't walk back and forth from here to town every day. It's too far. And too dangerous with the dusters coming through the way they've been."

She stopped and was quiet for a while. Woody just shrugged and continued washing out the beakers. Swish, rinse, dry. Swish, rinse, dry.

"You should live here," RJ said after a moment, nodding decisively. "We can fix up a nice spot for you in the barn loft. When the dusters hit, you'll take cover in here."

Woody placed the last beaker on the tray, wiped his hands dry on the towel. "Okay."

~~~

Harvey paced his kitchen, leaving a path in the dust on the floor.

"Have you lost your God-blessed mind, Rosa Jean?"

RJ stood with her arms folded across her chest, leaned her weight back against the sink basin. She said nothing. She simply watched Harvey march back and forth.

After a few more silent laps, he spoke again. "It ain't proper, having a man living with you."

RJ blew the bangs away from her eyes. She watched and waited a bit longer. When it seemed like he'd said all he could think of to say, RJ finally responded. "Lots of farmers have hired hands living on their property."

Harvey halted in his tracks, turned to face her. His eyebrows were cockeyed, his mouth fell open. "This ain't the same thing, Rosa Jean."

She wanted to tell him to close his mouth before he caught some flies, but she restrained herself.

"I'll fix up a room for him in the barn loft," she said. "We won't even be sleeping under the same roof."

Harvey shook his head. It was his turn to be silent. But RJ knew exactly what was going through his mind. It was true many farmers offered room and board to their workers, but she was a woman, a single woman. And people already gossiped about her driving around calling on the farmers when their wives were away. It was written all over his face.

"Harvey." She paused a moment, walked to him and took his hands in hers. "I know what people say about me. I hear the whispers."

His face contorted. "Then, how can you even suggest this? It'll only add fuel to the fire."

"Let 'em talk. I don't care anymore what they think of me," RJ said. "I *do* care what you think. And I figured you'd like the idea
~~~

of Woody living at the lab. Then, you wouldn't have to worry about me being alone."

Harvey's posture softened. Knowing Woody was just a stone's throw away would put his mind at ease. And everyone knew Woody would run into a burning building if he thought RJ was inside and needed help.

Still, Harvey was so stuck on tradition. The conflict in his expression was obvious. Harvey didn't like the idea of marrying a woman with a reputation, even if that reputation was pure gossip, a fabrication of petty minds.

RJ's mind raced with thoughts, searching for a way to sway him. Then an idea struck her.

"And the best part," she said, "is after we're married, I can move in with you here and Woody can move into the lab and take care of things there. That means we'll have more time together, just the two of us."

He melted a little more, and RJ could feel the scale tipping in her favor. She smiled at him and wiggled her eyebrows up and down. "*If* you know what I mean."

Harvey laughed and pulled her into a bear hug. "All right. You win, darlin'. You have my permission to move Woody into the barn."

RJ hugged him back and kissed his neck. *I wasn't asking for your permission*, she thought. *But I'm glad you see things my way.*

RJ pulled up the road to the Parkers' place. Woody was loading trunks and boxes of clothes and kitchen things into the Dodge sedan Pa had bought the day before. Ma was supervising. Woody had told RJ the family would have to leave behind most of their things. They could have brought more if they'd gotten a truck, but the car would allow Alice to lie down in the back seat for the long drive to Kansas City. Alice's comfort was more important than furniture and thingamabobs. At least, that's what Ma had said. And nobody argued with Ma.

RJ stepped out of her truck and waved to the family. Ma and Woody waved back. Pa emerged from the house, his arms loaded down, and gave her a nod. The family was eerily quiet. Even Woody. They were like a bright gurgling stream that had run dry. RJ was parched from the loss of their voices.

"Anything I can do to help?" RJ asked as she walked up.

"Naw," Woody said.

Pa tugged a rope over the mattress and boxes they had stacked on the roof.

Ma surveyed the car, pointed at a box here and a rope there. They all watched as Pa secured the last of the cargo. Then, they all stood silent for a moment more. Ma looked over the car again. Pa stuffed his hands in his pockets and inspected his boots. Woody looked up and away, and RJ kept him in her sights.

"Welp," Pa said at last. "I suppose that's everything. Don't you think, Ma?"

Ma agreed silently.

"I'll just go gather up Alice then," Pa said. He turned and headed back into the house.

Ma turned her attention to Woody. Her body tensed and she squeezed her hands together at her stomach.

RJ wondered what it must feel like for Olive to leave her only son behind. She realized the anguish her own mother must have felt in sending RJ away to live with her aunt and uncle. Growing up, she had never really considered her parents' anguish, only her own. A wave of guilt, of this sudden understanding, made today's events all the more painful.

Olive's intense desire to grip her son, to pull him to her, was obvious. And yet, RJ knew as well as Olive that doing so would make the parting that much harder on Woody. So Olive bore the pain alone.

"You take care now," Olive said. "Make sure you cut your nails when they get too long."

"Yes, ma'am."

Olive sniffed and cleared her throat. She flicked a tear from her cheek.

"And comb your hair every morning, so it don't get all knotted up."

"I'll be all right, Ma. You don't need to worry 'bout me."

That was more than Olive could take. She reached for Woody and embraced him. He stood stiffly, arms pinned to his sides, but he did not pull away. The embrace lasted only a heartbeat. Olive withdrew and brushed another tear from her face.

Then, Olive turned to RJ and drew her into a hug. RJ hadn't expected it, but she returned the embrace. The women held each other for a long time. RJ rubbed Olive's back.

"You'll look out for him?" Olive whispered.

"Of course I will."

Olive pulled back and looked RJ square in the eyes. She kept her hands at RJ's shoulders.

"I can't tell you how thankful I am that you came into our lives."

RJ wanted to tell Olive she felt the same way, but she couldn't speak. Her eyes burned and she blinked hard. Olive understood. The women embraced again, and RJ felt something tear open deep inside of her. She was eight years old again, losing her family for the second time.

Pa came out of the house carrying Alice, who was wrapped up in a quilt. The girl clutched her rag doll to her chest, rested her head on Pa's shoulder.

"Open the door," Pa said, and Woody quickly obeyed.

Pa crouched slowly and eased his little girl into the back seat. She whimpered softly, and then asked for Woody.

Woody hustled back to the open car door, folded his lanky body to lean in.

"Here I am."

Alice tried to speak, but was cut off by a fitful cough that shook her entire body.

"That's okay," Woody said when she quieted. "You don't have to say nothing. I know you're gonna miss me."

Alice smiled. Olive gave Woody a poke in his ribs.

"And I'm gonna miss you, too," Woody added. "Lots. You know that."

"I know," Alice whispered. "Will you visit me?"

Woody flinched as though she'd struck him.

"That's okay. You don't have to," Alice said and patted his hand. "I'll come back and visit you as soon as I'm better."

Woody let out a sigh of relief and smiled. "I'd like that. I'd like that a lot."

Alice tried to say something more, but was overcome with another bone-rattling cough.

That's when Pa spoke up and said it was time they got going. Woody backed out of the car and gently shut the door. He patted Olive on the back and opened the front door for her.

"Bye, Ma," he said after she had climbed in. He turned to Pa and held out his hand. "Bye, Pa."

The old man emitted a guttural sound and grabbed hold of his son. He pulled Woody into a bear hug. A long one. Woody tolerated it as long as he could and began to squirm to break free. Pa just laughed and held tight. After clinging to his boy just a bit longer, the old man stepped back and wiped his nose with his sleeve. "You behave yourself."

"Yes, sir," Woody said.

Pa turned to RJ and extended his hand to shake hers. RJ shook her head and pulled him in for a hug. He laughed and blinked a tear onto her cheek.

"Woody'll be all right," RJ whispered to him. "I'll see to it."

They broke their embrace. Pa coughed and climbed into the driver's seat. He fired up the engine and slowly drove down the drive so as not to stir up too much dust. RJ and Woody stood side by side and watched the car pull onto the road and disappear in the distant amber haze.

The August Farmers Union meeting was a disaster, and yet it was one of the most fruitful for RJ. After a brutally hot summer, the farmers were losing hope for rain in the fall. RJ encouraged them to continue replowing their fields after the dusters to help conserve what soil they had left. She talked a few into strip cropping, yet again, grass seed and winter wheat just in case the rain did come. She saw no spark of hope in their eyes. Still, some agreed, and those who refused did so with less venom than they had in the past.

For the first time, RJ felt like she belonged there, like she was on equal footing. Shared tragedy, it seemed, had a way of burying differences and bringing people together in their pain.

After the meeting adjourned, everyone poured out of the Town Hall and meandered down the street toward the Feed & Seed lot for the potluck. The women had the tables set with casseroles, salads, biscuits, cakes, pies. There were jars of pickles, jugs of lemonade.

Harvey winked at RJ and walked off with a group of men to continue talking about the weather and the price of seed. RJ smiled at him and wandered over to the buffet tables.

"Is there anything I can do to help?" she asked.

Mrs. Sharp was rearranging the food on the table – salads at one end, hot dishes together in the middle, desserts at the other end. She shook her head at RJ.

"No, thank you," she said, sliding one dish this way and another one that way. "We've got it covered."

"All right," RJ said. She glanced from the table, to the farmers, and back to the food.

"Why don't you grab yourself a plate and dig in," Mrs. Sharp said, just as RJ was turning to walk away.

"Oh," RJ was taken aback by the invitation. "Shouldn't I let the men go first?"

"Way I see it, you work just like a man," Mrs. Sharp said with a matter-of-fact air. "You ought to get some of the benefits."

RJ picked up a plate and asked which dish Mrs. Sharp had contributed. Then, she scooped up a healthy helping of the woman's famous hamburger pie, a way of saying thank you among women that meant more than words.

She worked her way down the line, and the men started filing in behind her. Mr. Meginnis led the group, piling his plate high with rabbit meat and corn muffins, scalloped peas and creamed onions.

"I hear you and Harvey is finally engaged," he said to RJ as they surveyed the spread side by side. She braced herself for some snide remark.

"That's real nice. You two make a fine couple."

RJ dropped the serving spoon into the scalloped peas, sending splatters of sauce onto the tablecloth. She felt her cheeks burn as she used her napkin to dab up the mess. Mr. Meginnis laughed from deep in his large belly.

"That'd be my fault, girly," he said. "Didn't mean to startle you with kindness."

RJ laughed, too, and gave him a sock in the arm.

"All right now you two," Mrs. Sharp said. "Break it up and move it along. The line's backing up."

RJ finished filling her plate and scanned the crowd for Harvey. He was still with his group, listening intently and chewing on his empty pipe as one of the farmers pantomimed his story.

"RJ, over here!" Woody waved to her from a table at the edge of the gathering. He sat alone, and the sight of it caused a sharp jab in RJ's gut. She understood the pain of losing one's family. Woody wasn't exactly an orphan, but in some ways the loss he suffered when his family moved away was harder to bear. She smiled at him broadly and hurried to join him.

"Thanks for saving us some seats, Woody," RJ said and sat down beside him.

Woody hunched over his food, his arms resting on the table circling the plate as if he were guarding it from predators. He filled his mouth with beans and took a swig of water while he chewed.

RJ tried to divert her attention away from him. It wasn't her place to correct Woody, she knew. He was a grown man. And yet he ate like a ravenous child. Didn't Olive teach him proper etiquette? To keep his elbows off the table? Not to speak with his mouth full? Of course the woman must have tried, RJ knew. She also knew you had to choose your battles with Woody. Heck, you had to choose your battles with everyone. But Woody was so smart, and handsome in his own way. He'd have himself a nice girl if he'd only fix some of his odd behaviors and poor manners.

Harvey joined them at the table, sitting on the other side of RJ. They all chatted and ate and laughed. Folks dropped by their table from time to time to offer their congratulations to the couple on their upcoming marriage. RJ couldn't help but notice the other seats at their table remained empty.

They fell into a comfortable silence as they finished off their lemonade and pie. The potluck crowd began to quiet down and thin out. The women started packing up the leftovers. When

Woody had cleaned his plate, he looked around, then looked at his friends and smiled.

“It’s just like you said a while back, Harv. We’re the Three Musketeers.”

A black two-door sedan rumbled up RJ's drive. She craned her neck looking out the window, struggling to see through the dust that now enveloped the vehicle as it stopped in front of the lab. A man in a dark-colored suit and wingtip shoes emerged from the driver's side door. He coughed and then sneezed and coughed again.

RJ grinned. "City slicker."

The man began to approach the house when Stormy charged from around the side, bellowed one warning bark, and stood in his path. She did not growl, but her posture was stiff and the muscles in her back quivered. The man in the suit seemed hesitant to test her mood.

"Hello," he shouted toward the lab.

RJ huffed, set down the beaker she had been cleaning and walked outside.

"Stormy, come." She called out from the front porch and the dog about-faced, ran to RJ's side and sat at attention. "You lost, sir?"

"No, ma'am, I don't believe so. I'm looking for Mr. Evans. I'm from the U.S. Department of the Interior."

"I see," RJ said, reaching down to scratch between Stormy's ears. After a brief pause, she added, "There's no Mr. Evans here. But if you're looking for RJ Evans, you're in the right place."

The man drew his eyebrows together, thrust his chin forward. "Miss, I'm looking for the man who runs the Soil Conservation Lab."

She stepped down off the porch, extended her hand. "Once again, you're in the right place. I'm RJ Evans. And you are?"

He shook her hand hesitantly, with the firmness of a dead fish. He stammered his name, Mr. Baylor. RJ smiled and welcomed him inside. She offered him a drink of water and a seat at the table. He lifted the beverage to his lips with a shaky hand. RJ worried over the man, and even Stormy softened to him.

"It takes some getting used to," RJ said. "The dust."

"Yes." He coughed again after he had downed the glass of water.

"So what brings you out, Mr. Baylor?"

He explained that since Black Sunday in April, President Roosevelt and Mr. Bennett in the Soil Conservation Service had dispatched men from D.C. to pay visits on the various soil conservation labs throughout the Great Plains to get a firsthand view of the battle they fought. Word of the devastation and loss had become all the more troubling when those in the East had gotten a taste of the dusters that folks on the plains endured on a regular basis.

"That's welcome news," RJ said. "It's hard to convey in my weekly reports, hard to give proper credit to the mettle of the folks around here."

Mr. Baylor nodded. He commented on how impressed he had been with her reports. Then he paused. He looked around the lab, seemed lost in contemplation.

"So you're the RJ Evans who attended the University of Wisconsin? You've been running the lab here? There's no other RJ Evans?"

RJ smirked, remained quiet for a moment. "Yes, yes and no," she said finally, then offered him a refill of his water.

He took his time with this glassful. RJ went back to cleaning. She had assumed he was rattled by the dust. She now understood he was rattled by her being a Miss instead of a Mister. It had been a while since RJ had had to deal with such nonsense. She had almost forgotten it still existed. *Just give him some time,* she thought. *Let it settle with him.*

After another minute or two had passed, RJ broke the silence. "I can give you a tour of the lab if you'd like. Show you the nursery. Take you out in the fields to see how we've used the lister plow to create terraces and contours."

Mr. Baylor blinked, snapped out of his trance and stood up. A tour of the operations was precisely the reason for his visit, he said.

"Excellent," RJ said. She took a set of goggles from the hook by the door and pulled a bandana from the drawer. She handed them both to Mr. Baylor. "You'll want these. Unless you've brought your own?"

He said that he hadn't any and accepted hers gratefully. RJ explained it would be best to tour the outside areas first, while the morning winds were still light. They donned their protective gear and headed outside. Mr. Baylor watched as RJ swept off the truck windows and cleared inside the engine. He raised his eyebrows with revelation. "I guess I need a broom, as well."

RJ smiled. "You figure things out as you go. Is this the first plains station you've visited?"

He said it was not, and she said she was surprised that the others hadn't helped him prepare for safer travels.

"I'll get you stocked up later, before you head out again. Goggles, mask, broom, water, shovel, the works. You'll never make it to your next stop if you get caught in a duster without them."

They drove past several of the properties of which RJ was most proud. The Clay farm, Tugwells and Sharps.

“These farmers have really embraced our conservation techniques, even though, without the rain, they haven’t yet reaped the benefits,” RJ said. “Still, they’re out there in the fields nearly every day, plowing dust, rebuilding the contours after the wind breaks them down.”

When they returned to the lab, RJ introduced Mr. Baylor to Woody. She showed the D.C. visitor the small nursery they’d built to protect the variety of grass seedlings they hoped to transplant to the fields if and when the rains came. Inside, she explained their daily routine of cleaning and covering to fight back the dust. She showed him how they’d sealed the tiny cracks and gaps in the walls, doorframes and windowsills with paste to keep out the dust.

“Somehow, it still finds its way in,” RJ said, running her finger along the table, drawing a line in the dust. “It’s fine as flour. Just works its way in through cracks too fine for the naked eye. The dust is everywhere. All the time.”

Mr. Baylor shook his head, taking it all in. The goggles and masks. The fields of dunes where wheat once flourished. The daily cleaning and sweeping and scrubbing before any scientific work could be done.

“How on earth do you keep from going mad?”

Woody and RJ exchanged glances.

“Not everyone does,” Woody said, looking down at his feet. He mumbled good-bye and slipped out the door.

Mr. Baylor watched Woody exit. He turned to RJ and asked, “Is he? Well, what I mean to say is, is that man all together?”

“Woody’s perfect,” RJ responded, perhaps a little too sharply. She swallowed hard. “It’s just that we’ve lost so many good people. To the black blizzards. To dust pneumonia. To despair. Those who remain keep working, keep fighting, keep waiting – for the rain, for some relief. But none of us are really ‘all together.’ Not anymore.”

RJ looked away. Mr. Baylor studied her for a moment, then followed her gaze out the kitchen window. Beyond the garden, Woody paced back and forth in the dirt, talking to himself.

RJ told Harvey all about the surprise visitor from Washington. It was exciting, she said, serving up their dinner as Harvey flipped the plates over on the table. She hoped the man's visit meant they would get more support from the government for their conservation programs, more relief for the folks in Vanham.

"I think I made a good impression on him," she said, "especially when I put together an emergency duster kit for his car. Can you believe he didn't even have a pair of goggles?"

Harvey said he couldn't believe it, and that Mr. Baylor was a lucky man to have crossed paths with her. Then he told her he had gotten some good news of his own that day.

"Tell me." RJ smiled at him and set her fork down to give Harvey her undivided attention.

"I got a letter from my brother Ben, up in Wichita," he said. "The factory he's working at up there just got some big new contract, and he said they're looking to hire another twenty men."

RJ raised her eyebrows. She worked hard at keeping her smile alive. She knew what was coming next.

"He said he could get me one of those jobs, no problem, if I wanted…"

Harvey's voice trailed off. He looked at RJ across the table, his eyes pleading.

"Ben says Wichita is real nice." Harvey dove back in, pulling the letter from his pocket and unfolding it. "He wrote, 'There's a nice little school not three blocks from our house. I bet your Rosa Jean could get a teaching job there, if she wanted. Wouldn't it be fun having her be your niece's school teacher?'"

Harvey looked up at RJ again, smiling.

"Oh, Harvey." RJ sighed.

"Wouldn't you have fun spending time with the little ones?" Harvey asked. "You like children."

"Of course I like children." RJ shook her head and sighed again. "But I'm not a school teacher. I'm a geologist, a scientist. And I already have a job that I like right here."

Harvey rubbed at his jaw. Then, he folded the letter and tucked it back in his pocket.

"It sure was nice of Ben to think of me, though," RJ said. "I like the idea of having a brother, once we're married."

She stood and walked around to Harvey's side of the table. She ran her fingers through his hair, smiled at him. He smiled stiffly. Then, he took hold of her waist and pulled her onto his lap. She laughed and kissed his ear.

"Some days, it feels like work just to breathe." RJ and Woody were cleaning the lab together, though she was talking more to herself than to Woody.

"It's the dust," Woody said.

It was true most people in Vanham had trouble catching their breath anymore. Their throats and eyes were always red and raw from the dust. Everyone had a cough they couldn't seem to shake. But that's not what RJ meant.

"No," she paused to think a moment. "It's not the dust. It's life. All the things I want to say and do. All the things I can't say and do. It's like I'm lying beneath a giant mound of dirt and everyone around me just keeps tossing shovelfuls onto the pile."

"Oh," Woody said. "I know what you mean."

"Do you?" There was no meanness in her voice, but RJ was surprised that Woody understood her analogy so readily. Even as she was saying it, she had been expecting him to take her literally, to question the lack of an actual dirt mound.

"Sure, I do," Woody asserted. "I feel that way too, most times. But it ain't dirt piled on. It's numbers."

RJ set down the rag she was using to clean her typewriter hammers and turned to look at Woody.

"You can't breathe because you have numbers piled on you?" Her tone was incredulous.

"Well, not literally," Woody said with some frustration. "It's a *metaphor*, RJ."

The tables had turned on them, and it made RJ laugh. Woody just smiled and continued wiping down the lab equipment.

"Okay, Woody, it's your turn to explain the metaphor. I'm afraid it's beyond me."

"You see things in your head like a pile of dirt. I see things as numbers," he said. "Some numbers are happy, some are angry. Some are light, others are heavy."

When folks make jokes about me and laugh, he continued, and I don't understand why they're laughing, that's a three. Three isn't super heavy, but it's odd shaped; it don't connect to itself at all. And it happens a lot, so those threes just pile up. When my ma hears folks laughing at me and it makes her sad, that's a big old nine sitting right on my chest. Heavy and upside down.

Woody paused a moment to take a deep labored breath, as though just talking about the numbers added to their weight. Eights are horrible. Double the weight, and all linked up, around and around in an endless loop. The eights pile up when I start thinking about all the things I want to do and say, but can't do and say. Just like you were saying.

Zeros are nice, he said. Open and light. Sometimes zeros will come along just when I'm feeling weighed down, and then I feel lighter. Like when Stormy smiles at me, a zero pops up in front of an eight and makes it go away. And when you gave me this job, it was like a hundred zeros popped up all around me, making the air light and open, giving me space to breathe again.

RJ leaned back in her chair as Woody spoke. She crossed her arms over her chest, watched him intently. *Who thinks in numbers this way?* She closed her eyes and tried to picture them as he in explained their weight.

"What's a four?" she asked.

"Fours are funny. They make me laugh."

"And twos?"

"Twos are complicated. I get lots of twos pulling me down when I'm confused about something. Like when someone says one thing, but really means something else, and they think I should know what they mean and I don't. Like when I was little and I'd get mad, and I'd pick something up and just smash it – maybe a plate or something like that. And then Ma or Pa or my teacher would say, 'Do you feel better now?' And I'd say yes, I do. And they'd get mad, because they really didn't want to know if I felt better. They really wanted me to say no and to say I was sorry, even though I wasn't. Boy, I had a lot of twos crowding me when I was little."

RJ smiled lightly and shook her head. "Sometimes you take my breath away, Woody. You really do."

"I'm sorry."

"No," RJ said and laughed. "In this case, I mean it in a good way. It's not like being buried beneath a pile of dirt. It's like running through a field of soft grass on a warm, blue-sky day. That kind of breathless."

"Oh, you mean like a cloud of zeros."

"Yes," she said, and swallowed hard to contain her emotion. "You're my cloud of zeros, Woody."

September 1935

RJ navigated the familiar road from town back to the soil conservation station, though road had become a mighty generous term.

Folks did their best to plow the dirt off the roads, to clear the dunes that collected along their fences and outbuildings, after the storms. Nonetheless, driving anywhere had become a daily adventure of traversing ruts and ridges. Every now and then, people would have to stop their vehicles, get out and shovel a path in the road to get through. Flat tires were a frequent annoyance.

These new travel challenges meant that Woody now accompanied RJ to town for her weekly errands. It was easier to clear the road and change flat tires as a team. So far today, however, they had been lucky enough to avoid both. RJ decided to take advantage of their good fortune and drive a bit out of their way.

"I'm going to drive past the Tugwell farm," she said. "I want to check and see if Ernie's had any luck keeping the field contours in place with all the dusters we've had rolling through."

"Okay," Woody responded.

RJ made a left and headed down the road past the Thomason farm. The wind blew a sheet of dust across the road, then settled down. A flutter along the barbed wire fence caught her eye. RJ slowed a bit to get a closer look.

"What on earth is hanging all along Mr. Thomason's fence?" she asked. "It looks like... I don't know..."

"Snakes," Woody said.

"Snakes?"

"Yes."

The snakes lay draped over the barbed wired, in various stages of decay, spaced ten or so yards apart. RJ shuddered.

"Why in heaven's name does Mr. Thomason have dead snakes hanging all up and down his fence?" she asked.

"His wife is Cherokee," Woody said.

RJ waited for Woody to continue with a lengthy explanation about why Mrs. Thomason being Cherokee was relevant. But he did not. They drove in silence a moment more. RJ glanced his way. Woody watched the landscape go by outside the passenger-side window.

"What does that mean? That his wife is Cherokee?" RJ broke down and asked.

Woody let out an exaggerated sigh and rolled his eyes.

The Cherokee Indians believe that killing a snake angers the rain god, Woody finally explained. Mr. Thomason kills the snakes and strings them up along his fence to make the rain god good and mad so it will bring down a long and mighty storm.

"That's ridiculous."

Woody shrugged.

"It's no wonder we have such a problem with jackrabbits," RJ added. "With fools stringing up the only predators we have left, all on account of some silly Indian superstition. Don't you agree, Woody?"

"No."

"No?" RJ asked.

"No," Woody repeated. "I don't agree with you."

"Why?"

Woody just shrugged his shoulders again and continued looking silently out the window.

After a few more minutes of silence, RJ spoke again. "Is something bothering you, Woody? It's not like you to be so tight-lipped. Especially with me."

Woody turned to look at her then. His face was void of emotion.

"I'm fine," he said and turned back toward the window.

"Okey-dokey," RJ responded, her voice dripping with sarcasm that she knew would be lost on him.

They continued their drive in silence. Past the Sharps', over to the Tugwells', then back toward home. Along the way, RJ made mental note of the progress she'd observed. Mr. Sharp seemed to be keeping up the terraces and contours despite the wind's constant effort to tear them down. Mr. Tugwell didn't seem to be fairing as well. It was harder on a man his age to mount the tractor and plow every day. She planned to add these thoughts to her D.C. report that evening.

Just before they reached the turn to the soil conservation lab, RJ had to stop so they could shovel a dune from the road. The two shoveled side by side without saying a word, laboring beneath their Red Cross masks, fighting against the wind that seemed hell bent on undoing their work.

Finally, they made enough progress to get the truck through and headed up the drive. RJ parked the truck and Woody leapt out, preparing to dart across the yard toward the barn.

"Woody, wait!" RJ shouted. "Something clearly has you upset. Is it because of what I said about the Thomasons? Why won't you talk to me? It does you no good to run off."

Woody clenched his fists at his sides and spun around to face her. "You're one to talk about not running off!"

The two had had their share of problems communicating, and Woody had stormed off in a huff more times than RJ could count. But he had never before turned on her in quite this way. He had never shouted at her with such anger.

"Woody, *what* is going on?" RJ felt her own frustration and temper rising.

Her friend began to pace back and forth. After a moment, he launched into a soliloquy, his frustrations spilling from him like a creek overflowing its banks in a monsoon.

"First off, that *was* a mean thing for you to say about the Thomasons and their Cherokee beliefs," he began. "I'm disappointed you said it. But that ain't the reason I'm mad."

Woody stared at RJ with an intensity that drilled down to her core. She nodded, signaling Woody to keep going, letting him know she would not interrupt.

"You think things are finally different," he continued, "that you finally got a friend. A friend who will always tell you the truth. Then, that friend goes and keeps a secret from you. That friend decides to run off to Wichita. But does she tell *you*? No, siree. It's a big ole secret. You wake up one day, and your friend, or at least the person you *thought* was your friend, is gone."

RJ hesitated to interrupt or ask questions, knowing the risk that he would just start again from the beginning. But he wasn't making any sense.

"Hold on." RJ raised her palms in front of her, patted at the air. "I don't know how you got this idea in your head, but I'm not moving to Wichita, Woody. I'm staying right here."

Woody stopped pacing. He turned to face her. His steady gaze unsettled her.

"I heard Harvey talking in town today. I heard him telling the fellas how you two are moving to Wichita after the wedding next week. How Ben got him a job at the factory."

RJ scrunched her eyebrows and shook her head.

"How could you plan to leave and *not even tell me*?" Woody asked, embittered and exasperated.

The pain in his voice stabbed at RJ's heart. She shook her head again.

"I would never do that. And I'm not going anywhere. I don't know what exactly Harvey said, but you must have misunderstood."

Woody pressed the heels of his hands hard against his temples and let out a guttural yell.

"You're just like everyone else. You think I'm stupid. I ain't stupid! I know what I heard!"

He turned and ran across the yard, disappearing behind the barn.

RJ resisted the impulse to chase after him. Partly because she knew he needed time to cool down; she had already pressed him too hard, too quickly. And partly because she was too rattled by what Woody had said to continue the conversation with him. She stood in the yard for a moment, then she got back in the truck and sped off to find Harvey.

"This is a nice surprise." Harvey grinned wide as he approached RJ's truck. He opened the door for her after she shut off the engine and reached for her hand.

"This day is turning out to be full of surprises." She took his hand and stepped out of the cab, but when he leaned in to give her a kiss, she turned and offered only her cheek.

Harvey raised his eyebrows. "What's wrong?"

RJ didn't answer right away. She'd been running the words through her mind the whole drive over. But now, saying what she'd come to say didn't feel right. It felt like she'd be crossing a line, one from which there might be no stepping back.

"Honey, you're worrying me," Harvey said. "What is it?"

"Woody's upset with me," she said.

"Oh." Harvey sighed with relief. "Shoot, you had me thinking something horrible had happened. Woody's always getting worked up over something. And he always comes around. Don't worry yourself over it, darlin'."

RJ just shook her head. Harvey turned stern.

"What's he done, Rosa Jean? Did he hurt you?"

"No," RJ answered quickly. "It's nothing like that. Woody would never hurt me. How could you even say that?"

Harvey threw his hands up in the air. "Well, what am I supposed to think? Why don't you just tell me what's on your mind, so I don't have to guess."

She told him what Woody had said, about Harvey talking to the men in town, about plans to move to Wichita after the wedding. Surely, Woody must have misunderstood.

"Damn that, Woody." Harvey shook his head. "It was supposed to be a surprise. My wedding gift to you."

RJ scoffed.

Harvey explained, the words shooting rapid-fire from his mouth. His brother found them a nice little place, a house they could rent to start with, and maybe buy once they'd saved up some money for a down payment. It's real close to the school.

RJ rubbed her forehead with the tips of her fingers. She covered her face completely with both palms.

"Sweetheart, this isn't the way I wanted you to find out." Harvey's voice softened, became pleading. He took her hands in his. "But you're going to love it in Wichita. We'll be near my family. We'll be happy."

"We already talked about this, Harvey. I told you, I don't want to be a schoolteacher."

RJ's hands were stiff in his, her words icy.

"You don't have to," he said. "You don't have to work at all. I'll be making a good wage at the factory. We can start a family right away."

She pulled her hands from his, turned and walked a few steps away. She looked out over the barren fields, her back turned to him. She imagined herself scrubbing Harvey's work shirts, with children underfoot and her stomach bulging with yet another. She'd cook every day and mend holes in the knees of tiny pants. She'd be stuck in the city, miles away from open fields or wooded trails. Her work as a scientist would be a thing of the past.

She folded her arms across her chest and turned to face him.

"The work I'm doing here is important. To the people here, to the future of our country. To *me*."

"I know that," Harvey said. He maintained the distance she had put between them.

"Then why? Why would you plan all of this? And why would you keep it a secret from me?"

Harvey approached her now. He stroked her arm.

"I thought it would be a nice surprise. I thought, I thought that once we were married, that being my wife would be more important to you than being a scientist."

RJ stared at him. A dull ache began to form in the pit of her stomach. Then she laughed – a jagged, bitter laugh that made Harvey recoil.

"What's so funny?"

She pondered his question for a moment before she answered.

"It's just ironic. *I thought* that once we were married, being my husband would help you see how important my work is to me."

Harvey shrank back. The wind began to grumble and virulent ribbons of dust began to unfurl across the barren fields. They watched the earth tumble and thrust itself up from ground. Harvey suggested they go inside, talk things through. RJ shook her head.

"I need to go," she said, moving toward her truck. "I need to think."

Harvey stepped aside to let her pass. When she climbed in the cab and pulled the door shut, he spoke to her through the open window.

"I'll come by your place on Saturday, like we planned, and we'll get married. It'll all work out."

RJ gripped the steering wheel with both hands. She stared straight ahead.

Harvey set his palms on the cab roof and leaned forward a bit, dropped his head, closed his eyes.

"I can't stay here any longer, Rosa Jean. Can't you see that? This place is killing me. I need to work, to earn a living, to see my efforts result in something. I need to *eat*, goddammit." He paused a moment, composed himself, then stood up tall and took a step back. "I'm heading up to Wichita on Saturday to start a new life. I hope you'll be with me."

RJ didn't respond. She sat in the truck another moment, then she fired up the engine and pulled away, tears welling up in her eyes.

Woody and RJ made amends as soon as she returned to the lab. Such things were easier with Woody. The two fell back into their daily rhythm. But RJ's mind was never far from Harvey or the decision she had to make by the week's end.

RJ walked the north field, measuring soil depth, scooping up samples, jotting notes. Even as she threw herself into the work she loved, RJ wondered, is this the last time I'll walk this field?

She ran scenes through her mind, contemplating the alternatives. The tearful scene in which she tells Harvey she'd be heartbroken to abandon her work. Then he breaks down, sweeps her into his arms and says he understands, should never have asked her to choose, will stay by her side.

Or the tearful good-bye when she embraces Woody, tells him she has decided to stand by her husband, as a devoted wife should.

And then there's the tearful good-bye in which she tells Harvey she cannot, will not abandon her work. He tells her, again, that he cannot stay. And can she blame him? He deserves all the things he wants from his life, from his work – all the same things she wants from hers.

Every scenario seemed to include tears and heartbreak.

RJ paused in her work. She looked up, across the landscape, toward the horizon. Her jaw tightened and heat began to fill her chest. *Damn you, Harvey Clay, for making me have to choose.*

The next day, working alone at her desk, struggling to type her notes, tears silently rolled down her cheeks. Staring at the nearly blank paper in the typewriter roller, RJ tried to push Harvey from her mind. She had made the decision to marry him, for better or worse, in good times and bad. Did it matter that they hadn't yet said their vows? How could she ignore his impassioned plea for them to begin their life together with a fresh start, with hope for a better future?

Of all the times RJ had felt alone in the past, they were nothing compared to how she felt at this moment. She longed for someone to hold and console her, for someone to give her the shrewd advice only a woman could. She ached for her mother, and for Ethel, and for Olive. Even one of Aunt May's stern lectures would have been a welcome salvation from such deep anguish.

RJ placed her elbows on the desk and buried her face in her hands. Her heart beat erratically. She couldn't seem to steady her breath.

Stormy crept up beside her and nudged RJ's elbow from the desk. The dog pushed her nose up under RJ's arm and pressed her head against RJ's stomach.

"It's okay girl. I'm okay."

RJ eased off the chair and onto the floor. Stormy climbed into her lap and bathed her face in slobbery kisses. RJ laughed, and cried, wrapped her arms tight around the dog. She did her best to draw oxygen into her lungs.

~~~

By midweek, RJ was numb. Her eyes were dry. Her mind was empty. She couldn't think anymore, and yet she still had no answer. She stood at the sink washing and rinsing beakers. Woody was out by the barn making repairs to the nursery.

The sound of a vehicle rumbling up the drive made RJ's heart leap. Harvey! She knew he would come around. She never should
~~~

have doubted him. She quickly dried her hands, smoothed her hair and licked her dry lips, then rushed out the front door to the porch.

But it wasn't Harvey's truck pulling in, and it wasn't Harvey who stepped out. It was a man in a fancy car and fancy suit.

"I'm looking for Rosa Jean Evans," he said and walked briskly toward the lab.

RJ said that was she. The man handed her an envelope containing the official seal of the U.S. Department of the Interior.

"What's this?" she asked.

"I regret to inform you this is your termination notice, Miss Evans."

He turned and walked briskly back to the car. RJ rushed after him.

"What? Why?"

"It's all in the letter. Good day, Miss."

Then, just as abruptly as he'd appeared, the man was gone. RJ stood dazed in the drive for a few minutes, unable to move. She stared at the envelope in her hand. Finally, she found the strength to turn and walk back inside. She sunk into a chair at the table and tore open the envelope, slowly pulled the thick stationery letter from its enclosure.

I am writing to inform you of your termination as Field Geologist of the Soil Conservation Station in Vanham, Kansas. It has been brought to our attention that you have misrepresented yourself in your employment with our department. Upon further review, we have determined you no longer meet the qualifications for employment with United States Government in this capacity. Your termination is effective immediately. You have thirty days to vacate the premises of your personal belongings...

~~~
~~~

RJ watched Woody walk from the barn to the house, his lanky frame a silhouette against the tangerine sky. She sat on the front porch step, a cup of coffee in one hand, the letter in the other.

When Woody spotted her, he waved wildly and broke into a trot, closing the distance between them in no time.

"Mornin', RJ. What you doing sitting out here on the porch?" Woody lumbered over and sat down beside her on the step, an arm's length away.

"Just looking at the land," she said.

Woody squinted in the same direction as RJ.

"And thinking," she said.

"About what?"

RJ wrinkled up her nose, handed him the letter. Woody took it from her slowly, eyed the government seal at the top. He gawked at her.

"Go ahead," she said.

He unfolded the paper, held it out at arm's length.

Dear Miss Evans, he read, and then his mouth fell open as he skimmed the first few sentences. He looked at his friend, searching her face for a clue, something that would tell him it was okay to continue reading.

RJ smirked, and Woody continued to wait, unsure. Finally, she nodded, yes, keep going.

"Dear Miss Evans," he began again, reading aloud this time. When he finished, he dropped his hand into his lap and whistled through his teeth.

RJ raised her eyebrows and sniffed. Words escaped her.

"Can they do that? Just fire you, 'cause you ain't a man?"

"It would seem so."

They sat for a moment without speaking, looking out at the land RJ had plowed and measured, at the soil she had tested and monitored, at the greenhouse seedlings she had sowed and nursed for the past year and a half.

"What did Harvey have to say about it?"

"I'm not going to tell him."

Woody blinked. "So I guess this means you're moving to Wichita."

RJ shook her head. "I don't know what I'm going to do yet."

Woody whistled again.

Tears welled in RJ's eyes. She blinked, and the salty droplets rolled silently down her cheeks, fell into her lap. She bit her bottom lip, fought back the sobs pushing up from her gut.

Woody swallowed hard. He shifted himself closer to RJ, wiped the sweat from his palms on his overalls, and then cautiously extended an arm around RJ's back and placed his hand stiffly on her shoulder. He patted her shoulder clumsily.

RJ looked over at his hand on her shoulder and let out a laugh that turned into a sob. Woody looked straight ahead, out into the fields. She looked up at his face, her emotions tumbling through her and out of her in a jumble of sorrow, and anger, and bewilderment, and gratitude, and uncertainty.

"Oh, Woody," she sobbed. "Thank you."

She turned her face into his chest, fighting the urge to wrap her arms around him tight, grateful for his arm around her. And she let go. She let go of it all.

Every muscle in Woody's body remained rigid, but he didn't release her.

"You're welcome, RJ. You're welcome."

~

What are you going to do? That's what Woody had asked her that morning, and she hadn't had an answer. The sun was slipping down below the horizon now, and RJ still didn't have one. She'd given Woody the day off. What was the point in working now? So he'd gone back to the barn to play with Stormy and read. RJ had gone into the lab.

Her mind was a jumble, as her options, which were precious few, bounced around her head. And Harvey would be by in the morning, on what was supposed to be their wedding day. She'd asked Woody to make himself scarce on Saturday. She needed to be alone to talk with Harvey.

Good Lord, how did everything get turned upside down so fast? For the first time since she'd come to Vanham, RJ prayed for a duster to roll in, to stop time until she could figure out what to do next.

The storm RJ hoped for never came during the night. The air was still and clear and crisp when she finally gave up on sleep at three o'clock. She wrapped herself in a quilt, sat on the front porch and waited for the sun to rise.

She studied the morning sky as it unfolded in a burst of color, from navy to marmalade, then from peach to pale blue. The ever-present prairie winds were nearly still. The air had only a hint of dust.

RJ shuddered. The last time she had experienced such a clear beautiful morning was Black Sunday. Was this an omen of darker things to come?

"No," RJ said aloud and shook her head. She stood, closed her eyes and drew in the fresh air. She told herself she'd be grateful for this day, regardless of what might unfold as the sun continued its journey across the sky.

As the morning crept along, RJ busied herself with cleaning and organizing.

She put on the pale green dress that Harvey had asked her to wear. It was his favorite, he'd said. Flattered her figure, he'd said. At the time, his request had made her stomach flip with delight. Today, as she pulled the dress over her shoulders and reached to ease up the zipper in the back, his directive left a hollow feeling in her gut. *Wear this. Move there. Do that.*

"Is there a man on earth who doesn't want to tell me what to do?"

She stared at herself in the mirror, waiting for her reflection to provide an answer. *Woody.* RJ shook her head.

"Is there a man on earth who *wants to marry me* and doesn't want to tell me what to do?" RJ said to her reflection.

She turned from side to side, checking her profile in the mirror, hoping she cast such a stunning image that Harvey would give up his plan to move, that he would stay by her side, no matter what the future might hold.

Then, and only then, would she tell him about the visitor from D.C., about the letter.

~~~

RJ watched from the kitchen window as Harvey's truck pulled off the road and up the drive to the lab. He turned off the engine and stepped out into the sun. Her heart leapt at the sight of him, looking dapper in a gray suit and polished shoes. It was the first time she'd seen him dressed up, and his effort to look sharp both thrilled and pained her.

She stretched her neck from right to left, front to back, to try to ease the tension knotting up her body. It was a futile effort, so she headed out to the porch.

Harvey looked up at her wearing the dress he'd selected and flashed his dimpled smile. He removed his fedora and walked up to join her at the porch step.

"You look beautiful, Rosa Jean."

"Thank you." She smiled through her fear. "You cut quite a striking figure yourself. Very handsome."

Harvey fiddled with the brim of his hat.

"I can't tell you how relieved I am to see you in that dress. We're going to be so happy, Rosa Jean. You're going to love my brother and his wife. We'll have a good life in Wichita."

RJ steadied herself. She shook her head, almost imperceptibly.
~~~

"I love you so much, Harvey, and I want to marry you." She paused. "But I can't give up my work."

Harvey exhaled and turned his head as though she'd slapped him. He ran his hand back and forth over his mouth. They stood silently for a moment, for a lifetime.

"So you're not packed?"

RJ shook her head slowly. She couldn't have spoken even if she had known what to say.

"Rosa Jean, please. Don't do this."

"Just stay here with me," she said, barely above a whisper and took a step closer to him. "Just for a little while longer."

He backed away from her as she spoke, shaking his head angrily. His eyes turned red and glassy. He tried to speak, stopped and cleared his throat. Then, he looked her square in the eyes.

"I can't marry a woman who doesn't trust that I know what's best for us, who doesn't love me enough to do as I ask."

His honesty made RJ laugh out loud with bitter, angry realization, even as her eyes filled with tears.

"Then why the hell did you even propose to me, Harvey? You know that's not who I am. Did you really think putting a ring on my finger would magically transform me into someone I've never been?"

"I thought you loved me." His voice matched the anger in hers.

"I *do* love you. And I know you love me, too."

"But that's not enough, is it?" his voice cracked as he spoke and he looked away now. It was too painful to look into her eyes and see the truth.

They stood quiet, still. Harvey pinched the bridge of his nose and squeezed his eyes shut tight.

After another moment passed, Harvey grunted and pressed his fedora on his head.

"I best get on the road before the wind starts to kick up," he said. As he turned toward the truck, he paused and angled his head slightly in her direction. "Good-bye, RJ."

It was the first and only time he had called her by her nickname, and it was a knife to her heart. She stood statue still, watched him drive out of her life in a tumble of angry red dust.

"Good riddance," she said. She pushed her shoulders back, wiped the tears from her cheeks, and headed back to the lab to change into her overalls.

Woody paced behind the barn. RJ had asked him to make himself scarce come Saturday. Woody had said that he was only one person, and there was no one else like him anywhere, and as a result he was already scarce. He didn't understand how to make himself scarcer, unless he was to disappear. That's when RJ explained it was a figure of speech, and that in fact she did want him to disappear, but only by going somewhere else, and only temporarily. She wanted to be alone when Harvey came, because the two of them needed to work some things out. So Woody disappeared behind the barn when Harvey's truck pulled into the drive.

The young man walked from one end of the barn to the other. Back and forth, back and forth, creating a furrow in the dirt. Stormy lay in the shade, panting, watching him. When Woody heard the crackle of dirt beneath tires, he peeked out from behind the barn and saw Harvey drive away, alone.

"He left," Woody said to the dog. "He left without RJ. Can you believe that, Stormy?"

Woody resumed pacing back and forth.

"And people's always calling me a dummy. Even I know better than to drive off and leave behind a woman like RJ."

Woody paced. He started listing all the reasons why Harvey had made a big mistake by leaving. Chief among them were all the things that made RJ so swell, like her laugh and the way her hair always fell in her eyes when she was working and how she'd puff out a lip and blow the hair up. And, of course, there were her eyes themselves, how they sparkled when RJ talked.

Stormy watched him a bit more, then she rolled on her side and plopped her head into the soft dirt. Little puffs of dust rose rhythmically as she panted in and out.

Then there's all the amazing work RJ does, Woody continued thinking out loud. And how she don't mind me borrowing her expensive books to read anytime I want.

Woody stopped pacing. He stared in the direction of the house.

"I hope she's okay over there. I hope she ain't crying. Do you think she's crying, Stormy?"

Upon hearing her name, the dog lifted her head and looked at Woody.

She wanted me to make myself scarce, Woody said and resumed his pacing. But did she mean all day? Or just when Harvey was here? I should have asked her that, so I'd know what to do. Harvey drove off and left her all alone. Does she want to be alone? Maybe I should go on over to the house and ask her if she still wants me to be scarce. But if she does, then she might get mad I came and asked, after she already told me so.

Stormy yawned and laid her head back in the dirt. And Woody paced and talked, talked and paced.

~~~

Late that afternoon, the sky fell dark crimson and the wind turned bad-tempered. RJ stepped out onto the front porch to survey the horizon. Woody walked slowly toward the house from the barn.

"Sandstorm?" RJ glanced toward the horizon.

"Looks like it," Woody said. "I wasn't sure if I shoulda hunkered down in the barn or if I shoulda come over."
~~~

RJ smiled at him. "Well, of course you should have come over."

Woody raised one eyebrow. "I *did* come over."

RJ thought for a moment to explain herself, then decided against it. She told him to come on inside. She whistled for Stormy, and the dog came running from the abandoned chicken coop toward the house. They all got settled in just as the wind got fierce.

Inside, Woody retrieved three small beanbags from his pants' pocket and began juggling. RJ sank into a kitchen chair and began shuffling a deck of cards. It was the deck Ethel had given her after RJ's first big storm alone. You can go batty sitting in the dark by yourself with nothing to do with your hands, Ethel had told her. After the months of dusters and shuffling since, the cards had a permanent crease down their centers, the suits had nearly worn away.

"I'm so tired of being in the dark," RJ said.

"At least the sandstorms ain't as bad as the dusters," Woody said, still juggling. "Don't usually last as long. Don't get so black."

RJ cut the deck and riffled the two halves back together. She thought about the wad of string Harvey kept in his pocket.

"I wasn't talking about the storms."

"Ah." Woody caught all three beanbags in one hand and then turned to face RJ. "You were speaking *metaphorically.*"

She flashed him a wistful smile.

"I'm glad you're here, Woody."

"Me, too," he said.

Woody resumed his juggling. RJ dealt a hand of solitaire. The wind howled and pounded the lab. The door rattled and fought its hinges. The world spun nevertheless. RJ gathered the cards, shuffled and dealt again.

"Knock, knock," Woody said.

RJ looked over at Woody. He was still juggling.

"What did you say?" she asked.

"It's a joke. I say knock, knock. And you say, who's there?"

"I'm not in the mood for jokes, Woody."

"How do you know? You ain't even heard the joke yet. Knock, knock."

RJ sighed heavily. She deliberated for a moment on what to do. Of course, she knew Woody wouldn't let it go. She looked at him, opened her eyes wide and said, "Who's there?"

"Tarzan."

"Tarzan who?"

"Tarzan stripes forever!"

Woody laughed. RJ rolled her eyes and shook her head at him. "That's dumb."

"I know," Woody laughed even harder. "That's what makes it funny!"

He dropped the beanbags and fell onto the floor laughing. Stormy pounced on him, slobbered kisses all over his face. RJ couldn't sulk any longer. She watched the two of them and set free the kind of laughter only they seemed to be able to coax from her.

When they all settled down, Woody sat up.

"Knock, knock," he said.

"Oh, for heaven's sake, Woody. No more jokes."

Stormy lay down beside Woody on the floor, and he scratched her belly.

"Knock. Knock."

RJ drummed her fingers on the table.

"Who's there?" she finally said.

"Wooden shoe."

"Wooden shoe who?"

"Wooden shoe like to hear another joke?"

RJ groaned. "That was even worse than the first one."

"Ok, then you tell one," Woody said.

RJ thought for a moment. "All right," she said. "You say knock, knock."

"Knock, knock," Woody said.

"Who's there?" RJ asked.

Woody opened his mouth to respond, but he didn't know what to say. "Wait a minute. You did it wrong," he said.

RJ giggled and slapped her knee. "That's what makes it funny, Woody."

His eyes glinted. "Now *that's* dumb."

RJ seemed to lose all her senses and laughed from deep in her belly until her sides hurt. Stormy barked and leapt around the kitchen table like a gazelle. Woody laughed hard, too, even though he still didn't think the joke was funny.

Outside the wind bellowed its objection to their merriment. The sand rained against the house in protest to their levity. Yet, for a brief precious moment, all RJ and Woody heard was the laughter.

"What are you gonna do, RJ?"

"Gosh, Woody. Would you stop asking me that."

Woody frowned, took a book from the shelf in the lab, wiped the dust off the top of the pages and placed it carefully in the packing crate. She had been avoiding the subject for three weeks. But she knew the uncertainty of things was like a big old pile of eights sitting on Woody's chest.

"You could go to Wichita. Marry Harv."

RJ shook her head no. She couldn't be with Harvey now, not after all that had been said between them. If she went to him now, it would be for all the wrong reasons. She would lose herself. But she didn't want to talk about Harvey, especially not with Woody.

"You could move to town and open Ethel's diner back up," Woody said.

"With my grand cooking talents?" RJ said. "I'd go out of business in two days."

Woody smiled.

"Besides," she added, "I don't think I could even step foot in that diner. My heart breaks all over again just thinking about it."

She let out a weary sigh, and sat down on the floor. Stormy took it as an invitation and trotted over, tail buzzing and slobbery tongue wagging. RJ patted the ground beside her. The dog plopped down at her side.

RJ reached up to the desk for her cigarettes and matchbook. She lit one up, took a long draw, tilted her head back as she exhaled.

"I wish you didn't smoke," Woody said without looking up from his work.

RJ's stomach plunged like a rock. She watched him a moment, then shook her head.

"Because women shouldn't smoke," she said, more to herself than to Woody.

He looked over at her, brows pulled together. "I don't know what being a woman has to do with it. I don't like the smell, no matter who's doing the smoking."

"That's the only reason you wish I didn't smoke?" RJ asked.

"That's the only reason," he said. "It stinks. It makes me want to puke."

RJ looked down at the cigarette between her fingers and chuckled.

"Well then," she said, and stubbed out the butt in the ashtray. "That's as good a reason to stop smoking as I've heard."

"So you're not gonna smoke anymore?"

"No, not if the smell bothers you that much."

"Thanks," he said, matter-of-factly.

Woody continued dusting and packing books. RJ lay back on the ground, folded her arms behind her head. Stormy snuggled in and put her chin on RJ's stomach.

"I could write to the university in Madison," RJ said, staring up at the ceiling. "Inquire about faculty positions. I might be able to get a job in research."

Woody nodded his approval. RJ scratched behind Stormy's ears for a bit. After a minute or two, she sat up and asked Woody what he was going to do now. Woody shrugged and tucked another book in the packing crate.

"You can stay here and work with the new geologist," RJ said.

Woody shrugged again. Deep down, they both knew whoever took RJ's place would never keep Woody on, would never see in him what she saw.

"You could move to Kansas City to be with your folks. Work at the GM factory," RJ said. *Maybe we could both move to Kansas City.* She thought about Woody living in a big city with its steady buzz of electric lights. She imagined him working in a factory every day, with the roar and the vibration, the constant reek of machinery grease.

"We'll figure something out," RJ said.

Woody hammered the crate lid into place.

~~~

RJ and Woody drove into town to pick up supplies and more empty crates for packing. She kept her eyes straight ahead, her fingers firmly wrapped around the steering wheel. Woody talked about an article he'd read in the newspaper about beer you could buy in a can.

They been working on it for years, Woody explained, but the carbonation kept exploding the cans. They finally figured out they could line the cans with the same lacquer stuff they use in kegs to keep 'em from blowing. You can go right into Krueger's and buy yourself a beer or a cream ale in a can. Ain't that something? Folks told the newspaper man the canned beer tasted just like draft, even better than bottled beer.

RJ nodded from time to time. Every now and then she'd make a sound as though she were following along. "Oh?" or "Hmm."

After a bit, Woody stopped talking and watched her drive. They passed Harvey's place. A little while later, they turned, just before the Sharp farm, and headed on the main road into town. Woody reached over and placed his hand on RJ's shoulder. She flinched, broken from the hypnosis of the road, surprised by his touch.

"You okay, RJ?"
~~~

"Yes."

She glanced his way for a second.

"You look sad," he said.

RJ didn't respond right away. She turned her attention back to the road. It struck her that Woody rarely took notice of how people felt. His observation made her heart flicker. "I am sad. But I'll be all right."

Woody looked out the passenger side window. "You miss Harvey."

RJ gave him another fleeting look. Woody's statement tumbled around in her mind as they bumped along the rutted road.

"Yes," she said. "But that's not the reason I'm sad."

"It's not?"

"No. Isn't that funny?"

Woody scrunched up his nose, furrowed his eyebrows. Finally, he shook his head.

"You'll have to explain it to me. I don't get the joke."

RJ smiled. She wondered if she'd ever get used to Woody's way of taking things exactly as they were said.

"I don't mean literally funny," she said. "I mean funny as in surprising, or… odd."

"Oh," he said.

"I mean, when I stop and really think about it, if I'm really honest with myself, I'm more heartbroken about losing my job than I am about losing Harvey."

Woody bobbled his head from side to side, mulling this new bit of information. "That's not really so odd."

"No, maybe it's not after all," she said. "But it *is* sad."

Woody scrunched his face up again. "Wait a minute. I thought you said you *weren't* sad about Harvey."

RJ drew in a deep breath and held it a moment, her cheeks bulging out as though she were under water. Then, she liberated the air in a big gust.

"Don't try to understand me, Woody. It's a fool's errand. Most of the time I don't even understand myself."

They entered the city limits and drove to the Nickel & Dime. RJ parked near the door and turned off the engine. The two sat motionless for a moment, each lost in his or her thoughts.

"You understand yourself better than you think you do," Woody said finally, then opened his door and unfolded his long legs from the cab.

RJ sighed and shook her head. *Maybe I do.*

RJ and Ernie Tugwell walked the perimeter of his land. They were quiet for a long time. Ernie had been doing a good job of keeping the field contours in place. He replowed after every duster, just as RJ had instructed him. He'd sown the grass seed where she'd said, had left fields fallow though it pained him.

"The fields are looking good," RJ said. "All things considered."

"Yap."

They continued their walk in silence. As they rounded the final field and headed back toward the house, RJ asked Ernie what he would do if the rain didn't come this year.

"Keep farming dust, I reckon," he said. He rubbed at the gray stubble on his chin. "Hope for rain next year. Don't know how to do anything else."

RJ nodded.

"So you want me to work with the new fella they hire on?" Ernie asked after they'd walked a bit further. "Or should I run him off when he comes around?"

That he would even ask the question made RJ's heart swell. She sighed and looked out across the fields.

"The land still needs help to heal," she said.

"Don't we all," Ernie said. RJ looked at him intently. He gave an awkward shrug, trying to shake off the embarrassment he seemed to feel at getting philosophical.

"I don't have anything against whoever takes my place," she said. "And it'll help you in the long haul. You should work with him, Ernie."

"All right. I'll stick with it, if you say so," he said. "But I'm still gonna give the new fella some grief, make sure he knows he's got some mighty big shoes to fill. Even if they're tiny women's shoes."

That made them both laugh. RJ threaded her arm behind Ernie's elbow and leaned into him just a bit as they continued to walk.

"I sure am going to miss you, Ernie."

"Yap."

~~~

After the Tugwell place, RJ drove into town to check the post office. First, she stopped in at the Feed & Seed to say good-bye to Mr. Meginnis. They hadn't exactly become best friends, but since Black Sunday and then Ethel's passing, the two had gained some respect for one another. Anyone who could get out of bed every morning and forge ahead in the dust had some common ground.

She headed down Main toward the post office and saw Mr. Sharp headed her way on the opposite side of the street. Their eyes met, and Mr. Sharp jogged across to join her.

"Hiya, Miss Evans."

"Hiya, Mr. Sharp. I'm glad we ran into each other. Saved me a drive out to your place."

She told him she would be leaving Vanham in a few days, that a new "pen pusher" would be coming around to introduce himself.

"Yeah, I heard you got sacked."

RJ forced a brave smile. She couldn't bring herself to say it out loud.
~~~

"Just 'cause you're a woman?" he asked.

"Yes, it would seem so."

"It ain't right," Mr. Sharp said and spat into the dirt to punctuate his point. "I'll admit I didn't like having a woman in that job either, at first. But, you work just as hard as any feller I've known, and it turned out you're smarter than half of 'em put together, too."

RJ swallowed hard. She didn't know whether to laugh or cry, whether to hug the man or sock him in the arm.

"That's about the nicest thing anybody's ever said to me."

Mr. Sharp plunged his hands in his jacket pockets and scuffed at the dirt on the sidewalk with the toe of his boot. "So, what are you gonna do now?"

RJ looked off in the distance and shook her head slowly.

"Eh, you'll figure it out," he said.

"I wish I had your confidence." She smiled at him. "How about you, Mr. Sharp? What are you going to do?"

"Same thing I've always done. Same thing my pa did before me." Now he looked off in the distance, glared at the horizon. "Hold out for the next rain."

They stood on the sidewalk together for another moment, staring in the distance, quietly reflecting their fates. Then, RJ extended her hand, smiled at him with her eyes. Mr. Sharp took her hand, gave it a firm shake, and walked away.

RJ swept her hair away from her face with both hands, then continued down the street. She moved briskly past the diner, kept her focus straight ahead. The windows had stayed shuttered since Ethel's death. The doors had remained locked since Marjorie had packed up her friend's personal belongings and shipped them to Ethel's sister in Ohio.

The wind kicked up a fresh cloud of dust that swirled in the street and across the sidewalk. But that wasn't the reason RJ's eyes stung and her throat constricted. She blinked hard and quickened her pace still more.

She slipped into the post office and leaned her back against the closed door as though she had just evaded an attacker.

"That a duster rolling in?" Bud asked.

RJ shook her head, took a moment to compose herself. Bud tilted his head and studied her. Just as he opened his mouth to question her further, RJ found her voice.

"Just the usual wind and haze," she said, abruptly adding, "Any mail for me?"

Bud paused only a moment before allowing her change of subject.

"A few things," he said, reaching below the counter and retrieving a small stack. He slid it across the counter to her. "Got a telegram, too."

RJ raised her eyebrows.

Bud handed her the sealed telegram. "Hope it's good news."

"Thank you," she said, barely above a whisper. She stared down at the envelope in her hand for a bit. "Well, I best be on my way."

She tucked the sealed envelope into her stack of mail, between a letter from Aunt May and the Sears & Roebuck catalog. She'd wait until she was home to read it and learn her fate.

"Good-bye, Bud."

"Good-bye. It was a pleasure to know you, Miss Evans."

"Oh." RJ was taken aback by the melancholy in his voice. She flashed him a tender smile. "I feel the same way."

She nodded to him one last time and slipped out the door.

"I got a telegram," RJ told Woody.

"I'm sorry," he said.

"Sorry? Why?"

"Telegrams is always bad news. Otherwise, whoever sent it would just send a letter. That's what my ma always said anyhow."

RJ smiled. "Well, this telegram has good news."

She told Woody she had received word from the University of Wisconsin in Madison in response to her job inquiry. They would be pleased to have an alumna return and had offered her a faculty and research position. She would teach a few classes a week and continue to research soil conservation.

Woody looked down at his lap with a stiff smile. "That is good news, RJ. For you."

RJ pulled a chair around the table so she could sit beside him. She touched his knee for half a second, then folded her hands in her lap. Woody looked up at her.

"It could be good news for you, too," she said.

"I don't see how."

"You could come with me."

Woody rolled his eyes and let out a blast of air like a punctured tire. He stood up from the table and began to pace back and forth across the room.

"Just hear me out," RJ pleaded gently. "I know you don't like new things. But you'd be with me, so it wouldn't be all new. We could find you a job on campus. You could live in faculty housing with me."

Woody expelled another violent gust of air and threw up his hands.

"I couldn't live with you like that. It wouldn't be proper."

"It would be if we were married."

With that, Woody froze. He swallowed hard and turned slowly toward RJ, eyes cast down.

"Woody, will you marry me?"

A long time passed before Woody responded. RJ waited, hands still folded in her lap. She watched him, waiting for him to look up, waiting for him to answer.

Woody breathed in and out slowly, deliberately.

"You want to marry *me*?"

"Yes, more than anything I've ever wanted."

Woody shook his head a little. "What about Harvey?"

"Harvey wanted to change me, and when he couldn't, he left." There was no anger in her voice. She simply stated a fact. "I know you'd never do that, Woody. I know that with all of my heart."

"That's true." He whispered so softly now that RJ could barely make out the words. But she knew what he had said. She stood and walked to him.

"I could be a good husband," he said, even more softly, more to himself than to her. RJ just smiled. Finally, he looked up, looked her right in the eye. "You think I'd be a good husband?"

"You'd be the best husband," she said. A flood of warmth surged through her. "You're already my best friend."

Woody smiled now, just a flash, then he looked up and away, the way he did when he was working hard to focus on something important.

"I don't like Madison," he said. "Don't like big cities."

RJ knew Woody had never been outside Vanham city limits, much less to a big city. But she didn't dispute what his gut told him.

"You'd like UW," she said instead. "It's like a small town, just like Vanham. It has everything you could ever want, right on campus. A little market, a cafeteria if you want to eat out, and a library. Oh, Woody, you wouldn't believe the library they have at UW. It's three full floors."

A library with three full floors. Woody couldn't help but smile at that.

"It's so green and lovely, with planters filled with flowers, and red brick buildings. And the snow in the winter is so beautiful and thick. You could create your beautiful paintings in the snow in every lawn on campus." RJ was almost giddy at the idea of it.

Woody's face went flush and his eyes went wide. RJ laughed.

"And I'll be there," she added.

Woody's face went serious again. He walked toward the table and sank back into his chair. RJ went to him, knelt on the floor in front of him, looked up into his face.

"I need you, Woody." RJ's voice broke as she said the words, as she realized the truth of them. "I won't go to UW without you. My heart would be broken forever."

His face contorted and he flinched as though he'd been stabbed.

"I know change is hard for you," she continued, almost desperate. "But I'll be with you to help. Just think of how well things went when you moved from your home to here at the lab with me. Just think of how wonderful it's been."

Woody continued to stare into the distance. RJ fell silent. She could think of nothing else to say to convince him, and the fear of him saying no began to grip her. Dread took over her body like a vice – tightening, compressing, suffocating.

"I'd like to be your husband," Woody finally said. "I'd like to take care of you."

His words released the vice, and RJ nearly collapsed with relief. She beamed at him.

"We'll take care of each other," she said.

"We'll get married, and we'll move to UW," Woody said.

RJ whooped with joy and threw her arms around him. He didn't hug her back, and she didn't expect it. She just hugged him even tighter and planted a kiss on his cheek.

"Aw geez," he said, but he remained still. RJ laughed and smooched him again.

"I said it when I first met you, and I'll say it again. You sure like to laugh, RJ Evans."

"Soon to be RJ Parker," she said, and laughed again. And Woody laughed, too.

~~~

RJ parked the truck in front of the Vanham City Hall building and turned off the engine. She looked over at Woody sitting beside her. "Ready?"

"Ready," he said. Woody opened the door and unfolded his lanky frame from the small cab. He reached down and smoothed the wrinkles from his pants, rubbed the toes of his shoes on the back of his calves to shine away the dust. RJ walked around the truck and stood beside him.

"You look very handsome, Woody."

"You do, too," he said, looking down at his shoes. "Pretty, I mean. Very pretty."

RJ smiled and thanked him. She straightened his tie a bit and then turned toward the building. Woody ran ahead, up the front steps and opened the door wide. The gentle morning breeze made RJ's peach polka-dot dress flutter against her legs. Woody paused to admire her silhouette as the sun shone through the fabric.

They walked inside and signed the commissioner's daily log book. On the line that asked the reason for today's visit, RJ wrote "marriage."
~~~

"Oh, hot diggity," said the woman at the front desk. "It's been ages since we've had a marriage."

She jumped up from her seat and hurried into the commissioner's office. Only a moment later, she and the commissioner emerged, the gentleman pulling a black robe on over his white button-down shirt and suspenders. He smiled at the couple.

"Mrs. Turner tells me y'all would like to be married today."

"Yes, sir," Woody said and took hold of RJ's hand. Her stomach fluttered with surprise at Woody's uncharacteristic gesture of closeness. She smiled and gave his hand a light squeeze.

They all walked into the commissioner's office. He directed where he would like the couple to stand and explained that Mrs. Turner would be their witness if they didn't have anyone else with them.

"It's just us," said RJ, and Woody concurred.

"Very well then," the commissioner said. "Let's begin."

He opened a leather-bound book and read a few quotations and other words of wisdom about love and matrimony. He asked if RJ and Woody had both come to be married willingly, and they both said yes. Then, he asked each if they would have the other, for better or for worse, in sickness and in health, until death they do part. RJ said, "I do." And Woody said, "You bet I do!"

Mrs. Turner chortled and rummaged for a hankie.

"Then, by the power vested in me by the State of Kansas, I pronounce you man and wife. You may now kiss your bride."

Woody turned to RJ, gently placed his hands on her cheeks. His expression turned serious.

"All right now," he said. "Just hold still."

RJ suppressed the urge to giggle and did her best to be still. Woody slowly lowered his face to hers, carefully angled his head to one side and lightly pressed his lips to hers. RJ felt a jolt in her chest she hadn't expected when his lips puckered tenderly. She leaned into the kiss, parting her lips slightly to embrace his. Her stomach fluttered for the second time since entering City Hall that morning. Woody lingered in the kiss a heartbeat more, then took a step back.

He let out a giant sigh of relief and wiped his forehead with the back of his hand. Then, he smiled, “Hey, that wasn’t so bad.”

RJ threw her head back and laughed. Mrs. Turner and the magistrate broke into applause.

“Not bad at all,” RJ said. Then, she stood on her tippy toes, threw her arms around his neck and planted another kiss on his lips.

Mrs. Turner dabbed at her eyes with a hankie. “Just goes to prove, there’s a key for every lock.”

May 1989

"Fifty years ago, rain returned to the Great Plains, ending a nearly decade-long drought that played a part in the worst man-made environmental disaster in our nation's history. The American Dust Bowl."

RJ addressed a gathering at the Wichita Art Museum. She wore comfortable shoes and a smart pastel blue pantsuit with padded shoulders. Her silver hair was swept back in the relaxed flapper-style bob that had been her trademark look for six decades.

"My late husband's art offers a glimpse into that time," she continued. "It captures both the desperation and the hope of the people who lived in the Dust Bowl, their suffering and their perseverance. It portrays both the devastation and the beauty of the land."

Her sister-in-law Alice stood beside her holding a giant pair of gold scissors. Behind them both was a wide red ribbon strung across the gallery entrance and a large plaque:

Peculiar Savage Beauty: A Window into the Dust Bowl
The mixed-media art of Woodrow Parker

Together, the women cut the ribbon. The crowd applauded and followed RJ and Alice into the exhibit. They dispersed in various directions, wandering slowly through the gallery, taking in the poignant beauty of Woody's dust paintings.

RJ had never seen so much of Woody's art displayed in one place before, and the sight took her breath away, took her back in time.

The move to Madison had been a shock to Woody, as they both had known it would be. He spent hours reading through the campus library's collection, which helped to calm his nerves. But RJ knew he needed something more, an outlet for his creative energy, his brilliance. She mentioned Woody's dust paintings to a colleague, who in turn reached out to a friend in the university's art department.

They set Woody up with a drafter's light table, where he could create dust art using his hands and tools and different shades of sand and dirt on the backlit glass. Many of their friends at the university were impressed with his work and encouraged Woody to develop a way to preserve the images. The museum exhibit was the result of that lifelong pursuit.

The display featured dozens of Woody's creations. The sand images were created on one sheet of glass, then sealed with a polymer resin and topped with a second layer of glass. They were framed in window molding or reclaimed lumber. Some were flanked by weatherworn shutters. On display in a darkened gallery, the windows were backlit by soft light in orange and pink hues.

"It's like we've stepped into a time machine," Alice said, shaking her head in awe. "I'd forgotten how the air was all rose-colored after a duster."

RJ could only nod. She had no words for the flood of feelings she was experiencing. She looped her arm around Alice's, and they walked together through the exhibit, taking in the images:

A skeletal tree alone on a flat barren plain.

Schoolgirls with their Red Cross masks, goggles and lunch pails.

A farmer plowing his fields, stalked by a cloud of dust.

Buildings and cars half buried by dunes.

A mountain of dust bearing down on the city of Vanham.

As the gallery filled with more people, RJ and Alice were drawn to different images. They parted ways.

Alice walked toward a pane backlit by soft blue light, depicting a field of wheat swaying in the prairie breeze. She pulled an oxygen tank on wheels alongside her, a lifelong reminder of the dust pneumonia that nearly took her life half a century ago.

RJ stood before an image of Ethel, alone in her diner, wiping down the lunch counter.

"It's breathtaking." A young woman walked up and stood beside RJ, pointing to the image. "She's beautiful, in a sad, lonely sort of way."

RJ smiled, her eyes transfixed by the image of her old friend. "Yes, she was."

After a moment, the young woman spoke again. "Dr. Parker, I'm sorry to disturb you, but I wonder if you would sign this." She held out a book, RJ's first of many that had been published about soil conservation.

"Of course," RJ said, turning to the title page. "Who shall I make it out to?"

The young woman said her name was Anna. She'd read all of RJ's books, and she was working on her master's degree in soil science.

"My grandfather encouraged me to study it," Anna said with an affectionate smile, a small dimple winked in her cheek. "You may have known him, actually. He was born in Vanham. He said he worked with the government's soil scientist there on sustainable farming in the 'dirty thirties' before he moved to Wichita."

"Oh," RJ gasped. "Your grandfather is Harvey Clay?"

"Yes!" Anna said. "You got it on the first guess."

RJ beamed and bit her lip.

"You have his smile," she said, shaking her head. "Harvey and I… well, your grandfather was a very dear friend, to both myself and my husband. How is he?"

The glimmer in Anna's eyes dimmed. "Oh, he passed away, almost ten years ago now. Emphysema, you know, from all those years in the dust and then working in the factory."

"I'm so sorry to hear that," RJ said. They stood quietly for a moment, then RJ added, "So, you say *he* encouraged you to pursue a career in science?"

Anna nodded enthusiastically. "He did. I remember one time telling him I was worried about how much time school would take. I wondered if going that route might cause me to miss out on getting married, having a family. Grandpa Harv said there was no reason I couldn't do it all. He said any man who'd pass me up because I wanted a career would be a damned fool, and that I shouldn't worry because someone smarter would just come along and swoop me up."

RJ's eyes turned watery. Her throat got tight. "That's excellent advice. Your grandfather was a wise man."

Anna's face turned serious again. "I'm sorry. I've upset you. Perhaps I shouldn't have…"

"No, no," RJ said, shaking a smile back into place. "It's just an emotional day for me. So many memories."

RJ returned Anna's book and asked her to keep in touch. Then she watched the young woman wander off into the exhibit hall. RJ sat down on a bench and watched the other patrons as they milled around examining Woody's art. After a bit, Alice joined her on the bench.

"This really is something, isn't it?" Alice said, inhaling deeply through the thin plastic oxygen tube and exhaling with a wheeze.

RJ agreed. She took hold of Alice's hand and said, "Come on, dear. Let's go for a drive."

~~~

The roads from Wichita to Vanham were all paved now. RJ steered her silver F-150 pickup down the empty interstate. Like her husband, RJ had always remained partial to Fords. Alice sat beside her on the bench seat, wrangling with the road map she'd purchased in the museum gift shop.

"You'll want to take the next exit, I believe, and then head west."

RJ thanked her sister-in-law, but she didn't really need navigation help. Vanham was a beacon, guiding her home. Besides, the town wasn't even on Alice's crinkled map. The last of its residents had moved away in the 1960s. Vanham, like many other small farming communities that had dotted the Great Plains, was now a ghost town.

They pulled off the interstate and slowed down to take in the surrounding sights. The grasslands had re-emerged in the past decades. As far as the eye could see, tall slender stalks rippled across the landscape, an ocean of emerald and gold.

When they approached the Vanham city limits, it was even more evident that the plains' rebirth was solidly underway there. Windows, doors and lumber had been scavenged from most of the buildings, leaving only foundation blocks poking up from the earth. There were a handful of skeletal brick structures left scattered throughout town, empty skulls with hollow eyes. Tall grass sprouted from cracks in cement slabs and asphalt lots.

RJ drove slowly down the main road, from one end of town to the other – past the remnants of the Motel Royal and the gas station, past empty lots that were once home to the post office and Ethel's restaurant.
~~~

When they reached the end of town and, quite literally, the end of the road, RJ put the truck in park and shut off the engine.

"Shall we explore a bit?" she asked.

"You go ahead," Alice said. She patted the oxygen tank beside her on the seat. "My pal and I will just enjoy the view from here, I think."

RJ hopped down from the mammoth truck and forged ahead through the grass and weeds where the road had been. A single wall of the Feed & Seed remained standing, shored up on one side by an embankment of earth and shrubs.

She walked past the ruins, out toward the vast meadow. How long had it been, she wondered, since she'd been this far away from the city, from the rumble of traffic and the hum of electricity? *Too long.*

At first, the quiet enchanted her. Then, her ears tuned to the sounds of the earth. How noisy it was after all. How alive! The crunch of stubby weeds beneath her rubber-soled shoes lured her further along. The chirp of crickets welcomed her home. *We've missed you,* they sang.

"I've missed you, too," RJ whispered as she walked deeper into the field, weaving between clusters of tufted blue grama grass.

The wind blew tenderly from the northwest, carrying echoes of voices from the past. RJ heard Ethel's heartfelt church hymns in the sway of the purple coneflowers. She heard Harvey's placid laughter in the rustle of the bronze-tipped buffelgrass. RJ stopped walking and took in a deep, cleansing breath of the sun-kissed air. She heard Woody's inquisitive banter in the buzz of the field grasshoppers.

RJ glanced back in the direction from which she had come. The remnants of the town had evaporated in the distance.

She slipped off her shoes and stood in her stocking feet, feeling the cool soil beneath her hammertoes. She closed her eyes. She waited for her pulse to quiet, for her breath to slow. She listened. A Cooper's hawk cried overhead. Field critters scurried for cover below. The wind blew across the plains, just as it had for centuries. The dust had finally settled. And RJ heard it, breathed it, felt it all.

She felt the earth move.

The End

Author's Note and Acknowledgments

Peculiar Savage Beauty is a work of fiction. Yet, the story was inspired by many real people and events. Dozens of letters, essays, photos, songs and books by individuals including Aldo Leopold, Willa Cather, Dorothea Lange, Woody Guthrie, Caroline Henderson, Daniel Tammet, Temple Grandin and Timothy Egan helped me view humanity and the earth – and their inextricable connection – through many eyes.

During my research for the novel, I was thrilled to learn about Frances Hammerstrom, the first female graduate student in wildlife management, who studied under Leopold at the University of Wisconsin (UW) in Madison. While RJ's character is not based on Hammerstrom, learning of her pioneering career certainly encouraged me to continue developing RJ's education and career as I did.

Living through the Dust Bowl and Great Depression was a challenge somewhat beyond comprehension for most of us today. The extreme hardship and daily grind required simply to survive are difficult to even imagine. For many people, the most common point of reference to that time is John Steinbeck's classic novel, *The Grapes of Wrath*, and the epic tale of the westward exodus of farmers driven from their land by drought, foreclosure and desperation. According to Timothy Egan's award-winning nonfiction book *The Worst Hard Time*, however, that represents only a small fraction of the Dust Bowl story. It's true, more than 220,000 people moved to California between 1935 and 1937. "But only 16,000 of them came from the actual Dust Bowl," Egan wrote. "A majority of people in the most wind-bared and lacerated counties in the southern plains did not move, or they relocated only a few hundred miles." It was the story of those who stayed, or who ventured only as far as the nearest big city, that intrigued me. It was that story I wanted to know and understand and, ultimately, to share.

As a novelist, I exercised creative license with regard to some dates and events of the era. This may have created a few anachronisms that die-hard historians will find irritating. For that, I apologize. My excuse is that such liberties, I believe, help to advance the story and portray the characters in the most compelling and entertaining way possible. And that, after all, is the ultimate job of the novelist.

Peculiar Savage Beauty does contain a few real-life historical figures who played a prominent role in the Dust Bowl story.

Hugh Hammond Bennet, dubbed the Father of Soil Conservation, studied and wrote about the perils of soil erosion throughout the 1920s and 1930s. One of his more influential pieces, "Soil Erosion: A National Menace," was published in 1928. In it, he challenged readers to consider, "What would be the feeling of the nation should a foreign nation suddenly enter the United States and destroy 90,000 acres of land, as erosion has been allowed to do in a single county?" (All told, more than 15 million acres of land in America's heartland were destroyed by tilling and erosion during the early decades of the 20th century.) Key political figures, not the least of which was President Franklin D. Roosevelt, took notice of Bennet's dire warnings and he was tapped to establish the U.S. government's soil erosion service in 1933.

Aldo Leopold was a conservationist, forester, educator, writer and outdoor enthusiast. He taught at UW, though his work there in ecology and his philosophy of conservation developed from the mid-1930s to late-1940s. Because I wanted RJ to have been a student of Leopold's, and because I wanted her well established at the soil conservation station in Vanham in April 1935, I took liberties with the years she studied at UW with Leopold as a mentor.

The timing is significant because on April 14, 1935 a terrifying, days-long dust storm began on a clear, peaceful Sunday morning. It would later come to be known as Black Sunday. It caused unthinkable devastation and struck terror in the hearts of many across the United States, in much the way it is described within these pages.

Just as a good magician does not reveal her secrets, I will refrain from citing the many research efforts and resources that went into creating this work of fiction. That said, there are handful of sources and people who warrant special notes and thanks.

For the character of Woody, I owe a debt of gratitude to the many individuals with autism whom I've had the pleasure of knowing, as well as to the writings and life stories of Daniel Tammet and Temple Grandin. Their collective courage in overcoming challenges and embracing differences is an inspiration. I hope that Woody's peculiar ways and unique talents are equally inspiring, though he existed in a time long before the complex neurological condition now known as autism spectrum disorder was diagnosed.

Online archives of the *UW Badger Yearbook* from the 1930s provided an invaluable glimpse into college life during that time. Thanks to the UW archivists who took the time to preserve this history and make it accessible to all. Thanks also to *The New York Times* best-selling historical novelist Sandra Dallas, who suggested yearbooks to me as a possible resource on college life in the 1920s and 1930s.

Likewise, online archives of *The Saturday Evening Post* helped me gain insight into what Americans were thinking, feeling and doing in the 1930s. Even the advertisements from the era proved entertaining and enlightening. Marybeth Lorbiecki's wonderful biography on Aldo Leopold, *A Fierce Green Fire*, was a tremendous help in my research about his life and work. The "Pioneers" section of the Association for Women Soil Scientists website also provided inspiration and gave me the confidence to place a female scientist at the center of this story.

Eric Brevik, Ph.D., chair of the Department of Natural Sciences at Dickinson State University, took the time to chat with me at length about the history of geological and soil science. He also provided a list of recommended reading that was invaluable to my research and basic understanding of field study. Any inaccuracies in soil science that may occur within these pages are entirely of my doing and are no reflection on his valiant efforts to educate me. He has my sincere thanks, as does Susan Fisk of the Alliance of Crop, Soil, and Environmental Science Societies for helping to put me in touch with him.

I'm grateful to Gladys, Jean, Lee and Linda McCann for sharing stories and genealogy research through the years, which painted vivid pictures in my mind's eye of farm and small-town life during the Depression. Thanks to author and friend Jewell Parker Rhodes for her early and ongoing encouragement of my writing – from her support of my first novel, to giving me her copy of *Out of the Dust* by Karen Hesse when she learned of this novel as an early work in progress.

Peculiar Savage Beauty went through many revisions and iterations (as all writing should). Its gradual improvement is the result of valuable feedback over several years from fellow writer and friend Melissa Crytzer Fry, and my niece Kristi McCann, who was an early reader. Deep appreciation goes to editor Anne Dubuisson for her insights and copyeditor Nancy Brown Prenzno for her thoroughness.

Without my husband's unfailing belief that my stories are worth telling, no matter how long they take to tell, neither of my novels would ever have been written. For this, Mike, and for so much more, I can never thank you enough.

Finally, my sincere gratitude goes to all who've opened this book and sacrificed the time required to read it. As 18th century English writer and literary critic Samuel Johnson once said, "A writer only begins a book. A reader finishes it." Thank you for helping me finish this book.

Recommended Nonfiction Reading

- *The Worst Hard Time*, by Timothy Egan (2006)
- *A Sand County Almanac*, by Aldo Leopold (1949)
- *A Fierce Green Fire: Aldo Leopold's Life and Legacy*, by Marybeth Lorbiecki (1996)
- *Daring to Look: Dorothea Lange's Photographs & Reports from the Field*, by Anne Whiston Spirn (2008)
- *Born on a Blue Day: Inside the Extraordinary Mind of an Autistic Savant*, by Daniel Tammett (2006)
- *Bound for Glory*, by Woody Guthrie (1943)

ABOUT THE AUTHOR

Jessica McCann worked for more than 25 years as a professional freelance journalist and corporate writer. Her articles have appeared in *Business Week*, *The Writer*, *Raising Arizona Kids*, *Phoenix* and dozens of other magazines. McCann's debut novel, *All Different Kinds of Free*, won the Freedom in Fiction Prize and was published by Bell Bridge Books. She lives with her family in Phoenix, Arizona.

CPSIA information can be obtained
at www.ICGtesting.com
Printed in the USA
LVHW09*1954220818
587766LV00006B/87/P

9 780999 460207